Join the army of fans of Scott Mariani's Ben Hope series . . .

1.1 million copies sold in the UK alone – and counting!

'For those who are yet to meet Ben Hope, beware – he is **highly addictive!**'

'Another **gripping** tale'

'Just when you think Ben Hope has settled into some kind of normality his life spins apart. **Amazing twists and turns** . . . plenty of action. **Never a dull moment!**'

'Once again Scott Mariani has **hit the bullseye!**'

'Yet again Ben Hope – **the man we'd all secretly like to be** – triumphs in the end!'

'Scott Mariani is a storyteller of the **highest quality**'

'Thank you, Scott, for keeping me so well **entertained** and **enthralled**'

'Isn't it about time Mr Mariani lets Ben Hope settle down? . . . I hope not! I am enjoying the series too much!'

'**Heart-stopping!**'

'Ben Hope is **the hero we all need**'

'One of the best thriller series of our time!'

'Just keeps getting **better and better**!'

'Only one word to describe it – **AWESOME**!'

'Loved every single page: the **style** of writing, the **detail** of plot, history, geography, technical **knowledge** and romantic **tension**. Thank you, Scott!'

'Constant **twists and turns** urging you to read the next page to reach the final **thrilling** conclusion'

'Ben Hope **at his best**'

'**Five stars are not enough**'

'Full of **action and fast-paced thrills**, these books are just fantastic'

'Makes you regret that you **read it too fast**'

'Thrills, spills, **terror** and **excitement**'

'Another **cracker** from Scott Mariani'

'Once again, Scott Mariani has delivered a **superb, action-packed, edge-of-the-seat adventure** that leaves you just wanting more. Bring it on!'

'Probably **the best Ben Hope yet!**'

'I read it in **one day**'

'Anyone who has not read this series of books should **do so straight away!**'

'My heart is still **beating furiously**'

'Ben Hope is **a thinking Jack Reacher**'

'**Fast and furious** as ever'

'**Action-packed** and forward-thinking **suspense** and **thrills** throughout . . . great for technology, history and action fans and those looking for a comfortable and **intelligent** read'

THE MARTYR'S CURSE

Scott Mariani is the author of the worldwide-acclaimed action-adventure thriller series featuring ex-SAS hero Ben Hope, which has sold over a million copies in Scott's native UK alone and is also translated into over 20 languages. His books have been described as 'James Bond meets Jason Bourne, with a historical twist.' The first Ben Hope book, THE ALCHEMIST'S SECRET, spent six straight weeks at #1 on Amazon's Kindle chart, and all the others have been Sunday Times bestsellers.

Scott was born in Scotland, studied in Oxford and now lives and writes in a remote setting in rural west Wales. When not writing, he can be found bouncing about the country lanes in an ancient Land Rover, wild camping in the Brecon Beacons or engrossed in his hobbies of astronomy, photography and target shooting (no dead animals involved!).

You can find out more about Scott and his work, and **sign up to his exclusive newsletter**, on his official website:

www.scottmariani.com

By the same author:

Ben Hope series
The Alchemist's Secret
The Mozart Conspiracy
The Doomsday Prophecy
The Heretic's Treasure
The Shadow Project
The Lost Relic
The Sacred Sword
The Armada Legacy
The Nemesis Program
The Forgotten Holocaust

To find out more visit **www.scottmariani.com**

SCOTT MARIANI

The Martyr's Curse

AVON

AVON
A division of HarperCollins*Publishers*
1 London Bridge Street,
London SE1 9GF

www.harpercollins.co.uk

A Paperback Original 2015

2

A catalogue record for this book is
available from the British Library

ISBN-13: 978-0-00-748618-2

Set in Minion by Palimpsest Book Production Limited,
Falkirk, Stirlingshire

Printed and bound in Great Britain by
Clays Ltd, St Ives plc

MIX
Paper from
responsible sources
FSC® C007454

THE MARTYR'S CURSE

Prologue

France
January 1348

The crowd looked on in awed silence as the pall of smoke drifted densely upwards to meet the falling sleet.

Four attempts to light the pyre had finally resulted in a dismal, crackling flame that slowly caught a hold on the pile of damp hay and twigs stacked up around the wooden stake at its centre. So thick was the smoke, the people of the mountain village who'd huddled round in the cold to witness the burning could barely even make out the figure of the man lashed to the stake. But they could clearly hear his frantic cries of protest as he writhed and fought against his bonds.

His struggles were of no use. Iron chains, not ropes, held him tightly to the thick wooden post. Rope would only burn away, and the authorities overseeing the execution wanted to make sure the job was properly carried out – that the corrupted soul of this evil man was well and truly purified in the cleansing flames.

He was a man of indeterminate age, thin, gaunt and known locally as Salvator l'Aveugle – Blind Salvator – because he had only a right eye, the left a black, empty socket. The robed and hooded traveller had first turned up in the village in late November. He'd declared himself to be a Franciscan priest on a lone pilgrimage to Jerusalem, where almost for the first time since its fall to the Muslim forces of Salah al-Din in 1187, Christianity was re-establishing a lasting foothold. Salvator's mission was to join his fellow Frenchman and Franciscan, Roger Guérin of Aquitaine, who had managed to purchase from the current Mamluk rulers parts of the ancient city, including the hallowed Cenacle on Mount Zion, and was in the process of building a monastery there.

But Salvator's long journey hadn't started well. He'd scarcely covered eighty miles from his home in Burgundy before a gang of brigands had beset him on the road, taking his nag and the purse containing what little money he had. Bruised and battered, he'd plodded on his way on foot for a month or more, totally dependent on the goodwill of his fellow men for shelter and sustenance. Finally, fatigue and hunger combined with the growing winter cold and the unrelenting rain had brought on a fever that had nearly ended his pilgrimage before it had properly begun. Some children had come across him lying half-dead by the side of the path that wound up through the mountain pass a mile or so from their village. Seeing from the dirty tatters of his humble robe that he was a holy man, they'd run to fetch help and Salvator had soon been rescued. Men from the village had carried him back on a wagon, he'd been fed and tended to, and fresh straw bedding had been laid down for him in an empty stable that he shared with some chickens.

During the weeks that followed, the priest's fever had passed and his strength had gradually returned. By then, though, winter was closing in, and he'd decided to delay resuming his journey until the spring. To begin with, most of the villagers hadn't objected to his remaining with them two or three more months. It was an extra mouth to feed, true; but then, an extra pair of hands was always useful at this hard time of year. During his stay, Salvator had helped clear snow, repair storm damage to the protective wall that circled the village, and tend to the pigs. In his free time, he'd also begun to draw a crowd with his impromptu public sermons, which had grown in frequency and soon become more and more impassioned.

Needless to say, there were those who were unhappy with his presence, and this became more noticeable as time went on. It was a somewhat closed community, somewhat insular, easily given to suspicion and especially where strangers were concerned – even when those strangers were men of God. And most especially when those strangers frightened some people with their odd ways.

The first rumours had begun to circulate about a month after Salvator's recovery. Just a few passing whispers to begin with, quickly growing to a widespread consensus that the presence of this itinerant priest was cause for deep concern. Increasingly, villagers complained that the content of his sermons was scandalous. He railed against core doctrines of the Church, even attacked the views of the Pope, which he declared to be ignoble and ungodly. But that wasn't the worst of it. What really worried people were the seizures.

Once while feeding the pigs and again in the middle of delivering one of his sermons, Salvator had been seen suddenly to go rigid, then drop to the ground and begin to thrash about in a way that absolutely terrified those who witnessed it. During these inexplicable convulsions, his limbs would twitch violently and his face would contort in the most horrible way, foam drooling from the corners of his mouth and his one eye rolled up in its socket so that only the white showed. Most alarmingly of all, it was reported that he would babble and croak in a strange, guttural language that none of the villagers had ever heard before.

As the rumours inevitably gathered momentum, so did the growing belief that Salvator was possessed by demons. They'd all heard of such things, though never before seen it with their own eyes. What else could explain these frightful episodes?

It was after the third seizure happened that the village elders convened to discuss the urgent situation. The assembly of greybeards unanimously decided that such evil could not be allowed to remain in their midst. Despite the risks posed by the weather, they all agreed that their best horseman, a young carpenter named Guy, should be dispatched at once to the nearby town to notify the higher church authorities. In the meantime, Salvator should be locked up in a stone barn outside the village walls and guarded day and night, so that whatever sinister forces had taken hold of him could do no further harm.

When, after several worrying days, Guy returned from his trek, he was accompanied by an envoy of the bishop and a small party of officials and soldiers, who rapidly set up court in the village's tiny stone chapel and summoned the prisoner to be brought before them. Covered in chains, Salvator was forced to prostrate himself in front of the bishop's envoy, explain himself for preaching such scandalous and profane sermons, and provide evidence to all present that he was not in league with powers of Satan.

The evidence Salvator gave them was all they needed. Right before their eyes, and to their horror and satisfaction in equal measure, he succumbed to yet another bout of convulsions that proved beyond any doubt that some devilish entity had taken possession of this man's soul. There was no alternative but to purge it out, to banish the demon and cleanse the corrupted fleshly vessel that had been its host.

Death by burning was the only way.

Bit by bit, the sluggish flames gained on the pyre, helped by a chill wind from the mountain that picked up and cleared the smoke. Salvator screamed in agony as the fire began to dance around his feet, then up his legs. Part of his robe burned away, exposing blackened and blistered skin.

'I curse you!' he screamed through the heat mist at the church envoy on his high seat, and at the lesser authorities and the soldiers gathered nearby to watch.

'And you!' Salvator bellowed at the crowd. 'Damn your souls, for what you have done today to an innocent man!'

The people shrank away, terrified in their belief that it was the voice of the tormented demon inside him that they were hearing. Children buried their faces in their mothers' robes; hands were pressed over their ears to protect them from evil.

The flames leaped higher around Salvator, and still he wouldn't succumb but kept on roaring at them.

'God sees the shameful sin that has united you all. May His eternal curse be on you all, and your children, and your children's children after them! May a thousand years of pestilence rot this unholy place and everyone in it!'

One of the soldiers glanced nervously at the bishop's envoy, ready to raise his bow and fire an arrow into the heart of the flames in order to silence the voice that was rattling the nerves of even the most hardened man present.

But the envoy shook his head. For purification to be effective, no mercy could be allowed. The heretic must burn to death.

And burn to death Salvator did, though it took an unbearably long time. To the villagers, it seemed as if the flaming human torch went on railing at them even as the sizzling flesh peeled from its bones. Then, finally, his cries diminished and he hung limply, no longer resisting, from the blackened chains that held him to the stake. The remnants of his robe burst alight. Then his tonsured hair. By now he could barely be seen for the flames. His one rolling eyeball seemed to peer balefully at them from the scorched ruin of his face.

Long after the carbonised skeleton had fallen into the cinders leaving the chains hanging empty, Salvator's voice went on ringing inside the heads of the villagers. They would never forget the promise of everlasting pestilence that had been heaped on them and their line.

Within months, Salvator's words would come true.

The martyr's curse had begun.

Chapter One

Undisclosed location
North Korea
3 June 2011

Not long after his entry team had penetrated the inner core of the building, Udo Streicher knew it was over.

His information had been first-rate. The materials he'd been looking to acquire were exactly where his sources had said they would be, and he'd come within a hair's breadth of having them. Millions had been spent on intelligence and equipment. An entire year had been devoted to planning. Twelve-hour days. Sometimes sixteen. Checking every possible detail. Obsessing over the layout of the hidden complex. Analysing the security systems. Evaluating the risk. Assessing their chances of making it out alive.

And for all that meticulous planning, now the raid had gone badly wrong. The mission was blown. The ten-strong group was down to nine. The equipment was lost. They'd ditched everything they'd brought with them, except their weapons.

Behind them in the white-walled, starkly neon-lit corridor, three dead bodies lay sprawled in pools of blood. Two of them belonged to the armed Korean security personnel who'd surprised the intruders just as they were about to make it through the final set of doors that separated them from their objective. The third belonged to an Austrian called Dieter Lenz, a follower of Streicher from the beginning. But Dieter wasn't important any more. What mattered was getting out of here. Streicher refused to consider the alternatives. He'd rather die by his own bullet than face a lifetime of incarceration in the roach-infested hellhole of a North Korean prison camp.

The nine remaining members of the team ran in tight formation, their clattering footsteps all but drowned out by the shriek and whoop of alarm sirens that were sounding off all through the facility. Hannah Gissel had her pistol drawn and her teeth bared in a kind of animal ferocity. Torben Roth was clutching the Uzi he'd gunned the guards down with. Bringing up the rear were the Canadian, Steve Evers, and Sandro Guidinetti. Guidinetti looked like he was losing it under the pressure.

'Which way did we come?' Wolf Schilling yelled as they reached a fork in the corridor. Every door and wall in the lab complex looked the same.

'This way,' Streicher said, pointing left. He gripped Hannah's arm and they raced on. The sirens seemed even louder, a wall of sound that permeated everything. Another door. Another bend in the corridor.

A side entrance swung open, and suddenly the way ahead was blocked off. A four-man security patrol, dressed in khaki paramilitary uniform and wielding Chinese-made assault rifles. Screaming at them in Korean. Streicher knew little of the language but the message was clear: DROP YOUR WEAPONS! SURRENDER OR WE WILL SHOOT!

The stand-off lasted less than two seconds. Torben Roth was the first to open fire, shooting from the hip and hosing nine-millimetre rounds up the corridor. Hannah snapped off three, four, five shots from her Glock. The guards crumpled up and fell. Streicher shot the last one with his own Heckler & Koch. He did it without hesitation or compassion. It wasn't the first time he'd shot a man.

'Come on!' Hannah yelled. Her eyes were flashing with a mixture of aggression and terror and pure adrenalin. She leaped over the heap of dead men. The other eight followed.

Streicher felt a strange surge of pride in his woman. Weeks earlier, he'd decided that in the event of the mission going bad, he would kill her before he took his own life. A wild, untamed spirit like hers didn't belong in captivity.

They ran faster. The alarms drowned out everything. Every door they passed, Streicher kept expecting to see fly open and hordes of guards swarming through. But so far there was nothing like the level of resistance he'd feared. The North Korean economy was dismal to the point that even a hard-core military dictatorship could be forced to make serious defence cuts. That might be the reason. After all, nobody knew about this facility. Security could have been pared down to the bone, with nobody any the wiser. Maybe the remaining few guards were locked down elsewhere in the building, unwilling to face the armed intruders' superior numbers. Maybe there were no more guards at all.

All of which was making him begin to wonder if they'd been premature in beating a retreat.

Before he could decide what to do, they'd reached the main entrance. The jungle air enveloped them like a hot, wet cloak as they burst outside. The alarm sirens were even louder out here, their echo bouncing off the buildings, distortion crackling in the team's ears. The compound was grey concrete, as vast and forbidding as a high-security prison yard, and ringed with a mesh fence supported on steel posts fifteen feet high and topped all the way around with coils of razor wire. The main building was far larger than the rest, white, squat, windowless, like a giant bunker. The smaller buildings clustered around it, mainly storage units and maintenance sheds, were painted in military drab green. The main gate was directly opposite the white building, eighty yards away. From there, a concrete road spanned the patchy open ground surrounding the facility, where the jungle had been roughly cut back to clear room for it.

Officially, this place had never been built. The North Korean rulers firmly denied its existence. US Intelligence had long suspected otherwise, but their satellites had never been able to distinguish the facility from hundreds of others across the country that looked outwardly identical.

The American spies were clever, thorough people. But Udo Streicher was cleverer, and took thoroughness to a level that verged on the pathological. If anyone could find out what was really in there, he could. And he had, though it had cost him a fortune and a lot of hard work.

Needless to say, Streicher and his people hadn't used the main gate to get inside. The hole they'd cut in the wire was a hundred yards along the perimeter fence, on the east side of the compound where the bushes grew closer and the no-man's-land was at its narrowest. Beyond, a thicket of trees hid the clearing where the team's two choppers waited on standby to whisk them and their precious spoils back over the border to the RV point on the coast, from where a motor launch would carry them eastwards to the safety of Japan. A chartered jet from Tokyo back home and dry to Europe, and the mission would have been accomplished.

A successful outcome would then have become the start

of the next phase in the plan, one that Streicher had dreamed about for a long, long time.

'We're clear,' Roth said, glancing around them. He seemed to be right. The compound was deserted and empty apart from a parked row of Jeeps in Korean People's Army colours.

'We've taken them all out, that's why,' said Hannah. 'There's hardly anyone guarding this place. Which means we need to turn around and go back inside and get the stuff. Right now. Before it's too late.'

Streicher said nothing. He stood still, his head cocked a little to one side as if he was smelling the air.

'She's right, Udo,' Schilling said. 'We have time. We can still do this.'

'It's what we came here for,' Hannah said. 'It's why we chose this place, remember? That's what you told us. Our best chance. Our only chance.'

Streicher said nothing.

'I'm up for it. Or else we came all this way for nothing,' Roth said.

'And Dieter died for nothing,' Schilling said.

Streicher said, 'There's no time. It will have to wait.'

'Wait how long? Months? Years?'

'As long as it takes.'

'No. I want to do this,' Hannah said.

So did Streicher. He wanted it more than anything in the world. But he shook his head. 'Listen.'

He'd heard it the moment they stepped outside. It had been barely audible over the sirens, but now the sound was growing. It was the growling rumble of vehicles approaching. Hard to tell how many. Enough to be a serious problem. Enough to have made him absolutely right about getting out of here, this minute.

'Oh, shit,' Hannah said, as she heard it too.

Then they saw where the sound was coming from, and suddenly things were very much worse.

The line of military vehicles emerged at speed from the jungle, roaring along the road right for the main gate. Six of them, ex-Russian GAZ Vodnik troop carriers, each carrying up to nine men. The column made no attempt to slow for the gate. The first vehicle crashed straight through, steel frame and galvanised wire mesh crumpling and folding underneath its wheels as it stormed inside the compound followed by the rest of the convoy. The vehicles fanned out and skidded to a halt. Their hatches flew open and a mass of men spilled out. More than fifty fully armed troops. Against nine.

'Fuck them,' Torben Roth said. He snapped another magazine into his Uzi. Hannah raised her pistol. Gröning and Hinreiner looked at each other, then at Guidinetti.

The clatter of small-arms fire filled the compound. Roth held his ground. A burst to the left; a burst to the right. Then he staggered and dropped his Uzi and blood flew and hit the wall behind him. Streicher ducked down low and ran to the fallen man and saw that his face had been ripped open by a rifle bullet. Streicher grasped him by the arms and began dragging him behind cover, helped by Gröning. Hannah kept on firing. Several of the soldiers were down, but now the Russian GAZ Vodniks were advancing and bringing their on-board heavy machine guns into play. The roar shattered the air; 14.5mm bullets ploughed through the parked Jeeps, gouged craters in the buildings, chewed up the concrete.

Streicher now knew beyond any doubt that he'd been right. Things were bad enough already. If they'd stayed inside the building a minute longer, none of them would have made it this far alive.

'Help me,' he yelled, dragging the bleeding, disfigured Roth. Between them, he and Wolf Schilling and Miki Donath managed to manhandle the injured man out of the field of fire and between the buildings while the others did what they could to hold back the soldiers.

The firepower coming at them was overwhelming. Hannah fell back when her pistol was empty. Guidinetti was hit in the shoulder and Evers was supporting him as they made their retreat. How so many of them made it back to the hole in the wire without getting shot to pieces, Streicher would never know. Staggering through the undergrowth towards the trees with Roth's weight slippery and bloody in his arms, he was praying that the soldiers hadn't already intercepted the waiting helicopters.

Sixty seconds later and the choppers would have been gone anyway. The pilots had heard the gunfire and were quickly powering up their turbines in desperation to get the hell away from here. Their skids were dancing off the ground and the vegetation was being flattened by the downdraught as the surviving team members clambered on board. Streicher, Hannah, Donath and Schilling and the injured Roth on one; Evers and Guidinetti and Hinreiner and Gröning aboard the other.

The soldiers were coming. Flitting shapes among the trees. Muzzle flashes lighting up the shadows of the thick green forest. Bullets cracked off the Perspex screen of Streicher's chopper.

'Take it up! Get us out of here!' he yelled to the pilot.

As the choppers lifted off, the thicket suddenly crashed aside. Like a great scarred green armour-plated dinosaur scouring the jungle for its prey, a Korean People's Army VTT-323 armoured personnel carrier lurched through the trees, flattening bushes and saplings and anything else in its path. Its twin machine guns swivelled up towards the escaping aircraft. But those weren't what Streicher was gaping down at from the cockpit of the rising helicopter. It was the turret-mounted multiple rocket launcher that was angling up at them, tracking its targets and ready to fire at any moment.

'Higher!' he bawled over the din of the rotors, thumping the pilot on the shoulder. 'Higher!'

Two rockets launched simultaneously in a twin jet of flame. They streaked through the trees and hit the second chopper and blew it apart in a blinding flash that gave way to an expanding fireball.

'NO!' Streicher howled as he saw it go down.

The burning wreck dropped from the air and crashed down on top of the armoured personnel carrier. A secondary explosion rocked the jungle, and then Streicher saw no more as his pilot spun up and away at full thrust, nose up, tail down.

They flew in numb silence over the forest. The green canopy zipped by below. Wolf and Miki were trying to hold down the bleeding, squirming Torben Roth and pump morphine into him from the first-aid kit. Hannah was lost in a world of her own, her face drawn and grim and spattered with someone else's blood. She made no attempt to wipe it away.

And Udo Streicher was just beginning to contemplate the scale of the disaster. It would be a long time before he was fully able to calculate his losses, both human and financial.

But he'd be back. This wasn't over. It would never be over. Not until he'd attained his goal. One way or another, the world would know his name before he was done.

It was, after all, his destiny.

Chapter Two

Hautes-Alpes, France
The present day

When they'd found the stranger, at first they hadn't known what to do with him.

It was nineteen-year-old Frère Roby, the one they affectionately called simple, who'd first stumbled on the camp high up on the mountainside during one of his long contemplative rambles one morning in early October. Roby would later describe how he'd been following a young chamois, hoping to befriend the animal, when he'd made his strange discovery.

The camp had been made in a natural hollow among the rocks, sheltered from the wind, out of sight and well away from the beaten track, only accessible along a narrow path with a sheer cliff face on one side and a dizzy drop on the other. It was like nothing Roby had ever seen. In the middle of the camp was a shallow fire pit, about two feet deep, over which had been built a short, tapered chimney made of stone and earth. The fire was cold, but the remains of a spit-roasted hare showed that it had been used recently. Nearby, almost invisibly camouflaged behind a carefully built screen of pine branches, was a small and robust tent.

15

That was where he'd found the stranger, lying on his side in a sleeping bag with his back turned to the entrance. To begin with, Roby had been frightened, thinking the man was dead. As he dared to creep closer, he'd realised the man was breathing, though deeply unconscious. The chamois completely forgotten, Roby had dashed all the way back to the monastery to tell the others.

After some thought, the prior had given his consent, and Roby had led a small party of older men back to the spot. It was mid-afternoon when they reached the camp, to find the stranger still lying unconscious inside his tent.

The men soon realised the cause of the stranger's condition, from the empty spirits bottles that littered the camp. They'd never seen anybody so comatose from drink before, not even Frère Gaspard that notorious time when he'd broken into the store of beer the monks produced to sell. They wondered who this man was and how long he'd been living here undetected, just three kilometres from the remote monastery that was their home. He didn't look like a vagrant or a beggar. Perhaps, one of them suggested, he was a hunter who'd lost his way in the wilderness.

But if he was a hunter, he should have a gun. When they delicately searched his pockets and his green military canvas haversack in the hope of finding some identification, all they came across was a knife, a quantity of cash, some French cigarettes and an American lighter, as well as a battered steel flask half-filled with the same spirit that had been in the bottles. They also found a creased photograph of a woman with auburn hair, whose identity was as much a mystery to them as the man's.

The monks were fascinated by the fire pit. The blackened mouth of the stone-and-earth chimney suggested that the stranger must have been living here for some time, perhaps weeks. The way it was constructed indicated considerable skill. They were men who'd been used to a hard, simple existence close to nature all their lives, dependent through the harsh Alpine winters on the firewood they'd gathered, chopped and seasoned themselves. They understood that the fire pit was the work of someone highly expert in the art of survival. That, as well as the green bag and the tent, made them wonder whether the stranger might at one time have been a soldier. Such things had happened before. A Wehrmacht infantryman had been found frozen to death not far from here in the winter of 1942, hiding in the mountains after apparently deserting his unit. As far as the monks knew, there weren't any major wars happening at the moment, down there below in the world they'd left behind. The stranger was dressed in civilian clothes – jeans, leather jacket, stout boots – and his blond hair was too long for him to have belonged to the military any time recently.

Whatever clues they could discern as to his past, it was his immediate future that concerned them. Despite their isolated, ascetic lifestyle, the monks were worldly enough to know about such things as alcohol poisoning, and were afraid that the stranger might die if left where he was. The monastic tradition of helping travellers was just one of the many ways in which they were sworn to serve God. The question was, what should they do?

There'd been some debate as to whether to bring him back to the monastery, where the prior would best know how to help him, or whether to call immediately for outside help. It hadn't been a hard decision finally. None of them possessed a phone on which to dial 15 for the SAMU emergency medical assistance service.

So they gathered up his things and carried him back along

17

the winding, steep and sometimes dangerous mountain paths to their sanctuary, Chartreuse de la Sainte Vierge de Pelvoux, where the stranger had remained ever since.

That had been over seven months ago.

Chapter Three

Ben Hope's awakening before dawn was sudden, as it always was these days. He couldn't remember ever having slept as deeply and restfully in his life before now. The instant he laid his head down and closed his eyes in the utter stillness of his living quarters, he was falling into a soft darkness where no dreams came to haunt him, and he became still to his innermost core. From that profound, total immersion in the void, one hour before daybreak each morning he snapped into a fully alert state of wakefulness, ready to begin each new day with all the energy and enthusiasm of the last.

This was not a familiar experience for Ben. Things hadn't always been this way.

His life, until the day the monks had found him half-dead on the mountain and brought him here, had been hurtling towards wilful self-destruction. The events leading up to that point were still just a painful blur in his memory. He couldn't, and didn't really want to, recall the exact course that his long period of wandering had taken him on.

He remembered a wet day in London last August, marking his return from a crazy journey that had led him from Ireland's west coast to Madeira and across the Atlantic to the Oklahoman city of Tulsa. He remembered the terrible emptiness and sense of bitter loss that had struck him like a bullet to the head the moment he'd stepped off the plane into the London drizzle and realised that he was now completely directionless. He had nowhere to go, except straight to the nearest bar to get wrecked. No home to return to, and nobody to share it with if he had. Not any more, not since Brooke Marcel had walked out of his life.

Or more correctly, as he knew too well, since he'd walked out of hers. It wasn't supposed to be that way. He truly hadn't wanted to hurt her.

But instead, fool that he was, he'd gone his own way, like always. The knowledge that he'd broken the heart of the woman he loved more than anything in the world – that had been just about the worst agony he'd ever had to endure. It had driven him to the very edge. And he'd have let it drive him right over into oblivion.

He couldn't even remember for how many drunken days he'd hung around in London after getting back from the States. Not long, though. The place held too many memories for him, because it was where Brooke had lived for most of the time he'd known her. He did remember getting thrown out of a couple of pubs – or maybe three – once with blood smeared over his knuckles, stumbling away down the street before the police turned up. It wasn't his blood. He didn't know whose it was, or what the fight had been about.

Somewhere along the dotted, meandering trail of bars that followed, one merging into another, people had started talking French at him instead of English. He'd no idea how that had happened, whether he'd crossed over the Channel by ferry or gone under it by rail. Whether he'd drifted back to France because his home for some years had been a former farm in Normandy, a place called Le Val. Or whether he might just as easily have ended up in the Netherlands, Norway or Iceland. None of this entered his mind at the time. All he'd wanted to do was lose himself. Didn't matter where. Didn't matter how.

Ben had been a hard drinker for many years, with a preference for single malt scotch when it was available to him. The habit had left its mark on his time in the military, and it had sometimes affected him in the career he'd pursued since. But there was hard drinking, and there was beyond hard; and then there was the kind of wild, insane, hell-bent suicidal self-poisoning where you didn't even give a damn what you threw down your neck so long as you could keep it coming and it blotted out all thoughts, blotted out everything, slammed down the iron portcullis on the whole world. The more he drank, the more he wanted to escape from himself, the more he needed to get away from other people.

Maybe that was why he'd made his way into the mountains. Or maybe he could have blindly wandered off anywhere. That was what lost souls did, after all.

When he'd woken in his strange new surroundings that evening over seven months ago, reeling and sick from the whisky still in his system, his first impulse had been to escape. If he hadn't been so dehydrated and weak, he'd have rejected the food and shelter offered by the monks and gone back to trying to kill himself in a new mountain lair – one where this time nobody could ever find him.

That was then. Something in him had changed. He felt strong now. Clean, clear, fit and alive. He hadn't touched alcohol for one hundred and ninety-three days straight. Today would be the hundred and ninety-fourth, but who was counting?

He wondered where Brooke was right now. Most likely she was still asleep in her bed, with a little while yet to dream whatever dreams were in her mind before her day began. He pictured her lying there. He hoped she was happy, and

21

thinking about her that way made him smile. There'd been so many days when all he could do was think about her and agonise over the love he'd lost and the life he'd walked away from. For the first months he'd been here, the mistakes he'd made still haunted him in the dead stillness of the night, when he'd light his candle and gaze at the photo of her that he'd been carrying for so long in his wallet that it had become frayed and worn. Sometimes it had hurt so much that he couldn't bear to look at it.

But the rawness of the pain had begun to fade imperceptibly with each day he remained here. He didn't fully understand why. Just knew that, thanks to this place, he'd slowly begun to discover within himself a strange kind of serenity. A feeling he'd never experienced before. One he'd been chasing all his life and never found. Until coming here.

Yes, he had changed, and he knew that it had been the Carthusian monks of Chartreuse de la Sainte Vierge de Pelvoux who had guided him on his path. For their friendship, and their trust, he owed them more than he could say.

Ben flipped himself out of his hard, narrow bunk. The stone floor was cold against his bare feet. Without hesitation, he dropped down on to his palms and did five sets of twenty press-ups, pausing a few seconds between sets, savouring the lactic-acid burn, letting the pain build up in his triceps and deltoids until the muscles screamed. Then he hooked his bare toes under the rough wooden edge of the bunk and did another five sets of twenty sit-ups. When he was done with those and his abdominals were cramping satisfactorily, he got to his feet and walked over to the massive stone lintel above the doorway connecting the small bedroom to the rest of his quarters. It had stood strong for a thousand years and could probably have held the weight of an Abrams main battle tank. He didn't think he was abusing it by using it as a chin-up bar. He jumped up, hung from his fingers with his feet dangling above the floor. Knees slightly bent, he lifted himself up so that his eyes were level with the lintel, then slowly down. He did five slow, painful sets of those before he dropped lightly to his feet and dusted off his hands.

Before the day was done, he'd have repeated the whole routine seven or eight more times. The solitary hours the Carthusian monks devoted each day in their cells to prayer, Ben spent on exercise. The pain of physical endurance was his purification, the endorphin rush his little piece of heaven. He'd never been much good at prayer. Maybe that would change too, with being here. One small step at a time.

Ben slowly washed himself in the stone cubicle that served him as a bathroom. The water was straight from a mountain spring, not much above freezing. It reminded him of the things he'd liked about the army. So did the uniform, although the plain robe of a lay brother was unlike any other garb he'd donned in his life. He was getting pretty used to it now. Something about it seemed to fit. He put it on, tied up the sash belt, stepped into the pair of plain sandals he now wore instead of boots, then left his quarters and went out into the stillness of the monastery to begin another day.

One small step at a time.

He was in no hurry to leave this place.

The magenta glow of the sunrise, shot through with streaks of gold, cast its light through the ancient cloisters as Ben walked the same route he walked each morning to attend to the first of his daily duties. Soon the slow, heavy tolling of the bell would signal Mass, the only sound to break the silence as the arched passages filled with a procession of silent robed figures heading towards the church. Some were young men, still strong and upright. Others were bent and old, on crutches, with long white beards. They must have lived there so long, they'd totally forgotten any other life.

After the first week, Ben had expected the monks to ask him to leave; especially as he'd been so aggressive with them at first, demanding they bring him the remaining bottles from his pack. Their gentle refusal had been like some act of love. They'd gone on serving him his food twice a day, and nobody had said anything about leaving. After two weeks, when he was feeling slightly stronger and the violent craving for alcohol had become more bearable, they'd moved him from the infirmary to a small house just inside the main entrance, which was used as guest quarters. Slowly at first, he'd started to explore the monastery.

Nobody was stopping him from walking out of the gate, but something inside him did. For the first time, he'd felt the power of the place. He'd looked out over the ancient stone wall across the mountainside and the forests down below, and thought there was something special here.

It was so easy to forget that Briançon was just a few miles away, the highest city in Europe, with a population of eleven thousand people. The world beyond, with all its wars and politics and deception and unhappiness, might as well have belonged to another galaxy. It felt to him like an existence he could comfortably leave behind, shut the door on and never return to.

By the fourth week, he'd begun thinking that he couldn't go on accepting the care of his hosts without giving something back. The winter was setting in by then, and you could smell the snow coming. From his walks about the monastery and its grounds, he could see there was so much work to do. So much he could offer in return, by way of thanks. Nobody had ever asked him, but from that day he'd

24

begun tending to the livestock, the goats and long-horned cattle whose milk the monks drank and used to make butter and cheese. He gathered eggs from the hen houses, chopped firewood, helped out with general manual tasks like carpentry or masonry repairs on the ancient, weathered buildings. The monastery was also home to a small population of cats, employed to keep down less welcome animal visitors. To them, it was permissible to talk, and Ben enjoyed feeding them.

His daily duties brought him into a little more contact with other inhabitants of the monastery. Through looking after the animals, he met Roby, the young man whom he had to thank for being here – for being alive – and each day they spent some time together. Silence was strictly observed even during work hours, but Roby would often have whispered conversations with him. Ben liked him a lot.

Roby wore the short cowl of a first-year novice, over which he put on a black cloak when the community got together. He was nineteen, with a disarming smile and a mental age of perhaps thirteen or fourteen. But what he lacked in quickness of intellect, he more than made up for by his devotion to Chartreuse de la Sainte Vierge de Pelvoux and everyone and everything in it, and he could speak and read Latin nearly as well as he could French.

As Ben discovered, Roby was a good teacher, too. Under his patient tutelage, Ben became pretty adept in the art of milking goats and cattle without getting butted or trampled to death or spilling milk everywhere. The only occasion when Roby burst out laughing was when Ben fell flat on his face trying to catch a running, flapping chicken that wouldn't let itself be herded into the hen house. Roby's mirth was like a child's, which just made Ben warm to him more. They'd laughed together for about half an hour that time.

Afterwards, Ben had realised that it was the first time he'd laughed in months.

His contact with the monks themselves was more limited. They were men whose stillness and calm fascinated him. Observing their vow of silence, they seldom spoke to one another as they went about their duties, let alone to him. One exception to the rule was the weekly visit Ben received from Père Jacques, the Father Master of Novices, a kindly man Ben put in his late sixties. Ostensibly, the visits were to find out how Ben was, whether he needed anything, how he was recovering. The Father Master of Novices never probed, but Ben could sense the man was curious as to the intentions of this stranger in their midst.

Little by little, the serene daily rhythm of silence, prayer and hard work had seeped into his bones until it felt like part of his life. Every morning at quarter to six, Ben would get up, complete his exercises and then go and see to the livestock. At eight the bell tolled for the first time, and the monks would assemble for Mass. Ben's morning was spent working, taking care of the gardens and the orchard. Lunch was at noon, a simple dish of vegetables, eggs or fish, eaten alone in his cell. The food was served by a monk pushing a wooden trolley down the corridors, on a tray slid through a hatch – like in prison, except here there were no locks on any door. Wine or beer were permitted in extreme moderation, though Ben avoided both.

The rest of the afternoon was spent working until Vespers at four, then there was a light supper. At seven the bell tolled again for prayer. An hour later was bedtime, but it didn't last long. The Carthusians believed in a semi-nocturnal life, on the grounds that the stillness of night invited them to more fervent prayer. At eleven-thirty the bell summoned the monks to a session of prayer in their cells; then shortly after

26

midnight the community made their way back through the barely lit cloisters and would sit in the darkness of the church in profound silence before the chanting of Matins began. It wasn't until deep into the small hours that they returned to their cells, for yet more prayer, before they finally retired to bed for just two or three hours' rest before the whole routine began again.

There was no TV. No radio, no phones. Secular reading material was strictly limited. Computers and the internet were unknown here. It was a life that had remained fundamentally unchanged since the founding of the Carthusian Order in the early eleventh century. The Order's motto was *Stat crux dum volvitur orbis*: The cross stands still while the globe revolves. The existence this place offered was designed to make you lose all interest in the affairs of the outside world, and it was effective in ways Ben couldn't have imagined.

Finally, one cold midwinter's evening by the glow of a crackling wood fire, as the snow fell silently outside over the mountains and layered the roofs and walls of the monastery buildings under the silver moonlight, without being asked, Ben had told the Father Master of Novices what was in his heart.

Jeff Dekker, the former SBS commando who had been his business partner and closest friend, would have thought Ben had lost his mind. This was the guy who'd never once turned away from trouble, even when the odds were at their suicidal craziest. Who'd taken down the worst of the worst and protected the innocent as if he'd been born to it. Adventure and risk were in his blood.

But not any more. Those days were now over for good.

Ben had said, 'I want to stay.'

Chapter Four

It had been after that discussion that Ben had been taken to see the prior. The head of the monastery lived in just the same kind of humble quarters as the other members of the order. His name was Père Antoine. He was over eighty, with a face deeply etched by wrinkles and what would have been a leonine mane of pure white hair if it hadn't been for the monk's tonsure shorn into it, symbolising the crown of thorns worn by Christ.

The first thing Ben noticed about Père Antoine was his eyes. They didn't belong in an old man's face. They seemed to glow like those of a happy child, as if filled with some kind of inner light that poured out of him. Ben found them mesmerising.

The two men spoke in French, after Ben explained that his was fluent and he had lived in France for a while. The old man smiled at the discovery that 'Ben' was short for Benedict, and addressed him by the French version of the name, Benoît. He gently invited him to talk about himself, which was something Ben found difficult. Secrecy was second nature to him, instilled by years of covert military operations and the work he'd done since leaving the army. But that wasn't the only reason it was difficult for him to speak openly. Here, now, in the presence of the old monk, Ben felt a sense of shame.

'I've done a lot of pretty bad things,' he confessed.

'Père Jacques tells me you were once a soldier. For how many years was that your occupation?'

'Too many.'

'During those years, Benoît, did you kill many people?'

Ben said nothing.

'The memory of your past pains you, I see. But you atoned for your sins by leaving that path.'

'I'm not sure if that counts as atonement, Father.'

'It depends on the reason why you left.'

'I didn't like people telling me what to do.'

'You have a problem with authority?'

'It depends on who's giving the orders. If it's someone I respect, that's one thing. If it's some government stooge with a secret power agenda who expects me to do his dirty work for him on the pretext of protecting the realm, that's another.'

'You did not find your realm worth protecting?'

'Not if it meant taking the lives of innocent people whose countries we invaded simply for reasons of territory and economics. That troubled me then. And it troubles me even more now, when I think about the things I did.'

'And if your order came from God?'

'I'm still waiting for that one,' Ben said. 'That's the truth.'

'Perhaps it has come already, but you do not see it.'

Ben didn't reply.

The old monk nodded thoughtfully and reflected for a few moments. 'By choice, I know little about the modern world. But history, I do know. These things you tell me – it was always so. This monastery was built during the time of the First Crusade. It is convenient for us to forget that the Christian forces who established the Holy Kingdom of Jerusalem, in so doing, carried out the wholesale massacre of thousands of innocent Muslim lives. It was not an act of faith, but of pure murder.'

Ben looked at him.

'The Church's past is tainted by many sins, and to force good men to do evil in the name of God is but one of them.' Père Antoine smiled sadly. 'It surprises you, to hear me speak this way.'

It did.

'You speak of your shame for the things you did then,' the monk went on. 'But the goodness in you prevailed, Benoît. You left that life behind.'

'I tried to,' Ben said. 'I wanted to use what I'd learned to do some good.' He paused as he tried to find the right words. 'Things happen in this world. Things you couldn't even begin to imagine from up here. K and R is just one of them.'

'You are right. I have no idea what that means.'

'Kidnap and ransom,' Ben explained. 'It's a business, and a big one. The trade in human misery for money. The men who do it are pure bad, and too often, there's nobody there to stop them. That was something I wanted to change.'

'And did you?'

Ben thought of the kidnap victims he'd removed from the clutches of their captors. A long list of names and faces that he'd never forget. Many of them had been children, snatched from their homes, from schools, from cars, so as to extort ransom from their families. He wondered where they all were now. Getting on with their lives, he supposed. He wondered if they too were haunted by old memories.

'Saving the lives of the innocent is not something of which you should be ashamed,' Père Antoine said.

'Yes, I saved people. But to save them, sometimes unpleasant things had to be done.'

'Violence?'

'Yes.'

'Killing?'

Ben shrugged. He nodded. He glanced down as he did it. It was the first time in his life he hadn't been able to look another man in the eye.

'I did what I had to do to resolve the situation. Or that was how it seemed to me at the time. Perhaps there might have been another way.'

'Perhaps. Or perhaps this was the duty that God set in your path. He has many purposes for men of courage and integrity.'

Ben smiled darkly. 'Next you'll be telling me that He moves in mysterious ways.'

Père Antoine was silent for a long time, reflecting. 'We have talked about the past. Now let us talk about the future. You have been here long enough to have seen a little of our life. The institutional framework by which we live is somewhat rigid, some might say uncompromising.'

'Believe me, Father, I've been used to that.'

'Very well. Then consider our vocation to solitude. It requires a strong will and a balanced judgement. It is not for everyone.'

'I love this place,' Ben said. 'I feel at peace here.'

'Because of what you have found here, or because of what you believe you have run away from?'

Ben didn't reply.

The old man smiled. 'You may wish to dwell a little longer on that question. And ask yourself how truly you would be suited to life here. It takes time to adapt to it, learning to still the mind, quiet the senses and calm the spirit. It is a purely contemplative life, leaving behind all that we have known previously. He who remains in the Charterhouse has felt in the very centre of his soul a call so profound that no words can truly describe it. It is the revelation of the Absolute. But even this is only the beginning of a quest to which one's entire life, in all its aspects and for however long we may continue in this world, shall be utterly devoted. We seek only God. We live only for God, to whom we surrender body and soul. "You have seduced me, Lord, and I let myself be seduced."'

'*Jeremiah*, chapter twenty, verse seven,' Ben said. He hadn't forgotten everything from his past theology studies, even though they'd been scattered across the course of twenty-odd years – a dismal stop-start pattern of failure and indecision. There'd been times in his life when he'd wanted nothing more than to enter the Church, convinced that was the only way he'd find the peace of mind he needed so much. At other times that notion had seemed ridiculous, a crazy and irrelevant pipe dream. In any case, life had always got in the way of his plans and he'd found himself being dragged around the world instead, with people endlessly trying to shoot him, stab him, or blow him up. Routine stuff. You almost got used to it eventually.

If the monk was impressed by Ben's knowledge of the Bible, he didn't say or do anything to show it. He went on, 'Therefore we cast ourselves into the abyss, and cut ourselves off from all that is not God. For our new life to begin, first there must be a kind of death. The death of our old selves.' He paused, and those glowing eyes seemed to bore into Ben. 'Are you ready for that, Benoît?'

'I've faced death often enough,' Ben said. 'And wished I could leave my old self behind somehow.'

'It is the reason you tried to lose yourself in wine.'

'That's one way of putting it,' Ben said.

'Can you live without it? The drink?' For a moment, the monk's eyes were as sharp as the directness of his question.

Ben paused before he replied. 'I won't lie to you, Father. It isn't an easy thing to give up. But I feel a little stronger every day.'

The old man smiled again and fetched a small bottle from the folds of his robe. 'Here. It will bring strength, health, and vigour.'

'What is it?' Ben said, gazing at the bottle.

'Just a humble tonic that I make myself, using water from the mountain and some simple ingredients. It contains no alcohol. I have been drinking it for many years. Try it.'

Ben uncapped the bottle, sniffed, sipped. It didn't smell of anything and had only a faintly bitter taste.

'A little each day is all you need,' the old man said, then fell into a state of very still contemplation that seemed to last for ever in the silence of the room.

Finally he said, 'Very well. I believe you should remain with us a little longer, so that you may decide whether it is truly the path you wish to pursue. There is no hurry. If, after this period of time, you still wish to remain and it is deemed that you are fit and suited for this way of life, you may formally request to be admitted to the order, subject to its rules, to live at God's disposal alone, in solitude and stillness, in an everlasting prayer and a joyful penitence. The Father Master of Novices will visit you regularly and watch over your training.'

'Thank you, Father.'

'Tomorrow you will move to your own monastic quarters, so that you may share the life we live. You will come and see me here once a week from now on, and we will talk.'

On his way out, Ben noticed the chessboard on a table in the shadows.

'I find that it quietens the mind,' the old man said. When Ben looked surprised that such things were allowed in the monastery, the prior explained that since the death of the very ancient monk who had been his chess partner, he'd had nobody to play against but himself.

'It's a win for white in four moves, maybe five,' Ben said, gazing at the board.

'You play? Good. Then when you visit me each week, we shall play together.'

Ben's cell was more spacious than he'd expected. It was on two floors, with its own carpentry workshop and even a little walled garden outside. He began to understand that a Carthusian monk's lifestyle of solitary contemplation required just a little elbow room to prevent him from going mad. He had the minimum of simple pine furniture, a small desk at which to read and eat, his bunk, and a lectern for praying on bended knees, where a member of the order would spend much of his day. A small, shuttered window in his main living space overlooked the mountainside and the forested valley below. With the coming of spring, he planted some seeds in his garden and watched the green shoots grow each day. He took some of the prior's 'little tonic' each day, too, after his morning exercises and again at night before bed. It seemed to be working for him. Whether it was that, or the fact that he'd stopped drinking for the first time in his adult life, combined with the simple diet of wholesome home-grown food, goat's milk and pure spring water, he'd never felt so healthy and full of vitality.

That spring, a new duty he added to his daily routine was helping the monks brew their beer, which they stored in kegs in a vault beneath the monastery and sold to make a little money for the place's upkeep. A few months ago, it might have bothered him to have been around the beer. Now, he was barely tempted by it.

Besides, he enjoyed the company. He was getting to know them all better now. With the onset of the warmer weather, more time was spent in the neatly tended gardens and the surrounding wildflower meadows where the long-horned cattle roamed and grazed. Away from the monastery buildings, Ben discovered that the rule of silence was far less strictly observed. The monks would sit clustered together on benches during their downtime in the spring sunshine, enjoying the Alpine views, their wrap-around shades and Aviator Ray-Bans a strange contrast to their robes as they shared animated discussions and laughed and joked together, like regular guys.

Now and then a jet plane would fly over, tracking across the pure blue sky above the mountains. It was becoming strange to imagine that there was a whole other world still out there.

This place grew on you, for sure.

Chapter Five

It was just after dawn on a late May morning, and Ben was finishing up the day's first punishing bout of exercises before going about his duties, when there was an unexpected knock at the door of his cell. He quickly shrugged on his robe, opened the door and saw that his visitor was the Father Master of Novices.

Père Jacques pulled back the hood of his habit to reveal his tonsured scalp, and spoke in his usual hushed, benevolent tone. 'I have come to ask a service from you, Benoît.'

Ben was getting used to being called that. 'Whatever I can do, Father.'

In as few words as possible, the monk explained that it was about the beer. Ben already knew that once every few months the store of monastic ale, that had been ageing in barrels in the cellar deep beneath the monastery, needed to be brought up and loaded on the prehistoric flatbed truck that was the monks' only motor vehicle. He also knew that it was the job of Frère Patrice, one of the lay brothers, to don everyday clothing and drive the laden truck down the winding mountain road into Briançon. There, it was passed on to the wholesaler's agent who handled the distribution of the quality brew across France. It was a useful source of revenue for the monastery, as well as a proud centuries-old tradition.

But, as the Father Master of Novices explained with a frown, Frère Patrice had twisted his ankle badly a few days earlier after tripping down the refectory steps, and was unable to fulfil his duty today. Would Benoît agree to take his place?

Ben said that he'd be delighted to help in any way he could. He felt pleased and honoured that he'd been asked. It meant that he was trusted. It meant he was starting to be considered one of the community.

Before anything else could happen, though, first the beer barrels had to be brought up from the cellars. Like everything else here, that had to be done the old-fashioned way, which meant the hard way: at least eight hours' worth of tough physical labour carrying and rolling each forty-gallon iron-banded oak barrel separately all the way up from the bowels of the monastery, to be loaded on the truck ready to be taken down the mountain first thing the following morning, in time for the rendezvous with the distributor in Briançon.

Ben welcomed the task. Soon afterwards, he joined a small gang of lay brothers assigned to cellar duty. Their names were Gilles, Marc and Olivier. After brief, solemn greetings they got started.

Ben had never visited this part of the monastery before, deep below the main buildings. Olivier led the way with a lantern down endless twisting, steeply descending passages. Their steps left a line of prints in the dust as they walked. The little light the swaying lantern threw off glistened against the condensation that trickled from the mildewed stone walls, and every sound echoed deep in the shadows. Ben ran his fingers along the damp rock and could feel the tool marks where this space had been carved out of the solid heart of the mountain a thousand years ago, a feat of unimaginable difficulty. The further they descended, the more it felt like going down into a mineshaft, and he wondered how the hell they were meant to drag the beer barrels all the way up to ground level. It seemed like the kind of punitive exercise the army would delight in inflicting on raw recruits.

He soon found out the answer. A system of ropes and pulleys had been in use for about the last five hundred years – pretty newfangled technology so far as the monks were concerned – to carry the barrels up from the murky cellar. Quite how not installing some proper electric lighting down there was supposed to bring them closer to God, Ben didn't know and didn't ask. At least the rope and tackle system helped them avoid the very real possibility of meeting Him all too soon by being crushed to death while hauling their load up the steep, narrow stone steps in the semi-darkness. But to shift them from the cellar's iron-studded oak doors all the way to the former stable near the main gate where the truck was housed, it was going to be a simple, old-fashioned muscle job. Whatever the monastery earned in the way of revenue from this, Ben and the gang were going to earn it on their behalf today.

After four hours of sweaty work, they'd managed to shift more than half the barrels up to ground level, and the lay brothers looked more than ready for a break. It was agreed that they'd take half an hour to rest their tired arms and backs, then meet up again here to finish the job.

While the others went off to nap, or pray, or however they saw fit to spend the next thirty minutes, Ben wandered the underground passages. He used the flickering lantern to light his way, marvelling at how few people must have been here over the course of so many centuries. Some of the passages went down even deeper; he reckoned he must be a hundred and fifty feet or more below the monastery. The floor was thick with the dust of ages.

He supposed these might have been escape tunnels for the monks during turbulent periods in history, or hiding places in which they could take refuge from marauding enemies. Nobody of a claustrophobic nature would have wanted to venture down here, especially as some of the carved-out stone channels weren't much more than child-sized. At just a shade under six foot, Ben had to bend right down to be able to explore them. He'd always been fascinated by secret passages, ancient tunnels, hidden places. Maybe Freud would have said he was subconsciously looking for somewhere to escape from the world, hide from life. Maybe Ben would have told the old boy where to shove his psychoanalytic theories.

Just as he was thinking he should start making his way back, Ben saw tracks in the dust. Moments later, he noticed a strange pale glow up ahead, shining on the rough rock wall like the kind of natural phosphorescence he'd seen in caves in the Middle East. He paused, mystified, then curiosity drew him towards the light.

Suddenly the narrow walls seemed to fall away and the echo of his footsteps sounded much deeper. Ben realised that the tunnel had opened up into an underground cavern. Its sides and ceiling were too angular to be natural. He raised the lantern to spread its reach and peered around him, fascinated and wondering what this place was, or had once been.

But he was even more fascinated by the strange glow, which he now realised was shining from the mouth of a secondary passage to the left that led away from the opened-out chamber. Looking down, he saw that the tracks in the dust were leading that way. He followed, having to bow his head in the constricted passage. After a few yards, he found himself advancing on the source of the strange light.

It wasn't any kind of natural phosphorescence, but very much man-made: a small illuminated rectangle surrounded by a halo of light. It was moving slightly as the person holding it sat crouched against the rock wall, hunched over the tiny screen.

As Ben edged closer, he heard a gasp and the light darted away and went out. He shone the lantern, and instantly recognised the startled face that was gaping at him from the darkness.

'Roby?'

'Oh – it's you, Benoît. You frightened me.' Their voices reverberated inside the tunnel.

'What are you doing down here?' Ben asked. He already knew the answer, and what the novice had whipped out of sight to hide in his robe. 'Where did you get the mobile phone from, Roby?'

Roby hung his head in embarrassment. 'I – I – you won't—'

'Tell?' Ben smiled and shook his head. 'Of course I wouldn't.'

'Thierry gave it me,' Roby said, referring to another of the younger lay brothers whom Ben didn't know so well. 'You can go on the internet with it.'

Even here, the lures of modern life managed to curl their tentacles around the impressionable. 'And you were scared someone would catch you with it,' Ben said gently. 'It's okay, kid. Your secret's safe with me. Just try to stay off the porn sites. They're bad for your soul. And I don't think Père Antoine would be too impressed.'

Roby looked penitent.

'So this is your little refuge?' Ben asked, smiling.

Roby nodded. 'Nobody ever comes down here.'

'I understand. Just be thankful it was me who caught you

and not the Father Master of Novices. Now come on, I think you'd better get back before they miss you.'

Roby reluctantly followed him out of the narrow tunnel. At its mouth, Ben turned again to examine the cavern. 'What is this place?' he asked, raising the lantern.

'Dunno. Maybe they used to keep things in it.'

Ben stepped over to the wall and ran his hand along it, wiping away dust and cobwebs. It was the same thick, craggy stone with countless pick and chisel marks made by the miners, probably monks themselves, who'd carved this space out of solid rock at a time when crusading Christian armies were fighting – and mostly losing – in the Holy Land. He followed the wall, shining the lantern to look for engraved Latin script or anything else that could explain what the place had once been.

He didn't find any, but he did find something else. The cavern had once been bigger, until at some point, a long, long time ago, a section of it had been bricked up. How big a section was anybody's guess.

'I wonder why they did that?' Ben muttered.

Roby just shrugged absently. He seemed more interested in the clandestine mobile phone he was fingering inside the pocket of his robe.

Ben ran his hand across the dusty brickwork. It looked centuries old, but the mortar had been carefully applied and was still solid. Finding a lump of rock on the ground, he used it to tap against the wall. It made a hollow sound.

'Something's behind here,' he said, mostly to himself. For all he knew, it stretched out cathedral-sized behind that wall. Had part of the chamber become unstable and needed shoring up? Or perhaps the walled-up section marked the mouth of another passage leading deeper into the mountain, perhaps even all the way through to the outside, like a true escape tunnel? If that were the case, it could have been walled up to prevent anyone making their way in from the other end. But then, the monastery was hardly built like an impregnable fortress. If an invading force had wanted to take it, they wouldn't have had too much trouble breaking down the main gates. They wouldn't have needed to mess about with tunnels.

Just one of those mysteries of the ancient past. He wasn't going to learn much by staring at a wall and it was time for him to go back and get on with moving the rest of the beer barrels up from the cellar. The others could be there already, waiting for him.

Ben tossed the lump of rock away. Some unconscious part of his mind expected it to hit the stone floor with an echoing thump. It didn't. Instead, it landed with a brittle, crackling *crunch* that caught Ben's ear and made him frown. Strange.

And familiar. He'd heard that sound before. It didn't have pleasant associations.

Ben lowered the lantern and saw what the rock had landed on. He crouched down and examined it. Then picked it up and gazed at it.

It was the shattered remains of a human skull.

Chapter Six

That evening before church, Ben sat by candlelight in Père Antoine's cell. The chess pieces cast flickering shadows across the board as the two of them faced each other, both deeply involved. Their weekly game had become a welcome part of Ben's routine and he'd felt himself grow closer to the prior, even if the old monk had turned out to be a fiendish player and nearly always beat him. Ben's black army was in serious trouble again, and he was damned if he could think of a way to thwart those white bishops ganging up on his queen. He pulled her back out of immediate danger, exposing his remaining rook to enemy forces. Nothing he could do to prevent the sacrifice. War is hell.

'Thank you again for agreeing to drive the truck tomorrow,' Père Antoine said as he nonchalantly captured the rook and set it down among his growing collection of Ben's lost men.

Ben shrugged, as if to say it was nothing. He contemplated his losing position for a moment or two, then said, 'I made an interesting discovery today, Father. One of the passages down below leads into some kind of chamber, but it looks like it's been walled up.'

The old man's eyes flicked up from the chessboard, fixed on him for a moment and then lowered again. 'May I ask what led you down there?' he asked quietly. His expression was inscrutable.

'I was just exploring,' Ben said. He didn't mention Roby, or the novice's reason for hiding down there. 'I wondered what the chamber had been used for, if anyone still knows.'

'That place has not been used for a long time,' Père Antoine said.

'That's what I thought.' Ben backed his queen another few steps out of trouble and launched a tenuous offensive against the white king. 'There's a lot of dust and cobwebs down there. And other things that I'm sure wouldn't have been left lying around if it was often visited.'

Père Antoine didn't ask what other things. Ben wondered if that was because he already had a good idea what they might be.

'A lot of history in this place,' Ben said after a long beat of silence.

'Indeed there is,' the old man replied, gazing at the board.

'A whole honeycomb of tunnels. Makes you wonder where they all lead. Maybe there are more chambers you don't even know about.'

'No. There is just one.' Père Antoine looked uncomfortable. He shifted a knight and Ben's offensive suddenly began to look like another retreat. 'I would respectfully ask you not to go there again.'

'In case it's unsafe? Is that why it was walled up, to prevent a collapse?'

The old man pursed his lips, peering at Ben over the chess battlefield. 'It is a place we here prefer not to speak of,' he said, his voice barely above a whisper.

It didn't seem appropriate to ask why. 'I didn't realise. I'm sorry.'

'You were not to know, my son. Every place has its secrets

from the past. Even here, some things remain that ought to be forgotten.'

'Secrets?'

'And ghosts. Things that should be left undisturbed.'

'I don't believe in ghosts.'

'Yet they haunt you still,' the old man said with a faint smile. 'The ghosts of your past actions.'

'But God forgives. That's what you told me.'

'Yes, He forgives. Even the worst and most shameful acts of man, if we repent fully enough and ask for His mercy.'

It seemed as if the prior was alluding to more than just Ben's own sordid history. He felt that in bringing up the subject, he'd unearthed something greater, something darker, than a forgotten skull from centuries ago. But it was obvious that the old man had no desire to dwell on the matter any longer. There was a firmness in the monk's eyes, the closest thing Ben had seen in him to a look of authority. In the gentlest way, it meant 'this subject is closed'.

'Check,' Père Antoine said.

The rain started some time before dawn the next day. Ben watched the spring downpour from the window of his cell as he got ready that morning. Big splashy raindrops burst on the flagstones below and trembled on the leaves of the trees that stood in the courtyard. It felt strange to be putting on his black jeans and denim shirt instead of the robe he'd become accustomed to. The prospect of leaving the monastery and venturing down to civilisation for the first time in six months felt strange, too. Maybe the world down there would be completely different from before. Maybe aliens had landed and taken the place over. From up here, there was no way to know these things.

Ben laced up his boots, shrugged on his scuffed old brown

45

leather jacket and left the sanctuary of his cell, grabbing his green bag on the way out. He walked through the cloisters and out across the high-walled yard to the building where the truck was kept. The tall double doors opened with a creak. The rain was drumming hard on the stable roof and a leak had found its way through the old tiles to drip down to the straw-covered floor. One of the cats, disturbed by his entrance, uncoiled itself from the nest where it had been sleeping, gave him a disgusted look and slunk away.

The truck was parked with its rear end facing the doors. Ben had been too occupied yesterday with the laborious loading process to take a closer look at the vehicle. He circled it, peering critically here and there, pausing to kick the big old knobbly tyres and wondering whether it was still running on the same tankful of diesel as it had been for its last outing several months ago. Diesel didn't go off as quickly as gasoline. But the state of the fuel wasn't really his main concern. It was the vehicle itself that troubled him a little. How roadworthy was it? He didn't even know if it would start.

The truck wasn't quite as ancient as the monastery, but that didn't exactly make it modern, either. The long flatbed was made of wooden planks that were crumbling and riddled with wormholes. The dark green paintwork was badly faded with age and the soft tonneau cover lashed in place over the precious cargo of beer barrels had been patched so many times that there wasn't much left of the original canvas. It was a 1966 eight-ton long-wheelbase Citroën of the type known as a 'Belphégor'. Ben wondered whether the monks were aware that their only motor vehicle was named after one of the seven princes of Hell, the demon primarily responsible for sloth and laziness and tempting sinners with the lure of fancy new inventions. Maybe that was a deliberate ploy to discourage monks from learning to drive, he thought as he hauled himself up inside the spartan cab.

After so many months spent mimicking the lifestyle of circa 1350, it felt weird to be back inside a motor vehicle. Especially one that officially belonged in a museum. The steering wheel was about the size of a ship's, positioned almost horizontally above a stamped metal dash fitted with instruments that could have been lifted from a military half-track of fifty years ago. But the old motor cranked into life at the first twist of the key and settled into a steady rumble, dispelling at least some of Ben's immediate concerns. He depressed the heavy clutch and eased the huge gearstick, a steel bar long enough to lever a wall over, into reverse. There was no grinding, crunching shearing of metal. So far, so good.

'Here goes,' he muttered to the truck. 'Don't let me down, now.' He re-engaged the clutch and the scarred old green monster backed rumbling out of the stable building. Ben spun the wheel about a hundred turns to manoeuvre it round to face the tall arched wooden gates, which two monks stood holding open. He found the switch for the windscreen wipers, then lumbered towards the entrance. The monks waved as he passed through.

He waved back, hauled the heavy steering wheel to the left in the direction of Briançon, hit the gas and was on his way.

'Just you and me now,' he said to the truck.

If he'd known then what he'd find on his return, he would never have left the place.

Chapter Seven

The articulated Volvo lorry had driven through most of the night, cutting southwards from Switzerland on a careful winding route through the Italian Alps. As morning came, the driver finally arrived at the rendezvous point. The chosen location was a quiet, high-altitude roadside spot a few minutes outside the Alpine town of Torre Pellice, forty-seven kilometres south-west of Torino and just fifteen kilometres from the Italian-French border, in a rocky, dusty plateau between two cliffs. On the right-hand side of the road was a stretch of crushed-stone layby three times the lorry's length. Eyes on his mirror, the driver eased the big trailer into it, perfectly parallel with the road and out of the way of what little traffic might pass this way. According to the plan, he brought the lorry to a halt in the centre third of the layby, leaving enough space in front and behind. Then he shut down the big diesel, settled back in his cab and drank coffee from a flask while he waited for the next step of the plan to happen.

The driver's name was Dominik Baiza. He hadn't been waiting long before three other vehicles arrived at the RV point. Three identical black Range Rovers, dusty from their long drive, travelling in convoy along the empty road. They pulled up in front of the lorry and their occupants got out.

Four to a car. Eleven men, plus the female driver of the middle Range Rover, the youngest of the group.

This was no social occasion. Baiza didn't get out of his cab to meet them, and there was little conversation among the twelve. A couple of them lit cigarettes and stood smoking at the side of the road, while the rest just bided their time, leaning against their vehicles or sitting in the shade of the big lorry trailer. The sunshine was bright and most of them wore dark glasses. They were dressed casually, most in jeans and T-shirts. The woman was wearing a leather jacket and combat boots, and a baseball cap covered her tied-back hair. The men paid her no more attention than they did one another. She was just one of the gang, there for the same purpose as they were. Some, like Torben Roth and Wolf Schilling, were old hands, veterans of the 2011 Korean mission. Roth still bore the scar from that operation, the whole left side of his face creased into a permanent scowl from the rifle bullet that had come close to killing him. Others were relatively new recruits, like Wokalek and Zwart, the Englishman Dexter Nicholls, and the woman herself, whose name was Michelle Faban. New blood, very carefully chosen, with the right background and the right mindset. The boss was careful about such things, as he needed to be.

The rendezvous was complete seventeen minutes later when they heard the thud of the approaching chopper. 'Here he comes,' Torben Roth said. Cigarettes were tossed away. Hands pulled out of pockets. Inside the lorry cab, Dominik Baiza quickly finished up his coffee.

The chopper was a Bell 429-WLG. That last part of its designation stood for 'with landing gear'. As it came in to land, sparkling white against the vivid blue sky, the undercarriage descended like that of a fixed-wing aircraft. The group on the ground backed away from the roaring noise and the hurricane of downdraught that whipped up road-side dust and loose gravel. Michelle Faban held on to her cap as the blast tore at her hair. The chopper came neatly down in the middle of the road, taxied a few feet forwards and to the right, towards the back of the articulated Volvo. Then it halted. The rotors began to power down, and the assembled twelve gathered round in a circle to greet their leader.

The tall, slim figure of Udo Streicher emerged from the cockpit, cool and unruffled from the flight, wearing a loose white shirt and Armani jeans, reflective Ray-Ban Aviator shades shielding his eyes. He was in excellent shape for a man of forty-six. The wind from the slowing rotor blades swept his silver-flecked hair back from his high forehead.

The chopper passenger was Hannah Gissel, Streicher's long-time girlfriend. Hannah was wearing a black combat jacket. Her long, slender legs were enveloped in skintight black leggings. Her hair, so blond that it was almost white, was spiked and cropped even shorter than she normally wore it. She looked mean and ready for anything. Appearances weren't deceptive. The newer guys on the team, with the exception of Michelle Faban, had been briefed on the rules when it came to Hannah. You didn't talk to her. You didn't even make contact with those pale grey eyes. Not just because she was Streicher's woman, and Streicher was known for his pathological jealousy. Even if Hannah had been single, it would have been a serious error of judgement for any man to get too familiar with her. A fatal mistake, literally.

Udo Streicher met his people with the cursory nod of a man used to being in command. He walked a few steps to where Dominik Baiza, inside the lorry, could see him clearly in his mirror, and raised his hand. At the signal, Baiza flipped a switch inside the cab. It activated the tailgate, which hinged downwards, supported by two thick hydraulic rams, to act as an access ramp. As it descended, all eyes were on the cavernous interior of the trailer.

Once the ramp was fully lowered, Torben Roth walked up it and disappeared inside, his footsteps ringing with a metallic echo. Moments later, the space filled with the growl of an engine firing up. Streicher and the others watched as the formidable vehicle that was the lorry's sole cargo reversed slowly down the ramp.

It was Udo Streicher's latest acquisition. He called it his BATT-mobile, standing for Ballistic Armoured Tactical Transport. The thing was even more robust than it looked. A Lenco BearCat, designed in Pittfield, Massachusetts, for SWAT-team raids and similar contingencies. It wasn't exactly a civilian vehicle. Its charcoal-grey bodyshell was rated to defeat small-arms fire up to and including .50-calibre M2 and 7.62 NATO armour-piercing rounds. Gun ports, three to a side, allowed its occupants to return fire at assailants. Streicher had toyed with the idea of having the optional roof-mounted machine-gun turret fitted, but decided that as the vehicle was to be used on public roads during the mission, that might draw a little too much attention.

In all other respects it was a full-on assault vehicle. The blast shield under the chassis rendered it impregnable to landmines, while the six-litre V8 turbo-diesel engine could propel it out of trouble very quickly. The finishing touch, and essential to the success of this mission, was the breaching device on the front – a massive steel buffer that looked like the cowcatcher on an old steam train. The BATT-mobile was an exercise in excess. But then, one of Udo Streicher's many philosophies was that if a thing was worth doing, it was worth overdoing.

'Pretty cool, huh?' Hannah said, standing surveying the vehicle with her fists on her hips. Her lips twitched into the merest smile. Coming from her, it was high praise.

Streicher had paid as much attention to the inside of the vehicle as the outside. It was fully kitted out for this mission, carrying a small arsenal of weaponry, as well as breaching munitions and some even more specialised equipment that he'd obtained from another of his illicit contacts. Naturally, such things didn't come cheap. He was aware of the hit that his financial resources had taken in order to put the mission together, but it wasn't a significant concern to him. Not under the circumstances, and he remained a very wealthy man. Wealthy enough to carry out whatever plans were necessary to attain the dream that dominated his whole life.

Things would soon begin to happen. They had a few miles to cover, some time to kill, some final preparations and checks to make. Nice and easy. No rush. No moves, until the time was precisely right. If all went according to plan – and Streicher had no reason to believe it wouldn't – they should have no problems. It was a soft target. A whole different proposition from the 2011 disaster. That had been a lesson learned the hard way.

Nothing was going to stand in his way this time.

Nothing, and nobody.

And all thanks to *his* genius. *His* hard work. *His* penetrating mind, that had put together connections nobody else had or could. That was what made him different from everybody else. That was why he deserved the future he saw for himself.

Baiza reversed the BearCat to the bottom of the ramp. Loose stones pinged and popped under the savage tread of its big tyres as he backed it right away from the lorry to make room for the chopper to taxi up inside the trailer in its place. Silvain Chavanne and Riccardo Cazzitti began unloading the necessary gear from the back of one of the Range Rovers: a special high-pressure spray to cool the rotor assembly, and a set of wrenches to dismantle the blades so that the chopper could fit inside the trailer. It would be Dominik Baiza's job to mind the lorry until the team's return. Streicher's thorough planning had seen to it that he had enough food and water, as well as a nine-millimetre pistol in case of any interference. Streicher had thought of everything.

'Everyone knows what to do, yes?' Streicher said, scanning the solemn faces. Several heads nodded. Stepping down from the BearCat, Torben Roth just gave a grunt.

'Then let's get rolling,' Streicher told them.

Chapter Eight

Ben's route snaked and twisted like a meandering river all the way down the mountain, in places flanked by lush verges bursting with spring wildflowers, in others teetering on the edge of vertiginous drops with little or nothing in the way of safety barriers. He soon discovered that the truck had steering as vague as a politician's answers, and learned to take it easy on the narrow bits. The brakes left something to be desired, too, which made interesting work of the frequent hairpin bends on a road made slick with rainwater. The heavy load made the suspension sway on every corner, and sometimes it felt as if the thing might tip over. But he felt happy to be doing this for his companions. It gave him a sense of purpose. Of belonging.

After a couple of miles, the rain stopped and the sun beamed out through parting clouds. Ben turned off the clattering wipers, opened the window and smiled as the fresh breeze streamed in. The trepidation he'd felt about leaving the sanctuary of the monastery began to melt away with each passing mile. Life was all right. It really was. He didn't even miss his cigarettes any more.

The drive took a little over forty minutes. It was the perfect kind of scenic yet challenging Alpine road that a gentleman of a sporting disposition would have relished tackling in something like a Porsche Cayman or a classic Morgan. But Ben took his time, rumbling along sedately, taking care not to overload the tired old brakes on the long, steep downward straights, slowing right down for the bends. As he drove, he drank in the spectacular views across the valley and let the sunshine soak into his soul. Yes, life was okay. By the time the road had wound its way down to Briançon, he was even getting to like the old demon Belphégor.

Approaching the town, Ben reached for the slip of paper he'd been given showing the directions for the rendezvous point. From the historic part of Briançon, which dated back to Roman times as Brigantium, the modern town sprawled south-westwards. The small industrial estate he needed to find was right out on the edge, and his directions allowed him to skirt around town and approach from the east side. The roads weren't badly congested, which was a relief to Ben as he'd worried about cooking the clutch in stop-start traffic. He guessed that this must be the quietest time of the year, well out of the snowy season when hordes of skiers descended on Briançon and the town's population tripled. Not that Ben had seen any from his remote sanctuary, not even when the snow lay thick all across the peaks and valleys and every day brought a fresh blizzard.

Filtering west, he passed a hospital, then a spread-out retail park. He saw a big Champion supermarket, some scattered industrial buildings and a tyre services place next to a garage. A little further on, he found the entrance he was looking for, a green steel gate in a mesh fence leading to a large concreted yard, empty apart from a Renault truck and a silver BMW. A short, badly overweight guy with sandy hair was leaning against the car. Three leaner, younger guys were hanging about the truck. Ben pulled up a few yards away, yanked on the handbrake and turned off his ignition. The Belphégor stuttered and fell silent.

Ben jumped down from the cab. It was approaching midday and the sun was hot and bright, making him shield his eyes. He looked around him as the sandy-haired man ambled up. The mountains were visible in the background, away beyond green hills overlooking the town that were dotted with little white houses and chalets sparkling in the sun.

'You must be Pierrot,' he said in French to the sandy-haired man. Pierrot was the rep for the distribution company that handled the monastery beer.

'You're not the regular guy,' Pierrot said, eyeing him.

'Just standing in,' Ben said. They shook hands and got down to business. Pierrot's crew of three quickly, efficiently switched the cargo from the Belphégor to the Renault while Pierrot spread a couple of forms out on the bonnet of the Beemer for Ben to read and sign on behalf of the monastery. Ben examined the small print carefully, checked the payment and bank details were correct, then reviewed everything again and found no problems. He signed on the line and handed the forms back to Pierrot. The man grinned, put the forms into a folder and then opened up the boot of his car.

'*Fait une putain de'chaleur, hein?*' he said, squinting up at the bright sun.

Ben nodded and agreed that it was pretty warm. Maybe if Pierrot lost a few pounds he wouldn't feel it so much, but Ben kept that opinion to himself. Pierrot had other solutions. From a cooler in the back of the car he produced a couple of chilled bottles of Kronenbourg. He offered one to Ben. Ben shook his head and said no, thanks.

Soon afterwards, the crew finished up, swigged down a

cold beer each and then piled into the Renault. Ben watched the truck drive off with its load, followed by Pierrot in his car. That was that. His job was done, his responsibility fulfilled, and it was time to go home. He walked back to the Belphégor. Clambered up into the cab, twisted the ignition key . . . and nothing happened.

He did it again. Again, nothing happened. Completely dead. Either the battery had suffered a total discharge in the time it had taken to transfer the beer to the Renault, or something more complex and sinister had just happened to the truck's electrics.

Wonderful.

Ben heaved open the bonnet and peered in at the grimy nest of ancient wiring. He was no mechanic. Like other SAS soldiers he'd had some basic training in fixing vehicles, in case of certain emergency situations on hostile ground that involved commandeering – or just plain stealing – civilian transport that might not always be in top condition. But he had a feeling that the SAS would have continued on foot sooner than give the Belphégor a second look. Set fire to it maybe, if they needed to create a diversion.

Bolted to the flatbed behind the cab was a tool locker. Nothing more than a metal box, battered and dented and speckled with rust, about four feet long by about two feet wide. Ben jumped up on to the flatbed and crouched down, hooking eight fingers under the flaky edge of the locker lid to lift it. The hinges were near solid with rust and old paint, and it gave a creak as it opened. He looked inside, and what he saw made his mind up not to bother trying to fix the truck himself. There was a removable compartment containing an assortment of spanners that looked as if they'd spent decades at the bottom of a river. The lower compartment contained no jack, no tyre irons or wheel-nut wrench, only a coil of greasy old rope and a pair of bolt croppers.

All of which was about as useful as having no tools at all.

The other thing Ben didn't have was a phone. The only items in his pockets were his wallet and the little bottle of Père Antoine's tonic that he was currently working his way through. However liberating the joyful technology-free monastic lifestyle might feel up there on the mountain, it had its practical shortcomings down here in the big, bad world.

Remembering the garage he'd passed a little way back down the road, he began walking.

Within five minutes, he was standing on the forecourt talking to a jovial guy in a grease-stained overall, explaining his situation. Within ten, he was riding back in a tow-truck to where he'd left the stricken Belphégor. The mechanic hooked it up and they towed it the short distance to the garage where more guys in overalls came to stare and grin as if they'd never seen anything like it before. Which, Ben realised, they probably hadn't. After a quick inspection, the mechanic in charge gave Ben the prognosis on the electrical system. The word he used was '*foutu*'. Not exactly a technical term. Not a very encouraging one, either, until the mechanic pointed to a rusted heap in the corner of the yard and told Ben that he should be able to cannibalise some parts from it.

Four hours, he assured Ben. Four hours tops, and the old Belphégor would be back in action.

Until then, there wasn't a lot Ben could do. Even if he'd had a phone, he couldn't call the monastery to tell them he'd be late coming back and not to worry. Not that they worried unduly about much, generally. They would have said it was in God's hands. For all practical purposes that was the only way Ben could see it, too.

So, there it was. Four hours to kill. It wasn't the end of the world.

He took a note of the garage's number and set out on foot towards town. The walk took him thirty minutes, by the end of which lunchtime had been and gone and he was hungry and thirsty. A few sips of Père Antoine's tonic did a little to quell the thirst. Ben still didn't know what it contained. He put the bottle back in his pocket and checked the contents of his wallet for the first time in months. In all that time he'd spent not a single penny, so there was still plenty of cash inside. Now to find a place to eat.

Briançon was a pretty place. Parts of the old town had once been heavily fortified, to defend the region from an attacking Austrian army. However many centuries ago that had been, Ben didn't know for sure – but when you lived in a medieval monastery, everything seemed recent and modern by comparison. He walked through narrow, winding grey-stone streets and up steep paths and steps, looking for a bistro or a sandwich bar. The streets were busy. Lots of colour, lots of noise and life. He wasn't used to it any more. It was a rhythm you had to get readjusted to, in the same way he'd often had to get back in synch with normal life after spending long periods away on military operations in jungles or deserts, back in the day.

Rounding a corner, Ben saw parasols and tables out on the street. This was the kind of bistro he'd been looking for, where he could get a snack like a *croque-monsieur* and a Perrier water. It looked like a welcoming place. A waiter with a tray was weaving efficiently among the tables. One table was occupied by an animated white-haired group who looked like a tourist party. At another was a middle-aged professional guy in suit and tie, maybe a local businessman or a bank manager, reading a newspaper. At another sat a couple, not old, not young, in their thirties. They were clasping hands across the table and obviously in love. The guy was heavily built, in jeans and a polo shirt. The woman was wearing a light sleeveless top and shorts and sandals, and had her back to Ben.

There was another table nearby that was empty. He walked towards it. His plan was to stay a while, watch the world go by, bide his time while the mechanics were doing their bit and then slowly wander back to the garage to pick up the truck. There was no hurry. No pressure. He felt relaxed and easy about the whole thing. The monastery had taught him to feel that way.

As Ben approached the café terrace, he did a double-take at the woman sitting with her back to him and suddenly halted dead in his tracks as if he'd been shot. He felt himself go very cold. He stood there, staring.

Her auburn hair was thick and loose, falling down in curls between her shoulder blades and moving nicely when she did. Her shoulders were slightly burned, a touch too much sun on her fair redhead's skin. Everything about her was stunningly familiar. He was certain he recognised the curve of her slim back. Her elegant posture, the way she had her ankles crossed under the chair as she leaned forward talking about something and gesticulating with her free hand. The fingers were tapered and delicate. She wore no rings.

A million emotions suddenly flooded through Ben's mind, stinging him like electric shocks. His hands began to shake. He blinked. It was her. He couldn't believe it.

She was oblivious of his presence, but as Ben went on staring, the guy she was with began to take notice of him.

Ben walked a few steps closer. His legs felt wobbly. He reached out to touch her shoulder. The guy she was with narrowed his eyes and looked to be about to say something, but Ben spoke first.

'*Brooke?*'

Chapter Nine

Ben couldn't help himself. He put his hand on her shoulder. Her skin was warm and soft and dry against his fingers. She flinched a little in surprise and let go of her companion's hand, breaking off from whatever she'd been saying to him in mid-sentence.

'Brooke?' Ben said again. He was positively amazed, *amazed*, to see his ex-fiancée here. It was like something out of a dream, the dream he'd had so many times.

She turned. Her mouth opened. Her eyes locked on to his, as blue as a summer sky.

Blue. Not green. Brooke had eyes the colour of emeralds.

It wasn't her. This woman was a couple of years younger than Brooke. Her mouth was thinner, her cheekbones higher, her features sharper. Especially with the hostile look she was giving him.

The millisecond that Ben realised his mistake, he withdrew his hand and stepped back. 'Please forgive me, Madame. I mistook you for someone else.'

Her blue eyes flared. 'It's *Mademoiselle*,' she snapped, as though calling her 'Madame' was a far worse crime than laying your hands in a familiar way on a total stranger. So much for the neo-post-feminist political-correctness movement in France.

Ben went on apologising, but it was too late. Now the guy with her was getting involved, standing up abruptly and scraping his chair across the terrace with the backs of his legs. He had to step away from the table to avoid butting the parasol, because he was a big guy. At least three inches taller than Ben and about a foot broader across the chest. The mild irritation in the woman's eyes was eclipsed by the fury in his. Ben couldn't entirely blame him. It was a normal thing. A male thing. Like a rutting stag wanting to win his mate by scoring over the potential competition, this guy obviously felt he had to put on a show. Naturally, he was going to make a big thing of wanting to protect her.

Too big a thing. Right away, Ben could see the signs of a situation about to turn ugly. He wasn't the only one. The businessman was watching over the top of his newspaper. The white-haired group had stopped talking and were throwing anxious glances at them.

'Hey, I said I was sorry,' Ben said, keeping his tone light and his body language unthreatening. 'Let me buy you a drink, okay? No hard feelings.'

'Get your fucking hands off her,' the guy raged.

'I did,' Ben said. He'd backed off two long steps and now couldn't have touched her if he'd wanted to.

'Who the fuck do you think you are?'

'I'm from the monastery,' Ben said.

The big guy sneered. 'Joker, eh?' He came around the table, brushed past his girlfriend and moved towards Ben with his fists clenched and raised.

'Let's not take this too far,' Ben said. 'It was a mistake. I apologised.'

The woman was saying nothing. There was a gleam in her eye. Maybe she was enjoying this. Maybe the idea of being fought over was making her day. Ben couldn't be sure, but in any case he was too busy watching her beau to take too much notice. The guy stepped closer, within punching distance. Which, with arms the length of his, was a fair stretch. 'I'm going to knock your damn head off, asshole.' Then the punch was on its way. Ben could have sat down, eaten his *croque-monsieur*, drunk his Perrier and maybe taken a little nap in the time it took coming. He stepped out of the way of the swinging fist. The guy's momentum carried him forwards, past Ben.

'You don't want to do this,' Ben said. 'Why spoil a beautiful afternoon?'

But now it was even more too late. This wasn't about the woman any longer. His face mottled with humiliation, the guy gathered himself up for a second punch. It was faster than the first, though not much. Ben had time to say, 'You're an idiot,' before he caught the fist that was flying towards his face. He twisted it. Just a little twist. Nothing too aggressive. Certainly not vicious. But once he had the guy's arm trapped, he wasn't going to let go either. A lucky hit from this opponent could break his nose, smash his teeth. Ben didn't much feel like returning to the monastery all banged up and bloody. He was fairly certain they had disciplinary rules against lay brothers who brawled in bars in their spare time. Père Antoine might just show him the door, and Ben wasn't ready to leave.

So as Ben saw it, he really had no choice. He twisted the guy's thick arm all the way around behind his back and used the painful leverage to dump him on his face. He hit the ground hard.

'Stay down,' Ben warned him. 'It's finished. You made your point. You're a hero.'

But the hero wouldn't stay down, which was a bigger mistake than the one Ben had made in touching his girlfriend's shoulder. He swayed up to his feet and came on again. Blood was leaking from his nose and spotting all down the front of his polo shirt. Ben stepped in between the flailing arms and hit him in the solar plexus. Minimum force. It didn't feel to Ben like much more than a tap, but the guy went sprawling backwards as if a horse had kicked him. He crashed into the table at which Ben would have been quietly enjoying his lunch now, if this hadn't happened. The table capsized, spilling the big man back to the ground. Bloody-faced and wheezing and clutching at his stomach, this time he didn't seem inclined to get up again. At that moment the waiter came bursting out of the bistro, along with a couple more guys. One of them pointed at Ben and yelled: '*J'appelle les flics!*'

'No need for the police,' Ben told them, spreading his hands. 'I'm sorry for the trouble,' he said to the staring auburn-haired woman, then turned and began walking away.

'Wait!' she called after him. 'What's your name?'

That just beat everything. Ben could hear the commotion as he made his retreat, but didn't look back. Turning the corner, he broke into a jog. His nerves were jangling badly. Not because of the fight. It was as if some huge, gaping wound inside him, which he'd thought had healed, had been ripped back open again even worse than before and his whole being was gushing out of it, draining him right down to the marrow.

A hundred yards up the twisting narrow street, he settled back down to a fast walk. The jangling wasn't wearing off, but becoming more intense. His thoughts and emotions were flying around inside him in so many directions at once that he could hardly even see where he was going. All he could see was Brooke's face. He kept going. Crossed the street without looking, heard the urgent blast of a car horn and ignored it. He wouldn't have cared if a bus had mown him down. Let it.

Four minutes later, he was inside another bistro. He walked straight up to the bar.

'What'll it be, monsieur?' the barman asked.

'Scotch,' Ben said.

'Which one?' the barman said, motioning at a row of bottles.

'I don't care. You choose.'

'Water?'

'As it comes.'

The barman poured out a glass. It was empty almost the moment it touched the bar.

'Leave the bottle,' Ben said.

It was going to be a long day and an even longer night. But nothing in comparison to what would come later.

Chapter Ten

The first thing Ben saw on awakening was the stained Artexed ceiling above him. With some effort, he shifted his gaze to look down the length of his body and saw that he was lying in a bed. He closed his eyes. For a few disorientated moments, it seemed to him that he was tucked up in his bunk in the safe haven of the monastery. That the discomfiting fragments of memory playing at the edges of his mind were all just a bad dream.

Except that they weren't. He opened his eyes and realised that he wasn't dreaming about the sour taste in his mouth or the thudding headache of a serious whisky hangover. Wedging himself up in the bed to peer at his surroundings, it also occurred to him that his cell at the Chartreuse de la Sainte Vierge de Pelvoux wasn't decorated with peeling posters of naked women and filled with bodybuilding equipment. A long bar resting on a flat weight bench was sagging with enough iron to make Ben's muscles hurt just looking at it.

Nor did his cell contain a wall-mounted rack full of guns. Confusing.

Ben's watch said it was 7.47 a.m. He climbed out of the rumpled bed and felt the full force of the hangover wash over him. He was still fully dressed. The bed was beside a small window. While his cell looked out over a sweeping eagle's-view vista, all that could be seen from here was the bare brick wall of a neighbouring building. He peered down and saw an alleyway, empty but for a couple of wheelie bins.

He threaded his way between the bench press set-up and stacks of weights over to the gun rack. They weren't replicas. He took one down. AK-47. Romanian, with a folding stock and unloaded thirty-round curved steel magazine. Old, but well looked after, the metal parts covered in a light sheen of oil.

Ben thought, *Hmm.*

He replaced the weapon on the rack and looked at the one below it. It was a FAMAS rifle, service weapon of the French army for the last thirty years or more. FAMAS stood for *Fusil d'Assaut de la Manufacture d'Armes de Saint-Étienne*. It was a strange-looking contraption, built on the design concept the military designated 'bullpup', with the receiver placed behind the pistol grip and trigger unit instead of in front of it. It was a way of creating an automatic weapon that was short and handy without sacrificing too much in the way of barrel length. Some hated it, some loved it. To Ben's eye the thing looked ungainly, but he knew it did the job it was built to do. This one was standard military issue with the twenty-five-round straight magazine, even fitted with the regulation bayonet.

The real question was what one of these was doing in the room with him. Ben was beginning to wonder now if he'd fallen down a cosmic wormhole and woken up in a parallel universe.

He tentatively left the room and found himself at the end of a narrow passage he was certain he'd never seen before. He followed the beat of rock music and the scent of fresh coffee to a door at the other end, and swung it open.

The other side of the door was a small kitchen. Seated alone at a scarred pine table, listening to a radio and holding a mug that said ULTIMATE WARRIOR, his host in this strange place flashed him a brilliant smile. Suddenly, Ben's fragmented memory was beginning to slot miserably back together.

'Hey, big man,' his host chuckled in French, rising to greet his guest. Maybe he was being modest. Six-six at the very least, with skin the colour of burnished ebony, he wasn't the smallest Nigerian guy Ben had ever seen. He made the muscle-bound oaf Ben had beaten up the day before look like a dwarf. He was somewhere in his late forties, his hair grizzled at the temples. A tattered Gold's Gym T-shirt showed off his weightlifter's shoulders and powerful, vein-laced arms.

Ben stared at him, struggling to recall the name. 'Omar,' he said at last.

The dazzling grin widened. 'Brother, I'm surprised you remember a fucking thing.'

Ben slumped in a wooden chair. 'That's about all I do remember.' But the rest was slowly coming back. He wasn't sure he wanted it to.

Omar filled in the missing pieces with obvious amusement. How he and his bar-room buddies had found a new drinking companion the previous evening when this already toasted English guy had wandered into their regular haunt clutching the remains of a bottle of scotch. It had turned into quite a night.

'Did I say anything?'

'Just kept rambling on about some woman. You got it bad, my friend. I know how that goes, believe me.'

'Nobody got hit, did they?' Ben dared to ask. He looked at his knuckles. No sign of fresh bruising, and they didn't hurt. Still, that didn't prove anything.

'Didn't get that far,' Omar told him with a booming laugh. 'Not quite. Shit, I never saw anyone put away that much whisky before. Me and the boys were taking bets on when you'd drop, man. Incredible.'

'Yeah, it's a real talent,' Ben muttered. 'I hope you won your bet.'

Omar shook his head, still beaming. 'Nah. You cost me big time.'

'Sorry to hear it. Did you bring me back here?'

'Wasn't going to leave you lying in the gutter for the cops to scrape up, now was I?'

'I appreciate that, Omar.'

'Hey, no worries. How'd you like the room?'

'Interesting,' Ben said, rubbing his eyes. 'Especially the wall decorations. I don't mean the posters.'

'Oh, that,' Omar replied dismissively. 'Just a few souvenirs.'

'That's a G2 FAMAS. You won't exactly find one in the local gun shop.'

The bright grin again. Ben was going to need sunglasses for the glare. Omar said, 'That one came home with me from a little spree called Opération Daguet.'

'You fought with the French Army in the Gulf?'

Omar shrugged it off. 'Long time ago.'

'1991,' Ben said. 'Around the time I joined up.'

'I knew there was something about you.'

'British Army. Special Air Service. Long time ago, too.'

'Want a coffee, bro? Look like you could do with it.'

'And a favour,' Ben said, nodding and then wincing at the pain the movement cost him. 'I need a lift. Have you got a car?'

Omar looked at him. 'Shit. Have *I* got a car?'

Chapter Eleven

Omar's pride and joy was a H1 Hummer, the civilian version of the M998 US Army Humvee, the nickname that was the nearest anyone could pronounce to HMMWV or High Mobility Multipurpose Wheeled Vehicle.

The last time Ben had been inside a real one had been on a classified SAS mission in the Middle East. The demilitarised version might not have been bristling with heavy armament, but it was still a monster of a truck that dominated the road by sheer force of intimidation. Painted a deep, gleaming metallic gunmetal that was halfway between charcoal grey and black and all tricked out with mirror-tinted glass and oversized wheels and crash bars and enough auxiliary lighting to fry an egg at thirty paces, it could have been custom-built to suit Omar's own huge frame.

'Won it in a poker game,' he explained loudly over the roar as they muscled their way across Briançon with all the noise and presence of a tank battalion, scattering lesser traffic into the verges. 'I can hardly afford the insurance, but what the hell, I like it.' Ben might have appreciated it more if every jolt of the off-road suspension hadn't sent another arrow of pain through the middle of his skull.

The garage opened for business at 8.30. As the Hummer

roared up on to the forecourt, Ben saw the Belphégor truck sitting waiting there for him.

'Thought you weren't coming back,' the mechanic said. 'Had her all fixed up and ready for you yesterday afternoon.'

'Don't ask,' Ben replied.

The mechanic tossed him the keys. 'Wouldn't take her on a grand tour of Europe, but treat her kind and she'll do fine.'

Ben waved a final thanks to Omar, and the Hummer took off with a large hand extended in a goodbye wave from the window. Ben watched it roar away. Now he just wanted to get out of Briançon as fast as possible and try and put this shameful episode behind him. He paid the repair bill from his own money, and clambered into the truck. It rumbled into life at the first twist of the key. As long as it got him back, that was all he could ask.

It was coming on for 8.45 as Ben set off. His thoughts were dark and brooding on the drive back to the monastery. It was another bright and sunny morning, but he was too swallowed up in self-loathing and penitence to take much notice. He'd let himself down, and not just himself. He'd turned his back on the monastery for just a few hours, and look at the result. This relapse meant there was a lot more work to do.

His stomach felt queasy and his blood alcohol level was probably still too high for him to be driving. He swigged down an extra-large emergency dose of Père Antoine's tonic en route, thinking it might somehow purge the toxins from his system, or at least help clear his head. It did neither, but was a small comfort to him nonetheless. The greater comfort was knowing he'd be home soon.

Home. It really was beginning to feel like that to him. Secure, closeted. A safe zone. He yearned to be there.

He drove doggedly on. The mountain road lifted him up

and up, until the pine forests were far below and he could taste the pure mountain air that whistled in through his window. The closer he got to the monastery, the more the darkness in his mind seemed to lift. When at last the walls came into view, he felt a surge of optimism.

But as he neared the gates, he sensed something that unsettled him. Because the gates were normally shut, and now they were open. Maybe the monks had been anxious about his return after all, and had left them open as a gentle hint to God to speed him safely home. Or because everyone was at prayer. Or maybe not. It wasn't that. There was something wrong.

Then he got closer to the gates and he saw what was wrong. The gates themselves, for a start. They'd been built to open outwards, but now they were hanging open inwards. Ben saw shattered wood. Buckled hinges. One of the gates was listing at an angle where its mountings had been ripped from the stone pillar.

Ben stopped the truck. He stared at the smashed entrance. Something had happened here while he'd been away. Something significant and irreversible and not good.

Those gates had withstood centuries of weathering. The steel-banded oak was eight inches thick, age-hardened, tough as slabs of slate and locked from the inside by an iron deadbolt you could have hung a battleship from. To smash them open would require an immense force. An extremely violent impact from a very heavy object moving at quite some speed. Like a seriously large and powerful battering ram.

Ben drove through the broken gates and rolled the Belphégor inside the yard. Then he stopped again.

And stared.

Chapter Twelve

He stopped, because of what he saw in front of him.

The crow that had been pecking at the body spread its wings and flapped away. There was blood on the pale cloth of the monk's robe. Blood spread across the ground underneath him. He was sprawled face down in the dirt with his arms out to his sides and one leg crooked, as if he'd been trying to crawl forward on hands and knees before his limbs had given way under him.

Ben's stomach clenched like a fist and he shut off the truck engine, ripped the key from the ignition and booted open the door and jumped down from the cab. His first illogical thought was that the monk had suffered a heart attack or a stroke. He ran towards the body, then abruptly halted a few yards short of it. He looked around him, and blinked, and his stomach clenched even more tightly when he saw that there were other bodies in the yard.

They were everywhere.

He could see five, six, seven of them from where he stood gaping in disbelief. Then an eighth, spread-eagled face-up in the shadow of the store building. Then a ninth, hanging out of the low arch of the cloister wall as if trying to clamber through it. More blood. Blood all over the place. Spatters of it on the stonework. Pools and spots and trails of it on the ground, congealing and going dark and sticky in the morning sun. There was a hum of buzzing flies in the air, dark clouds of them swirling and hovering over and around the bodies.

Ben hurried towards the nearest body and felt something small and hard under the sole of his boot. Even through thick rubber, he could tell right away that the object wasn't a stone. He crouched and picked it up. A dull brass cartridge case. Its circular base was concentrically stamped in small lettering WIN 9mm LUGER.

It might have been an incongruous sight here in Chartreuse de la Sainte Vierge de Pelvoux, but it was an extremely familiar one to Ben's eyes. Standard nine-millimetre ammunition, the casing manufactured by the Winchester Repeating Arms Company under licence to Browning Arms of Morgan, Utah. A relatively diminutive cartridge, but famously effective. High-pressure, high-velocity, beloved of practically every military force on the planet since its invention in 1902, making it the world's most popular combat handgun and submachine gun round. It also lent itself very well to being downloaded to subsonic velocity levels, eliminating the ear-splitting crack that a bullet makes when breaking the sound barrier, and allowing the report to be further subdued by a sound suppressor. In layman's terms, it was easily silenced. Which made it a natural for any kind of covert work, or the kind of criminal operation where a lot of shots would have to be fired without drawing unwanted attention.

Ben turned the spent cartridge over in his fingers and sniffed at the blackened case mouth. The whiff of cordite told him it had been recently fired. No surprises.

And it was no surprise either to see plenty more of the cases lying about the ground. Random patterns and clusters of them all over the place, scattered little yellow sparkles catching the sunlight.

Ben tossed the case away and clenched his jaw and assessed what he was seeing. One gunman hadn't done this: that much was fairly obvious to him. It was the work of a team. How many strong, Ben couldn't say. To carry out an orchestrated attack of this scale, he'd have estimated the need for upward of six, maybe eight shooters. That left the question *why*. And that was a question he couldn't even begin to answer.

He crouched by the body. The man's white tonsured hair was matted with blood that was dried almost black. Where the crow had been pecking at the blood-soaked cloth of his robe, there was a bullet-hole between his shoulder blades. A trail of blood led back a few paces. He'd been shot in the back, probably while fleeing. He'd fallen on his face and then managed to crawl a little way before his killer had stepped up close and fired a second shot to the back of the head.

Ben reached out and grasped the monk's shoulder to roll him over. His skin was cool. There was little point in checking for a pulse as the body was stiffened up like a board with the onset of rigor mortis. The point-blank headshot had exited the middle of the monk's forehead, an exit wound big enough to drop a golf ball into. It had made a mess of his face, but Ben was able to recognise him. It was old Frère Robert, who'd helped him rebuild part of the frost-damaged outer wall in the wintertime. Ben had liked him. He'd liked them all.

He stood up and stepped across to another body, then another. Then a fourth, and a fifth. Same result. All dead, all cooling, all stiff, all shot with what looked like nine-millimetre expanding hollowpoints. Small entry hole, tapering out to a big exit hole. Very lethal, and very messy. And expertly executed. From the quantity of brass on the deck and the way that every victim had been double-tapped, one to the chest and one to the head, Ben could tell that the killers had been armed with pistols. They'd done their work the same way he had been taught to do it in the army: the first shot snapped off centre-of-mass to bring the target down, the second aimed more closely to finish the job. Brutal and effective. No quarter given, no survivors left behind.

The trail of death led him from the yard to the store building to the church. Everywhere he went, he kept finding more of them. There was Frère Patrice, slumped in a sitting position against the low wall of the little garden that surrounded the church, still wearing the support bandage on his twisted ankle, his walking stick on the ground next to him, blood spattered across the stonework from the through-and-through headshot that had taken away part of his skull. Then a few yards on there was the lay brother Olivier, who'd been on the work detail carrying up the beer from the cellar. Then there was Frère Gaspard, the greedy one. Shot in the belly and the throat, as if the killers had been starting to get bored by the time they got to him and were experimenting with variations.

Ben walked on. His head was spinning and he wanted to wake up from the nightmare.

It was beyond imagining. Who had done this? What had happened here?

Ben wasn't a pathologist. But he'd seen a lot of death in his time. Enough to know that a human body loses approximately 1.5° centigrade per hour after death until it reaches the ambient temperature around it. The colder the environment, the faster the cooling. It was a pleasantly warm morning for the time of year, by Alpine standards, maybe eighteen degrees. Living human body temperature was nearly twenty degrees warmer, at thirty-seven point five. Which would mean a rough maximum of thirteen hours for the corpses' temperature to drop to the same level as the air. Allowing for the lower temperature of the early morning and therefore a faster rate of cooling, probably less than that. Say, ten hours. But the bodies felt a little warmer than ambient temperature. They were still cooling, not yet stabilised. Without a thermometer it was impossible to gauge accurately, but Ben estimated that the attack had taken place about five hours ago. That gave plenty of time for rigor mortis to set in, which generally happened sometime after the first couple of hours.

Ben looked at his watch. It was coming on for 9.30 a.m. At an educated guess, the slaughter had happened around half past four in the morning. Just before dawn. A time when the monks had wrapped up their final night-time prayers and would be slowly returning to their cells to take some rest before the day began again.

I should have been here, he was thinking over and over.

If he hadn't been delayed, he would have been. *If he hadn't been drinking himself stupid in some bar with a bunch of strangers.* The truck would have been ready for him to collect and drive home. He'd have got back yesterday afternoon. He'd have been here, with his friends, when the attack happened. He might have been able to do something to stop this.

But he hadn't. And there wasn't a damn thing he could do to change that sorry fact.

He spent the next twenty minutes checking inside each and every one of the monks' cells. Most were empty. Some weren't. He found no survivors. Then he checked the Father Master of Novices' quarters, and the prior's. The two monks were nowhere to be found.

Until Ben moved on and ran to the church.

A thin white-haired body lay sprawled on the church steps. His robe had ridden up his legs as he'd fallen. The blood pool had trickled down three of the stone steps before it had begun to congeal.

Ben recognised him and said, 'Oh, no.'

It was Père Jacques, the Father Master of Novices. The palm of one outflung hand blown through by a gunshot; the same shot that had hit him above the left eyebrow as he'd tried to shield himself from the bullet. The nine-millimetre round had exited the crown of his skull and made all the usual ugly ravages on its way out. Ben didn't want to have to look too closely, but then something drew his eye and made him bend to scrutinise the gruesome mess in more detail.

Among all the blood, something appeared to be sticking out of the centre of the monk's forehead. It took him a moment or two to understand what he was seeing; then he reached down and gently grasped the small foreign object between finger and thumb. It came away easily, because it was only lightly stuck to the skin by a crust of dried blood that had formed around it. It was just over an inch long, cylindrical, maybe quarter of an inch thick. It shone the same colour as the spent cartridge cases that littered the ground, but it was softer than brass between his fingertips, and weighed almost nothing.

It was a cigarette butt. A very particular and distinct type, a brand Ben had come across before. The shiny foil filter was emblazoned with a minuscule Russian imperial eagle, emblem of the Czars. The filter was pinched and crumpled from the pressure of stubbing it out. The smoked end was blackened, crushed and trailing bits of unburned tobacco soaked with blood. Ben flicked the thing away in disgust.

It had left a small circular burn mark on the dead monk's brow.

To shoot a defenceless man in the head was one thing. To stub your cigarette out on him when he was down, that was another. The ultimate insult added to the ultimate injury.

Bastards.

Ben made himself remain calm. He stepped around the blood and walked inside the open door of the church. The cool interior smelled of incense and death. The mosaic stone floor laid centuries ago by master masons was smeared with more blood.

There were thirteen bodies inside the church. Either they must have congregated in here when the shooting began or they'd still been at prayer when the attackers hit.

One of the bodies was Père Antoine's.

The old prior was as dead as the rest. The final expression frozen on the octogenarian's face was one of serene calm. He looked almost beatific. As if he'd met his end in the quiet certainty that he was going to meet his maker, that this life was just one small stage in the journey and there was nothing to fear in leaving it behind.

That didn't make it any easier for Ben to deal with. He crouched over the prior for a long moment, remembering their conversations and their chess games and the old man's kindness to him.

He said out loud, 'I'm going to find who did this.'

Vengeance is mine, saith the Lord. Ben was pretty certain that would have been Père Antoine's reply. Or words to that effect. He'd have counselled Ben to leave it be. To find within himself the strength to walk away and resist the growing urge that was firing up his veins and making his hands shake and his heart pound and his breathing heave with anger. To go with God, walk the path of peace. Or as Jesus had said,

Love your enemies and pray for those who persecute you, so that you may be sons of your Father in heaven.

Ben wished he had that strength. He wasn't the man Père Antoine had been. He wasn't Jesus either. Not by a long shot. And the path of peace was no longer his to walk.

He stood up and left the church. Headed slowly back down the bloody steps. He made his way through the arch that led into the shady cloister and found three more bodies spread out on the stone floor.

Including one in particular who shouldn't have been there at all.

Chapter Thirteen

The man was no monk, that was for sure. He was from the outside, but he was no ordinary outsider either. It seemed strange to see anyone here not clad in monastic garb, and even stranger to see a man in black combat trousers, black high-leg military boots, black multi-pocket tactical vest, black ski mask, shooters' gloves and utility belt. Then again, under the circumstances, maybe not so strange.

The dead man had been packing some sort of semi-automatic pistol before someone had disarmed him and left him with an empty holster. Presumably, the same somebody who had shot him twice in the head with the same nine-millimetre ammunition that had been used to dispatch the other victims. The empty shell cases were lying nearby. His eyes were open and glazed in the holes of the ski mask.

Ben touched three fingers to the guy's neck and held them there for a moment before he whipped off the ski mask and looked at his face. The guy was somewhere in his mid-thirties, white, dark-haired, not ugly, not handsome, not a memorable face, but one Ben wouldn't be forgetting for a long time. It wasn't a monk who'd shot him. Aside from the obvious reason why that couldn't be the case, Ben could think of an even more compelling one. This guy had been alive much more recently than any of the monastery's dead residents. He wasn't quite warm to the touch, but he was in a considerably fresher state than they were. Ben grabbed the black-clad right arm and wagged it from side to side and up and down and then let it flop limply to the guy's side. No sign of rigor mortis yet. The shoulder and elbow joints were loose and flexible. The blood on his face and all down the front of his combat vest was still wet, barely tacky. He'd been dead for well under two hours. Maybe even less than one.

Which told Ben two things. Firstly, unless something extremely bizarre had taken place involving two rival armed gangs happening to choose this spot for a shoot-out and managing to hit almost nobody except bystanders, this fellow had been killed by his own team. The precision of the gunshot wounds in his head made it impossible that he could have accidentally taken a stray bullet intended for one of the monks. This had been deliberate. Ben had absolutely no idea why.

Second, it told him that the perpetrators hadn't long since left the monastery. If he'd turned up even just an hour earlier he might not have missed them. In turn, if he was right that the attack had happened at around 4.30 in the morning, it meant they'd lingered here quite some time. After killing everyone and securing the place for themselves, they'd then hung around for the next four or so hours.

Doing what? He had no idea about that either. What had they wanted? What could have kept them busy for so long?

Ben kneeled by the body and removed both gloves to examine the dead guy's fingers for nicotine stains, wanting to know if this was the bastard who'd stubbed the cigarette out on Père Jacques. No stains. He let the hands flop in the dead guy's lap and next frisked him for any kind of ID. No big surprise to find none, but he did find a phone. He slipped it into his own pocket with a view to checking through it later, and then turned his attention to the small black zippered haversack the guy had slung over his left shoulder. It felt unnaturally heavy, for all the size of it. The black nylon strap was dragging on the man's clothing, weighing him down. At first Ben thought of spare armament, extra magazines, boxes of ammunition.

But then he unzipped it and looked inside, and frowned. Now he was really confused.

There were two items inside the bag, both identical in size and shape, both cool and smooth and hard. Between them, they accounted for the unusual weight. They weren't boxes of ammo or backup weapons.

Ben lifted one out with each hand and stared at them.

The gold bars glittered in the sunshine.

Chapter Fourteen

Ben remained kneeling, the dead man half forgotten, blinking in amazement at the items in his hands.

The last one of these he'd been this close to, years ago, had been part of an old cache of Nazi gold, marked with a German imperial eagle perched atop a swastika. That had made it pretty easy to identify, as well as to take an educated guess that it had been manufactured sometime between 1933 and 1945. He hadn't known if it had been minted or cast or whether the highly recognisable emblem had been stamped or moulded on to it. Only that it was shiny yellow and damned heavy, damned valuable and had some major history behind it.

These two were shiny yellow and damned heavy as well. They were bright and smooth, each about twelve inches long and about four inches wide by three inches high. Solid, dense lumps of metal. Each weighed somewhere between six and eight kilos, making him straighten up and pivot his body weight slightly backwards to counter the tug on his arms. He put one of the bars down on the ground, rested the other on his knee as he reached into his pocket for the truck ignition key. Gripping the shaft of the key tightly, he dug its tip at an angle into the top of the bar. Steel was much harder than gold. The tip of the key easily left a jagged score mark as long as his thumb and maybe a millimetre deep.

Ben examined the scratch very closely. He was looking for dark grey underneath the gold. He'd heard of solid lead ingots, melted and moulded into the right shape out of wheel weights or roofing lead, being painted or even plated to fool the unwary.

But this was no lead ingot dressed up, and when he tested the second bar he got the same result. Apparently, they were the real thing. Which he had to presume meant they were pretty seriously valuable. At this moment, that was the absolute limit of his knowledge. Neither bar had any visible markings on it anywhere. Nothing to indicate their provenance, their age, or what the hell they were doing here.

That was just one more thing he was going to have to figure out.

Ben laid the two bars side by side in the dead man's lap and covered them with the bag. He didn't think the guy would be going anywhere with them. He stood up and walked on down the cloistered passage.

Soon afterwards, he picked up the blood trail. It started out of nowhere, the way blood trails so often did. Its source was marked with a splatter against a wall and a nearby spent nine-millimetre shell case. From there, a heavy line of spots, each the size of a large coin and serrated like a circular saw around its circumference where it had splashed to the ground, led through archways and down steps and along paved aisles for about fifty yards, until it disappeared through an open doorway. There was a russet-coloured partial palm print on the door from where the injured person had stumbled into it with their hand extended in front of them, crashing through in a hurry.

Ben meant to find out where it led. He might find another

dead monk at the end of the trail, or he might find a second shooter. Preferably one who wasn't yet expired, so that he could milk some information out of them before they were. Or before he made them that way.

But Ben knew he had to hurry. Whoever it was, they'd been losing a lot of blood.

The doorway was the one leading down to the cellars, along the same route Ben had travelled back and forth two days earlier with the work party bringing up the beer. He walked in and smelled the faintly musty odours that came up from below. It was full of shadows down here and his eyes were adjusted to the bright sunshine, but he could make out the regular spots of blood that dotted the way ahead. If anything, they were becoming more frequent. As if the bleeding had been getting worse, or the person had been slowing down, or both at once.

The trail led downwards into the maze of passages beneath the monastery. More handprints and smears, the colour of autumn leaves, appeared on the bare stone walls. Ben blinked to make his eyes reset themselves to the growing darkness. His footsteps began to echo more deeply around him as he ventured further underground. He wished he'd had a torch, then remembered that he had the dead man's phone in his pocket. He paused to turn it on. It had a built-in light that he used as a torch, sweeping the weak beam ahead of him left and right as he made his way onwards.

Without the light there to guide him, he might have tripped over the heavy object that was lying in his path. He nudged it with his foot, then crouched down to examine it. It was another gold bar, apparently identical to the two he'd found on the dead man. He picked it up. Same weight. He brushed it all over with his fingertips. No markings, just plain smooth cool metal.

Ben laid the bar back down and moved on. Down, and down. Then the passage levelled out. He'd been here only once before, but he knew exactly where he was. The place seemed familiar to him, yet different. It wasn't just the blood trail that hadn't been here before. It was all the tracks in the dust. Lots of them, adding considerably to those that the work party had made trekking to and fro to shift the beer up from the cellars. It looked as if a whole procession of people had come this way, and back again. Perhaps several times, judging by the confusion of prints. One thing was for sure, these prints hadn't been made by monks. Monks didn't wear deep-tread combat boots.

He kept moving urgently forward. The light flicked this way and that, casting shadows on the rough walls and picking out more splashes of blood. And more. The dark passage curved left, then right, carving into the mountain like a mole tunnel. Ben moved quickly but cautiously, one eye on the ground. Any time soon, he'd be approaching the place where the walls opened up into the man-made cavern he'd discovered two days earlier. That seemed to be where both the blood trail and the multiple tracks were leading him.

Now he came to a fork in the path as the blood trail and the tracks diverged. The tracks kept moving straight ahead towards the cavern, while the blood trail veered off to the left, into the craggy entrance of the secondary passage Ben remembered from before. That was the direction he opted for, bowing his head to avoid the low, rough ceiling. The tracks could wait. This might not.

Just a few yards on, he came to the end of the trail.

Ben had thought he would find a dead monk there, or maybe a live bad guy. He found neither.

Chapter Fifteen

Up ahead in the tight passage, the blood spots terminated in a pool that had spread and gathered in the recesses of the uneven floor. Ben's light flicked from side to side and settled on what looked like a heap of old sack-cloth dumped against the rough stone wall.

The heap moved. Only very slightly, but it moved.

Ben hurried forward, shining his light. He'd realised who it was.

He said, 'Roby.'

Falling to his knees next to the slumped figure, he saw he was right. Roby's eyes were shut and his face was ghastly white and slick with sweat. A fringe of dark hair was plastered across his brow.

Ben understood what the boy was doing here. Pure animal instinct. When any creature, small or large, was frightened or hurt, it was nature's way for it to return to the burrow. This had been Roby's little hideaway out of habit, the place he knew his fellow monks wouldn't come looking. Except that on this occasion, he hadn't come here to get away from the monks. He'd come here to get away from the men who'd shot him.

Ben shone his phone light over the boy's robe. The blood was soaked everywhere, the thick material saturated with it.

It was a stomach wound. One of the cruellest and slowest and most painful ways to die from a bullet.

Roby stirred. His eyes flickered open, then closed again, then reopened. They were dull, bloodshot and unfocused. He seemed to sense the presence next to him and tried to move his head, but didn't have the strength. He whispered, 'Benoît?' His voice was just a shadow of a breath.

'It's me, Roby. I'm right here with you.'

The tiniest of smiles curled the corner of the boy's mouth and then it drooped, as if even that effort was too much. His energy was almost gone.

'I knew you'd come back,' Roby breathed. He tried to reach out his hand. His fingers were thick with blood, some of it dried, most of it fresh.

Ben swallowed. 'Stay still. You're going to be okay.' Which he knew was a lie. Roby was not going to be okay at all. He was going to die. It was a miracle he'd lasted this long. Or maybe it was just a cruel prolongation of his agony. Ben knew he couldn't move him and that nothing could save him. They could have been within yards of a hospital, and the outcome would still have been the same.

But Roby was fighting it. He hadn't had sixty years of serene devotional meditation to help him calmly accept, even embrace, death. He was as terrified as most other people would have been. With a supreme effort that must have used up nearly all his fading reserves, he gripped Ben's hand in his bloodstained fingers. The movement shot a bolt of pain through him that sent a ripple of shock across his face. The agony was awful, Ben could see that. Roby gasped and a stream of garbled words hissed out of him. Ben strained to listen and caught none of it.

'What happened here, Roby?' He kept his voice gentle and soothing, fighting his emotions.

Roby's eyes rolled back and the lids fluttered. His head lolled, and for a bad second Ben thought he'd lost him. But then the boy fought his eyes back open and mouthed more words, almost soundlessly. 'They came . . . it was before dawn . . . I was . . .' The whisper trailed off to nothing.

'Who? Who did this?'

The effort was killing Roby. But he had nothing to lose any more. His breath was coming in gasps and his hand was trembling in Ben's. Sweat beaded all over his pallid face and pooled in the hollow of his throat. His eyes opened a little wider, and the terror in them flashed brightly for an instant, a gleam that caught the light from the phone Ben was shining over him.

'Benoît . . . I saw . . . I saw *demons*.'

Ben looked at him. The young man was raving, that was all. His brain was closing down. Random neurochemical impulses firing off as the nerve endings died and the mist of darkness rose up to take him away. People at the very point of death often talked gibberish or seemed to experience hallucinations, for the same reason. 'It's all right, Roby,' was all Ben could say.

But whatever it was that Roby was trying to say, he was desperate to get it out. 'No . . . not demons. *Ghosts*. I saw . . . they were . . . all white . . .'

And then the boy could say no more. His chest heaved with his last breath. His spine arched. A juddering spasm, and then Ben felt the life go out of him and his body go rigid and then relax and become limp.

Ben closed his eyes and held Roby for a few seconds. Then he let go of the dead boy's hand and let his body slump gently to the floor. He stood up, said a silent goodbye and moved on.

From the mouth of the secondary passage he turned left again, in the direction of the tracks. It was virtually a thoroughfare along here. Twice, he kneeled down to inspect footprints that hadn't been obliterated by others overlaid on top of them. One set of prints was distinctly smaller than the rest. Which was clear enough evidence that the tracks had been made by at least two people, as opposed to one person doubling back and forth many times. The smaller print had the same kind of large tread as the others, indicating some kind of standardisation of their footwear. Ben thought about the combat boots the dead shooter in the cloister had on. They'd come down here. Why? He thought of the two gold bars in the dead guy's bag, and of the third one he'd nearly tripped over in the passage. Had there been a treasure buried beneath the monastery? Had the killers come here to raid it?

That would have explained the hours they'd hung around after the killings. Any kind of a sizeable haul of gold would take as long to lug up to ground level as a truckload of beer. Maybe even longer, depending on how much of it there was to shift. Maybe there'd been so much gold that one bar dropped here or there didn't make any difference.

Maybe so much of it that the killers had begun to argue among themselves. Hence the dead guy in the cloister. There wasn't always honour among thieves.

Ben moved on a few more yards towards the carved-out cavern he'd visited two days ago with Roby. Two days ago wasn't a long time for someone who tended to notice small details the way Ben did. And while he could have sworn that the passage walls and ceiling had been smooth and un-damaged before, now he was noticing a widespread lacework of cracks and fissures, some only hairline, others wide enough to stick his thumb into, on both sides and above his head. The dust underfoot was deeper and his boots crunched on small pieces of stone that had been dislodged from gaps that hadn't been there before. Ben might have been worried about it, if he hadn't had worse things to worry about.

Now the passage opened out into the cavern that had been dug out of the rock. The place Père Antoine hadn't wanted to talk about. Where Ben had found the skull, and the section of brickwork that walled off the way ahead. The skull was still there, crushed from the rock Ben had dumped on it. It lay half-buried in fresh dust, from the cracks that had opened up everywhere. Next to it lay a fourth gold bar, apparently dropped in the same careless way as the last, gleaming dully in the light from Ben's torch-phone. But he paid it only a moment's attention, because he was distracted by a far bigger discovery.

The partition wall blocking off the cavern wasn't there any more. It had been blown away.

Chapter Sixteen

Ben held his light up at eye level and examined the hole where the brickwork had been. It was almost perfectly circular, about five feet in diameter, a circumference of just under sixteen feet as neatly blasted away as anything he had ever seen. The rubble lay scattered about on both sides of the hole. It looked as though a giant bullet had punched right through the wall.

Now Ben understood the cause of the cracks he'd noticed in the walls and ceiling of the passage leading up to it. Only one kind of munitions could have produced such a perfect hole. A shaped charge. Plastic explosive, wired in place and remotely detonated. That wasn't exactly the kind of hardware you could get via mail order. And whoever had rigged it was some kind of artist. It must have been a delicate operation. A fraction too much charge, and he could have brought the whole mountain down on top of himself and his team. Ben could still smell the faint tang of cordite from the explosion.

The tracks in the dust headed right through the hole. Evidently, whatever they'd come for lay beyond. Ben ducked and clambered over the rubble and followed the tracks into the blackness.

The first thing that hit him was the smell. The air had been trapped in here for who knew how many centuries,

94

but that alone couldn't explain the sickening rankness of the stench that made Ben want to gag almost at the first breath. He pulled up the hem of his shirt and clamped it tightly over his nose and mouth as a rudimentary filter. It helped, but only slightly. He took a few more steps inside and cast the light around him. Its glow didn't reach the sides, and there was no telling how big the space around him was. The ground sloped away gently, rough and stony. He advanced one cautious step at a time, feeling his way. He could have done with a brighter light, and was certain that the intruders had come a little better equipped than he was. Head-torches, maybe, or six-cell Maglites enhanced with LED bulbs that could slice through the murk as well as a car headlamp. His light was beginning to dim as the phone's battery faded. Now and then it gave a little flicker, and its colour was yellowing. He might have ten more minutes before it gave out entirely, or he might have five. Either way, it wasn't reassuring. He could smell and hear better than he could see.

What he could hear was the echo of his footsteps resonating inside the dark space, and something else. A scuttling sound, furtive and intermittent. He raised the light higher and ventured forward a few more steps. His right foot made contact with something soft and mushy. It felt like stepping into a pile of rotten fruit. He shone the light downward, saw the glutinous yuck he'd stepped in and smelled its awful stench through the material of his shirt. It was the decomposing flesh of something furry, half-eaten and extremely dead. Now he understood the cause of the stink in here, and he understood the scuttling noises that echoed all around him.

The place was full of rats. Hundreds of them, or thousands, everywhere. He saw their dark shapes flitting from shadow to shadow as they scattered and hid, disturbed by his presence. The chamber was strewn with their carcasses and bones. A few yards away lay the body of the biggest rat Ben had ever seen. It had to be two foot long from nose to tail, but what struck him more than its size was that it was deformed, twisted and apparently eyeless. They must have been living down here in the darkness for so many generations that they'd lost their sight.

Ben had no great love for rats, but they possessed certain qualities it was hard not to admire in a morbid kind of way. When it came to survival skills, rats left humans far behind, simply because of their sheer adaptability. They could thrive in the very worst conditions, drink water that would poison most other creatures, devour things that not even a starving dog would go near. If required, cannibalism was not an issue for them. And that was how Ben realised they must have been living down here, subsisting off the flesh of their own kind. Which perhaps accounted for the deformities. Maybe eventually they would die out, given enough time, but they seemed to have managed to keep going for a few thousand generations at least. There must have been enough moisture in the dirt to keep them hydrated, just enough oxygen filtering in through minute cracks in the mountain to prevent asphyxiation. Millions of them, being born and surviving and dying and giving sustenance to their fellows, while the sorry saga of human history rolled meaninglessly onwards through the ages, above them and below them and all around them.

Ben lifted his boot from the stinking ooze he'd stepped in and moved deeper into the cavern, straining his eyes to see in the slowly, steadily dimming light.

Then he stopped and stood still and gazed at the sight that greeted him a little way further from the entrance.

96

A wide section of the cavern floor was covered with human bones. Mounds of them, several feet deep in places. Ribcages and fibias and tibias and sticks of spine and skulls, all piled and tangled up. It was impossible to tell how many skeletons were strewn among the rocks and the dust, because so few of them were still intact. They'd fallen apart with age, or been picked apart by rats. Many of the bones were partially eaten away. There was no telling how many must have been gnawed into calcium-rich dust by generations of sharp little rodent teeth. Maybe they were too ancient now to offer any nutritional value to the rats. Ben didn't know. All he knew was that he was looking at the remains of an awful lot of people.

He stepped closer and shone his light down at the grisly boneyard. He knew how to tell a female skeleton from a male by the shape and relative width of the pelvic bone, and he could see female remains among the piled mass. Children's bones were easier to tell apart, and he saw those, too. Then he looked more closely and saw more. Lengths of iron chain, red and pitted with corrosion, lay twisted and coiled among the human remains. Iron shackles were riveted at intervals along their length, still tightly clamped around the skeletal wrists and ankles of men, women and children alike. Iron plates bolted into the rock, with iron rings holding the chains securely to the floor. These people had been bound up like galley slaves.

You didn't put the dead in irons.

And that was because this wasn't a grave. The place told its own story. Once upon a time, many centuries ago, hundreds of men, women and children had been dragged in here alive, shackled in chains and then left to rot as the chamber was sealed shut behind them. No food, no water. No light, little air. Maybe they'd survived a while, the way the rats had. Ben could almost hear their screams of desperation. How long had they echoed for, until they'd finally died away to the last whimper, and then to nothing at all?

The Church's past is tainted by many sins, and to force good men to do evil in the name of God is but one of them.

Père Antoine's words. Had the prior known about this place, about what was hidden behind the wall?

Whether he had or not, someone else had known something.

The skeletal remains apparently hadn't been the only secret contents of the walled-up cavern. The gold had come from here, too.

And that was something that made absolutely no sense to Ben. None of it did, as he stood there in the darkness, staring at the pitiful spectacle all around him and trying to understand.

His light was fading for real now, slowly dying from white to yellow to amber. The little halo around him was shrinking, and the darkness was encroaching all around him like a black fog, slowly enough to allow his vision to adapt.

And in the midst of the fog, a tiny movement caught his eye and made him turn. Not a movement, but a small blinking glow of light.

A series of red light-emitting diodes. A row of digits. Glowing faintly from an unseen panel somewhere in the darkness. A decidedly non-medieval device. One that someone had left behind not very long ago.

Counting down.

Counting down very rapidly, tenths of a second ripping into seconds, rolling into minutes. Minutes that had already run out.

The digital readout showed:
00:00:16:08.

In the time it took for Ben to blink and realise what he was seeing, the numbers raced on downwards. Now the panel showed:

00:00:15.57—

—Time to move. *Now.*

Ben turned and ran through scattered bones and splashed through rotting filth and sprinted for the entrance faster than he'd ever moved in his life.

And then the cavern blew.

Chapter Seventeen

It blew with a shattering detonation and a shock wave of expanding superheated gases that instantly vaporised the contents of the cavern, both the dead and the living. The whole mountain rocked with the violence of the blast. First the explosion, then the implosion as the cavern fell in on itself. An avalanche of car-sized pieces of rubble came crashing down. Millions of tons of stone and dust tumbled and poured and slid and obliterated everything as the walls and ceiling gave way under the vast weight that had been bearing down on them for centuries. The neatly blasted-out circular entrance of the cavern collapsed like a giant mouth snapping shut, swallowing up everything that had been inside it seconds before.

Ben just made it through the hole before the roof came crashing down. The shock wave saved him, and almost killed him at the same time. It lifted him off his feet and propelled him out of the exploding cavern, all arms and legs. Tumbled him through the air and cannoned him against the rocky wall of the passage and flung him down on his side, knocking the wind out of him. The dragon's breath of the blast erupted from the cavern, close enough to sear his skin. Just as it seemed as if the fireball would engulf him, the collapsing ceiling swallowed the explosion. Then, suddenly, deafening silence.

The air was filled with dust and smoke. Scorched, battered, stunned and blinded, barely knowing if he was dead or alive, Ben somehow scrambled to his feet and ran, utterly convinced that the whole rock tunnel was going to fall in and bury him down here for all eternity. But he kept running anyway, feeling the way ahead, blinking dust out of his eyes and coughing up the crap that filled his lungs, stumbling over the uneven ground, scraping his shoulders and elbows against the rough walls as he sprinted like a crazy man through the darkness. Showers of dust and stones rained down on him as he went. He couldn't tell whether the ground was still shaking, or whether he was just unsteady on his feet.

He kept going. No fear, no restraint. No thoughts at all, just pure animal energy driving him forwards through the darkness, his muscles working like pistons and his heart thudding like a demented thing that threatened to burst out of his chest. And the ceiling didn't come down to bury him. He made it through the twists and turns of the passage, and then to the fallen gold bar. This time he did trip over it, and tumbled headlong. He landed hard on his hands and heaved himself up with barely a pause, and kept running, upwards and upwards towards the light and the air. Then suddenly he could breathe, and see.

The glare of the sun hit him in the face as he reached ground level. Ben burst out of the doorway, caught it with his shoulder, spun and fell in a wheezing heap in the dirt. It took a few seconds before he fully realised that he'd made it out alive. Or just about. His hair was singed and the skin on his left cheek felt tender where the heatwave of the blast had scorched it, his hands were cut and bleeding and embedded with grit, and every muscle in his body was screaming in agony. He sat up and leaned against a wall, wiped the stinging dust out of his eyes and coughed up more of it that he'd swallowed. All the time, he was thinking furiously.

The killers had used a shaped charge to blow through the cavern wall, only to take what was inside and then plant a second, delayed, much bigger charge to seal the cavern off again.

Why would they do that?

Right now, he had no idea.

He rested five minutes, then another five, until his breathing had settled and he was convinced he had no major injuries. Just dozens of minor ones. Which was fine. He was functional, and that was all he needed to be.

Smoke was drifting from the doorway leading to the underground passages as he gathered himself up, dusted himself off and began walking back down the cloister. He was dizzy and nauseous, and a loud constant whine had set up in his ears from the explosion. He could see in his mind the faces of the dead. Roby, Père Antoine, all of them. He should have been able to do more for them. Many had been his friends, and many more he knew he'd have befriended if he'd been able to spend more time with them.

He couldn't bury them. It would take him a month on his own with a shovel. The cops would have to deal with the clean-up. Ben felt obliged to call them in, but he didn't intend to be here to face questioning when they turned up. Nor did he have a lot of confidence in their ability to sort out what the hell had happened here. Generally speaking, and for a variety of reasons that could be more or less summed up as professional differences, Ben and police officers didn't mix well. It might have had something to do with the fact that he tended to obtain results, when they tended to fail. On occasion, it might also have had something

102

to do with the kinds of methods he employed to get those results, which they didn't always appreciate.

Ben limped back to his personal quarters, knowing he was seeing them for the last time. The first thing he did was use a rag to wipe down every surface he'd ever touched. Sooner or later, the monastery was going to be the subject of a major crime investigation, and the last thing he needed was for the cops to know he'd been here. With his past record, he was the perfect patsy for frustrated local detectives looking for someone to pin this on. Once he was satisfied that all his prints were erased, he gathered his few possessions and stuffed them inside his canvas bag, then slung it over his shoulder and left with a final glance at the rooms that had been his home.

After that, he headed back to the cloister where the dead shooter was still sitting exactly where Ben had left him, minding the two gold bars. Ben relieved him of them and put them in his own bag along with the rest of his stuff. The extra kilos hung uncomfortably from his bruised shoulder as he returned to the main yard, threading a path between the scattered bodies of the monks. The crow was back, continuing the meal Ben had interrupted earlier. He felt like flinging a stone at it, then reasoned that it had as much right to survive as anyone else.

With a painful effort, Ben hauled himself into the truck's cab, dumped his heavy bag on the passenger seat and then started up the engine. It sounded quieter than before, but that was only because he was a little deaf after the blast. He forced the gearstick into first, touched the gas and the truck lumbered deeper into the yard. He brought it to a halt, crunched the stick into reverse and twisted the huge ship's wheel to U-turn right around to face the gates, then straightened up the wheels and turned round in his seat to look out of the rear window as the truck backed up with a nasal transmission whine. He reversed as far as he could towards the buildings, careful not to let the knobbly tyres run over any of the dead monks. Leaving the diesel running in neutral, he jumped down from the cab, walked back to the dead shooter and grabbed him by the collar. 'You didn't think I was going to leave without you, did you?' he said as he started dragging the body towards the truck.

It was a short drag and the guy wasn't terribly heavy. Ben slalomed him in between the drying blood pools, then when they reached the truck he let go of the dead man's collar and his forehead smacked limply to the ground. Ben undid the ties holding the tonneau cover down to the truck's flatbed on one side, then turned back to the body. Rolled him over with his foot, bent over him and grabbed him by both arms to yank him into a sitting position before heaving him upright. The dead man's knees kept giving way, and Ben supported him like a drunk carried from a wild party. He slammed him against the side of the truck's flatbed and let his upper body topple backwards through the loose canvas, then bent down and grabbed his ankles and lifted both floppy legs off the ground, one after the other. With some twisting and heaving, he managed to get the body lying flat on the pitted wooden cargo bed.

Ben jumped up next to him. He looked at the rusty old tool locker bolted down behind the cab. Four feet long, two feet wide. The dead man wasn't a huge guy. Ben raised the creaky locker lid, propped it up and lifted out the removable compartment full of crusty old spanners, which he shunted to the edge of the flatbed and let fall to the ground. The locker was empty now, except for the coil of old rope and the pair of bolt croppers lying in the bottom. But it wouldn't be empty long.

'In you go,' Ben said. If he had to share the truck with a dead man, he'd rather not have the guy stinking up the inside of the cab. Besides, nosy cops had a tendency to spot dead men in the passenger seat quicker than they might check on-board tool lockers. With more heaving and twisting, he manhandled the dead man's torso into the box, shoulders twisted diagonally, his left arm under him and the right folded across his chest. The guy's head was up at an angle, as if peering down his body to see what was going on. Ben shoved him down deep inside the box with the heel of his boot. Not a big man, but not a midget either, and his legs wouldn't fit. They overhung the edge of the locker, no matter which way Ben tried to squeeze them in. Which was easily remedied, by means of three or four judicious bone-crunching stamps to his knees that allowed them to be folded up sideways and crammed into the tight space.

People talked about having respect for the dead. Ben didn't like having to break the guy's legs this way. He'd much rather have done it while he was still alive.

Once the body was all tucked in, Ben covered him up with the lid and banged it down tight. Then jumped down from the flatbed, quickly fastened up the tonneau cover and climbed back behind the wheel. He crashed the lever out of neutral and into first, pressed down hard on the pedal and the truck lurched forwards with a dieselly rasp.

He didn't look back as he steered it across the yard, towards the open gateway. The truck lumbered through the gates. He twisted the wheel to the right, heading in the opposite direction from his route to Briançon the day before. Leaving behind the dead bodies of his friends, and the place he'd called home.

He didn't know where the road was going to take him. Not yet.

At this moment, he knew just one thing. That whoever had done this wanted blood.

And that blood was what they were going to get.

Chapter Eighteen

If she leaned her head close to the window and peered downwards, Hannah Gissel could see the shadow of the Bell 429 flicking and rippling over the picture-perfect pasture-land below them as they flew northwards towards their destination. The roar of the rotors was muted in her radio headset. She turned and smiled at Udo Streicher, sitting shoulder-to-shoulder alongside her in the pilot's seat, and gazed at him for a few seconds with a secret look of admiration. His face was set in an expression of concentration, his eyes hidden behind his aviator shades. He appeared outwardly calm, but Hannah could tell from the way he held himself that there was a bright twinkle behind those dark glasses, and that inside he was bursting with glee and leaping about like a lottery winner, pumping his fists in the air, roaring with laughter. She felt exactly that way herself, though like Udo she was far too restrained to let it show.

In fact, her heart was thumping almost as fast as the heli-copter rotors. They'd done it. They'd damn well done it. Even after the devastating setback of the failed North Korean attempt, she'd never doubted her man's ability to pull this off. Now they were almost home and dry. Ready for the next phase to begin.

Then things would really start to get interesting.

Hannah twisted further around in her seat and looked at the eight white oblong containers secured inside the passenger space behind them. Securely locked, carefully strapped down to prevent them from tumbling about in flight. Their shiny white super-tough plastic shells gleamed in the bright morning sunlight that filled the cabin. The fruit of years of planning and sacrifice. Theirs at last.

Oh, yes, things were definitely going to start getting interesting from here on.

Before too long, the chopper overflew the twisting blue river that marked the western boundary of the hundred-acre organic dairy farm. Streicher gave a little smile of satisfaction as they entered what he considered his own airspace. Like all his real estate holdings, he owned this land in a company name that could never be traced back to him personally. It had been the best investment he'd ever made, even though he had absolutely no intention of ever selling it, and even less interest in organic dairy farming. All but a ten-acre chunk of the land had been leased for the last twelve years to a reliable, hard-working couple named Lili and Jens Mosman, who employed enough hands and did a good enough job of the day-to-day running of the farm to turn a reasonable profit. The Mosmans enjoyed a harmonious rapport with their landlord, whom they knew only as 'Herr Schumann', and who left them alone to do their thing, never interfering, seldom seen, and then only from afar. The one time they'd actually met face to face was to sign the lease on the farmland, years ago.

In return for Herr Schumann's generosity and fairness towards them, the Mosmans never expressed curiosity about, and gave a wide berth to, the ten-acre patch that he kept for himself, circled by trees and securely fenced off from the rest of the spread. As far as they were concerned, it was just a convenient location for their colourful landlord to keep his helicopter and a few other of his possessions.

Which, as far as that went, was no word of a lie. At the heart of the ten-acre patch was the large hangar that housed the Bell when it wasn't in use. A private road ran through the trees and between fields along the edge of the farmland; now and again the Mosmans might catch a distant glimpse of Herr Schumann and his wife, to whom they'd never been introduced but whose name they'd been told was Ulrike, zapping off in one of his collection of expensive motor vehicles. It was no longer much of a topic for discussion in the Mosman home. Herr Schumann was obviously wealthy and possibly slightly eccentric in his ways, but hardly nuts enough to warrant much in the way of speculation, let alone gossip. In any case, the Mosmans were not the most imaginative of folks, and generally too busy with the running of the farm to think about much else.

The chopper rattled over well-kept farm buildings and neatly fenced green pastures dotted with grazing cattle. Jens Mosman's bright red tractor was cutting across one of the lower fields, looking like a shiny toy from high above. Soon after, Streicher dropped altitude as the circle of pine forest surrounding his personal acreage came into view. At its centre, the big hangar with its wood cladding and pitched roof looked archetypally Swiss. It was surrounded by an apron of concrete, connected to the perimeter fence and high gates by the private road.

Streicher activated the landing-gear controls. The helicopter sank gently downwards, treetops blotting out the view of farmland all around. It touched neatly down on the concrete apron and taxied towards the huge steel shutter that was the only entrance to the hangar.

Hannah pointed a small, custom-made remote control.

It had a ten-digit keypad, and below it two coloured buttons, red on the right and green on the left. She pressed the green button with a manicured nail and the shutter instantly began to wind open. The rotors slowed from a roar to a lazy *whoop-whoop-whoop* and the whine of the turbine deepened in pitch. Streicher waited until the shutter was fully elevated, then taxied inside the wide rectangular entrance. Hannah pressed the remote again and the door began to close behind them.

Lights came on automatically, filling the huge hangar with brightness. The concrete floor was gleaming red. The walls were dazzling white. Parked tight against one wall, taking up less than half its length, was the Volvo articulated lorry that Dominik Baiza had driven back alone. Baiza was one of very few people trusted with access to the hangar. As instructed, before leaving he'd unloaded the Lenco BearCat from the trailer and parked it neatly to one side. Across the hangar were a few of Streicher's more leisure-orientated vehicles: his classic Benelli six-cylinder motorcycle, his fully dressed Honda Gold Wing Aspencade, his Harley, and the impossibly low, sleek shape of the Pagani Zonda supercar that looked more like a carbon-fibre space fighter than an automobile.

Streicher finished taxiing the Bell into its designated space, which was marked out in neat white paint lines on the floor. He and Hannah waited a few moments until the rotors had slowed to a standstill, then he disembarked first and stood by the hatch as she carefully passed out the white containers one by one. With equal care, Streicher laid them in a neat row on the carry rack of a specially adapted electric golf buggy. When the eighth container was securely in place, the two of them clambered aboard the open-sided buggy. Streicher pressed the accelerator pedal and the little vehicle whooshed off silently across the shiny floor.

An intruder peering in through the window would have been baffled by the sight, because there was apparently nowhere inside the hangar for the golf buggy to ferry its cargo to. No storage facilities of any kind, no other visible rooms. It was just a vast open rectangular space, like an enormous garage.

Until Hannah produced the little remote handset she'd used to open the shutter doors. She entered a six-digit combination code and pressed the red button.

Nothing happened for a few moments.

Then the near-invisible hairline seam that traced a ten-metre square in the floor began to widen to the whoosh of hidden hydraulic gears, and the secret trapdoor opened up in front of them.

Finally, now that he was truly home and dry, Streicher allowed a wide grin of triumph to spread across his face.

'We did it, Udo,' Hannah said. It was a rare thing for her to show emotion, but at that moment she could have cried.

'We did, didn't we?' he replied with a chuckle, and directed the silent vehicle down the ramp into the underground domain below that virtually nobody else in the world knew existed.

Chapter Nineteen

Ben drove aimlessly for fifteen minutes, approximately south-east, just to put distance between himself and the monastery. The unfamiliar road curved and looped around the mountainside, then dropped steeply in altitude and took him down into thick deciduous and coniferous forest, the trees arching over the road in places to make a tunnel. Just one car passed in the opposite direction and his mirrors were empty. The sun was shining. It should have been another beautiful day in paradise.

He slowed as a narrow forest track appeared on his right, pulled in and drove the Belphégor fifty yards, rocking and lurching over the uneven ground until he came to a clearing, about thirty yards wide and roughly circular. The ground was hard-packed earth, littered with bark chippings and moss and last autumn's leaves. At the centre stood a wooden picnic table, and at its edge was a block-built toilet facility. If the place had been developed as a travellers' rest for road-weary tourists, it was too well-hidden to have ever had much use. Today, at any rate, it was completely deserted, and that suited Ben fine.

He stopped and killed the engine, but he didn't get out of the truck. The deafened whine in his ears was beginning to wear off. He could hear the birds chirping overhead, the whisper of the breeze in the leaves and the soft hum of forest insects. Sunlight filtered through the foliage and dappled the windscreen. He sat motionless for a long time, staring dead ahead into space over the top of the wheel. Slowly, he was beginning to unwind. His jaw had unclenched, his fists loosened on the wheel and his heart had returned to its normal resting rate of forty-five beats per minute. Before, he'd been upset and angry. Now he was upset, and angry, and focused. Calm. Clear. Cold. And very dangerous.

'All right,' he said at last.

He took out the dead man's phone. It was a cheap pay-as-you-go item, shiny and new with the standard bells and whistles, including a built-in camera. He scrolled over to the screen icon labelled Call Records, and opened up the menu. It was blank. No calls either made or received, unless the dead guy had deleted them all. Ben backtracked to the main menu. Picture files: blank. Calendar: blank. He back-tracked again and selected contacts.

This time, he found something. There were ten numbers in the list, but no names. Over the next few minutes he dialled each one in turn, and each one in turn came back with a generic answerphone recording.

'Fine,' he said, and slipped the phone back in his pocket. He climbed down from the cab, stretched his sore muscles and walked over to the toilet block. The washroom facilities were basic and neglected, with a grubby sink and a cracked mirror, no soap, no towel, cold water only. He peered into the glass and saw a wild man looking back at him. Hair almost white with dust, red-rimmed eyes staring out of a face that was gaunt and unshaven and streaked with soot and dirt, like a soldier slathered in facial camo cream before going into battle. He spent the next few minutes cleaning himself up as best he could, splashing cold water over his face and brushing the worst of the dust out of his hair. The result wasn't perfect, but marginally decent enough to frequent human society again.

He walked back to the Belphégor, restarted the engine and jammed it in gear, and spun the wheel round and round to full lock to U-turn back out of the clearing and down the narrow lane to the road. He pulled out and continued in the same direction, the road twisting and bending through the trees, now and then a break in the overhead canopy offering a glimpse of the mountains against the clear blue sky.

After another fifteen minutes he saw a sign for a filling station coming up on the right. Fifty yards later, he toed the brake and leaned across the transmission tunnel and the massive gear lever to wind down the far-side window and get a good look at the place as he drove past. The filling station shop was a low, weathered wooden building about forty yards back from the road, attached to an old open-fronted tin-sheet barn that would have had some agricultural use back in its day but now served as a storage shed. Firewood was stacked high in one corner, rows of butane cylinders stood in another. A pair of old-style pumps stood out on the patched concrete in front of the shop, one for gasoline and the other for diesel. A sign over the doorway read GAZ – TABAC – LOTERIE. Parked at the side of the building was a hard-used Peugeot 505 pickup truck with rusty skirts and a taped-up headlamp, the only other vehicle in sight. A bent old guy in a Breton cap, whom Ben took to be the proprietor of both the business and the pickup truck, was pottering slowly about the storage shed, seeming to be doing not much of anything.

Ben drove on a hundred yards, then flicked his indicator and pulled into the roadside. Leaving the truck running and the driver's door open, he got out and walked back along the road to check out the filling station more closely. His first impression had been right. It was a useful place for his purposes, selling everything he needed. Best of all, it was a suitably old-fashioned kind of establishment. The kind he favoured most at times like these, which was to say the kind with no security camera keeping tabs on the vehicles that rolled in and out. He walked back to the truck, then reversed the hundred yards back down the road and pulled up on the patched concrete.

It wasn't that the Belphégor needed diesel. Ben had another errand on his mind. The bent old man in the cap emerged from the workshop and greeted him with the customary and more formal '*Bonjour, Monsieur*' that older folks in quiet parts of France still observed. Ben purchased four plastic five-litre petrol cans, a Michelin map of the local area, a roll of absorbent paper towel, and the first pack of Gauloises he'd bought in over seven months. He waited patiently while the old man pumped twenty litres of Eurosuper 98 Sans Plomb into his four cans, then paid cash and smiled a polite goodbye, carried his purchases to the truck and was on his way.

He pulled the Belphégor around in the road and headed back the way he'd come earlier. Fifteen minutes later, he'd returned to the clearing. The place was just as deserted as before. He parked the truck as close to its centre as he could, next to the picnic table, then shut off the engine for the very last time and climbed down from the cab with his bag, weighed down by the gold bars inside. He carried it to the edge of the clearing and dumped it at the foot of a tree. Returning to the truck, he undid the tonneau cover fastenings once more, then clambered up on to the flatbed and opened the tool locker. Reaching inside with both hands, he grabbed its occupant by the collar and sleeve and yanked him upright.

It took a few moments to drag the dead man out and lay him on his back on the pitted slats of the flatbed, his broken legs splayed out at odd angles. The guy's skin had turned a sickly grey-green and rigor mortis was beginning to stiffen him up. Ben took the phone out of his pocket and used its built-in camera to take a mugshot of the corpse.

He quickly examined the picture on-screen. It wasn't the most flattering of portraits, but it would serve its purpose perfectly well. Satisfied, he put the phone away and stepped back over the body to the open tool locker. He lifted out the pair of bolt croppers, the only component of the truck's useless toolkit that he hadn't discarded earlier.

'This won't hurt a bit,' he said to the dead man.

When the unpleasant part was over, Ben left the bolt croppers lying across the corpse's chest. Then he unscrewed the top of each of the four plastic fuel cans in turn. Taking care not to get any on himself, he sloshed their contents all over the flatbed, over the corpse, inside the cab, everywhere. The volatile petrol fumes filled the air with their sharp tang and shimmered up like heat ripples in the dappled sunlight as they quickly began to evaporate. Ben left the upturned cans where they lay, then walked away from the truck. He reached in his pocket for the cigarettes he'd bought. Tore open the pack, drew out a Gauloise, put it lightly between his lips. It felt as if it belonged there. He lit it with his old Zippo and took a deep draw of the smoke, letting the acrid taste of it fill his lungs. His first cigarette all year. Unlikely to be his last.

He sucked it hungrily down to its last inch, then plucked it out of his mouth and walked a few steps back towards the truck and flicked the burning stub on to the flatbed.

Twenty litres of spilled Eurosuper 98 caught light almost instantly with a big, gushy *WHUMPF* and a hot expanding breath that Ben felt on his face as he retreated to a safe distance. The fire spread everywhere at once, licking and rolling and consuming all it could find, until the Belphégor and the picnic table next to it could hardly be seen behind a curtain of flames that danced and leaped up high in the centre of the clearing. A tower of black smoke caught the breeze and drifted and dissipated over the forest.

Ben gazed at the blaze for a few moments, then turned, picked up his bag from the foot of the tree, slung it over his shoulder and started walking back towards the road.

Chapter Twenty

The underground passage beneath Udo Streicher's hangar was like a subway tunnel, its curved walls tiled shiny white, brightly lit by rows of neon strips that ran its entire considerable length. The floor was made of a rubberised compound, allowing the buggy's chunky tyres to adhere to it safely as it plunged down over a hundred metres at a steep angle into the ground. By the time the tunnel levelled out it was already far from the hangar, directly beneath the fields, with an impenetrable thickness of reinforced concrete between it and the distant surface.

For all his wealth, Udo Streicher couldn't have come close to affording the subterranean complex that stretched far and deep and totally hidden below the rolling greenery of the beautiful Swiss countryside. Rather, it had been the brain-child – and in retrospect the ruinous folly – of a business entrepreneur named Helmut Batz.

Batz had made the bulk of his money in shipping, an occupation that enriched him magnificently but failed to satisfy deeper needs. By the time he'd reached the age of fifty in 1977, he was not only one of the wealthiest men in Europe but also one of the most profoundly unsettled, convinced as he was of the imminent total war set to engulf the world at any time. In 1982 he finally completed work on the giant bunker in which he planned to harbour, in long-term safety, an extended circle of his relatives and friends in the event of the much-anticipated nuclear holocaust. Unfortunately for Batz, not even his robust shipping fortune could survive the project's astronomical costs, while meantime his business interests suffered due to his single-minded obsession with it. Financially crippled and suffering from depression, he somehow managed to hang on for another eighteen years before his spiralling debts and failing health finally got the better of him and he was forced to sell up for a painful fraction of what he'd ploughed into his pet project.

One man's loss is another man's gain, and for Udo Streicher the chance that had come his way that fateful day in October 2000 had been the golden opportunity of his life, one he'd unhesitatingly snapped up. Never mind the hundred acres of prime pastureland and the farmhouse that came with the property: the bunker itself was what drew him, and couldn't have been better suited to his unique needs. Thanks to Batz's almost maniacal perfectionism, the place had been built to such high-level specifications that it would last literally for ever. It was a veritable fortress, capable of withstanding a one-megaton bomb blast detonated half a mile away: the equivalent of seventy Hiroshima bombs dropped all at once right on his doorstep. Not that Streicher worried about nuclear war, unlike his predecessor. He had other interests.

In addition to luxuriously appointed reception rooms and sleeping quarters for up to eighty people, the bunker's grand design comprised a command post and armoury, a gym, an operating theatre and medical lab, and even a cell block in case the long-term cohabitation of an isolated community anxiously facing a post-apocalyptic future led to cabin fever and social disorder. Necessities such as a richly stocked wine cellar had not been overlooked either, along with the essential gigantic food storage facilities, tanks for water and for fuel to power the generators and heating system. The water-purification and air-filtration systems had been space-age technology back in 1982 and were still highly advanced even by modern standards.

In short, the bunker was a self-contained haven for a man of Udo Streicher's disposition and future plans. Secrecy was, always had been, his highest priority. Just days after the property had been officially transferred into the untraceable company name he'd carefully set up in advance, the architect's offices in Geneva where the plans were stored had burned to the ground in a mysterious night-time fire. Soon afterwards, the one-time engineer in charge of the building project, one Leon Landenberger, now retired, had fallen to his death from the high Titlis suspension bridge in an apparent suicide while on a skiing holiday. The unfortunate Helmut Batz himself had perished later in the same year when his Porsche had spun off a twisty section of mountain road near Chamonix. One by one, all remaining ties to the existence of Streicher's new subterranean paradise were severed.

Meanwhile, he sold off the penthouse apartment in Lausanne and the chalet in Zermatt. He no longer needed them. At the age of thirty-one, as far as official records showed, he became homeless. The richest homeless person in Switzerland.

Now, fifteen years later, far below the rich organic pastures where cows grazed contentedly against the mountain backdrop, the golf buggy whooshed silently through a storage warehouse that resembled the hold of a giant supertanker. Streicher had not been idle for the last decade and a half.

He'd spent a great deal of that time, and a great deal of money, in vastly supplementing the existing stores he'd inherited from Helmut Batz with enormous quantities of equipment and materials. He'd travelled to Colorado and Montana to learn from hard-core survivalists there, folks who'd left behind conventional living to fence themselves off from a world they regarded as doomed by coming catastrophic events, natural or otherwise. He'd learned a lot from them, returning to Switzerland full of ideas about the requirements for long-term post-apocalyptic survival.

And not just survival. Streicher wasn't simply a 'prepper'. His ideas went much, much further.

Mere survival wasn't the issue.

And to that end, the bunker's storage spaces were filled floor to ceiling with industrial shelving packed with anything and everything that could help him in his quest. The armoury section alone was more than fifty metres from end to end, three racks high, along both walls. It housed enough military-grade small arms to comfortably equip a medium-sized private army. The guns that didn't stand in glistening oiled rows, butt down with their muzzles pointing upwards, were still packed in their original armourers' crates, unfired and untouched until the day they'd be put into action. Everything that could ever be put to good use in the after-world, as Streicher called it, was stockpiled there. Each variety and calibre of weapon was amply catered for among the endless stacks of olive-painted ammunition boxes. Streicher prided himself on what was most certainly the largest and most secret private arsenal in Europe. He often thought about the man who'd helped supply much of it. Miki Donath, his friend, close ally and future lieutenant, temporarily indisposed at the hands of a corrupt judiciary system that treated great men like common criminals.

Hannah's thoughts echoed his own as their conveyance glided between the towering racks of hardware. 'Poor Miki,' she mused out loud. 'I wonder how he's doing right now. I can't bear to think of him rotting in that prison.'

'When the time comes, he'll be back with us,' Streicher said. 'None of us is going to have to wait much longer.'

Hundreds of metres further on, he braked the golf buggy to a smooth, silent halt as they reached the part of the bunker he and Hannah had come down here to visit. Until now, it was a section that had stood empty, like a missing tooth in an otherwise perfect smile, an ever-present symbol of failure that he'd found hard to bear. Not any longer.

The massive safe stood as tall and wide as a very large human being. Its steel walls could neither be drilled nor pierced with the hottest cutting torch. Nothing short of a tank shell could have busted the hinges and locks that held the thick door in place.

The two of them stepped out of the vehicle. Streicher walked over to the safe and entered the combination code he alone in the world knew. The steel door swung open, revealing its electronically temperature-regulated interior and four shelves, stacked vertically one above the other.

Streicher turned back towards the cart. Carefully, he picked up one of the eight white containers from its carry rack and placed it on the upper shelf. Hannah passed him another. He laid it delicately beside the first. They took their time filling each shelf in turn, neither of them speaking, each smiling a little smile of pleasure. This was a moment to be savoured.

Afterwards, in the warm luxury of their personal quarters, reclining on a soft rug in front of a crackling log fire with a Chopin Nocturne playing in the background, Streicher and Hannah clinked glasses. The champagne was an old vintage, one that he'd been storing for a long time in the hope that, one day, this celebration would be a reality.

'To the future,' Streicher said. 'To our dream of the after-world, soon about to come true.'

'The afterworld. And to the martyr's curse,' Hannah said, raising her glass, which sparkled in the firelight.

'Yes, indeed. To our dear Salvator. If he had only known that his words would one day make history.'

'To Salvator.'

They clinked again with the delicate, chiming ring that only the best crystal can produce. The two of them, far below ground, hidden from the world, safe and secure and completely in control. Not only of their own personal destinies, but those of millions of other human beings. It was a heady feeling. Streicher took a long sip of the ice-cold champagne, feeling the bubbles on his tongue.

'I'm so proud of you,' Hannah said.

He grinned and shrugged modestly. 'I've been working on my revised list. Would you like to see it?'

Her eyes sparkled. 'I'd love to.'

He slipped the piece of paper from his pocket, and care-fully set down his glass. The writing on the list was messy, with a lot of corrections and crossings out. 'Eight cities,' he said. 'That's just to begin with, of course.'

'Tell me them,' purred Hannah, raising her glass to her lips. They'd been having this discussion for years, but only now was it finally becoming a reality. Lottery winners got to indulge themselves by spending hours picking out the model and colour of that Bentley or Ferrari they'd always wanted. For Udo Streicher, for whom wealth had been a fact of life since childhood, self-indulgence came in other forms.

'Here they are,' he said. 'Berlin, Brussels, London, Madrid, Paris, Rome, and Vienna.'

Hannah pursed her lips. 'That's only seven, Udo.'

'So it is. I left out Prague.' He looked up from the list. 'Do you approve of my choices?'

'Hmm,' she said. 'It's a bigger world than that, my love. What about China and Japan and Australia? What about America?'

'It'll take care of itself, you know. By its very nature.'

'Darling, of course it will. But we want to give it all the help we can, don't we?'

He frowned at his piece of paper. 'You're right. This list is too thin.'

Hannah took another sip of champagne and fell silent for a moment, her brow furrowed with reflection. 'I'm thinking, only one in the whole of the United Kingdom? London's right down at the southern end of a long, thin island. Think of the more northern populations.'

'Leeds, Manchester, Edinburgh,' he said, nodding. 'We should probably fit one more in, at least.'

'This is fun, isn't it? So exciting.' She beamed, and the firelight gleamed on her teeth and in her eyes. He'd never seen her looking so beautiful.

'You might say it's *intoxicating*,' he said, and they both laughed for a long time.

Chapter Twenty-One

Ben had a way to walk before he was able to thumb a lift from a passing car. His rescuers were two elderly and quite batty sisters in a Renault 5 who obviously weren't afraid of picking up lone male hitch-hikers carrying military haversacks, somewhat dusty and battered and smelling faintly of petrol and smoke. Ben smiled and tried not to look like someone who'd just disposed of a dead body in the woods. The only occupant of the Renault who seemed suspicious of him was the cantankerous white miniature poodle who sat guarding him in the back seat and bared its teeth at his every move.

After listening politely to their life stories for a dozen kilometres, Ben parted ways with the sisters on the edge of the village where they lived. They drove off with big smiles and waved goodbyes, and he watched the Renault disappear before setting off in search of a bus stop. His map told him he was still sixteen kilometres from Briançon, which was where he was headed on his next set of errands.

He found the bus stop and spent half an hour waiting on a bench in the sunshine, hunched forward with his elbows on his knees and his bag between his feet, systematically working his way through the pack of Gauloises. They tasted good, and he needed the lift they gave him.

By the time the silver Autocars Resalp coach finally rolled up the dusty road and halted by the stop with a squish of airbrakes, he was buzzing and light-headed from the nicotine. He flicked away his half-smoked cigarette, boarded the bus and settled in a vacant window seat near the back, then closed his eyes and didn't open them again until he was in Briançon.

The town's main bus station was a busy place, the hub of routes radiating in all directions, to Grenoble and Avignon, all the way north to Paris, south-eastward into Italy and north-eastward into Switzerland. Ben made his way to the exit through the crowd of travellers and headed on foot towards the centre of town. His bruises ached and the weight of the bullion in his bag was pulling on his shoulder. His body was telling him he was hungry, but he had no stomach for food.

He soon found the place that was to be his first port of call. The office supplies store was empty, cool and airy. Beyond the racks of shelves for computer sundries and print cartridges and stationery, various kinds of paper and packaging materials, there was a separate workstation area offering do-it-yourself photocopy and fax services. The shop was staffed by a young woman with a pleasant smile and shoulder-length fair hair. Hers evidently wasn't a very busy job, as Ben could tell from the half-read romance novel propped open on the desk in front of her. He smiled back and did his best to look friendly and inoffensive.

He bought the thinnest sheaf of plain white general-purpose office paper he could find on the shelf, a black permanent marker pen and a little set comprising a stamp and inkpad. He asked if he could use the workstation, and the pleasant young woman said that of course he could, showed him a sheet of tariffs and gave him brief instructions on how to use the all-singing, all-dancing combined photo-copier and fax machine.

He walked over to where the machine sat just below chest height on a worktop surface and dumped his bag at his feet, glad to be relieved of its weight for a couple of minutes. It had been a while since he'd used technology like this, but he knew more or less what he was doing. The copier was a large cream-coloured plastic cube with rounded edges and a top lid that opened to expose the flat glass scanner screen. He flipped it up to hide behind, then dug nonchalantly in his pocket, took out five sausage-sized packages rolled in absorb-ent paper towel and laid them in a little row on the worktop. Then he opened the stamp and inkpad set and placed it beside them. He wouldn't be requiring the stamp, only the pad, which was just a rectangle of some kind of felt material soaked in black ink. He tested it with his fingertip. It was moist and his finger came away stained black. He wiped it on his jeans. Next, he opened up the thin sheaf of office paper, drew out a single sheet and laid it down beside the other items. Finally, he took out the phone he'd inherited, turned it on and scrolled through the menu to bring up its own number.

So far, so innocuous.

Before he went any further, he glanced over the top edge of the open lid at the woman behind the counter and saw that she was engrossed in her romance novel and not paying him any attention. He unrolled the first package.

The severed finger was pale and bloodless. The small amount of fluid that had leaked from its raw end had been absorbed into the paper. Index finger, right hand. Ben casually picked it up, like the uneaten cold chipolata left over from last night's barbecue. He pressed the fingertip into the pad, made sure it was good and inky, then carefully applied it to the paper, rolling it gently left and right the way cops did when they were fingerprinting suspects. Lifting it away, he saw that it had made a pretty good impression, the minute lines and grooves and whorls showing up neatly on the paper. One down, four to go. He replaced the ink-stained finger in its wrapping, laid it to one side and moved on to the next, and repeated the operation until he had a row of prints that any jailhouse duty officer would be proud of. One hand was enough, for his purposes.

As he waited a moment for the ink to dry, he noticed the shop assistant glancing up from her book and smiling at him. He smiled back. This could turn into a beautiful friendship. He picked up the marker pen and wrote in capitals beneath the line of prints: THE LONE WOLF SAYS HELLO. Below that, he copied out the number of the phone.

He placed the sheet on the scanner, made sure it was properly squared up, then lowered the lid. Took out his wallet and riffled through the pocket containing the various business cards he'd collected over the years, found the one he wanted and slipped it out. It had been waiting in there for a long time. The top right corner of the card bore a little emblem of a blue globe nestling in a laurel wreath, superimposed over a set of golden scales and pierced vertically by a golden sword. The scales and sword of justice: at least, that was the principle. It was the emblem of Interpol. The name on the card was Commissioner Luc Simon.

Luc Simon was that rarest of creatures, a senior police officer whom Ben had worked with and come away liking and respecting. When Ben had first crossed paths with him, Simon had been a simple Detective Inspector in Paris. Nowadays he was well up the food chain and riding a desk somewhere on the top floor of the Interpol HQ in Lyon, almost exactly a hundred miles north-west of Briançon. His promotion hadn't come as any surprise to Ben at the time: the guy wasn't just a flashy dresser. He was as skilled and clever and rigorous as they came. Good-looking bastard, too, oozing Gallic charm like a leading man from the heyday of French cinema.

It had been Luc Simon who'd once said to Ben, 'Men like us are lone wolves.' He hadn't been talking about solitary lupine predators; he'd been talking about their dealings with women, and the sad plight of men whose difficult occupations and single-minded direction in life seemed to doom them to eternal bad luck and trouble when it came to relationships. Luc had been having marital troubles back in those days. Ben knew the feeling.

Lone wolf. He had never forgotten that conversation, and he was pretty sure that Luc would remember it, too.

Luc Simon was the one cop in the world Ben would turn to at a moment like this. If not for help, then for information. There was a fax number in tiny print at the foot of the card. Ben keyed it into the machine, pressed the button the woman had instructed him to press, and the technology went into action. There was some humming and clicking from the works, and then a message appeared on the digital readout to tell him his fax was winging its way to the recipient. He lifted the lid, pulled out the sheet of paper and folded it into his wallet. Gathered up his stuff, paid for the fax, exchanged a last smile with the nice young woman behind the desk and stepped back out into the sunshine.

He dumped the fingers and the stationery in a waste bin up the street.

Chapter Twenty-Two

Ben's second task was to find a public phone situated in a discreet position well away from prying eyes and ears. It was a strategy he'd decided on during the rambling bus ride to Briançon. He couldn't bear the idea of the dead monks rotting away up there on the mountain where nobody might find them for weeks, even months. And he didn't want to use his newly acquired phone to make the call, because he didn't want the regular cops to have the number. In Ben's world, trust had strict limits.

The telephone box he found was on a quiet street corner, a good distance away from anything. Maybe the last proper phone box in France. He glanced up and around before he approached it, checking for CCTV cameras. Street surveillance had quadrupled in France over the last few years, and even though the country still had only a small fraction of the four million cameras spying on British citizens from every corner every day, the spread of the European police superstate dictated caution. Ben dialled 17, waited to be put through, and then in an altered accent and as briefly as possible he informed the switchboard operator about the multiple shooting at Chartreuse de la Sainte Vierge de Pelvoux. He hung up quickly and walked away, wondering how long it would be before a fleet of emergency vehicles screeched their way up the mountain road to find what he'd found earlier that day.

'Fuck it,' he muttered, and lit another cigarette as he walked. Slipping back into his old ways didn't make him feel especially great about himself. The tobacco hit was headier than usual, because he hadn't eaten a scrap since breakfast in the monastery refectory the day before. He still didn't feel much like food, but now his body was telling him he needed to refuel before he fell down. Further down the street, he found a shady, half-empty little bar, where he took a corner table and ordered a half-baguette *jambon beurre* and a glass of red house wine. The first was just to keep him going, the second to settle his nerves. Just one glass, he promised himself. The sandwich, when it came, was heavily buttered and filled with thick-cut ham and Gruyère cheese. He tore into it, ripping chunks off and wolfing them down and realising how hungry he actually was. The wine was delicious.

As he ate, he took out the mobile phone, used it to go online and dial up a search engine to find out the value of gold bullion. What he found out was no less impressive than expected. Next, he clicked back into the phone's list of contacts and retried each of the ten numbers he'd tried earlier. Same result as the first time. As before, he hung up on each in turn without leaving a message.

No word yet from Luc Simon. Ben wasn't disappointed. He believed that the Frenchman would get back to him, but he knew it might take a while. Which left him time to ponder the evidence in front of him, and to plan his next move.

Ben finished the half baguette, washed it guiltily down with the last of the wine and then sat back and thought about explosives. More specifically, about shaped charges. He'd already established in his mind that whoever had blown the near-perfect five-foot circular hole through into the sealed chamber under the monastery had a deadly talent that must have been honed by years of experience. Military training? Possible. Likely, even. Which narrowed the field by some degree, but not far enough by any means to have a place to start looking.

Setting that aside, Ben pondered the chances of tracing the perpetrators via the source of the explosives themselves. He knew a number of ex-military guys who'd moved on to deal in the arms business, legally and otherwise. They were just a phone call away, and one or two of them might even have been happy to hear from him and to know that he hadn't just vanished off the face of the earth after all.

But Ben was also very much aware that those same guys, for all their wealth of knowledge and insider contacts, wouldn't tell him anything he didn't already know. The fact was that explosives, and even the rarer sub-variety of shaped charges, could be obtained just about anywhere, by anyone. It wasn't like a tank or a rocket launcher or a surface-to-air missile or an attack helicopter, any of which could potentially, with a little insistence and the right kind of persuasion, be traced back through a web of middlemen and dealers to whoever had paid hard cash for the thing. Explosives weren't specialised, ultra-sought-after military equipment, commanding eye-watering rates from those willing to approach the go-to underworld guys who could supply them. Using them wasn't the specific domain of high-level crooks or international soldiers of fortune. Even the most advanced and powerful shaped charges were widely and cheaply available: to the steel industry, for instance, to blow out blocked dies or cut girders. To the timber industry, to fell large trees or clear log-jams. Just as they were commonly used for demolition, quarrying and ice-breaking and blowing out post-holes in hard ground, by thousands and thousands of operators all over the world. Licensing was complex, not always strictly enforced, and open to all kinds of cash-in-hand, under-the-counter abuses.

In short, there would be no simple trail of breadcrumbs. Even assuming Ben could find a lead to follow, he could easily end up spending weeks chasing down a hundred avenues, kicking down a hundred doors, and getting precisely nowhere.

One thing was for sure: he wasn't going to get very far at all without certain bare necessities. Money wasn't a big problem – he still had plenty of cash, and when that ran out, the remainder of the Caisse d'Epargne bank account left over from his days of living in Normandy would last him for a while. He needed transport, which wasn't a problem either; but the third of those bare necessities wasn't such a simple matter to get hold of.

Unless you had the appropriate contacts. And it just happened that Ben had one of those, right here in Briançon.

He left the bar carrying his heavy bag on his shoulder and made his way on foot across town, retracing the route he'd taken by car as a passenger that morning until he arrived at the three-storey apartment building next to the bare-brick alleyway with the wheelie bins. He ran his finger up the list of names next to the door buzzers. Third from the top was the name O. Adeyemi, with an apartment number. He pressed the buzzer, and a few moments later a deep voice sounded out of the raspy speaker.

'Yeah?'

'Come to repay your lost bet,' Ben said into the intercom.

There was a pause, followed a few seconds later by a click, and he pushed his way inside the building. He trudged up the stairs, reached the apartment and banged on the door. It opened, Omar filling the whole doorway.

The big Nigerian grinned another of his dazzling grins. 'Hey, man. S'matter, van broke down again?'

'Don't you have a job to go to?' Ben said.

'Gentleman of leisure, bro,' Omar said graciously, ushering him into the poky passage. The same aroma of strong coffee was wafting from the kitchen.

'I'll take a cup, if there's any going,' Ben said.

'Hey, Café Omar, always open for business. I'm honoured. You came all the way back just for that?'

'Actually, I came to ask three more favours.'

'Oh, yeah? Three?'

'The first one's just small, number two's a little bigger, and number three's a little bigger again.'

'That's a lot of favours, man,' Omar said, showing Ben to the same chair he'd sat in before and pouring steaming black coffee into a mug. 'Especially as I already saved your butt last night *and* this morning.'

'Brothers in arms?'

Omar's chair creaked as his giant bulk settled into it. He took a slurp of coffee, smacked his lips and raised a suspicious eyebrow. 'Start with favour number one, and we'll work our way up from there.'

'Sounds fair. First, I'd like a shower.'

Omar ran his eye up and down Ben and gave a rumbling bass chuckle. 'You need it, all right. Be my guest.'

'Thanks. Now, ready for the big stuff?'

'Try me,' Omar said.

'Favour number two, I need your FAMAS rifle, your Kalashnikov and every round of ammo you've got squirrelled away under the floorboards. Favour number three, I have to borrow your Hummer. I don't know how long for, and I can't absolutely guarantee that you'll get it back in one piece.'

Omar's eyes boggled for a moment. He began to roar with laughter and then stopped as he realised Ben was serious. 'I want to help you, man, but—'

'Let's call those last two more of a trade,' Ben said. He reached down to the bag at his feet, undid the buckles and flipped open the canvas flap. He hefted out one of the gold bars.

'Take it,' he said.

Omar took it. Even his muscle-bound arms sagged an inch under the weight. He turned the gold ingot over and over in his hands. Stared down at it bug-eyed and speechless for a long minute, then stared up at Ben. 'Don't fuck with me, man,' he finally said in a low voice. 'What is this?'

'It's not brass,' Ben said. 'That's for sure.'

'I'm not even gonna ask where it came from,' Omar said.

'Always a wise policy,' Ben said.

'Are you drunk?'

'Never,' Ben said.

'I don't want any trouble.'

'You won't get any,' Ben said. 'No comebacks, no strings attached. It's yours. I've never met a bodybuilder who didn't have a set of scales. Weigh it. My guess is seven and a half kilos. Twenty-four-carat gold is going for over thirty thousand euros a kilo, today's price. You'll lose a bit, because there's no hallmark. But you'll still do okay.'

Omar paused a moment to do the arithmetic, and said, 'Holy shit.'

'Now you're a gentleman of leisure, for real. Don't spend it all at once.'

'Hold on, bro. When you said about maybe not bringing my Hummer back in one piece . . .'

'Just in case,' Ben said. 'Thought I should warn you.'

135

'You any idea what it takes to bust one of those things up? They're indestructible.'

'In my experience, nothing's indestructible,' Ben said. 'But now you can afford to go out and buy three more. One other thing. If anyone should come around asking questions, you've only just realised the vehicle's been stolen and you were about to report it, okay?'

'Anyone, as in the cops?'

'For your own protection,' Ben said. 'So, do we have a trade?'

Omar looked at him very carefully, very seriously, for another full minute as he decided. 'I have a couple of big cases of ammo,' he said.

'I'll take the lot,' Ben said.

'What are you gonna do, man?'

'Nothing that will come back on you. That's a promise.'

Omar nodded. He paused again, for fifteen long seconds. Ben could see the wheels turning in his head. Then Omar went to fetch the FAMAS, the Kalashnikov, the ammo cans and the keys to the Hummer.

Chapter Twenty-Three

Briançon was a pleasant, polite, civilised town. Far too much of all those things to attract the kind of people Ben needed to find next, and for the kind of further enquiries he needed to press on with. Pleasant, polite, civilised people couldn't help him in his quest.

And so Ben had pictured a map in his head, with Briançon marking its imaginary centre, and started thinking of where he might begin looking for less pleasant people who could. Four hours' drive to the south lay the deceptively named city of Nice, a place whose darker side Ben wasn't unacquainted with. Once upon a time, its undisputed kingpins had been the Sicilian crime bosses, but nowadays the prostitution and drugs rackets were an open market to any number of ruthless and ambitious hoodlums. If you were looking for a particular class of low life, there were worse places to start turning over rocks and kicking down doors.

But then there was Marseille. About two hundred and fifty kilometres to the south-west on Ben's mental map, just a little under three hours' drive from the cosy tranquillity of Briançon. If Nice scored an approximate seven out of ten in the Sin City leagues, then Marseille was way off the scale. An erstwhile haven of sea and sun that had decomposed into a festering lair of organised crime and police corruption. Provence's own answer to South Central LA, where the litter-swirled streets were pockmarked from repeated drive-by shootings; officially Europe's most dangerous place to be a young person growing up, and a land of opportunity for the Milieu or French criminal underworld. The days of legendary gangsters like Marseille godfather Jacky 'The Madman' Imbert, glamorous figures who'd lived the dream rubbing shoulders with the likes of Alain Delon, were gone. They'd long since been displaced by cut-throat gangs of Corsicans, Turks, Maghrebis, *Pieds-Noirs*, Senegalese and ethnic Manoush and Yeniche gypsies, all continually disembowelling one another over rights to control arms and drug trafficking, the sex trade, illegal gambling, extortion and protection and murder rackets, money laundering and fraud, arson and theft and, finally but not least, kidnapping.

Human trafficking was the reason Ben had become familiar with the less salubrious districts of Marseille, back in the days when he'd called himself a 'freelance crisis response consultant'. He didn't suppose the place was any less of a sanctuary for scumbags than it had been then. In fact, he was fairly certain it was even worse than he remembered, and he had his reasons for thinking that way.

It was well known in certain circles that a fresh team of players had increasingly become established as the new-generation crime bosses of Marseille, and that was what interested him. Walking tall, like lions among the hyenas, the Russian mob now lorded it over the gang scene. Under their rule, the number of bloody turf wars and feud killings and execution-style assassinations had rocketed to unprecedented levels. The Russians had virtually uncontrolled access to a river of illicit weaponry coming out of Eastern

Europe, as well as to trained men happy to make use of it. Many of their enforcers were battle-hardened ex-military, tough, beefy, crude and violent men recruited from former Soviet territories like Chechnya and Georgia, for whom the act of murder was so casual and human life so cheap that they scared the crap out of the rest of the Milieu gangs, whose territories they were snapping up one by one.

Nowhere else on Ben's mental map, within a radius of two hundred and fifty kilometres, a circle ranging one hundred and ninety-six thousand square kilometres in area, would you find anything like such a high concentration of professionally trained and equipped criminals ready to rock 'n' roll at the drop of a hat. Exactly the kind of people you could expect to carry out a military killing operation against a community of poor innocent monks who just happened to be sitting on a hoard of gold that maybe they didn't even know about. Exactly the kind of people who might be looking to finance themselves and their organisation through an easy heist against unarmed, defenceless opponents.

Not to mention, exactly the kind of people you might also expect to find smoking Russian cigarettes like the one that had been stubbed out on Père Antoine's forehead. Ben had tried them once, didn't much care for them. A particular and distinctive brand that had been manufactured in the Ukraine until 2005, and since then in Russia itself. Considered one of the country's finer blends, the sophisticated choice of rich Russian society folks, and maybe rich Russian gangsters, too.

All of which made Marseille the top spot on Ben's mental map. And which was exactly why, at this moment, he was barrelling south-westwards down the motorway towards Marseille in a gleaming dark H1 Hummer. Blasting through the hot afternoon with a cool wind roaring in through the wide-open windows, two hundred thousand euros' worth of gold weighing down the passenger seat the other side of the massive transmission tunnel, and a couple of automatic rifles plus over five hundred rounds of ammunition stuffed in a holdall in its cavernous rear space. The Hummer was perfect for him. It was fast, it would go absolutely anywhere he wanted it to, and it was big enough to set up a mobile camp in if it came to it. No amount of civilianisation could completely smooth away its military origins. The thing was a battle wagon, aggressively functional in every way, and Ben was grimly at home in it. He settled back inside its armoured shell and kept his foot down and felt as if he was going to war.

The late afternoon was still hot when he came into Marseille. From a distance it was a beautiful city, framed by a backdrop of high country, rock and scrub wilderness that the French called *la garrigue*. Up close, you could see the decay anywhere you chose to spot it. Ben avoided the bustle of the centre and picked his way around the outskirts, navigating from memory to a place he'd been before and hadn't ever been too eager to revisit. The area he was aiming for was a stretch of districts to the north of the city, a sprawling zone of neglected apartment blocks that had been knocked up cheaply and never knocked down, but should have been a long time ago. Isolated, almost self-contained, the area was like a city in its own right – one where the normal rules no longer applied.

Specifically, Ben was headed for a district called La Castellane. It was a close-knit cluster of estates hastily erected in the early seventies for a population of itinerant blue-collar workers who'd never been meant to stay, until worsening economic conditions and factory closures had made prisoners of them. In the span of not too many years, the place had become the most notorious ghetto in Marseille. It still was. The Hummer rumbled its way through dismal, colour-washed streets that could have belonged in a Mexican barrio. In some places, he could have imagined himself part of a military patrol threading its way through war-torn Baghdad, 2003. There was rubble everywhere, and now and then the shell of a burned-out vehicle. Any intact wall was covered in graffiti and every lower-floor window was barred like a prison block. Sun-blanched grass grew in patches between derelict buildings and stalled construction projects from ten or fifteen years ago, surrounded by dusty vegetation and the incessant chirping of cicadas. Strings of cars were parked along the streets, most of them white or silver or grey, adding to the impression that the colour had been drained out of the place along with any kind of happiness or hope. Feral packs of olive-tanned shirtless youths roved the streets, yelling and fighting among themselves and chucking things at passing cars.

But not at the Hummer. As Ben cruised by he saw the reaction of the kids, and it didn't surprise him. In the context of a place like Briançon, Omar's battle wagon was just an overblown, gas-guzzling folly of a car. But in these mean streets, its menacing appearance and black-tinted glass had a whole other meaning that these kids understood very well. The kind of people who drove about the ghetto in such vehicles were the kind who owned it, ruled it, who collected the money and dictated who lived and who died. Even think about throwing a can or a stone at a car like that and you'd better start running before its occupants casually pulled up, stepped out and mowed down everyone in sight with automatic gunfire. Then they'd hunt down your friends, your family, everyone you'd ever known, and kill them all. It was about respect.

Ben felt sorry for the kids. Many, perhaps most, would get caught up in the drugs scene, if they hadn't done already, looking for ways to gather easy cash and often catching a bullet or a blade in the belly for their efforts. Life expectancy wasn't high. He rumbled past another wreck of a burned-out car, and thought about what had happened to it. One of the methods the gangs used to dispense with rivals was to shoot them through the windows of their vehicles and then set them alight. It was called 'barbecuing'. Guns were everywhere. Rule of law was just a faded memory here.

Ben's prediction had been more than right. The area's decline since he'd last seen it was worse than he could have imagined. Then it had been a sinkhole of despair. Now it was just lost, irredeemable. Something had rotted the heart out of the place and it needed to be levelled and the whole thing rebuilt afresh. Except you couldn't change the people who'd brought about the rot, and they would just keep bringing it until there was nothing left. The only way to change them would be to kill them.

The place had indeed changed, but not so much that Ben couldn't find his way to his particular destination. The building he was looking for was a five-storey apartment block deep inside the La Castellane estates, filthy and neglected and looking like a penitentiary among the unkempt greenery.

He parked in the shadow of the trees fifty yards from the building's entrance, killed the engine and settled back in his seat. Watched the entrance from behind his tinted glass, and waited for darkness to fall.

Chapter Twenty-Four

It was a long wait, but Ben was very good at waiting. All Special Forces soldiers were, out of ingrained habit after years of hanging around on standby for brief, explosive bursts of action that more often than not were postponed. His body was calm, his breathing and pulse rate just ticking over somewhere above dormant. Mentally, he was coiled like the mainspring of a gun, ready at a fraction of a second's notice to drop the hammer on a live round and shatter the silence into a thousand pieces.

He watched and smoked, and then kept watching as evening turned to night and the expected events began to unfold, like a strategy developing on a chessboard in a game where Ben was already several moves ahead. He saw the kid in the blue hoodie, faded jeans and white trainers, scrawny, North African, about fifteen, take up position across the street from the building's entrance. Moments later he saw the three others, ganglier, taller versions of the first, in their late teens or very early twenties and wearing similar outfits, get out of a battered BMW, lope up to the grimy glass double doors and disappear inside. Ben knew they didn't live there, even if they acted as if they owned the place.

Aside from utter ruthlessness and vaulting greed, one of the things that made the drug gangs such a successful organisation was their strictly observed sense of hierarchy. Entry level for the novice was the job of '*guetteur*', a lookout posted to watch the entrance of a building where deals were going on inside. The potential dangers they looked out for included roving unmarked police cars, although that posed a small risk in the core of the police no-go areas. More likely was the threat of rival gang members busting in on their business, which happened frequently and with bloody results. Any sign of trouble, the lookouts would bolt and phone the guys inside, whereupon the guys inside would scram as fast as their feet could carry them. They were the next level up, known in Marseille gang-speak as the '*charbonniers*'. Literally, the coalmen. The shovellers, the drones, the ones who kept the fires burning and the money rolling in. On a good night, the dealers might conduct enough small transactions to rake in 12,000 euros, maybe 15,000, selling anything from cannabis resin to crack. They tended to work the stairs, where they could bolt at a moment's notice without getting boxed in.

The night was sultry and starless, and there was the smouldering electric smell in the air that hinted a thunderstorm might be on its way before too long. The street lights cast a dim ochre glow over the front of the building and the dealers' white BMW, giving the colourless scene the look of an old sepia-toned photograph. It was after ten. It wouldn't be long before the first of the night's customers would start to turn up. Right now, the street was nearly empty. Ben swung open the door of the Hummer and walked out from under the shadows of the trees with the rifle under his jacket. The buttstock jammed tight under his right armpit, the end of the stubby barrel protruding downwards at his waist. Benefits of a bullpup layout, making a full-bore military assault rifle as concealable as a submachine gun. At first glance, it was invisible. At second glance, it was time to run. But the lookout didn't get as far as the second glance, because his on-the-job experience didn't include spotting someone like Ben Hope approaching him through the darkness.

The FAMAS was out of the jacket and the muzzle was in the kid's face before he could react. Up close in the halo of the street light, he was nearer to sixteen than fifteen, with a bumfluff moustache shading his upper lip. Still a kid, but learning fast. His eyes opened wide at the sight of the gun and the stranger behind it.

Ben held the rifle in one hand and extended the other, palm up, fingers splayed. 'Phone,' he said.

The kid narrowed his eyes slightly, then reached for his phone and dumped it in Ben's hand.

'And the other one,' he said, nodding at the oblong lump in the kid's back pocket. Tricksy, these apprentice gangsters. The kid didn't move. Ben drew in his outstretched hand, gripped the rifle's black polymer fore-end to support its weight, quickly moved his trigger hand back from the pistol grip to the receiver and jacked a round of Omar's standard 5.56x45mm NATO ball ammunition into the chamber. There was nothing like that metallic *shlak-schlunk* to get people motivated. The kid instantly obeyed, whipped out his second phone and held it out for Ben.

'Now beat it,' he said. 'Go home to your mother and don't come back here.'

The kid took off without a second glance at the building he was guarding. Ben slipped the rifle back under his jacket. Looked right, then left. Nobody was around. The dealers would be in place by now, waiting for their first score. They'd be expecting a visitor any moment, but not the one they were going to get. Ben walked under the lights and shoved open the grimy glass doors. They led into a foyer that smelled like a urinal and doubled back on itself after a few metres, where it met a plain metal railing and the foot of the stairs. Graffiti was the only paint the walls had ever seen. The stairs were bare concrete, stained with piss and beer and blood and vomit and whatever else had been spilled on them for nobody to clean up. The sounds of thudding rock music and rap and a baby crying and a woman's angry yelling all merged together in a cacophony of noise that funnelled down the stairwell from the flats above.

As Ben had expected, he found the three *charbonniers* hanging about the first landing, guarding a bulging sports bag whose contents were probably worth the value of a brand new Mercedes. The one on the left had glazed eyes and looked as if he'd been smoking his own stash. The one on the right was too obese to move very fast. The one in the middle looked sharp and alert and useful. Ben instantly knew he was the one to watch. And he was watching Ben, as Ben climbed the stairs towards them, reached the landing and walked by, turned and started climbing up the next flight.

Ben walked up three steps before he turned and swung out the rifle. He had the high ground, blocking their escape upwards. No escape downwards either. They'd be thinking he wasn't alone, that his gang buddies would have the door covered already.

Ben kept the rifle trained on the sharp-looking one in the middle. If anyone was going to try anything, it was him. Not that these small-fry dealers generally went armed with much more than a switchblade. The heavy artillery didn't make an appearance until the next step up in the hierarchy, the guy to whom these three directly answered. That was the '*gérant*', meaning the manager, who recruited, controlled, and now and then weeded out by means of a bullet or a knife the small guys. Each *gérant* was responsible for his own block, running two or three dealers and up to a dozen sentries at a time. The small fortune each block could generate in a day was spouted up to the next level, the '*patron*' or mid-level boss who ran as many buildings as his level of seniority, the size of his balls or the limits of his territory would allow. The *patron* was the first of the big guys on the ladder. The ones Ben was interested in. One in particular. But to get to him, you still had to go through the small guys. Which was one key reason why the small guys needed regular culling, to prevent careless talk and to encourage loyalty. Not the most stable working environment.

'Eriq still running this place?' Ben asked, holding the rifle steady. One round of high-velocity 5.56 NATO in the concrete stairwell would blow out his eardrums just as surely as the bullet would blow out the brains of whichever dealer he shot at first. He didn't want to have to hurt his own ears.

The dopey one on the left just stared. The fat one looked like an overweight rabbit frozen in the beam of a hunting lamp. The middle one, the sharp one, frowned. Thinking this wasn't what it looked like. Not a rival gang hit. Something else. He nodded.

'Tell me who Eriq runs it for,' Ben said. He wanted this done fast, before a customer turned up or any of the block's residents wandered down the stairs and became an audience.

'For Rollo,' the dealer in the middle said.

'Rollo who?'

'Rollo le Tordu.'

Le Tordu wasn't his real surname. It meant 'the twisted one', and for good reason. 'Okay,' Ben said. 'Call Eriq. Tell him I want to see him. Here, in person, alone, right now. Tell him I just want to talk. There'll be no trouble, unless he's not here in five minutes flat. Then I'm going to shoot you three and help myself to all the merchandise. After that I'm going to burn this building to the ground and move on to the next, and the next. When I'm done, I'm going to make sure Rollo hears it was Eriq who made the move on him.'

The dealer in the middle took out a phone and thumbed a couple of keys without taking his eyes off Ben. 'Who'd I say wants to talk to him?'

'Just describe me to him,' Ben said. 'He'll know.'

The dealer waited for a moment while his call went through. Then, still not taking his eyes off Ben, he said, 'Dude, there's a guy asking for you.' Pause. 'He's here right now. Says you know him.' The dealer related the threat, down to the last detail, then listened, eyes still fixed on Ben and the rifle. 'Oh, yeah. He means it, all right. I think he'll do exactly what he says, you don't get over here right now.' Another pause. 'White guy. Not French. Speaks it pretty well, but he's a *rosbif* or something.'

Roast beef. One of the gentler terms of abuse the French had for the Brits. Ben hadn't even eaten the stuff in years.

'About forty,' the dealer said into the phone. 'Blond hair. Five-eleven. Leather jacket. Big fucking gun. Looks like a serious motherfucker, boss. We need to do what he says.'

There was a silence as Eriq on the other end of the line digested the information. The dealer listened, nodded, put the phone away. 'Eriq's on his way,' he said.

Ben lowered the rifle and tucked it back inside his jacket. 'Good. Then let's sit here quietly and wait for him.'

They waited. Nobody spoke. Ben lit a Gauloise and sat on the stairs with the FAMAS hidden at his side but ready for instant use if anyone tried to get away. Which nobody did. At ten to eleven a thin white guy with a ring in his nose

148

who looked like a potential dope customer appeared at the bottom of the stairwell, stared at the three dealers then at Ben and appeared to sense trouble, beating a quick exit. The woman upstairs was still raging and screaming, the baby went on crying, the mixed cacophony of music wafted down from above.

At 10.56 Ben heard a screech of brakes from outside, followed by the sound of running footsteps and the slap of the double glass doors being batted open.

Two seconds after that, Eriq Sabatier appeared at the foot of the stairs. He was a small, crumpled man in a flowery shirt. Dark-skinned, with the complexion of a used teabag. Bald on top, the sparse remaining hair scraped thinly back into a raggedy ponytail. He looked a little greyer and a little more haggard since Ben had last pointed a gun at him.

He stared at Ben. 'Oh, Jesus Christ. Oh, fuck me. It *is* you. I thought I'd never see you again.'

'Never is an awfully long time, Eriq,' Ben said. He flicked away his cigarette. Stood up and walked down the stairs, past the three dealers.

'What the fuck do you want?' Sabatier asked, shaking his head in dismay.

'I want you, Eriq,' Ben said. As he reached the bottom step he took out the FAMAS and walked right up to the *patron* and belted him once, hard, across the side of the head with the stubby barrel. Sabatier's eyes rolled up into their sockets, his knees buckled under him and he slumped to the floor. The three dealers gaped, but didn't move and didn't try to come to their *patron*'s aid. Ben reached down, grabbed a fistful of Sabatier's collar and dragged him out through the glass doors, down the steps to the street, and all the way over to where the Hummer was parked in the shadows. Dark clouds churned ominously overhead and the electrical static

149

build-up ahead of the coming storm smelled like burning plastic in the air. It was going to be a violent one.

Ben blipped the Hummer's locks open with the key fob remote, a non-military refinement. Stashed the rifle on the passenger seat, deprived the unconscious drug dealer of his phone and the nickel-plated Beretta semi-automatic he was packing in a behind-the-hip holster, and tucked the pistol in his own belt. Then he bundled Sabatier into the back of the Hummer with little more care than he'd shown the dead man he'd loaded on to the Belphégor. Climbed behind the wheel and fired up the engine and the headlamps and the Hummer's dazzling panoply of auxiliary lighting, and sped off with a screech of tyres.

Three kilometres down the road, Ben hit the brakes and pulled up. He arranged his collection of phones on the Hummer's centre console. He had four now: the two he'd confiscated from the lookout, the one from the dead guy, and the one he'd just taken from Sabatier. He tossed both of the lookout's phones out of the window. Picked up Sabatier's. It had just one contact number listed on it, and he knew whose that would be. He dialled, heard the ringtone and then a gravelly voice he remembered from long ago. He smiled.

'How are you, Rollo?' he said.

Chapter Twenty-Five

They didn't call Rollo le Tordu because he was psychologically twisted or ethically corrupt, even though there was no doubt he was both of those things and a lot more besides. He'd earned the name as a younger man, when some members of a rival gang had shot him eight times with pump shotguns and slung his smashed, bleeding body off the highest bridge in Marseille. The fact that he'd survived gave him a kind of legendary status in the underworld, while his horrific injuries had left him with a permanent severe curvature of the spine and a crippled leg: hence, le Tordu.

Rollo had done okay for himself. He wasn't rich by crime boss standards, but he wasn't poor either. He did a lot of seamy business around Marseille, as well as running a few legit bars and clubs. While he was established and respected within the illegal drugs racket, he wasn't so thick with his competitors that he hadn't been amenable to selling the occasional tip-off in the past when one of them was dealing in something more than dope. That was how Ben, while searching for the missing teenage daughter of a businessman from Cannes, had come to deal with him. Ben had eventually found the girl before her abductors were able to sell her on to the Moroccan flesh trade, though he'd had to lean a little on Rollo to get the information in a hurry. Rollo had survived with just a few bruises to his pride. The kidnappers hadn't fared so well.

'Thought you must be dead,' Rollo said on the phone. There was no smile in his voice.

'No such luck,' Ben said.

'So you're back in the game?'

'This time it's a personal thing,' Ben told him. 'I need to meet.'

'I'm a very busy man. What do you want?'

'The usual. To be pointed in the right direction.'

'I can already tell you, I don't know shit about shit.'

'You know everyone, Rollo. There isn't a rotten little scam going in this town that you don't hear about.'

'Yeah, well, I'm not in the information trade any more,' Rollo said. 'I've got bigger fish to fry these days. And besides, I don't like the way you do business.'

'Five minutes,' Ben said. 'That's all I ask. For old times' sake.'

'How sweet. What's in it for me?'

'Same as last time,' Ben said. 'I let you hobble away no more of a fucked-up cripple than you are already.'

'See, that's what I'm saying. I'm not feeling the love.'

'Plus, I'll let you have Eriq back,' Ben said.

There was a long pause on the line. 'What makes you think I want the fucker?'

'You don't have to be coy,' Ben said. 'I know how things are with you and Eriq. Though it's hard to tell who's got the worse taste in partners.'

'Five minutes.'

'Not a moment longer.'

'No funny business?'

'Not unless you start it,' Ben said.

'I'm at Club Paradis. Rue du Vallon Montebello. Know it?'

The time was 11.16. 'Give me thirty minutes,' Ben said.

He was there by 11.35. He left the Hummer a hundred metres away, as tucked out of sight among the parked cars as a vehicle of its size could be, shouldered his bag and marched the now-conscious and very unhappy Eriq Sabatier all the way up the street already crowded with nightlife, past the hookers and the brightly lit shopfronts and the two hairy idiots cruising the kerb on chopperised Harley Davidsons with ape-hanger bars and open exhausts that sounded like a bad case of flatulence. None of the ravers in the street seemed to care that the heavens were about to open. The first rumblings were already sounding from up above. Any minute now, big raindrops would start spattering the pavements.

Club Paradis was exactly what Ben expected it to be from the flashing pink neon sign over the door shaped like a naked woman. He supposed it made sense for a gay gangster to run a strip joint. It showed a certain kind of professionalism, like a teetotaller running a pub. The music inside was raucous, the crowd was heaving and swelling, the girls were doing their thing at their poles and attracting howls of enthusiasm from a couple of hundred sweaty punters, while another hundred thronged the bar. Nobody paid any notice as Ben shoved Eriq Sabatier through the middle of the throng, towards the door at the side of the bar marked PRIVÉ. Ben's progress was unobstructed, until he came to the door and a very large, square-shouldered, shaven-headed guy with a pointed goatee beard and a Slayer T-shirt two sizes too small for him stepped up to block his way. He towered over Ben by about a foot and a half. The bouncer, Ben guessed. Or Rollo's personal minder. The huge man glared at him and pointed at the sign with a heavily muscled arm.

Ben gave him a wintry smile, nodded his head back at Eriq and said over the noise, 'Delivering a package to Rollo. He's expecting me.'

The big man pursed his lips, made a fair show of looking as if he was thinking, then lumbered aside and let Ben through. Behind the door was a dingy passage with three more doors off it. One to each side and one straight ahead. One of Ben's mottoes from SAS days was *if in doubt, bear dead ahead.* Still keeping a tight grip on Eriq, he strode up the passage and shoved open the door in front of him without knocking.

'You truly are moving up in the world, Rollo,' he said.

The office was square and dark, lit by a single desk lamp. The walls seemed to throb with the muted beat of the loud music from the club. Cigar smoke swirled in the light and clung to the ceiling like a thick layer of fog. Rollo le Tordu apparently existed on carbon monoxide. He was the only person in the room, lounging in a huge reclining leather chair at the desk, facing the door. Behind him stood a big black steel safe, hanging ajar far enough that Ben could glimpse stacked bricks of banknotes inside. Business must be good.

'You haven't changed much, Hope,' said Rollo with the kind of smile a crocodile gives a baby wildebeest before dragging it into the river. His skin was like parchment. He wore small round glasses and nearly all his hair was gone. He was dressed in a silk Armani suit, but he didn't wear it well. Even sitting, his spine looked more twisted than ever.

Ben shut the door. 'Wish I could say the same about you, Rollo. Did your friends come back and throw you off another bridge?'

'Charming as ever,' Rollo said. He took a draw on his cigar and reclined further in the chair.

'Here's your errand boy back.' There was another leather-covered chair in the corner. Ben flung Eriq into it.

'He just walked in and—' Eriq began explaining.

Rollo turned the crocodile look on him. 'You're a fucking imbecile, you know that?'

'What was I supposed to do? Said he was gonna burn the building down.'

'Still standing,' Ben said. 'That's my side of the deal honoured.'

'Except for the part where you don't try any funny stuff,' Rollo said warily.

'That part's up to you,' Ben said.

'So what do you want?'

Ben stepped up to the desk. It was broad, dark wood like the rest of the office, topped with green leather. He dumped his bag down in the middle of it. The thump of something solid and heavy inside wasn't lost on Rollo.

'I don't deal in guns,' Rollo said.

'Different kind of hardware, Rollo.' Ben unstrapped the bag, reached inside and took out the gold bar. He held it up for Rollo to see, letting the light glitter along its surface, then allowed it to fall to the desktop. It hit the wood with a crash. Rollo didn't seem concerned about his dented desk. He was too spellbound by the gold bar. 'Is that what I think it is?'

'A lot more where that came from,' Ben said. 'At least, there was. And that's why I'm here. I need to know if anyone's brought a shipment into town in the last twelve hours or so. Handlers, fences, middlemen. You know them all. I want names and addresses.'

'How big a shipment we talking about?' Rollo said, staring at the gold, eyes bulging, not blinking, behind the little round glasses.

'Considerable. I'm thinking Russians.'

Rollo nodded pensively, anxiety flashing in his expression. 'The Russians are into some big deals, all right. But what makes you think it's them?'

'Somebody left a calling card behind when they took the gold. Someone with a liking for black Sobranies.'

Rollo finally tore his gaze from the gold bar and looked long and hard at Ben, his glasses glimmering in the light. He stubbed the cigar out on the onyx ashtray at his elbow. 'Have you any idea what you're getting into, if the Russians have anything to do with this? How'd you get involved, you crazy English bastard?'

'Half Irish,' Ben said. 'They involved me when they shot a bunch of my friends. They opened that door. Not me. Now they'll have to deal with what they find on the other side of it.'

'You go anywhere near those people, they'll gut and fillet you like a fish. They'll nail you upside down to a wall and slice your balls off.'

'We'll have to see about that,' Ben said.

'These friends of yours, do they have names?'

'They weren't exactly the kind of people you'd have in your address book, Rollo. Not in your class.'

Rollo pursed his lips again and returned his attention to the gold bar. He picked it up in his long, thin hands, hefted it and turned it over under the light with a look of adoration.

'Don't get too attached,' Ben said.

'I don't know how you think I can help you,' Rollo said.

'You're in the business.'

Rollo put the bar down and looked up sharply. The crocodile expression was back. 'That's right, I am. I'm in the getting my fair share of what's going around business. If I help you, there's a price to pay. Especially if the Russians are involved.'

'I told you what's in it for you if you help me. You can still get around with the help of a stick, and you can still chew solid food.'

'You're not such a nice guy, are you?'

'You don't want to know.'

Rollo sighed. 'All right. I can ask around. Give me forty-eight hours.' He paused, caressed the gold bar as if it was a purring cat. 'Leave this with me. I might need to show it to a couple of people.'

Ben shook his head. 'I wouldn't leave you alone with that for forty-eight seconds, Rollo. You can unglue your eyes from it, because this is the last you'll see of it.'

'We trade,' Rollo said. 'The information, for the bar.'

'Don't push me,' Ben said. 'That wasn't the deal.'

Rollo laid four thin fingers across the top of the gold bar. 'You put something like this on the table, that's where it stays. You think you dictate terms around here, smart guy? Who the fuck do you think you are?'

Ben gazed steadily at him. He concentrated hard on putting as much meaning into his gaze as possible. *You're a hair's breadth from finding out exactly who I am. I'm the guy who's going to break you in pieces.* It was a look of final warning. He was down to his last drop of patience. 'The information. Now.'

'Here's some information for you,' Rollo said. 'You're going to die, Hope.'

Chapter Twenty-Six

Rollo banged on the desk. Yelled, 'Jean-Claude! Bruno!'

The office door burst in and crashed juddering against the wall. Behind it, one big hand splayed out like a battering ram, came the huge square-shouldered guy in the Slayer T-shirt. The bouncer. Behind him came another man who might have been his younger brother, an inch shorter and a foot wider, with a crab-apple face and an arrowhead haircut. Both had to duck for the doorway and turn a little sideways to squeeze their bulk through it. Once inside the room, the tops of their heads were lost in the cigar haze that covered the ceiling, like mountain peaks shrouded in cloud. Between them they carried about four times Ben's weight in lard and muscle. They must have been standing right outside the door, waiting for the order from their boss. It seemed a little too prearranged for Ben's liking.

'Kill this fucker for me,' Rollo told them, with a wave of his hand.

Ben didn't much like the look of what they'd brought with them either. Slayer reached into his back pocket and yanked out a length of slim steel chain that he held in both fists and stretched out taut, like a garrotte. Little Brother was clutching a double-barrelled shotgun that had been sawn off at both ends to make a pistol out of it, eighteen inches long. The kind of idiot weapon that could kill everyone in the room with its indiscriminate spray.

Ben would have liked to get the gun off him as a matter of priority, but Slayer was standing in the way, snapping the chain tight in his fists and looking as if he could twist a man's head off with it. Which, Ben understood, was probably the case. All the more reason for not letting the chain get around his neck. He could worry about the shotgun afterwards. If there was an afterwards.

Ben flexed his legs into a fighting crouch, shifting his weight from foot to foot. He circled his fists like a boxer and threw an upward punch at Slayer's face. Slayer saw it coming and ducked his head back, and the punch fell short. But it was meant to. Its purpose was just to draw the guy's attention to what Ben's upper body was doing. Slayer's little pig eyes were fixed on Ben's moving fists, which was where Ben wanted them. He'd see a punch coming, but not what was following it. A certain kind of bar-room brawler always seemed to forget that the strongest limbs of the human body weren't the arms, no matter how muscle-bound they might be. Ben bounced once, twice, then launched a kick into Slayer's groin. He rotated all his energy and weight into it. The toe of his boot connected like a baseball bat with soft flesh, and Ben knew it was a good one. Slayer's big fleshy jaw dropped open and the piggy eyes widened in pain and shock. The chain jangled out of his fists and he fell to his knees. So far the fight had lasted about two seconds.

A certain kind of bar-room brawler also liked to shave his head, to prevent an opponent from grabbing a handful of it to their advantage in a fight. Which made good tactical sense to Ben. But what he'd never been able to understand was why those same guys often sported goatee beards. Maybe they thought it made them look wicked and intimidating.

To Ben, they just looked like a convenient handle, an alternative way of grabbing someone's head that defeated the whole object of the shaven head thing. As Slayer fell to his knees, and before the howl of pain had burst from his lips, Ben took hold of the goatee with his left hand. It was rigid with hairspray, like a strange black horn attached to the guy's chin, forming part of his jawbone. Ben gripped it tightly and jerked it hard towards the floor, plunging Slayer's head violently downwards straight into Ben's rising right kneecap. Another hard impact, this time not against soft flesh. Bone on bone, and Ben's knee was considerably more solid than Slayer's face. He felt the crunch as the guy's nose burst all over the place. Ben let him flop to the floor and stamped on the back of his head. A little disincentive to stop him from getting up again too soon.

Four seconds into the fight, one down, one to go.

Little Brother's red face was contorted with rage. He raised the shotgun, teeth bared. Then realised that his boss was directly behind Ben and right in the field of fire. He hesitated, began to shuffle sideways to get a clear shot at Ben, but he was slow. Much slower than Rollo, who was jumping out of his chair with surprising speed and hustling around the side of the desk towards the open door. Ben would have blocked his exit, but he had to do something about the shotgun before Little Brother realised he had a clear shot. Ben's hand whipped back behind his right hip and tore out of his belt the nickel-plated Beretta nine-millimetre he'd taken from Eriq. He brought it up faster than Little Brother could get the shotgun aimed. Flicked off the safety as he swung it, and was about to yell at Little Brother to drop the shotgun when Eriq Sabatier saw his chance and launched his wiry frame out of the chair in the corner to try and make a grab for the pistol in Ben's hand.

Ben clubbed Eriq in the face with it and sent him sprawling into Little Brother. Eriq was no heavyweight, but the force of the impact knocked the shotgun off course just as Little Brother was squeezing the trigger. It went off like a bomb detonating inside the office. Blasted a broad furrow out of the top of the desk and blew apart the leather chair Eriq had been sitting in. Ben felt the heat of the muzzle flash and the pain of the deafening noise lance his eardrums. With no shoulder stock to cushion the gun against the shooter's body mass, and most of the counterbalancing weight of the steel of the barrels cut away from the front, the sawn-off twelve-bore was virtually uncontrollable in recoil. All brute force and no finesse, like the ape holding it. Even the strongest hands couldn't stop it from bucking violently upwards with the power of the blast.

Before Little Brother could get back on target for a second shot, Ben was on him, gained control of the weapon and swept his squat, thick legs out from under him with a scything kick.

Gravity did the rest. Little Brother went down faster and harder than his elder sibling had. Ben kicked him again before he could scramble upright, a single brutal blow just behind the ear. Not hard enough to tear his head off and launch it into the far wall, but he wouldn't be back on his feet for a while either. He heaved once and went slack and inert on the floor.

Eriq was backing away, showing Ben his palms and shaking his head in supplication, as if to say 'Please, don't hurt me'.

Ben wasn't interested in Eriq. Rollo was gone. Ben trampled over the slumped mound of Little Brother to get to the door, hurried out into the passage beyond and saw one of the side doors hanging open. Through it, he could see brick

161

wall. An alleyway running along the back of the strip club. He ran to the exit. No sign of Rollo. He could move fast for a crippled guy, and there were a dozen ways he could have gone. There was no point in going after him. An uncomfortable feeling was growing on Ben that Rollo couldn't help him anyway.

'Damn,' Ben muttered.

Back inside the office, Eriq Sabatier went down on his knees, pleading for his life. Ben stepped over the unconscious bodies of Bruno and Jean-Claude, whichever was which. He raised the Beretta and pointed it at Eriq's head. If the blast of a twelve-bore wasn't raising any alarms thanks to the blare of the music next door, then the comparatively quieter snap of a nine-millimetre wasn't going to draw attention either.

'Please,' Eriq said.

Ben hesitated with his finger on the trigger. Saw the bodies of his dead friends. Saw the look on Roby's face as he died.

Then he looked at the pitiful crook kneeling in front of him. The guy was guilty of a thousand crimes. But not that one.

Vengeance is mine, saith the Lord.

And in any case, Ben wasn't going to bring down the Marseille crime scene with a single bullet. This wasn't his war.

So instead he just clubbed Eriq over the head with the pistol, and knocked him out. He slipped the gun back in his belt. Picked the gold bar off the desk and turned to the two unconscious heavies and used the bar edge-on to break all sixteen of their fingers. Just in case of repercussions, and it did the job better than a pistol butt or the heel of his boot. Rollo wasn't the most forgiving kind of person. Now, whenever he came skulking back thinking the coast was

162

clear, he'd find he had some extra personnel issues to consider. These two would be in plaster for a while.

Ben's hands were shaking a little and he was breathing hard as he replaced the gold bar in his bag. It had been a long time since he'd been in a real fight. The adrenalin was still rushing through his system. His right trouser knee was wet with blood from Slayer's mashed nose, and inside his right boot the toes were tingling from the hard kicks and would feel tender later. No other damage, but he'd risked serious hurt for nothing by coming here. He'd wasted time and he was annoyed with himself.

He stepped behind the desk to the big steel safe that Rollo had abandoned in his haste to get away. Opened the door wider. There was a lot of cash in there, bundled bricks of well-worn hundred-euro notes. Fifty to a brick. Five thousand euros. Forty bricks, in four columns of ten each. In total, something approaching the value of the gold bar. Ben lifted out half the cash and crammed it into his bag. Call it expenses money. At least his visit to Club Paradis hadn't been entirely pointless.

He left the place the way he'd come in, through the crowd and past the girls, with the heavy, bulging bag on his shoulder. Nobody paid any attention. He stepped outside into the night, took a deep breath of the sultry air and raised his face towards the churning clouds. The electricity in the atmosphere was reaching its peak, voltage mounting for the storm. He felt the first splat of warm rain on his face. As he started walking back towards the Hummer, it was followed by another, then another; then the murky sky let go and the deluge came down. It soaked his clothes and trickled through his hair. Within moments the pavements were slick and glistening, neon lights reflected under his feet as he walked. Thunder growled and boomed high above. He didn't try to hurry out of the rain. He had no idea where to go next.

That was when he felt the buzzing vibration of the phone going off inside his pocket.

Chapter Twenty-Seven

He reached for the phone, thinking at first that it was Rollo calling Eriq to find out what was happening and whether it was safe to come crawling back to Club Paradis. But it wasn't Eriq's phone that was ringing. It was the one Ben had taken from the dead man at the monastery.

Ben hit the reply button and pressed the phone to his ear, standing still in the pouring rain. This had to be the call he'd been hoping for from Luc Simon at Interpol. It was nearly midnight, but Luc worked crazy hours. He'd sacrificed his marriage for it.

The caller wasn't Luc Simon.

Instead Ben heard a woman's voice, speaking English with the typical transatlantic accent of a bilingual European, as if she'd learned most of the language from watching American movies. She sounded anxious and relieved, both at once. Talking low, like someone afraid of being over-heard. 'Dexter? It's . . . it's Michelle. Are you okay? Thank Christ. I was so scared, then when you called . . . Dexter? Talk to me.'

Ben hesitated, realising that his mystery caller must be one of the contacts he'd tried on the dead man's phone before, returning the call. His pulse quickened as his mind flashed through the possibilities. It could be someone trying to find out who'd taken the phone. Alternatively, it could be someone who didn't know the guy was dead. Or it could just be the guy's wife or girlfriend calling him. But then, what did she have to sound so nervous about?

He thought hard, knowing he had to make some kind of reply. Seconds counted. The name Dexter could be a first name or a surname. Either way, it wasn't French. It could be British, or American. He cupped his hand over his mouth. Put on a hoarse voice and an accent that was as neutral as he could make it. It was going to be tricky. One slip, and he'd lose her.

'Yeah, it's me,' he said.

There was a long pause on the line. Ben held his breath. Then the woman's voice said, 'Where are you? What happened back there? They said you got hit in the crossfire. They said it was an accident.'

Which told Ben very clearly this wasn't a call from a wife or girlfriend. She was one of them. He had one chance, one tiny fragile candle-flame of a chance, to find out more. He cupped his hand more tightly over his mouth and held the phone a little distance away. 'I'm okay, Michelle,' he muttered hoarsely.

'You sound strange.'

'I'm hurt,' he muttered. 'I got out. But I need help.'

'Where are you?'

Ben's mind raced. She seemed to believe he was this Dexter. The fish was tentatively hooked. Now, very gently, he had to try to reel it in. He tried to imagine a wounded man, running and desperate. He'd been that man himself, more than once in his time. How far could he have got from the scene in a few hours? Where might he have run for shelter? He thought about the spot from where he'd tried Michelle's number the first time. The place he'd abandoned the truck.

He spoke in monosyllabic bursts, covering it with spasms of coughing, like someone would if they'd been shot in the ribs. 'There's . . . kind of a picnic area . . . Clearing in the woods . . . Down the mountain, maybe fifteen minutes' drive, south-east. I . . . hitched a ride. Got to . . . get help. Bleeding bad.'

The story was full of holes. Ben couldn't imagine anyone giving a ride to a guy in bloody tactical clothes with a bullet in him, any more than he could imagine a badly injured man getting his bearings so right. But it was the best he could do. And the woman called Michelle seemed to buy it. 'Fifteen minutes south-east of the monastery?' she repeated anxiously. 'Is that right? Is that where you are?'

'Yeah,' he coughed hoarsely. 'I'm really hurt.'

'I'll come for you. I'll help. Hold tight, okay? Give me . . . oh, Jesus. It's a long way. Two hours. No, better make that three. Quick as I can, I'll be there. I'll find you. You hear me?'

'Hurry,' Ben croaked. 'I don't know if I can . . . urgghhh . . .'

A young couple scurried past in the rain. The girl gave him a very strange look.

'Hold on,' Michelle said on the phone. 'Hang in there. Three hours. On my way.' She ended the call.

Ben put the phone away and started walking faster towards where he'd left the Hummer. The call had left him totally baffled. Two things he knew for sure: firstly, he'd been following a complete blind alley with the Russians. People with names like Michelle and Dexter were about as Russian as he was. Forget the cigarette. Forget Rollo. So far he couldn't have been more wrong. He shouldn't even be in Marseille. Secondly, he had three hours to get back to the clearing. Less, if he wanted to get there ahead of her in time to lie in wait. It had taken him three hours from Briançon, and the clearing was a good way further. But he could make it. He'd just have to speed like a madman.

She wouldn't come alone, he knew that. The set-up screamed *trap*. What she'd said about this Dexter being hurt in the crossfire struck Ben as obvious bullshit. She was trying to trick the man into trusting her. She wasn't going to help him. She and the others were going to finish the job they'd started, and kill him. Which was fine by Ben. If he could have resurrected the real Dexter for the occasion, he'd have happily watched while they did it. And then the rest of them would be his.

The sudden twist in events was bewildering. But it was infinitely more than Ben had had just a few moments earlier. His fast walk elongated into a slow run, and then he was sprinting down the slick, shiny pavements with the driving rain stinging his face, until he reached the Hummer and unlocked it and threw his bag inside and himself behind the wheel. Fired up the engine with a roar and squealed the tyres on the wet road as he floored the pedal. He twisted the wheel and slewed the massive vehicle around in the road to point the way he'd come. Less than three hours to retrace his steps all the way back to the first stop he'd made after leaving the monastery.

Full circle. But now he had something to show for it.

Ben sped out of Marseille as fast as he dared. Hitting the open road, he was glad of the Hummer's battery of lights. He let them blaze mercilessly in the face of oncoming traffic. People flashed and honked at him. He was in too big a rush to care. The wipers worked double-time to slap the rain off the screen as his instrument panel glowed like a fighter pilot's cockpit. His speed crept up to a hundred and fifty kilometres an hour, a hundred and sixty, a hundred and seventy on the long empty straights.

Fatigue was creeping up on him, too. It had been a hell of a long day, and he faced a long night. Music was the best way to stay awake on a fast night drive. Omar's on-board CD collection was mostly Motown stuff: a lot of Marvin Gaye and Stevie Wonder, some Jackson Five. Ben hunted through radio stations until he found a late-night concert from the summer jazz festival in Juan-les-Pins. It was jazz the way he liked it: wild and frenetic. He cranked up the volume until the Hummer's cab was vibrating to the sound of wailing tenor saxes and crashing drums while he kept piling relentlessly through the night with his eyes glued to the road speeding by and his mind set on reaching his destination in time. He'd make it.

And he did. The Hummer's clock was coming up on 2.45 a.m. as he descended the twisting route beyond Briançon and found the little track leading off-road through the trees. The rain had stopped and the night had cleared, the Milky Way shimmering above the mountains. He killed the lights and engine and let the vehicle coast down the track, peering into the starlit darkness. The clearing was empty, apart from the burned-out wreck of the Belphégor, still sitting there undiscovered since Ben had left it the previous morning. There was no sign of the woman called Michelle.

Ben let the Hummer trundle on through the clearing and deeper into the trees, until he was confident that it couldn't be spotted. He climbed out and crept back towards the edge of the clearing. A clump of ferns made a hiding place where he could watch and wait, unseen, for whoever might come down the track. He settled down on the damp, rich-smelling forest floor and made himself as comfortable as he could with his back resting against a tree and the FAMAS rifle across his lap. The glowing hands of his watch read 2.51. He closed his eyes and let himself slip into a half-doze while his senses remained on standby. One hand on the pistol grip of the rifle. Finger lightly resting near the trigger.

Three o'clock came, and nobody turned up.

Three-thirty. Still nobody. Nothing but the busy silence of the forest around him. The call of an owl from somewhere in the dark trees. The tiny scuttle of insects among the greenery. The sound of things growing.

Twenty-five to four in the morning. Ben opened his eyes and wondered if anyone was coming at all.

Five minutes later he saw the first flash of vehicle lights glimmering through the trees. Heard the purr of a powerful engine and the creak of suspension, the rumble of big tyres rolling down the rutted track. Slowly, silently, he lowered himself deeper behind the ferns and watched.

The vehicle's lights swept above his head, across the burned-out shell of the Belphégor, the little toilet block and the empty picnic table. From its silhouette it was some kind of large, dark-coloured SUV. It stopped. The engine and lights died. The handbrake ratcheted on. Doors opened. Torch beams flicked this way and that around the clearing.

Ben had been dead right. The woman hadn't come alone.

Chapter Twenty-Eight

The two figures separated in opposite directions from the SUV. The taller, wider silhouetted figure moving towards Ben's right; the smaller, slighter one to the left. A man and a woman. Ben couldn't yet see if they were armed, but they were certain to be. It was obvious they were expecting company. Their torch beams cast trembling spotlights that searched slowly around the edges of the roughly circular clearing. If Ben's hidden position was at the six o'clock mark, the woman was at ten o'clock and her male companion at two o'clock.

Ben remained perfectly immobile, barely breathing, his pulse slow and steady. Stiller than the stillest part of the landscape, yet completely aware of his environment. It was a skill he'd mastered many years ago. In his SAS days he'd come within three feet of the enemy on several similar occasions, without them having the first idea of his presence so close by. Sometimes he'd stayed hidden until the threat moved on. Sometimes it had been he who was the threat, striking out of nowhere with all the speed, aggression and use of surprise that his training had instilled in him.

Tonight was going to be one of those kinds of nights.

The woman's torch beam swept slowly away from the edge of the clearing and dwelled for a few moments on the burned-out remains of the Belphégor, as if wondering about any possible connection between its being here and her mission. She'd stopped moving. Her male companion was working his way clockwise, probing into the darkness as if studying every leaf and twig. He stepped a little closer to Ben. Five o'clock. Then a little closer still. He was just a yard away through the curtain of ferns. Ben could hear his breathing. He could smell him. He could make out the recognisable boxy profile of the black pistol in his right hand.

The torch in the man's left hand swept over Ben's head. The wobbling pool of light hovered a metre above where he was crouched.

And Ben moved. Like a section of the darkness detaching itself from the rest, nothing more than a flitting shadow. Faster than it was possible for a human being to react, the man was gripped and helpless in an inescapable chokehold. The torch dropped out of his left hand and hit the ground with a thud, rolled and lay there, its strong beam projecting tiny stones as giant rocks against the edge of the clearing. Ben twisted the pistol clear of the man's right fist and let it fall. Spun him around, holding him in front of himself like a gasping, choking human shield. The stubby muzzle of the FAMAS hard up against the base of his skull. Said in a calm, clear voice that cut through the night, 'Drop your weapon.'

The woman froze for an instant, her torch beam pointed immobile at an empty patch of ground. Ben saw something small and dark fall from her hand and hit the dirt with a thump.

Ben said, 'Shine the light on yourself. Do it now. Both hands in plain view. Make no mistake, I'll shoot you.'

The woman hesitantly turned the beam on herself and stood there dazzled and blinking, spotlit like an actress on a dark stage who'd suddenly forgotten her lines. The man in Ben's grip was gasping for air. Ben let the pressure off his throat, shoved him a few staggering steps towards the middle of the clearing, then swung the rifle up and jabbed him hard in the back of the head with its butt. Steel and plastic connected against bone with a meaty sound. The man let out a grunt and collapsed on to his face, a few yards from the ruined truck.

Ben picked the man's pistol from the ground and instantly knew from the feel and weight of it that it was a Glock 19: mid-size nine-millimetre semi-automatic, fully loaded. Expensive, professional hardware. Only the very best lowlifes could afford them. He stuck it in his belt and moved towards the woman, training the rifle on her. She was still standing there, lit up like an apparition near the far side of the clearing, blinking and screwing up her face while trying to peer past the bright beam at whatever was happening. He hadn't been bluffing her. If she tried to bolt, he'd gun her down without thinking twice. He wasn't given to shooting women. But there were exceptions to every rule.

He studied her as he stepped closer. She looked young, fresh-faced, no more than about twenty-five, twenty-six. Not tall, but athletic in build, muscular without being bulky, light on her feet. Chestnut hair, pulled back in a ponytail under a plain black cap. She was wearing faded jeans and a well-worn Highway Patrol-style black leather jacket.

Ben snatched the torch from her as he got close. A solid aluminium tube, heavy with the weight of four large-cell batteries. As good a club as it was a flashlight. He kept the beam in her face and the FAMAS aimed a little way below, at her centre of mass. At this range it would blow a fist-sized hole right through her, and she seemed to know that. He stepped around her right side and shunted her forward with the barrel of the rifle.

'Over towards your friend,' he said. She began to walk stiffly towards the middle of the clearing. Her companion was beginning to stir, clutching his sore head and groaning in misery. Ben paused a step behind the woman to scoop up her discarded weapon. More of the same serious hardware. A Glock 26, same calibre as the other, a streamlined sub-compact model suited to a smaller hand. Ideal for concealed carry. It fitted comfortably in Ben's hip pocket.

'That's close enough,' he said when the woman was within two yards of her injured companion. 'Turn round and keep your hands where I can see them.'

The woman stopped walking and slowly turned to face him, with her arms held stiffly out at her sides, fingers splayed and palms to the front as if to say 'What did I do wrong?' She blinked in the torchlight and obviously wanted to shield her eyes, but had the good sense not to make any sudden moves. Her face was tight with tension. She flicked a rapid glance down at her companion, who was struggling to get up to his knees.

'Time for some introductions,' Ben said. 'You're Michelle, is that correct?'

She nodded, grimacing in the light.

'You have a second name?'

She hesitated. 'Faban. Michelle Faban.' She had the same transatlantic way of speaking English that he'd heard on the phone, but she looked as French as her name suggested.

'And him?' Ben asked, flicking the torch beam sideways at the man. He was on his knees, head hanging, breathing hard. He was blond, angular in his features. Scandinavian, Ben thought. Or Dutch, or German.

'His name's Breslin,' she said. 'Kurt Breslin.'

'Michelle, you're going to shine the light on Kurt while I frisk him. Think you can manage that without doing anything silly?'

She nodded.

'I hope so,' Ben said. 'Because if you even think about trying to take a swipe at me, I'll know before you've made a move. And you'll be dead.'

She nodded again, and he handed her the heavy torch. He said, 'On your feet, Kurt. I didn't hit you that hard.'

Breslin slowly, warily, pulled himself upright and stood there unsteadily in the brightness of the torch beam. The woman trained the light on them while Ben quickly went through her companion's pockets. The man's features were tight and angry in the white beam. Ben found nothing of interest, except a switchblade knife and a roll of duct tape. A few euros in any hardware store, one of the handiest accessories in a kidnapper's toolkit. He confiscated both the tape and the blade. 'Now it's your turn, Kurt. Same goes for you. It's not a good time for clever ideas.'

The woman handed over the torch. Breslin gritted his teeth in rage and held it steady while Ben patted her down. Up close, he could smell her subtle perfume. He did the job quickly, then snatched the torch from Breslin and backed away a step so he could shine the light on the two of them together. He kept the rifle in a one-handed grip at waist height, the muzzle wavering between them.

'Now let's talk,' he said.

'Where's Dexter?' the woman asked.

Ben stuck the torch under his gun arm so it stayed pointed at them while he slipped out his phone. He turned it on and scrolled one-handed to the mugshot picture file he'd taken of the dead man shortly before burning the truck. He flashed the picture at the woman. 'Look familiar?' he asked.

Michelle Faban flinched and her eyes clouded briefly. 'You killed him,' she said, tight-lipped, staring into the light.

'No, he was dead when I found him,' Ben said, putting the phone away. 'He had a couple of nine-millimetre bullets inside him. Something tells me he had it coming. But my friends didn't. Someone's going to pay for what happened to them, and right now you're top of my debtors' list.'

She frowned, narrowing her eyes, trying to peer at him more closely. 'You were there, at the monastery?'

'I should have been,' Ben said. 'I live there. Or I did, until you people came along.'

'You're no monk,' she said.

'Is it that obvious?'

'Who are you?'

'Every plan has a flaw,' Ben said. 'That's who I am. The guy you didn't account for. The small oversight that's come back to bite you on the arse. You're going to wish I *were* a monk.'

'You're getting this wrong,' she said. 'You need to let me explain.'

'That's exactly what you're going to do,' Ben said. 'You and Kurt here. It's just us. We're all alone out here. Shout for help, nobody's going to hear you. Nobody's going to come and rescue you. A bit like the situation at the monastery, except now you're on the receiving end. That doesn't feel so good, does it?'

'Let me explain,' Michelle Faban said again.

'I think Kurt should open the discussion,' Ben said. 'He hasn't said a word yet.'

Breslin didn't speak, just stood there breathing hard, every muscle tensed. Ben could see the tendons in his neck standing out like cables.

'You're a real tough guy, aren't you, Kurt?' Ben said. 'Or

trying to look like one, at any rate. So tell me, tough guy. How many of my friends did you kill?'

Breslin still said nothing. But the answer was there in his eyes. As if at the mention of them, he couldn't help but replay the events of the previous morning in his mind. Relishing them. Savouring them.

So Ben shot him.

The crashing boom of the rifle shattered the stillness of the dark. Night birds exploded in alarm from the treetops. Breslin caught the bullet precisely where Ben had been aiming, at the middle of his chest. The high-velocity round burst his heart and lungs apart. The force of the impact slammed him down on his back as hard as being hit by a freight train. He was dead while he was still in mid-air.

Ben turned the gun to point at the woman. She was frozen in shock, eyes wide open. Flecks of Breslin's blood were spattered on the side of her neck and face that had been closest to him.

'I'm not going to waste a lot of time here,' Ben said quietly. 'You're either going to give me some answers, or I'm going to put you down next to your friend and leave you both here for the rats.'

Michelle Faban looked down at the dead body. She seemed to have recovered quickly from the shock. The sight appeared not to bother her unduly, nor the blood on her. Ben even thought he saw a flicker of satisfaction pass over her face.

'It's all down to you now, Michelle,' he said. 'Better talk to me.'

'Did you have something to do with that?' she asked, nodding in the direction of the burned-out truck.

'You're a quick study,' Ben said. 'Smarter than your friend. The brains of the operation.'

'He wasn't any friend of mine,' she said. 'He was a

degenerate piece of trash. I'm glad you shot him. I've wanted to do it myself, many times.'

Ben stared at her over the top of the rifle. 'Is this how you think you're going to talk your way out, by appealing to my sense of empathy?'

Michelle Faban gave a shrug. 'I suppose not,' she said. 'I suppose you might as well shoot me too. Because now I'm not so sure if you're going to believe what I'm about to tell you. Just know that if you do shoot me, you'll open up a world of trouble for yourself that you can't imagine.'

'I don't know, I can imagine quite a bit,' Ben said. 'But as for believing you, you have nothing to lose by trying me.'

She shrugged again. 'Okay. I wish I could show you some official ID. Under the circumstances, you'll understand that's not a practical option for me right now. I'm not really Michelle Faban. That's an undercover identity. My real name is agent Silvie Valois of the DGSI.'

Chapter Twenty-Nine

DGSI was the acronym for Direction Générale de la Sécurité Intérieure. The French government agency responsible for counter-intelligence, counterterrorism and surveillance of threats against French territory and national security. As spook agencies went, it wasn't one of the best known. Back in the day, Ben and his team at the Le Val tactical training centre had run a few of them through their paces in advanced pistol-craft and hostage rescue skills, and not found them to be too badly lacking. They were a tough, well-drilled and intensively selected bunch. If Silvie Valois was telling the truth, it explained to Ben why she hadn't freaked out on being spattered with the blood of the man who'd accompanied her. But he still had more questions than answers.

'I knew it,' she said. 'You don't believe me.'

'Some verification would be nice,' Ben said.

'Like I told you, I haven't exactly been in a position to carry my agency ID card around. For the last four months I've been Michelle Faban, posing undercover inside Streicher's organisation as part of an agency investigation.'

'Who's Streicher?'

'Udo Streicher. Their leader.'

'Leader of what? A criminal gang?'

'You could call them that. They call themselves the Parati. It's Latin.'

'I know what it is,' Ben said. 'It means *the prepared ones*. Prepared for what?'

She shrugged. 'Well, that's a very good question, isn't it?'

Ben's mind was spinning as he stared at the woman telling him this wild story. The mystery was deepening faster than he could make sense of it. 'All right,' he said. 'What colour's your agency HQ building in Neuilly-sur-Seine?'

'None,' Silvie replied, straight off the cuff. 'It's in Levallois-Perret.'

'How many departments is the agency divided into?'

'Eight.' She rattled them off. 'Economic, Terrorism, Intelligence Technology, Violent Subversion, General Admin, Support, Counter-espionage and Internal Affairs.'

'There's a senior agent there. Big guy, six-three, scar on his cheek, bushy moustache. What's his name?'

'Jean-Loup l'Hermite,' she replied without hesitation. 'He took early retirement a couple of years ago.'

'Tattoo on his arm. Left or right?'

'Left arm, high up.'

'What was it of?'

'It was a mermaid,' she replied.

'What was his wife's name?'

'Didn't have one. She'd already been dead for five years when I met him. He's never looked at another woman since.'

Ben stared at her, long and hard and penetratingly. She might be telling the truth. Then again, she might just be a genius at preparation. It was still too early to say for sure, but he let the rifle muzzle droop towards the ground and clicked on the safety.

'You haven't told me who you are yet,' she said. 'Someone who seems to know a lot about my agency, that's for sure.

And someone who can get hold of a military-issue rifle. You know as well as I do that thing's off-limits to civilians.'

'I told you, I'm not a monk,' he replied. 'And I'm asking the questions here. Who was Dexter?'

'Dexter Nicholls,' she said. 'You mean, apart from being the dead man you impersonated tonight to get me here?'

'You seemed especially anxious about him. Why?'

'Dexter was one of ours, too,' she replied after a beat.

'He wasn't French.'

'English,' she said. 'Like you. Am I right?'

'Just keep talking.'

'I never knew his real name, only that he was with British Intelligence. It's a joint investigation.'

'Bullshit. He was one of the hit team.'

'He didn't harm anyone,' Silvie protested. 'You can be one hundred per cent certain of that. He had no choice but to be there. And now Dexter's body is among the dead, for the cops to find. If they haven't already. That could cause a lot of trouble for the agency, if they identify who he was.'

'I wouldn't worry about that,' Ben said. 'Because Dexter was properly cremated. There'll be no trace left of him on the mountain, or anywhere else.'

'Cremated? What the hell are you talking about? Where?'

'Right there,' Ben said, pointing at the dark shell of the Belphégor. 'The tool locker. I had to fold him up a little to get him in.'

She turned to stare at the truck, then back to gaze in horror at Ben. 'Jesus Christ. Who *are* you?'

'Someone who doesn't have a lot of sympathy for anyone who was present at the scene of the crime with a gun in their hand.' He looked her up and down. 'What's your height?'

'One seventy-one,' she said, taken aback by the question.

He shone the torch down at her feet. She was wearing high-leg combat boots. They were small. 'Shoe size?'

She frowned. 'Thirty-seven. Why the hell do you need to know that?'

'I found footprints at the scene. Combat boots, just like the ones you're wearing. One set of prints was smaller than the others. As if they belonged to a teenager. Or a woman with small feet.' He stared at her questioningly.

'Those weren't my prints you saw. They must have been Hannah's.'

'Who the hell's Hannah?'

'Hannah Gissel. Streicher's girlfriend. She was part of the team. She hardly leaves his side, and she's as dangerous as he is.'

Ben looked into her eyes. There was a truthfulness in them that would have been hard to fake. Hard, if not impossible.

'You have a lot more explaining to do,' he said. 'But not here.'

He walked her at gunpoint through the trees, shining the torch ahead towards the concealed Hummer. Twigs crackled underfoot. The night birds had returned to their roosts after the gunshot and were calling nervously in the darkness. Ben marched the woman up to the passenger door and held the gun on her while he yanked it open.

'Get inside,' he said.

She put one boot on the high sill of the door, found a purchase and hauled herself inside. Ben leaned the rifle against the Hummer's dull metal flank and took out the switchblade and the roll of tape. The blade flicked out with a click and glimmered in the moonlight. Ben pulled a length of tape off the roll and sliced it off. He used it to bind her right wrist to the tubular frame of the seat, another length to tie her ankles together and a third to connect them to her bound wrist. Then he slammed her door, walked around to the driver's side, stashed the rifle behind his seat and climbed in and used a fourth length of tape to attach her left wrist.

When he was satisfied she wasn't going anywhere, he climbed back out of the Hummer, locked it and walked over to Breslin's body. He grasped the dead man by both limp wrists and dragged him into the bushes. Then he strode fast across the clearing to the SUV his two visitors had arrived in and left blocking the mouth of the track.

It was a Nissan hardtop pickup truck, black and filmed with road dirt, the legend OUTLAW splashed in big letters down its flanks as if to proclaim the bad-boy virility of its driver. The keys were in it. Ben climbed up behind the wheel. The car smelled new. Nothing of interest in the glove compartment. He fired up the engine and lights, engaged gear and drove the big car across the clearing. He parked over Breslin's body, straddling it with a chunky off-road tyre either side. Not perfect, but better than nothing. Ben didn't have time for burials.

He returned to the Hummer and clambered in next to his prisoner. The engine growled into life and the lights glared back at them against the close cover of the trees. He let it idle for a moment as he took the woman's compact Glock from his trouser pocket and laid it in his lap.

'A gorilla couldn't break free from this tape,' she said, eyeing the gun. 'You don't take a lot of chances, do you, mister whoever-you-are?'

'That's why I'm still here,' he replied. 'And the name's Ben.'

He put the Hummer in gear and they lurched away over the uneven ground, crushing a semicircular path through the bushes until the lights washed over the space

183

of the clearing. He drove past the Belphégor for the last time. Down the rutted track, he reached the junction with the lonely, winding dark road, and hesitated. Right would take him back in the direction of the monastery, left in the direction of the old rural filling station. He swung out left and gunned the throttle, the Hummer's headlamps carving a channel down the empty night road like the beam of a lighthouse.

Chapter Thirty

'Where are we going?' the woman asked.

'Nowhere yet,' Ben said. 'You still have some explaining to do, Silvie. Or is it Michelle? You still have time to change your mind.'

'It's Silvie.'

'What about your pal Breslin? Was that his real name?'

She nodded. 'It's the one on his police file. Pretty unpleasant record, I might add.'

'So you're still sticking with the government agent story.'

'Of course I am. It's the truth.'

'All right,' Ben said. 'Then tell me about Breslin's record. Any military past? Explosives experience?'

'Just your run-of-the-mill criminal stuff,' she said. 'Breslin was one of the bad ones. The guy was known to be hanging around the fringes of the reformed Red Brigade when it carried out a number of murders of prominent liberals and anti-fascists in the late nineties. He was a crony of convicted European terrorists like Roberto Morandi and Marco Mezzasalma, before he fell in with Streicher. More recently he was suspected of keeping himself financially stable by dabbling in the odd ransom job. Often hauled in for questioning, never convicted. Streicher turns a blind eye to his gang's extra-curricular activities. The rest of the time, he keeps them busy.'

'Busy with what?'

'His grand plan.'

'Theft and murder's not much of a grand plan,' Ben said.

'It goes beyond that. Above my pay grade.'

'Are you saying you don't even know?'

'I know as much as they wanted me to know. Which isn't a lot.'

'Sounds like a shitty assignment,' Ben said.

She let out a sarcastic laugh. 'Really? A hundred and twenty-four days without any backup or contact with the outside sounds shitty? It was like living in a pressure cooker. Day to day, never knowing when they might bundle me in a car, take me out into the middle of nowhere, force me to dig my own grave and then put a bullet in my head. It wasn't until two months in that Dexter identified himself to me as an agent.'

'That was taking a risk.'

'He knew who I was,' she said. 'Even my real name. Somebody screwed up with that one. But Dexter must have figured that an ally on the inside was worth taking the risk for. I didn't believe him at first. I almost cut and run, thinking that they were on to me and it was a trick to flush me out. Took a week before I started to trust him. From then on, we tried to communicate when we could. We had to be so damn careful.'

'Obviously not careful enough, in Dexter's case.'

Her lips tightened. 'I have no idea how Streicher made him. Maybe it was during the attack. Maybe Dexter openly refused to harm anyone. Or maybe Streicher got suspicious before, and put Dexter on the team so he could kill him.'

Ben asked, 'So how did the agency get you in there? Download an application form from Streicher's website?'

'He surrounds himself with all kinds of fanatics and

crazies. Michelle Faban had to fit a certain profile. In her case, it was eco-terrorism and extreme animal rights stuff. The car bombing of a pro-vivisectionist. Arson attacks on fast-food restaurants and fur farms, breaking into animal research labs, harassment, intimidation, that kind of thing. DGSI inserted me into the group by setting up a chance meeting with a guy called Willi Dorn, a Green anarchist and sometime bank robber who'd been seen meeting up with Streicher. The insertion took time. Finally, Streicher met me in person.

'He was very suave and charming, not what I'd expected. He asked me a lot of questions about my experience, my philosophy of life, how I viewed the world, how I'd like to change it. Then asked me if I'd like to get involved in an organisation with a very special future and some really big ideas. When I asked what they were, he just smiled. Then I was introduced to some of the others, and before I knew it I was one of them. DGSI didn't even know where I was.'

'They let you go completely off the radar?'

'I wasn't very happy about that. I wanted a GPS chip hidden somewhere in my personal effects, but they wouldn't take the chance. Phone tracking was out of the question, too. Streicher doesn't let anyone carry their own phones, in case they could be tainted. He issues everyone with new ones, the numbers all pre-allocated and entered. He's fanatical about security. You saw how hard it was for me to get away alone tonight. It's virtually impossible to move without one of them breathing down your neck.'

Ben took out the phone he'd taken from Dexter's body and held it out for her to see. 'Dexter's phone,' he said. 'I called every number. You were the only one who returned the call.'

'The other numbers are the rest of the gang.'

'Then a law-enforcement agency could easily trace them.'

'To what? They're just ghost numbers. No contracts, no registration, no names, all cash. Streicher can change everyone's number whenever he wants, and he does, often.'

Ben laid the phone in a nook in the centre console between them. He jerked his thumb over his shoulder. 'Your pal's not going to stay hidden back there for ever. Someone's dog will sniff him out sooner or later. When he's found and you're still AWOL, it's not going to do your cover any good. Streicher's going to get suspicious of you, too.'

She shrugged, her movement restricted by the tape around her wrists. 'Too late to worry about it now. I'm out of there. And don't call him my pal.'

'Let me think about that. You were supposed to come alone. Instead you bring Prince Charming along for the ride, both of you all tooled up and ready to shoot me, stab me, tape me up and kidnap me, or whatever you were planning on. It doesn't help your credibility much.'

She sighed. 'Try to look at it from my point of view, okay? You really had me fooled with your call. Maybe because I wanted to believe Dexter was still alive. I suppose I was flustered and on edge, caught off my guard, less careful than I might have been about slipping away unnoticed. I was just about to take off out of there when he stopped me, asked me where I was going in such a hurry, so late at night. What could I do? I couldn't afford for them to get suspicious. So I went along with it. Told Breslin about the call. He figured it was a trap. Hence the hardware. I was scared he might run off and report it to Streicher, but I think he wanted to curry favour by handling it himself. Insisted on driving. The arsehole wagon was his, by the way.'

'Makes it sound as if you lived together,' he said. 'A cosy little nest.'

Silvie shook her head, watching the road. 'Hardly cosy. Streicher keeps his people together like some weird kind of commune.'

'He lives with them?'

'He comes and goes. Turns up now and then, hangs around for a few hours, has these little meetings and discussions, then disappears again. Nobody knows where.'

'So where did you come from tonight that took three hours to drive here?'

'Switzerland. It's a townhouse in Lausanne. One of Streicher's safe houses. I don't know whether he owns it or rents it. All I know is, he's got no shortage of places to move around. He can afford them. It's part of his strategy. The guy's insanely suspicious, even about his closest associates. The inner circle are his A team. Himself, Hannah, and a very small and select number of others. Then there's the B team, the ones he keeps a little closer, but not too close. Then there's the C team, the outer circle. That's as close as I got in four months to the heart of the gang. Dexter did a little better. He managed to get closer, into the middle circle. That's why Streicher had him on the assault team, along with B-circle guys like Breslin. I was just part of the logistics.'

'Meaning what?'

'We came in a convoy,' she explained. 'Twelve people in three vehicles, from the base in Lausanne to a meeting point just the other side of the Franco-Swiss border. Streicher provided the vehicles. Identical Range Rovers, black, top of the line, seven-seaters. I was driving one of them. Another of his people, Dominik Baiza, was there waiting for us with an articulated Volvo rig. Where he'd come from in it, I have no idea. It was transporting the attack vehicle. A BearCat. The kind of armoured truck used for SWAT raids on heavily armed drug gangs. It's fitted with a special ram that can breach any kind of barricade.'

'I know what it is,' Ben said grimly.

'Streicher and Hannah arrived by chopper soon afterwards. I don't know where they came from either.'

'Fifteen people in all,' Ben said. The list was already taking shape inside his head.

'Two of his guys, Chavanne and Cazzitti, took the rotors off the chopper, so it would fit inside the trailer. Baiza stayed behind to mind the lorry while the BearCat joined the rest of the convoy with Streicher at the wheel, and the other fourteen of us headed over the border into France. All lonely, empty mountain roads. No cops. At that point neither Dexter nor I had any idea where we were going, or what was happening. Only that it was a huge deal, some plan that Streicher had been working on for months. We stopped at a second point, off the road, way up in the mountains. We made camp for a few hours there while final preparations were made. There was a lot of activity happening inside the BearCat. Dexter and the rest went inside and didn't come back out. I suppose they were getting tooled up, checking weapons, having their final pre-operational briefing.'

'The attack happened around four-thirty in the morning,' Ben said. 'Is that right?'

'How did you know?'

'Forensic pointers,' he said. 'Plus common sense. It's what any half-decent tactician would have done. They could have hit the place by day, but at this time of year some of the monks might be out working in the fields or tending to the animals. No guarantee they'd get them all, and too big

190

a risk that one or two might be able to slip away and raise the alarm. The time to get them all together in one place, without having to go cell-to-cell rounding them up or sweeping every part of the monastery, was before dawn as they were getting together for morning Mass.'

Silvie went on. 'Nobody was saying much. It was very tense. Finally, sometime before four, the assault crew went off in the BearCat.'

'Names,' Ben said.

'There were eight of them. Streicher and Hannah Gissel, of course. Torben Roth and Wolf Schilling, two of his A-team crew who've been with him for ever. Then Breslin, whom you've ... ah ... met. Cazzitti and Chavanne. Lastly, Dexter.'

Ben ticked off the names on his mental list. 'Leaving six of you behind.'

She nodded. 'Me, a guy called Stefan Ringler who was always hitting on me, then Holger Grubitz. Another creep. Then the nerdy one, Anton Lindquist, kind of a bookish type, thick glasses. I don't quite know what his involvement is, but he's definitely no tough guy. Then there's the Pole, Tomasz Wokalek. A real shit-kicker, that one. Finally, the Dutchman, Rutger Zwart. None of us with much to do but twiddle our thumbs waiting for the others to return.'

'Which was about four hours later,' Ben said. 'Correct?'

She looked surprised that he could know that. 'More forensic pointers?'

'Three indicators that they hung around the monastery for quite some time,' he said. 'Firstly, the bodies of the monks were cold when I found them, but Dexter's was still reasonably fresh. Suggesting a lengthy interval between the killings. Secondly, the timing of the explosive charges. The initial one was intended to open up a space underneath the monastery. The next was designed to close it again, which it very nearly did with me still inside. It had been set just an hour before I got there. And thirdly, they had a heavy cargo to shift, and a long way to shift it.'

She glanced sideways at him, as far as she could turn against her restraints. He saw the gleam of her eyes in the darkness. 'What heavy cargo?' she asked.

'That's what this is about,' Ben said. 'You know it as well as I do. The gold that was under the monastery. Bullion. A ton of it. What other reason could there be?'

'I don't know anything about any gold,' she said.

Chapter Thirty-One

The Hummer barrelled on into the night, its low rumble and the thrum of its heavy-duty tyres filling the cab. Now it was Ben's turn to take his eyes off the road and glance sideways in puzzlement. 'What are you saying?'

'That this mention of gold bullion is absolutely the first I've heard of it,' Silvie replied.

'Then why else did you think they hit the place, if not to steal something of value?'

'I don't know.'

'How can you not know? You were part of the gang.'

'A peripheral part.'

'Whose job it was to infiltrate them, apparently. And gain information.'

'Which I tried very hard to do. So you believe me now?'

He shook his head impatiently. 'You must have heard something. Or seen something.'

'All I saw were those white containers,' she said.

'Containers?'

'When they returned from the raid, the BearCat's doors didn't open for maybe twenty minutes. Finally, Streicher came out. He looked jumpy. Buzzed. More excited than I've ever seen him. He'd changed out of his tactical clothing, but he smelled of cordite, like someone who'd just come off a shooting range. I saw inside the BearCat's open doors for a moment. That's where I saw them. Oblong, with rounded-off sides and corners, and locks and handles on. Like a cross between a briefcase and a military ammo can, except a little larger, made out of some kind of shiny white plastic or fibreglass. Plain, unmarked. Maybe six or eight of them, all lined up and securely fastened in an interior load bay. I have no idea what was in them. Maybe it *was* gold. Nobody said anything about it. All I could gather was that Dexter had been left behind for some reason. I was too afraid to ask questions.'

Ben listened and drove.

'My role post-operation was to dispose of the kit,' she went on. 'All their clothing was sealed up inside these big plastic bags. Or I assume it was their clothing. It felt bulky and soft, like bedding. Sort of crinkly when you jiggled it around. Also boots, judging by the weight. I was told on no account to open the bags, just to burn them. So that's what I did. There was a hollow in the rocks a little way off. I and a couple of others carried the bags over to it, piled them up, doused them with petrol and torched them.'

Thorough, Ben thought. But he was less interested in the contents of the bags than in other kinds of contents. 'And you're certain there was no mention of what was in the containers? Not even a hint?'

'None. Obviously, I never got the chance to talk to Dexter. Breslin might have known something, but it's too late for that now, isn't it? He was much closer to Streicher. Deeply loyal to him. They all are. He seems to have an effect on them. Like he's a god or something. Like they have an oath of fealty to him, as if he were their liege and they his vassals. It's weird.'

'What happened next?'

'The convoy split up. Nine of us got into two of the Range Rovers and headed back to Lausanne. I was still on driving duty. When I realised Dexter wasn't with us any longer, I started to get very worried, but I couldn't say anything. Torben Roth was right next to me, so I had to look cool. Cazzitti and Chavanne took the third Range Rover and went off in tandem with Streicher and Hannah Gissel in the BearCat. I assume they returned to the rendezvous point where the lorry and trailer were still waiting, then Cazzitti and Chavanne put the rotors back on the chopper, then the BearCat took its place inside the trailer, then the artic went one way and the Range Rover set off for Lausanne, while Streicher and Hannah flew back to wherever they came from.'

'Carrying the white containers.'

'That's my best guess,' she said.

'Cazzitti and Chavanne. Ex-air force?'

'Cazzitti did a four-year stint in the Italian Parachute Infantry Brigade. Might have picked up a few aero-mechanic skills there. Nothing on record about Chavanne.'

'Tell me about this Torben Roth.'

'Plenty on him. He was a PMC before he hooked up with Streicher.'

Ben nodded. Private military contractor. A mercenary. Torben Roth was suddenly his number one choice to be the explosives expert on the team. 'Is he good?'

'He's got the look of a killer, that's all I can tell you. Doesn't say much. Face was messed up by a bullet.'

Ben asked, 'Does he smoke?'

'Not that I've ever seen. Why are you asking?'

'What about Streicher?'

'He won't even let people do it in the safe house.'

'Then you never saw him light up a Russian cigarette. A black Sobranie.'

She shook her head emphatically. 'Never.'

'Okay. Just wondered.'

Ben drove on a while in silence, frowning as he pieced everything together in his mind. The pieces seemed to fit, but the picture they formed didn't make sense to him.

'I still don't get it,' he said. 'Why are DGSI so worked up about this Streicher? A joint operation like this is the kind of stuff they keep in reserve for the big fish. Major terror suspects. International crime rings. They wouldn't even bother with the drug syndicates in Marseille. They leave that to the regular police to deal with. So who is he?'

'He *is* a big fish,' Silvie said.

'Then fill me in.'

'You'll be disappointed with how much I actually know.'

'Let me be the judge of that.'

She hesitated. 'Before I say anything else, I should know a little more about who I'm talking to.'

'I told you who I am,' Ben said. 'A concerned individual, nothing more. I was just a guest at the monastery.'

'No ordinary guest, that's for sure. Since when did monks let someone like you come and live with them?'

'Someone like me?' he echoed, bristling a little.

'I mean, you're not exactly gentle Jesus meek and mild, are you?'

'I have a past,' he said. 'I was hoping to put it behind me. The monks showed me hospitality. They were good people.'

'How did you know about Jean-Loup l'Hermite?'

Ben didn't like being pressured for answers. Silvie Valois might have been the one tethered and captive, but it didn't seem to make her any less assertive. 'I met him once,' he said.

'Can't have been just a casual acquaintance. You know too much about him.'

'We did some training together,' Ben admitted after a restless silence. 'A few years back.'

'What kind of training?'

'The kind you might have benefited from tonight,' he said.

She gave a dark kind of laugh. 'Thanks for that. So this past of yours – would it be in law enforcement?' She thought about it for a moment, then shook her head. 'No, you were never a cop. I get the impression you don't like them much.'

'Most cops I know feel that way too.'

'You're not the type. You were a soldier.'

'Don't let the car fool you. It's borrowed from a friend.'

'I'm not talking about the car. Talking about you. You have the look.'

He didn't reply.

'Sure, you do,' she said. 'That look that never goes away. The way you handle yourself. The way you move, even the way you talk. It's indelible. Like a stain. And you're English, so it's a no-brainer. British Army, correct?'

Ben said nothing, just kept driving into the night.

'I knew it. And you were an officer, I'll bet.'

He looked at her. 'Really. You can tell that, can you?'

'Take it as a compliment.'

'Or an insult,' he said.

'A captain, at the very least. What unit?'

'Drop it,' Ben said.

'So I'm getting close. Let's aim for the top and work our way down from there. Special Forces?'

'How would you figure that one out?'

'Oh, from the way you jumped us tonight. You're right about the training. I thought I was good, and I am. But you made me feel like a total amateur. So, UKSF it is. Not too many divisions to choose from. SF Support Group? Special

197

Boat Service? You don't strike me as the navy type. Special Reconnaissance Regiment? That's a possible. But I'm going to plump for Special Air Service. How am I doing?'

Ben shook his head. 'You know something, Silvie Valois, or whoever you are? You're a little too smart for your own good.'

She smiled in the darkness. 'I'm right, though.'

'Right about to get thrown out of a speeding car if you don't start whistling a different tune.'

'Then you'd have to cut my tapes first,' she said.

'Or else slap another piece over your mouth.'

At that moment, the phone on the centre console between them began to vibrate and buzz in its plastic hollow. They both looked down at it.

'Aren't you going to get that?' she asked.

The phone gave two more pulses before Ben reached down and picked it up. He thumbed the reply button and pressed it to his ear, saying nothing, waiting for the caller to speak first. He eased off the throttle to quieten the resonance of the Hummer's engine note inside the cab.

'From one lone wolf to another, hello back,' said a familiar voice that Ben hadn't heard in a long time.

Chapter Thirty-Two

'It's been a while, my old friend,' said the smooth, warm, Gallic voice of Commissioner Luc Simon. 'Thought you'd dropped off the face of the planet.'

'Still keeping those healthy work hours, I see,' Ben said.

'Glutton for punishment,' Luc said. Ben could picture him sitting at his desk in a darkened office on the top floor of the Interpol HQ in Lyon. The expensive suit jacket hung crisply over the back of his chair. Tie loosened, but not too much. The ubiquitous cup of coffee steaming at his elbow, black as pitch and strong enough to stand a spoon up in. Luc Simon's hard-driving work schedule depended on a diet of heavy fuel.

'I thought about replying in some cryptic form to the rather unconventional communiqué that appeared on my fax machine,' he said, 'but I lack your imagination in these kinds of things. And besides, I didn't know where you were.'

'I'm in between places,' Ben said.

'Heading away from trouble rather than towards it, I hope.'

'A little of both.'

'That's what I was afraid you were going to say. In fact, I knew it. You worry me, Ben.'

'That's sweet of you to say,' Ben said, but he detected an emerging seriousness in the Frenchman's tone.

'Seriously. I have to ask myself what kind of mayhem your unexpected reappearance on my radar is going to spark off this time.'

'If you're referring to the thing in Paris,' Ben said, 'it really wasn't such a big deal.'

'A memorable high point in my police career. Wrecked cars and dead bodies all across the city, carnage and devastation, a one-man army on the rampage.'

'Don't exaggerate,' Ben said.

'And now, just when I was enjoying the peace, here you are again.'

'I only need a quick run on those prints,' Ben said.

'So I gathered. And I wish it were that simple. But I need to know where you got these from, my friend.'

Here comes the serious bit, Ben thought. The prelude was over. Now it was time to talk business, and it was clear that something was troubling Luc Simon. 'Off the guy's fingers,' Ben said. 'The rest is classified, as you might say. But from the question, I'm sensing you already know who they belonged to.'

'*Belonged*. Past tense. What am I to infer from that?'

'The obvious,' Ben said.

'See, now, that's a real problem,' Simon said.

'He was already dead when I found him,' Ben explained for the second time that night. 'If it's any consolation.'

'That makes a refreshing change, coming from you. And may I ask where he is now?'

'Don't worry, he's nowhere that's going to traumatise some unsuspecting member of the French public. Don't play games, Luc. If you know who he was, give me a name. You owe me that.'

'I do know who he was. Though it took a little finding. First place I looked was the Interpol criminal data management system covering France. The computer drew a blank. No trace of him there, no criminal history anywhere in this country. So then I ran a wider search. As an authorised user I can cross-check all European law-enforcement databases on suspected criminals or wanted persons. No sign of him there either. I had to dig deeper. And this does go deep. Which is why I said we have a problem if you're telling me this person is dead. It's going to cause more than a few ripples. If you want me to be forthcoming with you, you're going to have to reciprocate. Quid pro quo.'

Ben was a very close and secretive person, partly by nature, partly by training, mostly from long experience that had taught him a cardinal rule: *never tell anyone anything that you don't absolutely have to.* In this case, he knew he would soon have a decision to make. Opening up to Luc Simon represented a big tactical gamble. It would help establish the veracity of what Silvie was saying, one way or another. Which was important information to Ben. On the other hand, he hated exposing himself. Luc Simon was an old friend, but he was also a cop: the shrewdest and canniest Ben had ever met. Yet, if Ben didn't take the risk, he stood to find out nothing of any value. Choices.

He eased off the throttle and braked the Hummer into the side of the road. He leaned back in the driver's seat and twisted round a few degrees to face Silvie Valois. She was looking at him keenly, watching his face, studying his expression and straining to hear what was being said on the other end of the line.

'Come on, Luc. It's only a name. For old times' sake.'

'It's a little more than that. The subject whose prints you sent me was one Dexter Nicholls. He was an intelligence

201

operative. Not one of ours. He was working with French agents on a joint operation that I definitely, categorically *can't* talk about. Not even for old times' sake.'

Decision time. Ben thought, *Fuck it*, and jumped in with both feet. Cards on the table. All the way in.

'A joint operation involving MI6 and DGSI,' he said, 'investigating the activities of a Swiss called Udo Streicher.'

Luc Simon's composure slipped for a moment and he let out a sound that was halfway between a choking cough and a horrified gasp. 'Jesus Christ. You're not supposed to know anything about that.'

'I don't want to,' Ben said. 'I didn't choose to get involved. They crossed the line, not me. I was in peace.'

'Then stay that way. Keep out of this. For your own sake. You don't know what you're getting yourself into.'

'Too late for that, Luc.'

A long, pondering silence, then Luc Simon laid another of his hidden cards on the table. 'You know, I lied to you. Before, when I asked you where you were. I pretended I didn't know. The fact is, I know exactly where you are, Ben. I put the track on your phone before this conversation even began.'

'It's the least I'd expect of you, Luc.'

'Right at this moment, I'm looking at a wall-sized digital map of France with a flashing red dot on it. That's you. Which puts you uncomfortably close to the scene of a serious recent multiple homicide in the Hautes-Alpes region that the police are dealing with as we speak. I would be very, very concerned to think you had any kind of involvement in that situation.'

'I was the one who called the police,' Ben said. 'Just so you know.'

'You need to come in. We have to talk.'

'Sorry, Luc, that's not really on my agenda,' Ben said. 'I still have plenty of talking to do with Agent Valois here.'

Silvie's eyes opened wide, flashing in the darkness of the Hummer's cab.

There was a stunned silence on the phone. 'What did you say?'

'You heard me, Luc. For the record, she's not here of her own volition.'

All the way in. Ben was fully committed now. Nowhere to go but straight ahead, come what may.

'Where is she?' Luc Simon demanded.

'Right here sitting beside me,' Ben said. 'Safe and sound. I'm afraid I can't let you talk to her.'

'I'm warning you not to interfere with justice, Ben. You have no idea how deep a mess you've got yourself into already.'

'I'm not interested in your kind of justice, Luc. Or in any of your intelligence bullshit. I'm interested in one thing only, and that's finding the people who murdered my friends. There's nothing more you can do to help me, and nothing you can do to stop me.'

'I know you well enough,' Simon said. 'That's for damn sure.'

'Then you know to stay out of my way.'

'You realise that's something I can't do,' Simon said. 'Not even if I wanted to.'

'That's what I thought you'd say. Then consider Agent Valois a hostage until further notice.'

'Don't do this to yourself. We'll find you. You can't get away.'

Ben gave a dark smile. 'I thought you said you knew me, Luc.'

Then the call was over. Ben turned off the phone. There

was silence inside the cab of the Hummer. Just the muted growl of the idling motor and the crackle of duct tape as Silvie Valois shifted in her seat and shook her head at him in disbelief. 'Smart move,' she said. 'You just screwed yourself.'

'I don't think so,' Ben said. 'What I did was to verify that you were telling me the truth. That was worth taking a small risk for.'

'A small risk? You're crazy.'

Ben didn't reply. He went back to thinking. By now, Luc Simon's office would be a hubbub of burning phone lines as Interpol fell over themselves scrambling troops to the triangulated location of Dexter's phone. Police could be mobilised on the ground pretty damn fast, twenty-four-seven, even in remote Alpine areas, but not half as fast as by air. Ben knew that the Gendarmerie Nationale airborne division had helicopter bases all over France. Given the local topography, the difficulty in tracking targets by road in a mountainous region, the occasional necessity of locating and rescuing lost climbers and skiers, they'd almost certainly have a helibase in Briançon.

The GN chopper squadrons went all the way back to their role flying combat sorties in Indochina in the fifties, before the debacle of Vietnam had kicked off. These pilots had a long legacy of expertise. It would take just a few minutes before they were in the air, and hardly any time at all before the helicopters were homing in on a target so close to base. Meanwhile, Luc Simon would have been sure to order police roadblocks all around them. Those might take thirty minutes to set up. In that time, on twisty unlit roads, even the most determined driver couldn't realistically have covered more than about forty kilometres in any direction, dictating a minimum diameter for the cops to encircle. That didn't give Ben a lot of wiggle room, but it gave a little. The incoming airborne units gave him much less.

In short, it was time to get moving.

Chapter Thirty-Three

'What are you doing?' Silvie asked as he flipped open the glovebox and started rooting around for a bit of paper. Finding one of Omar's insurance documents that had a blank reverse side, he scrolled up the list of contact numbers on Dexter's phone and used the marker pen he'd bought in Briançon to write them down. The old-fashioned way, untrackable, untraceable. He folded the paper into his pocket and spent exactly two seconds deciding what to do with the phone. Keeping hold of it was out of the question. It was a virtual target hanging around his neck. Destroying it would simply kill the signal, which was the next best option. But he wanted the cops to be deceived for as long as possible into thinking they knew exactly where he was. He stepped out of the vehicle, waded into the long grass at the roadside and dropped the phone into the bushes, still switched on and screaming 'Here I am!' to his pursuers.

Jumping back into the Hummer and ignoring Silvie's questions, Ben took off and drove like a wild man. The road snaked and looped. The Hummer roared up inclines and squealed around hairpin bends. The lights carved a dazzling tunnel out of the trees that hugged the verges. Ben checked his mirrors every few seconds, half-expecting to see flashing blue lights chasing them, but the mirrors showed only darkness.

After a few more minutes, the deserted road climbed steeply for two kilometres and the trees fell away either side to reveal an open vista. The mountains all around them, the forested valley below, the night sky spangled with billions of stars that threw a diaphanous glow over the landscape.

Ben braked to a halt. Silvie watched as he got out of the Hummer, walked round to the front, stepped up on the bumper then on to the bonnet, then clambered up on the flat roof. Standing high above the road, he had a sweeping three-sixty view of the terrain. Everything was still. No screech of sirens, no thump of approaching helicopters. To the west, there was nothing but dark wilderness. North and south, the road was an undulating strip of ribbon shining under the stars. To the east, the ground fell away beyond the roadside barrier in a staggered rocky slope strewn with thorny bushes and clumps of pine. About three hundred metres below and three-quarters of a kilometre away across the valley, Ben could make out the shapes of agricultural buildings clustered under the trees, surrounded by a large walled yard with a farmhouse at one end. Its windows were unlit. The good folks inside were fast asleep, as all good folks should be at this hour.

Ben jumped down from the vehicle and opened the passenger door. 'Are you going to tell me what's happening, or what?' Silvie demanded. Without replying, he took Breslin's switchblade from his pocket and popped it open, then carefully slashed the tape holding her right wrist and ankle to the seat frame. Then he trotted round to the driver's door, leaned in over the transmission tunnel and did the same for her left side. She sighed with relief and shook her arms and rubbed her wrists to get the circulation flowing again.

'Out you get,' he said. 'There's a farm down there. That's where we're going.'

Silvie clambered out and started walking towards the edge of the road, peering down the slope. 'Not so fast,' he said, motioning her back to the car. 'Lay your hands flat on the wing.'

'You love that stuff, don't you,' she muttered as he looped a fresh length of tape to bind her wrists together.

'We get down there, no noise. Any tricks, I'll snap your neck.'

'So before you didn't believe me, and you were threatening to kill me; and now you do believe me, you're *still* threatening to kill me?'

'Life's tough for hostages,' he said. He tore off another five inches of the broad, strong tape, and before she could dodge backwards he slapped it across her mouth as a gag. 'Don't move.' He grabbed everything necessary from the Hummer. Slung his green bag over his left shoulder and the holdall containing the guns and ammo over the right. He had three pistols in various pockets, the two Glocks and Eriq Sabatier's Beretta. The combined weight of the weaponry, the gold bar and the stacks of cash he'd stolen from Rollo was close to crippling. About the equivalent of the heavy pack the SAS slave-drivers had expected their recruits to tote up and down the rugged slopes of Pen y Fan Mountain in the Brecon Beacons, way back in Ben's training days, on the same selection course that had since caused the death of a dozen men from exhaustion and heart failure. But this would be easy, nearly all downhill.

'Let's go,' he grunted at Silvie, motioning the way ahead, and they left the Hummer at the roadside as they stepped over the barrier and started threading a zigzag descent down the slope, Ben leading the way, keeping a watchful eye on his prisoner. His pang of regret at losing the Hummer didn't last long. Easy come, easy go, just like it had been for Omar.

The guy was probably still too much in love with his gold bar to care about a vehicle he'd won in a poker game.

It took more than twenty minutes to negotiate the tricky slope, loose stones and dry earth sliding in miniature landslips under their boots as they worked their way down to level ground. Where the decline bottomed out, the trees grew thicker and they crossed half an acre of woodland before a starlit meadow opened up in front of them. At its edge was an old post-and-rail fence marking the edge of the farm boundary. They climbed the fence and walked on in silence, cutting due east towards the farm buildings nestling in the trees up ahead. To Ben, laden down with kit, it felt like one of the night marches from his army days. He felt strangely excited, invigoratingly alive. All five senses on full alert, constantly vigilant, taking in every detail, every smell, every sound. Like the distant thud of choppers, at least two of them, bearing down through the night sky on a target they would soon find was nothing better than an abandoned phone tossed in the bushes.

He smiled. Luc wouldn't be a happy man.

From far above on the road, the farm had looked like a dainty model. Up close, it was a mess. Discarded machinery lay scattered about the yard and the sides of the rough, neglected buildings. The house was old stone, with a red-tiled roof and a squat chimney stack at each end. A dog barked from somewhere inside, but it was ignored and the farmhouse windows remained in darkness behind their louvred shutters. In front of the house was a large vegetable garden skirted by a stone wall. Parked face-out along the wall was a motley collection of tractors and old cars. Last in the line was a battered workhorse of a Toyota Hilux crew-cab pickup. The load bed was empty, apart from a diesel jerrycan and a rolled-up plastic tarp. No flat tyres, no missing lights.

It looked serviceable enough. Ben motioned to Silvie to stay in the shadow of the wall. He gave the jerrycan a nudge and heard the slosh of fuel inside. Gently, he eased open the Toyota's driver's door and saw the key dangling from the ignition.

Country life. The benefits of a relaxed low-crime environment where nobody expected thieves to come in the night, and few folks bothered locking their vehicles.

Crouching down with the pickup hiding him from the house, Ben unslung his green bag and felt his right shoulder begin to decompress. Rooted around inside, pulled out a brick of Rollo's cash and split it in half. 2,500 euros was more than the well-worn Toyota was worth. He hoped that the generosity of the exchange might entice the owners not to report the theft to the police. He left the money trapped under a stone on the wall, where it couldn't be missed in the morning. Eased open the rear cab door and loaded the gear inside. There was a pair of rubber wellingtons in the footwell, crusted with dried dirt. A tattered flat cap and a rumpled boiler suit that smelled strongly of chicken shit lay on the back seat. Ben closed the door, waved Silvie over from the shadows and bundled her into the front passenger seat. He eased in behind the wheel, took a deep breath and twisted the ignition. The diesel started up with a rasp, loud in the night. He quickly engaged gear and they took off. Still no lights came on in the farmhouse. Heavy sleepers.

The farmyard led to a private track that wound its way between sheds and barns and finally out through a set of gates to the open road. Silvie rolled her eyes angrily and muttered from behind her tape gag. Maybe she was complaining about the smell of old boots and chicken shit inside the truck.

The road snaked up the valley until a junction took them

back the way they'd come before. Ben drove fast for five kilometres, the Toyota's maladjusted headlights a pale candle glow compared to the supernova of the Hummer, its worn engine and suspension and tyres all protesting loudly from the punishment. Still ignoring Silvie, he stopped the truck and got out. He reached in the back, removed his jacket, took out the boiler suit and put it on. It smelled even fouler up close, but he'd worn worse things in his life. He unlaced his boots, took them off and slipped his feet into the damp wellingtons, thinking about trench foot. Finally, he opened the passenger door and yanked the tape from Silvie's mouth.

'There was no need for that, you know,' she said irritably.

'We needed something a little less conspicuous,' Ben said. 'Out here in the boondocks that Hummer stuck out a mile.'

'I don't mean the car, *imbécile*. I mean the tape. I'm getting tired of being trussed up like a prisoner.'

'You're a government agent. As of tonight, I'm effectively a fugitive. Figure it out.'

'If I wanted to resist you, don't you think I would have by now? I could handle you.'

'Don't even think about it,' Ben said. He put on the flat cap. Crouched down and poked a hand under the truck's dirty sill, felt about among the dirt-encrusted suspension members and came up with fingers caked in black grease. He smeared a little on his face and wiped the rest down the front of the boiler suit.

'It's a great look,' she said acerbically.

Ben grabbed the tarp from the load bed. 'We'll be coming up on a police roadblock soon. I'm going to have to ask you to snuggle down in the footwell for a while. If I don't think you can manage that without complaining or making noise, I'll have to tape your mouth up again.'

211

'You're just going to drive on through? These are trained police officers. Do you think they're stupid?'

'If they're not, then I'll just have to shoot my way through.'

'You really are crazy.'

'You want the tape?'

She shook her head. 'I'll be quiet.'

'Good.' He racked the passenger seat back as far as it would go to give her space to cram herself down as low as possible, then covered her with the tarpaulin. He got back behind the wheel. Lying in the nook of the steering column and the dusty instrument panel was an old briar pipe, filled with some kind of tobacco that might have been dried horse manure. He clamped the worn stem between his teeth and lit the bowl with his Zippo as he drove. He coughed at the first acrid sting of the awful smoke.

'Something's burning,' said a muffled voice from under the tarp.

'Shush,' Ben said. He drove on. The rubber boots gave little clutch or throttle control, but then the pickup was no thoroughbred. After rattling along for another kilometre, they rounded a bend and Ben saw his guess had been right. A pair of Renault Mégane police cars flanked the road up ahead, their headlights bright, their roof bars casting a blue swirl over the roadside bushes and trees. Two uniformed cops saw the truck approaching and stepped up to meet it. They were holding torches and both had holstered pistols on their utility belts. One was carrying the reliable old MAT-49 submachine gun on a sling, dangling at an angle across his chest. The other waved the Toyota down.

Ben stopped, and the two cops walked up to the vehicle. The one with the submachine gun stood blocking the way with a scowl on his face, as if all he wanted in the world was to get into a shoot-'em-up with a carload of villains.

This was probably the most exciting night of his career. The other came round to the driver's door, an older man, paunchy and jaded-looking. Ben wound down his window and a cloud of pipe smoke wafted out to meet the torch beam that panned around the inside of the cab. The light hovered over the plastic tarp that covered a kidnapped government agent, then flicked up at Ben, dazzling him. Then it did a quick tour of the back seats, flashed over the green canvas of Ben's bag containing stolen cash and gold bullion, and over the black fabric of the holdall stuffed with military rifles and ammunition.

Ben sat calmly behind the wheel, the pipe dangling casually from his mouth. His right hand lay relaxed in his lap, just inches from the Glock 26 that it would have taken him less than half a second to draw and put in the cop's face.

'Where are you headed this time of night, monsieur?' the cop asked.

Ben shrugged. He put on a gruff local accent. 'Looking for Max.'

'Who's Max?'

'My dog,' Ben said. 'Gone and run off again. Bitch in heat somewhere, is my guess. You haven't seen him, have you?'

'No, we haven't seen your dog,' the cop said irritably. 'What kind of dog is it?'

'Wolf dog,' Ben said, which was the commonest French slang for a German shepherd, *chien loup*. 'Big shaggy bastard. Goes for miles. Should've shot the randy fucker a long time ago.'

The light shone in Ben's face a moment longer as the cop took in the dirty boiler suit, the nasty old hat, the grease stains, the pipe, the whole look. Unshaven and dressed like the roughest backwater hick, Ben could be pretty certain he didn't bear much resemblance to any photo that had been circulated to the police. Probably the one that his former business partner Jeff Dekker still hadn't taken down from the company website, last time Ben had bothered to look. He'd had his hair cut military-short and worn a tie for that one, to impress potential clients. It seemed like another lifetime.

'So what's up?' Ben asked in the gruff accent. 'You looking for someone?' He took another puff of the pipe. The choking fumes swirled like ocean fog around the torch beam. The cop gave a splutter and stepped back from the window. Ben wasn't sure if it was because of the pipe or the chicken-shit smell of the boiler suit. Either way was fine by him.

'Not you, that's for sure,' the cop said. 'Okay. Move on. Hope you find your dog.' He signalled to the one with the submachine gun, who stepped aside to let the truck pass. He looked disappointed, but maybe the next vehicle they'd stop would be full of Mafiosi bristling with automatic weapons. Ben wound up his window and drove on with a rattle of loose exhaust. In the mirror, the two cops ambled back to their cars and then were lost from view.

Ben replaced the pipe on the dashboard and said in his own voice, 'You can come out now.'

The tarpaulin crackled as Silvie shoved and crumpled it aside and heaved herself up on to the seat. She looked at him. '*Max?*'

Ben shrugged.

She shook her head. 'I take back what I said. Maybe they really are that stupid.'

'Thanks for acting like a model hostage. I'm glad I didn't have to shoot you.'

'You're welcome. So what now?'

The first streaks of dawn were breaking over the mountains. 'I'm hungry,' he said.

Chapter Thirty-Four

The *routier* café was open early in the hopes of catching some business from passing long-haul truckers. It was a low, stretched-out building off the road, with a car park big enough to turn articulated lorries but mostly empty apart from a panel van and a smattering of early-bird customers' cars. The sun was coming up. It was going to be another warm day. By now, Ben had already discarded his farmer's disguise and flung the stuff into the pickup's load bed. The worst of the greasy dirt on his face was wiped off with a rag. They wouldn't have let him into the Ritz, but he was presentable enough for this place, all right.

He was light-headed from lack of sleep and couldn't remember his last meal. 'You know the routine,' he said as they crossed from the parked Toyota towards the café entrance. 'Try not to look like a prisoner, and don't forget I have a gun in my pocket.'

The place didn't look too appetising, or even too clean, but Ben was too tired and hungry to care. He walked Silvie past the few occupied tables, where people who looked even wearier than him tucked into brioches and breakfast fry-ups. The aromas of sizzling bacon and fresh coffee reached Ben's nose and made his mouth water. He ushered Silvie to a table right at the back, away from the other diners.

They sat opposite one another on soft vinyl bench seats, next to the window from which Ben could see the Toyota. The glass was grimed with dust and dirt on the outside and grease and fingermarks on the inside, and had a faded sticker saying *Défense de fumer*. Ben dumped his green bag on the seat, took off his jacket and laid it next to him with the hidden butt of the Glock close to his hand. When a bored-looking waitress descended on them moments later, he ordered a large pot of coffee, sausages and bacon and mushrooms and fried bread. Silvie asked for fruit juice and a croissant. Ben took out his cigarettes.

'You always smoke this much?' she asked as he lit up.

'I had seven months off. Making up for lost time,' he said. He leaned back and puffed away.

'It's unhealthy.'

'So's hanging out with guys like Kurt Breslin,' he said.

'There's a No Smoking sign there right next to you.'

'So arrest me,' Ben said. He reached over and pulled open the straps of his bag, dipped his hand down to the bottom and found the cool smoothness of the gold bar. He lifted it across with both hands and laid it on the thin wood veneer of the table, which seemed to sag under its weight.

'Evidence,' he said.

Silvie's eyes widened at the sight. 'You weren't bullshitting me.'

'Your man Dexter had two of them on him.'

'Why?'

'You tell me. Looked like he'd taken them for himself.'

'I can't believe that.'

'Aside from those, I found another two lying around, as if they'd been in a hurry and weren't too bothered about losing the odd one.'

216

'Which suggests that there must have been a hell of a lot of it,' Silvie said, staring at the bar.

Ben nodded. 'My thoughts exactly. Enough to keep them busy for hours bringing it up and loading it into the raid vehicle.'

She frowned. 'That's what troubles me. Surely a load like that would have filled up most of the vehicle. It's big, but it's not that big. And it was carrying a full complement of passengers, plus all kinds of other equipment. How come I didn't see anything, when I got a peek inside?'

'I don't know,' Ben said.

'And why would Streicher have kept the entire haul on board a single vehicle when the smart thing to do would be to distribute it among several? It doesn't make sense.'

'That's not all that doesn't make sense,' Ben said. 'I still don't understand why they needed the second charge.'

'To seal off the hole? Cover their tracks?'

'Then why didn't they drag all the bodies in there too? Including the body of their own man, which they left lying out in the open for anyone to find?'

'I don't know,' she said.

'And why go to the trouble of setting up a timed charge to seal up the hole, if they'd already emptied the treasure out of it? There was nothing more to hide.'

'Maybe they just wanted to create a diversion. The hour's delay would give them plenty of time to get far away. Maybe it was intended to take out anyone who might come snooping. Or maybe the timing device was faulty.'

'Too many maybes.' Ben saw the waitress approaching and slid the gold bar back into his bag. The waitress took no notice of Ben's cigarette, instead dumped her tray on the table between them and left without a word. Ben stubbed out the Gauloise on his saucer and launched straight into

217

his food. For two minutes he said nothing more as he demolished most of his plateful and drank a pint of hot black coffee. Silvie sipped her fruit juice and picked at her croissant.

'Then there's the matter of how he even knew the gold was there,' Ben said at last. Full of protein and carbohydrates, fats and caffeine, he felt halfway human again already. All he needed now was about twelve hours' sleep.

'If Streicher makes it his business to find out about something, believe me, he does,' Silvie said. 'I told you he was insane, and I wasn't kidding. He has the kind of abnormal capacity for single-minded focus that's associated with all kinds of psychiatric conditions. Like an obsessive-compulsive disorder, but apparently without any of the anxiety. Once he gets fixed on a subject, he can literally talk about it all day and all night. It's way beyond normal enthusiasm. I've witnessed some of his monologues. One night, weeks ago, before he moved us to the house in Lausanne, he was there with Hannah Gissel and some of the others. They were in the living room, drinking wine. I overheard some of the conversation, except it wasn't so much a conversation as Streicher himself just talking, and talking, and talking, almost as if he didn't care whether anyone else was listening, or even there. He gabbled on and on about a crypt. Deep underground, carved out of solid rock. But no mention of where it was, or in what kind of place. He said it was full of secrets.'

'Secrets?'

She nodded. 'Ancient secrets. Ones that had been almost completely forgotten over the course of centuries. Only he had been able to connect the facts. How he was going to make history. How he was going to be remembered. And on, and on.'

Ben said, 'Père Antoine talked about secrets too.'

'Père Antoine?'

'The prior of the monastery. I got to know him well, though not so well that he'd confide anything more. Something about the place's history seemed to trouble him.' Ben told Silvie about his discovery of the walled-up crypt, and how the old monk had been unwilling to discuss it. 'When I tried to press him, he clammed up and changed the subject.'

'He must have known they were sitting on a pile of gold,' Silvie said. 'There are probably hundreds of ancient treasures all over France, waiting to be dug up, and thousands of speculators who'd do anything to get a piece of them. The last thing a very private, secluded place like a monastery needs is a load of noisy attention. Maybe he was nervous about people finding out, the media getting wind of it, all kinds of hysteria and TV crews and crowds of idiots with cameras gathering outside the gates.'

Ben considered the idea for a few moments as he chewed on a piece of fried bread with mushrooms and washed it down with more coffee. 'It didn't sound to me as if he was talking about treasure. He mentioned ghosts from the past. Things that ought to be forgotten about. Like a dirty secret. Something shameful from days gone by. Something so terrible that it was still impossible to talk about it. That was the impression I got. And there was more down there in the crypt than just gold bars. I saw it for myself.'

Silvie frowned over the rim of her glass as she sipped the last of her fruit juice. 'What?'

'Old bones,' Ben said. 'Human skeletons. Piles of them. It was hard to tell how many. Scores of them, maybe hundreds. Men, women and children.'

'A mass grave?'

'More than a grave,' Ben said. 'Worse than a grave. They were shackled and chained to the floor. Nobody does that to a corpse. These people had been taken down there, walled up and left to die, a very long time ago.'

'Underneath a monastery? Who would do something like that?'

'The church authorities of the day,' Ben said. 'Nobody else would have had the power. And I think that Père Antoine knew about it. I think that was the secret he wouldn't talk about.'

'Horrible.'

'Yes,' Ben said. 'Very horrible.'

Silvie leaned forward with her elbows on the table, gazing emptily down at the wood veneer, her brow slightly furrowed and her lips pursed, as if she were thinking hard.

'What?'

'This may sound weird, but did Père Antoine ever talk about a curse?'

Ben looked at her. 'A curse?'

She nodded. 'Don't ask me for details. All I know is what I heard Streicher talking about that night. I remember that he kept mentioning something about a blind man's curse.'

'What blind man?' Ben said, baffled.

'In history. I think he was the one who cast the curse, or whatever it was. A priest, I think. I'm trying to remember his name. Damn it, what was it? Someone the blind.'

'That would make sense, I suppose,' Ben said, barely interested.

She ignored him and clicked her tongue in frustration. 'Salvator. That was it. Salvator l'Aveugle.'

The name reminded Ben of Rollo le Tordu. Funny how a person could become so inextricably associated with their disability that it merged with their identity. Right now, he was Benoît le Confondu. Benedict the Confused.

'Well, I don't believe in curses,' he said.

'But secrets are another matter,' Silvie said. 'This has something to do with the monastery, I'm sure of it. If we could understand it, I think it would explain how Streicher knew about the gold.'

Ben was silent for a beat. 'This isn't getting us anywhere. You promised you'd tell me what you knew.'

'I also warned you how little that was. Like I said, you'll be disappointed. It wasn't exactly a successful mission as undercover insertions go. It's not a career-maker. In fact, in four months I was able to discover virtually nothing more than what I was briefed on going in.'

'Which was?'

'Key facts,' she said. 'That Udo Streicher is Swiss, that he's forty-six years of age, that he has absolutely no criminal convictions or record of any kind, not so much as a library fine, and that he's very wealthy. His family made their millions in shoes, although he never worked for the business. He trained as a dentist. For a time he owned a private practice in Geneva. All totally legitimate and above board.'

'A dentist,' Ben said blankly.

'He's also a certified pilot, holds a Swiss private licence. He's exactly six foot tall, weighs about a hundred and fifty pounds, has dark hair greying at the temples, grey eyes, has no known home address whatsoever and is of prime interest to certain government agencies, who it seems have closely guarded reasons for believing he's on the verge of something big.'

Ben stared at her. '*On the verge* of something big?'

'I know. It's a hell of an insult to the people he's already hurt. But my superiors wouldn't consider what he's done

221

to your friends as something big. Take it from me. What they're thinking of is in a completely different league. Killing a few monks is nothing by comparison. Minor collateral damage. That's just the way it is.'

'All right,' Ben said. 'So just what is this master plan they're all so het up about? What is it we're supposed to be waiting for Streicher to pull off next? Was the raid on the monastery some kind of dry run for something? Was the idea to steal the gold to finance a bigger project?'

'I've already asked myself those same questions.'

'And what about answers?'

'For that, you need to be talking to DGSI.'

'I thought that's what I was doing. So far you're not giving me much.'

Silvie gave a short laugh. 'Pay grades, remember? You think my superiors tell me everything? I'm just a plain vanilla field agent. Way down the chain of command. Expendable. Not someone the agency trusts with privileged information. If Streicher's people had got suspicious of me and applied pressure, that is to say whatever kind of torture they might use to make me talk, waterboarding or hot irons, they'd quickly have realised I knew nothing. They'd simply have disposed of me, and the agency would come up with another plan for getting inside the operation. In effect, I was piggy in the middle. Which pisses me off, more than a little bit. In no way is that what I signed up for.'

Ben quietly finished his coffee, then sat back. 'So I'm back to square one. Which is to say, nowhere.'

'I'm sorry. I know you were counting on me for information.'

'It's a setback, that's all.'

'I know you're upset about your friends. I'm sorry about that as well.'

He said nothing.

'What are you going to do?' she asked.

Ben said, 'I'm going to find him, hunt him down and put him in the ground. Him, and whoever else was involved.'

'He has a lot of protection.'

'He's one man down already.'

'There are plenty more, and Breslin wasn't the worst.'

'It won't do him any good. I'll go through his people, layer by layer, one by one, whatever it takes, until I get to him.'

She looked at him. 'Are you really good enough?'

'This kind of thing isn't exactly new to me. And I'm still alive.'

'I was right about you, wasn't I?'

'I was in the SAS, yes. For many years. About half your lifetime.'

'I'm older than I look. And I was right about the officer part, too?'

He shrugged. 'Final rank of major. Not that it matters.'

'It says a lot about who you are.'

'No. It says nothing about who I am.'

'Why did you leave?'

'I wasn't happy in my work,' he said. 'I didn't like the way they did things, and I didn't always agree with why they needed doing in the first place. Politics isn't my game. I wanted to do good, to help people. That's why I left.'

'I can sympathise,' Silvie replied.

'Sure you can,' he said.

'I mean it. I'm not happy in my work either. I don't like being put into a vulnerable situation like that without being told the full story. I don't like taking orders from faceless bureaucrats who keep their cards close to their chests. I don't like the way they allow innocent people to be murdered, like some kind of acceptable sacrifice, while they wait in the wings playing the bigger picture game. And I want to get Streicher for what he did. No way they'd let me back on the case now. I'm compromised. But no way am I going to let myself be reassigned to some second-rate posting, to sit gnashing my teeth and twiddling my damn thumbs while all this is going on.'

Ben could see a spirited flash in Silvie's eyes as she talked. He liked it.

'So?' he asked.

'The way I see it, being your hostage gives me an opportunity. A time window. I don't have to return to base with my tail between my legs, at least not yet. I'm free, for as long as we can stay a step ahead.'

Ben smiled and lit another Gauloise. 'Are you trying to tell me you want to team up? Because the answer is, forget it. I don't need you any more. I'll go it alone from here.'

'Meaning what? That you'll just let me go?'

'The door's over there. I won't stop you. An hour from now, you'll have no better idea of where I am than Luc Simon or any of them.'

'And I tell them what?'

'You could just tell them you got away. Make up all kinds of harrowing stories about your ordeal and how you risked your life escaping from me. You'll be a hero.'

'Think again. You might find me useful to have around.'

He shook his head. 'You'll slow me down. I work alone.'

'Don't give me that "I work alone" crap. A lone man on the run is an easy target. Especially when they plaster your face all over the news, because everywhere you go people will be afraid of you. A man and a woman together don't arouse suspicion. Just a normal couple, going about our business.'

'You don't have the training. You said so yourself.'

'I'm a quick study. Anyway, I might surprise you.'

'Surprise is the last thing I need.' He yawned. Waves of fatigue were hitting him. The caffeine in his system had taken only the slightest edge off it.

'Rest is what you need,' Silvie said. 'You look exhausted.'

'And I want to sleep easy,' he replied, 'knowing that I won't wake up with a gun in my face.'

'You're scared I could arrest you?'

'Given what you do for a living, it crossed my mind.'

She smiled. 'The fact is, Ben, I could have arrested you any number of times. The moment we got out of the Hummer, for instance. When you cut me free of the seat, before you taped my wrists back together. The whole time you had me hiding under the tarpaulin. Or before we walked into this place, and any time since. Right this moment.'

'You think so?'

'I know so. Your weapons are all in the car, except for my Glock there in your jacket pocket. You're tired, your reactions are slowed. You'd never get to it in time. Not before I got to mine.'

'You're not even armed. You thinking of pronging me with a fork? Taking my eye out with a sugar spoon?'

She smiled again. 'They didn't teach you to frisk girls in the British Army, did they? Or maybe you were just too gentlemanly to check my underwear.' Her right hand emerged from under the table. It was holding a tiny black automatic, just a few ounces of polymer and steel, as smooth and rounded as a sucked sweet. Then it was gone, as the hand gripping it ducked back under the table.

'Say hello to my micro Kel-Tec,' she said. 'Seven rounds of .380 that have been with me the whole time, and that I could plug you with right here, right now. The law would

225

be on my side. Kidnapped government agent, defending herself against a heavily armed, highly dangerous desperado? No problem. And before you ask, yes, I have shot a man before. In fact there are three of them on the other side of the grass because I put them there. So you need to ask yourself: *why doesn't she shoot?*'

Ben said nothing. The gun was out of sight but he could feel it pointing at his belly under the table, the way you could sense someone watching you across a room. A .380 auto was no man stopper. It wasn't a .44 Magnum. But at close range a full magazine of those stubby, zippy little copper-nosed rounds would tear through him and make a real mess inside. It would kill him stone dead. That was for certain.

'The fact is, Ben, I can take you hostage just as easily as you can me. We can keep passing the baton back and forth, switching hats, captor and captive, all day long, until one of us gets hurt. But we don't have time to waste on silly games. What you and I need to do is make a deal. Work together. Partners, until this is over and we go our separate ways. Agreed?'

Ben said nothing.

'Trust me,' she said.

Chapter Thirty-Five

The first act of the newly formed alliance was to leave the *routier* café in search of somewhere to hole up and rest a while. 'I can sleep fine in the car,' Ben kept insisting as they headed down the road. Silvie drove, with her Glock back in her pocket.

'Don't tell me – you've slept in a lot worse places. You Special Forces characters seem to take some weird pride in subjecting yourselves to shitty conditions. What's wrong with us getting a room, with a proper bed in it?'

'Partly that I wouldn't want you to get the wrong idea about me,' he admitted.

She laughed. 'A gentleman to the last.'

The gentleman sat and kept a lookout for police, until his eyes wouldn't stay open any longer and he fell into a doze. Just seconds seemed to pass before he sensed the pickup had stopped, and opened them again to see that Silvie had pulled up in front of a roadside motel. 'This place looks like it might do us,' she said, getting out.

Within five minutes, they were unlocking the door to room twenty, which was situated at the far end of a block around the back of the motel, with a designated parking slot just a few steps away. Silvie grabbed the weapons holdall from the Toyota while Ben wearily brought in his green bag. She was strong and handled the heavy weight easily.

The room wasn't big, and it offered nothing more than the barest essentials. A pair of worn single beds, a wardrobe, a utilitarian bathroom, a lopsided standard lamp in one corner, a flimsy table in the other with a phone, cheaply framed bad art on the walls.

'Is this place scummy enough to satisfy your delicate sensibilities?' she said, smiling.

'Perfect,' he replied. He locked the door, walked straight back to the left-hand bed, nearest the window, and collapsed face down on it without taking his shoes off. The hard, lumpy mattress felt like feathers to him. He shut his eyes, breathed once, breathed twice, and then was spinning downwards into a dark deep pool where there were no thoughts or dreams and nothing really mattered.

More than five hundred kilometres to the north, Luc Simon hustled off the Learjet at Le Bourget airport, dived into the waiting black Citroën sedan and let himself be driven into the heaving traffic of Paris. He was restless and irritable. Irritated that he'd had to abandon his frenetic command post in Lyon just to report to a bunch of government suits. Irritated that he hadn't had a decent cup of coffee for the last several hours. Most of all, he was irritated that the high-powered and very secret meeting he was about to attend couldn't have been held in a simple boardroom. Trust these damn politicians to piss around at the Georges V when there was so much at stake and so little time.

When he walked inside the grand hotel's ridiculously opulent lobby and was ushered up to the Presidential Suite on the third floor by dark-suited men with radio earpieces and concealed weapons, his expectations were proved sadly correct. The silver platters of gourmet finger food and champagne on ice were already disappearing fast. It wasn't even lunchtime yet. And still not a decent drop of coffee to be had.

Present around the palatial room were several important faces he hadn't seen before, along with some that were more familiar. Jean-Yves Saunier, Central Director of the DGSI, was accompanied by the agency's Terrorism Division chief, Patrick Bideau. Keith Hillier, fresh off a flight from London, was MI5's liaison officer overseeing the joint Streicher operation. Simon knew Jürgen Ganz of the FIS, the Swiss Federal Intelligence Service, only by sight. Likewise François Aumont, the French Minister of the Interior, who was taking up most of a Louis XV settee and helping himself liberally to the Dom Pérignon. After a long round of introductions and hand-shaking and several infuriating minutes spent politely refusing food and drink, Simon was grateful finally to get down to business.

Central to the agenda was the worrisome figure of Major Benedict Hope, who overnight had rocketed from total obscurity to being considered a high-priority fugitive in connection with the ultra-secret Streicher operation. Thankfully, the intelligence guys were all up to speed on Hope's military file – made available courtesy of the British Ministry of Defence and the involvement of MI5 – and on what little information existed on the man's activities in the years since he'd quit the army. Police reports on the crime scene at the Chartreuse de la Sainte Vierge de Pelvoux had been more or less skimmed by everyone in the room, so Simon didn't waste too much time in delving straight to the heart of the matter.

'The latest developments, gentlemen. This morning the Briançon gendarmerie received a report of a stolen Toyota pickup truck, taken some time in the early hours from a farm less than a kilometre from where our air search team discovered the abandoned H1 Hummer. Police are hunting for the Toyota. The Hummer's owner is one Omar Adeyemi, forty-eight years of age, currently unemployed, a resident of Briançon. He told the police he'd only just realised it had been stolen, and was about to report the theft.'

'Think he's telling the truth?' asked Bideau, the terrorism chief.

'Frankly, there's not much we can do to prove otherwise,' Simon said. 'Meantime, one of the search teams combing the Hautes-Alpes area came across two more abandoned vehicles, just a few kilometres from the monastery. One was a Nissan SUV. Chassis and engine numbers filed away, stolen plates tracing back to a scrapped Peugeot that was written off in an accident last year. Fingerprints and DNA samples found inside the Nissan match up to our missing agent, Silvie Valois, and one Kurt Breslin. Who, as you all know, is, or as it now appears *was*, one of Streicher's followers. Breslin's body was recovered nearby. Looks like someone shot him with a high-velocity rifle at close range. We're still looking to determine the calibre and possible provenance of the weapon.'

'But we can safely assume this Hope pulled the trigger,' said one of the lesser government suits whose name Simon hadn't made a priority of remembering.

'I don't think we can safely assume anything about this case,' Simon replied. 'But right now, that's a realistic scenario, yes. It's possible that Hope managed to arrange some kind of rendezvous with them, whereupon he shot Breslin and took Valois prisoner, believing at that point that she was one of Streicher's team. Which is, obviously, the impression we've been working very hard to convey. Most of all to Streicher himself.'

'Looks like it's gone and backfired on us,' came the helpful comment from the Minister of the Interior.

'But now Hope knows who she is,' said the DGSI director,

Saunier. 'Which says the bastard must have tortured her. My agents don't give up information readily. Christ knows what shape she must be in now.'

'That's not his style,' Simon said. But the notion of the young female agent being sadistically tortured by a ruthless fugitive seemed to strike a chord and had the whole room rumbling speculatively for a few moments, until Simon patiently managed to regain their attention.

'The other vehicle is the recently burned-out wreck of an old Citroën truck. Not a lot left of it, but enough to trace its ownership back to the monastery of Chartreuse de la Sainte Vierge de Pelvoux. Forensic examination revealed charred human remains inside a tool locker on board. They're still working to identify them, but my instinct tells me it's going to turn out to be our second missing agent, Jon Ruddock, alias Dexter Nicholls.'

'Murdered by Ben Hope,' growled Keith Hillier, the MI5 man, who was into his third flute of champagne since Simon had entered the room.

'He says not.'

Bideau peered at Simon over the top of his spectacles. 'You trust him?'

'One thing Ben Hope isn't is a liar.'

'These SAS are psychopathic killers,' another nameless suit ventured. 'Everybody knows that. It's so trained into them that it takes nothing at all for them to turn bad.'

'You've had dealings with this man in the past, Commissioner,' Saunier said, flicking a report in his hand. 'Some years ago, matter of an abduction case while you were still with the police here in Paris. Hope was involved in some shadowy private capacity that I don't believe was ever fully explained. Never mind that for the moment. The question is, how well do you really know him?'

Simon heaved a sigh. 'Well enough to know that we have a problem. Bringing Hope into a situation like this is like sticking a live wire into a ton of high explosive.'

'I still don't understand,' the Minister of the Interior said. 'How is he involved?'

'The truth is, we don't know for sure,' Simon said. 'You can see from the transcript of my brief phone conversation with him that he said "I was in peace". That suggests to me that he'd been living at the monastery. As you can see from his record, he has a background in theology.'

'A warrior monk,' Jürgen Ganz scoffed.

'It's the warrior part that concerns me,' Simon said. 'These people were his friends. He's angry and he's on the warpath. Put that together with the kind of specialist expertise he's already amply demonstrated, and that makes him just about the most deadly person imaginable. The real problem is that he has no idea what he's dealing with here. More specifically, *who* he's dealing with. Our greatest concern at present is that he's liable to force Streicher's hand and aggravate the current crisis in a critically dangerous way. A very great deal is at stake here, gentlemen.'

Bideau nodded. 'We've got one crazy guy going after another crazy guy. It's a volatile situation, to say the least.'

'How do things stand on the Streicher front?' the Minister of the Interior asked, turning around towards Bideau and Saunier. 'I mean, do you people even know where he is?'

Bideau swallowed, pursed his lips and said, 'No.'

'We haven't been able to locate him,' Saunier said.

The minister turned the other way, to glare at Jürgen Ganz. 'And what about our Swiss colleagues?'

'We don't know where Streicher is either,' Ganz admitted sullenly after a beat. 'All our efforts have turned up nothing. No addresses. Not even an email or phone. He pops up, eludes us completely and then disappears again before we have time to react. It's as if he vanishes into the ground.'

'But Hope will find him,' Simon said. 'Rest assured of that. He can find anybody. That was his job. Which is our biggest problem. And which, as of now, makes stopping him just as much of a priority, before he sets the whole damn tinderbox alight.'

The Minister of the Interior shifted his bulk to the edge of the Louis XV settee and slammed his empty glass down on the table. 'Then what the hell are we wasting time for?'

Excellent question, Simon wanted to say, eyeing the half-empty platters and bottles that littered the Presidential Suite.

'I want a national television campaign,' the minister rasped, and two aides instantly started scribbling notes. 'Effective immediately. Half-hourly newsflashes showing Hope's face and that of his hostage. If the poor girl's even still alive. I want everyone in France to be on the lookout for this maniac.' He wagged a thick finger at Simon and showed his teeth. 'Meanwhile, Commissioner, you're author-ised to do whatever it takes. Mobilise armed response teams. Stop and search vehicles. Scour the countryside. Man like that, he'll have gone to ground in the woods or holed up in a derelict barn somewhere, planning his next kill. I want you to throw everything we have at the bastard.'

'This is no ordinary fugitive,' Simon said. 'Hope is a product of his training, combined with exceptional ingenuity. Talk to his former military superiors, and they'll tell you he's the best they ever had. Even though he's been years out of the SAS, he still operates like one of them. He travels light and unseen from place to place, using the resources that he finds on the ground. Capturing enemy ordnance and transportation whenever possible, and making use of their communications. He's a guerrilla. Just when you think you're closing on him,

233

he's slipped right through your fingers and he's miles away. The normal means are hopelessly inadequate.'

There was a lull as the whole room stared at Simon. 'What are you saying?' Saunier asked numbly. 'That he *can't* be caught? How is that possible?'

'He can be caught,' Simon said. 'We just have to understand the way he thinks.'

'I hope to God,' the minister said, 'that you're going to tell us *you* do?'

Simon paused. 'Here's what I propose, gentlemen.'

Chapter Thirty-Six

When Ben bobbed slowly back up to the surface and opened his eyes, the first thing he saw was the bad watercolour landscape on the wall by the bed. The second thing he saw was a figure crossing the room. He blinked, still not fully awake, reality slowly returning. It wasn't Luc Simon come to arrest him, two armed Interpol heavies guarding the door and more waiting outside in a car to whisk him away in manacles and leg irons. It was a female figure. Silvie. He watched her cross the room, backlit by the rectangle of bright sunlight that shone through the window. She was fresh from the shower, wrapped in a towel that covered her from chest to mid-thigh. Her hair was dark with moisture and loose over her shoulders. She walked to the window, checked outside with a cautious glance, saw that all was quiet and then padded barefoot back to the bathroom to finish getting dried off.

Ben could see her holstered Glock flung carelessly down among the pile of clothes on the other bed. She hadn't looked at it once.

Trust me.

He yawned and propped himself up on one elbow, then swung his legs off his bed and planted his feet on the floor, leaned forward with his elbows on his knees and ruffled his hair, rubbed his face and yawned again. He looked at his watch. Nearly quarter to one in the afternoon. He'd napped far longer than he'd meant to.

Moments later Silvie came back, this time with her hair wrapped in a smaller towel and wearing a motel bathrobe.

'You should have woken me sooner,' he said.

'I didn't have the heart to. You were out for the count. Sleeping like a little boy.'

'Thanks a million.'

'Besides, I can't have a partner stumbling about in a daze. We have work to do.'

He craved coffee. The room came complete with a jug kettle and a few sachets of instant stuff that barely qualified, but it would do. 'What about you?' he asked her. 'Catch some rest?'

She shrugged, bending over the other bed and tossing her gun to one side as she snatched up pieces of clothing. 'A little. Then I went out to get some things. There's a Carrefour up the road.'

'That's tactically smart,' he said. 'Last I heard, hostages don't generally walk around free. Or go off shopping in a hot car.'

'Relax. I told the receptionist my phone battery was dead, asked her very sweetly to call me a taxi, for which I paid cash out of your little bundle. That's a lot of money you're carrying around.'

'Spoils of war,' he said, standing up and heading for the table where the kettle was.

'I won't ask,' she said. 'But it came in useful. I got us some more food, if you're hungry. Got you some clothes, too.' She pointed at a plastic bag on the floor. 'Fresh jeans and a couple of shirts. Had to guess your size.'

'I've been buying all my own clothes since I left the forces, but thanks anyway.' He reached the table and reached for the kettle to check its water level before turning it on. Then stopped and frowned. 'What's this?' he asked, looking down at the compact laptop computer that was sitting in the middle of the table, wired up to the landline phone socket.

'Oh, I got us that too,' she said nonchalantly, unwrapping the towel from her hair. It fell loose and thick over her shoulders and face, curling and lightening as it dried. It looked good. He could smell the apple scent of the shampoo she'd washed it with.

'Why do we need a bloody computer?' he asked. Perhaps he wasn't wide awake yet, but it seemed like the strangest thing to him. Seven months living in a monastery, he'd almost managed to forget the abominable things existed.

'You're so old school,' she said. 'Everyone else has them, including the opposition, so why shouldn't we? They're kind of essential equipment now, you know?'

Ben shook the kettle, felt the slosh of water inside, thought about rinsing it out and topping it up with fresh but couldn't be bothered, turned it on and ripped open three sachets of instant coffee and emptied them into a cup. She was only fifteen years younger than him, but she was making it feel like thirty.

'Besides,' she said, 'I've been thinking over what we talked about. Secrets and ghosts. I couldn't get out of my head that maybe what Streicher knew about the monastery is key to understanding what he's really up to. So while you were sleeping I ran a few internet searches based on simple keywords: the name of the monastery, the blind guy Streicher talked about, the mass grave you found.'

Ben poured hot water into his cup and stirred the contents up into a brown goo that vaguely resembled coffee. 'Waste of time,' he said. 'Why is it that everyone under the age of

237

thirty seems to think all the mysteries of the world can be solved on Google?' He took a slurp of the scalding liquid and pulled a face at the taste of it.

'Well, as it happens I didn't do so badly,' she said. 'I turfed up this guy called Jehan de Roucyboeuf. Ever hear of him?'

Ben gulped down more of the coffee-surrogate and looked at her. 'Any particular reason why I should have?'

'He was a chronicler in fourteenth-century France,' she said. 'One of these itinerant scribes who used to go around writing about stuff they observed. Because so few people were literate in those days, the chronicles have actually become one of the most important sources for modern historians. Anyway, it so happens that this Jehan de Roucyboeuf's writings tell, among other things, the story of what happened to Salvator l'Aveugle. Of course it's all in medieval French, which is almost like another language.' She raised an eyebrow. 'Interested?'

'Spellbound,' he said, and took another slurp.

'My, we *are* a grumpy one in the morning. You will be. Turns out Salvator was a friar who was travelling through France with the ultimate goal of joining the Franciscan monastery founded in Jerusalem in the 1340s by Roger Guérin of Aquitaine. The writer doesn't say much about that, but I can fill in the blanks for us.'

Ben scowled at her. 'I see, so you're some kind of historian now.'

Silvie grinned back at him. 'Top of my class at the Sorbonne. It was my first degree, before I studied law. And what Roucyboeuf says is dead right. Guérin did succeed, after a lot of negotiations and using funds provided by the King and Queen of Naples, in purchasing the Cenacle. You know, the room where the Last Supper was held?'

'You're not the only one who's been to college,' Ben said. 'I am aware of what the Cenacle is.'

'He also bought enough land around the holy site to set up a new Christian community there. Even though Jerusalem was occupied by the Egyptian Mamluk sultanate, political relations with the Christian West were favourable enough to allow it.'

'All right,' Ben said irritably, 'so please tell me why this should possibly matter to us.'

'Because it supports the integrity of Roucyboeuf's chronicle,' she replied. 'It's important for us to verify it checks out historically, since some of these old sources can be wildly off the mark when it comes to factual accuracy. The chronicle tells us that Salvator never made it to the Holy Land. In fact, he never even made it out of France. After becoming ill and taking refuge in a mountain village in the Alps near Briançon, he fell foul of church authorities, was eventually accused of all kinds of devil worship and witch-craft, and was sentenced to death by burning.'

'Nice.'

'According to the chronicle, the key evidence for his condemnation by the authorities was the seizures that would make him fall to the ground, writhing and speaking in tongues.' She snorted. 'Sure sign of demonic possession, naturally.'

'I get it,' Ben said. 'Epilepsy. A lot of sufferers got a raw deal back in those days. Fear and superstition are a powerful combination.'

'But reading between the lines, his medical condition just gave his accusers a handy pretext for getting rid of him,' Silvie said. 'The real reason for his execution was that he was outspoken against the Church and highly vocal about the papacy, which at that time wasn't centred in Rome but

239

in France, in Avignon. Salvator was a Franciscan, meaning he was sworn and devoted to a life of poverty in Christ, and it's little wonder he nursed grievances against the religious establishment. The pope at that time, Clement VI, loved luxury and high living, and issued a papal bull in 1343 to justify his use of indulgences. Meaning, basically, cash for forgiveness. The Avignon papacy was notoriously corrupt, selling everything from remission from sins to high-ranking ecclesiastical office. Even holy relics were for sale to the highest bidder, to keep the senior church authorities in the luxury to which they were accustomed during this so-called "Babylonian captivity" period of the Church's history.'

'You found all this online in one session?' Ben said, staring at her.

'No, silly. Some of us were paying attention in history class. So, without actually spelling it out, the chronicle tells us that Salvator's burning at the stake was really a political assassination, sanctioned simply to eliminate one of the Church's critics.'

'I'm sure you're right,' Ben said. 'But—'

'Let me go on. Now, according to the chronicle, as the poor man hung there burning alive in front of the church authorities and all the villagers who'd gathered to see him die, he screamed out a terrible curse against them. Do you begin to see?'

The connection clicked like an electrical circuit in Ben's mind.

'You told me that Streicher talked on and on about a curse,' he said.

Chapter Thirty-Seven

Silvie nodded. 'He was obsessed with it. It's something important to him, and now here it is. Salvator l'Aveugle wished for a thousand years of pestilence to descend on his tormentors, the villagers, their children, and all the way down the line, as punishment for what they'd allowed to happen to an innocent man.'

Ben went on drinking the bad coffee as he listened, trying to decide whether this was getting them anywhere.

'Now, these were medieval times,' Silvie said. 'An era of widespread superstition and ignorance, especially in the Christian West, while in the Islamic world and the Far East science and mathematics were light years ahead. Curses and prophecies of doom were ten a penny across Europe back then. People really did fear them, and if by pure coincidence one of them appeared to come true, they were very quick to fall for it wholesale. Like if some clergyman told the people God was angry with them, and the next thing their crops were washed away by a bad storm or blighted by a drought, this would be taken as cast-iron evidence that the clergyman really did have word from the Lord. All about luck and timing.' Silvie smiled grimly. 'And you couldn't ask for better timing than Salvator's curse. I mean, this *was* 1348.'

241

'So what's so special about 1348?' Ben said, not getting it.

'Oh, nothing much,' she said. 'Apart from the fact it was the year that the Black Death first swept through France, taking with it about half the population. Just months after Salvator's curse was still literally ringing in their ears, the people began to drop dead like leaves off a tree. An isolated community, way up in the mountains with little to no contact with the outside world, wouldn't realise that the rest of the country, in fact the whole of Europe, had it just as badly as they did. Easy for them to remember Salvator's words as he burned alive, and to assume the plague was a visitation on them, God's punishment for their sin of colluding in an innocent man's execution. Too late to repent, though, when everyone around you is dying. Some of the local villages died out completely. So did most of the clergymen who'd attended Salvator's execution. Roucyboeuf gives some pretty vivid accounts of the bodies heaped up in mounds, the plague dead being loaded on carts while the living prayed for Divine mercy. They were so overwhelmed by the scale of the disaster and the sheer number of dead and dying, the bishop decreed that the victims should be entombed in a mountain cave beneath the nearby monastery. No prizes for guessing which monastery we're talking about?'

Ben said nothing, just grimly nodded.

'Not just the dead, but the living, too,' Silvie went on. 'Anyone thought to be infected was taken and thrown in alive with the hundreds of corpses. No mention of them being chained up, but it figures, doesn't it? Afterwards, the cave was walled up and became a mass tomb. Anybody left alive inside would have died a slow, agonising death.'

Ben put down his unfinished coffee and tried not to think too hard about what it must have been like for them down there. In the pitch darkness. The stench of the dead all around them. The squeak and scuttle of the rats. The moans of the dying and the weeping of those awaiting the same inescapable fate.

'The chronicle goes on to tell the story of Eloise,' Silvie said. 'She was the leader of a group of heroic nuns who had been trying to help the sick, and who for their troubles were taken and walled up along with them. The legend tells how Eloise's screams could still be heard echoing down the mountainside long after the mouth of the cave was sealed up.'

Every place has its secrets from the past. Even here, some things remain that ought to be forgotten. Ben remembered Père Antoine's words. So this was the shameful episode in local history that the old monk had been so unwilling to reveal. It explained why he'd become cagey when Ben asked about the walled-up crypt. It explained the scores or even hundreds of men, women and children whose bones Ben had discovered under the monastery.

But it still didn't explain everything. Far from it. All it did was open the door to more questions.

'Not a bad morning's research, hmm?' Silvie said.

'It's a start,' Ben said. 'As far as Streicher's concerned, it doesn't take us anywhere.'

'I don't agree. It has to mean something, if we can just figure it out. We know he was obsessed with the curse.'

'But we don't know why,' Ben said. 'Why would that be his reason for launching a raid on the monastery all these centuries later? What's the connection with the gold? Did the chronicle mention anything about that?'

'Nothing,' she admitted.

'None of it makes sense,' he said. 'Why would the church authorities seal hundreds of plague victims inside their own treasure vault, knowing they were sealing off their gold with it?'

243

She shrugged. 'Maybe they didn't know it was there.'

'In which case, Streicher couldn't have known about it either. Not from the story of Blind Salvator, and not from the writings of this Jehan what's-his-name?'

'Maybe there's more in the chronicle,' Silvie said. 'Something that we're missing.'

'You said you read the whole thing.'

'Just what's viewable online,' she said. 'There could be more of it that isn't yet digitised. France has an awful lot of history. We're still working on the National Archives. It's a big task that will take years, decades even. Meanwhile, there are still hundreds of kilometres of shelves of original ancient documents that can only be accessed physically, in person.'

He looked at her, sensing her intention. 'We'd have to travel to Paris,' he said.

'So?'

'So Streicher is in Switzerland,' Ben said.

'This could be the key to understanding his plan.'

'Or it could be a complete blind alley,' he said. 'What are you doing?'

'Looking up a number,' she said, stepping quickly over to the laptop and flipping up the lid. The screen flashed into life. She clicked a few keys. 'French Ministry of Culture website. Contact details for the Archives Nationales centre in the Marais, in Paris. Here we go.' She picked up the phone from the table, dialled the code for an outside line and quickly punched in the number from the screen.

'I'm going for a shower,' Ben said, and let her get on with making the call as he grabbed the bag of fresh clothes and headed for the bathroom. He could hear her talking as he locked himself in. The tiles and mirror were still steamed up from Silvie's shower earlier. He undressed quickly, letting his dirty clothes fall to the floor. He turned the water up high, and as he waited for it to come to temperature he inspected his bruises. They were still livid, but less tender now. His hands hurt worse, and there were still a few bits of grit embedded in his palms. He stepped under the hot water and spent ten minutes blasting away the last of his weariness.

After his shower, he opened up the bag of fresh clothing and found that Silvie had also bought a pack of disposable razors and a can of shaving foam. He rubbed a squiggle with his finger in the condensation in the mirror above the sink, and gazed at himself. His burned cheek was red and felt a little tight. It would look worse before it looked better. There wasn't a lot he could do about the patch of singed hair, either. But after washing away the last of the grease stains from his face and a careful shave, he decided that, all in all, he wasn't looking too terrible. The clothes fitted him well, too. Silvie had a good eye.

When he walked back into the bedroom he found her dressed and sitting on the bed. Her hair was brushed and hanging loose down her back. 'Hey, look at you,' she said. 'You don't clean up too badly.'

He grunted. 'Your phone call didn't last long.'

'It certainly didn't,' she said. 'I used my credentials to get through to the head curator of the archives. Had him look up the chronicles of Jehan de Roucyboeuf, asked if they were available to view in their entirety. He was very helpful and efficient.'

'And?'

She sighed. 'And then he told me I couldn't view them. Simply not possible.'

'Too old?' he asked. 'Too fragile to expose to the air? Too valuable to handle?'

'They're missing,' she said. 'Listed as stolen during a

break-in last April. Two nightwatchmen had shotguns stuck in their faces and were tied up and hooded while a gang of raiders ransacked a section of the archives. And guess what? Nothing else was taken. It was a targeted robbery. The cops have nothing. No clues, no suspects.'

'Looks like someone else was interested in the same thing we were,' Ben said.

'Streicher,' Silvie said. 'Got to be. I told you, there's something about all this. The chronicle forms part of his plans. I just wish I knew what, and how.'

'If it does,' Ben said, 'we've hit a wall. There's nothing more we can learn for the moment. Let's get out of here. You're going to take me to the Lausanne safe house.'

'All the way to Switzerland in a stolen car?' she said.

'We have enough cash to buy another.'

She shook her head. 'Not from a legitimate dealer, not without a paper trail. We'll have to go searching for some backstreet chop-shop that'll take your cash in exchange for a hunk of unroadworthy shit that's liable to break down on the motorway and draw all kinds of the wrong attention.'

'All right, partner,' he said. 'What do you suggest instead?'

'I say we play to our strengths here,' Silvie said. 'Nobody expects a kidnapper and their hostage to walk about in the open. They expect us to move furtively, unseen, probably by night and in stolen cars or vans, with me trussed up out of sight in the back.'

'And our strengths are?'

'Like I said before, that we're just a regular couple going about their business. We're closer to Grenoble than we are to Briançon. We could get a train from there and be in Lausanne in a couple of hours.'

'Tactically unwise to be seen in public,' Ben said. 'It's taking a risk.'

She smiled. 'And that's something you would never do?'

For the second time that day Silvie worked her charms on the motel receptionist, who was persuaded to drag herself away from the TV to call up the local taxi service. As they waited for the cab, Ben moved the Toyota pickup and left it discreetly half-hidden right around the back of the motel, next to a row of garbage bins where it didn't look at all out of place. The taxi driver turned up moments later, a cheery guy with a big overhanging gut, who loaded their luggage in the back of his Mercedes, commenting on the weight of the holdall and perfectly oblivious to what it contained. Ben returned the room key and settled the bill with Rollo's cash. Then they took off in the direction of Grenoble.

Five minutes after they'd gone, the motel receptionist was bored with the comedy show she was watching. She idly reached for the remote control and surfed from channel to channel in search of something more exciting. Click. A romantic movie, two dead film stars kissing. Click. A Japanese cartoon about giant monsters battling it out. Click. A cereal advert featuring a toothy kid with a spoon in his mouth. Click. A newsflash, some big deal going on with a senior police officer looking serious and faces of wanted fugitives popping up on-screen. Click. A prehistoric *Starsky & Hutch* rerun, with pistols popping and big barge-like American cars screeching around the littered streets of Bay City, California.

Then she stopped, and frowned, and clicked back a step to catch the tail end of that newsflash, and frowned again, and her eyes opened wide.

'*Merde*,' she said out loud.

The couple from room twenty were on TV.

Chapter Thirty-Eight

When they reached the railway station in Grenoble, Ben paid and generously tipped the driver with more of Rollo's useful cash. Then he and Silvie made their way to the platforms. The only train going in the right direction was due to depart at 3.45 that afternoon. Its destination fell sixty kilometres short of theirs, terminating in Geneva. Lausanne was just a short bus trip beyond, nestled between the shores of Lake Geneva and the Swiss Alps.

Ben paid cash for two tickets. Right on time, the long train rumbled and clattered up to the platform and halted with a hiss of airbrakes. They boarded the fourth carriage from the front, grabbing a pair of facing window seats with a table, and Ben stashed the heavy holdall and the green bag in the rack overhead. The train began to fill up around them. Most of the passengers were tourists, huffing and straining red-faced as they dragged their bulky cases and rucksacks down the aisle, manhandling them into the luggage racks, checking their reservations, fussing over seat numbers, arguing about who got to sit by the window, fiddling with their electronic gadgets the instant they were seated as if unable to resist the siren song of technology for more than a couple of minutes at a time. Ben saw a guard stride down the platform. Heard the old-fashioned whistle signalling that the automatic doors were about to close. Then the carriage vibrated gently underfoot as the engines powered up, he felt the familiar heave and stretch of the couplings as they took up the strain, and the train began to pull out of the station.

Silvie sat on the edge of her seat with her elbows on the table and her loose chestnut-coloured hair framing her face, gazing out of the window at the sunny white-capped mountains as they left Grenoble behind, rocking gently to the muted clatter of wheels on tracks. Ben ignored the picturesque view. He was thinking more about what they could expect to find at the end of the line.

'Fifteen of you met up at the rendezvous before the raid,' he said, keeping his voice low so that only she could hear him over the noise of the train. 'Twelve in the cars, plus Streicher and his girlfriend, plus the artic driver. Correct?'

She nodded. 'So,' Ben said, 'minus two dead men, Breslin and Dexter, makes thirteen. Minus you makes twelve.'

'Streicher, Hannah Gissel and ten of the loyal,' she said. 'But he's got the money to take on all the help he wants, whenever it suits him. There could be more, I can't possibly say.' She gave Ben a look. 'And they're all going to be armed to the teeth. Told you it'd be dangerous. Are you having second thoughts?'

'I'm not worried about myself,' he said. 'I'm worried about you.'

'Thank you, but don't be.'

'Nobody's making you do this. You're free to get off at the next stop. Run back to DGSI. Tell Interpol you gave me the slip.'

'Like that guy Simon would believe me.' She smiled briefly, then looked serious again. 'Anyway, I thought we already had this discussion.'

'We did,' Ben said. 'But in my experience it's a discussion you can't have often enough. There are potential negative outcomes here that should be carefully considered.'

She cocked an eyebrow. 'Meaning one of us might not make it out.'

'Two against twelve or more. It's a possibility. As is neither of us making it out. Either is more likely to happen than coming away with a zero casualty rate against big odds like that. So, I'm just saying. The door is open. You can get out before it's too late, go back to your job, home, boyfriend, whatever's back there waiting for you.'

'I broke with him before I went undercover,' she said. 'He was an asshole anyway.'

Ben smiled. 'Fair enough.'

A moment of warmth passed between them. 'You have a nice smile,' she said. 'Should use it more often.'

'When this is over,' he said. 'When Streicher's in the ground. I'll be smiling then.'

'Then what? Do you have someone to go back to? It's strange, I feel like I know you, but I hardly know anything about you.'

'I did have someone. That's all done with now.' After he'd said it, the truth of his words hit him like a punch. It really was over. He went quiet for a moment.

'I'm sorry,' she said.

Ben snapped out of his reverie and looked at her. 'What for? It's not your fault.'

'You want to talk about it?'

'Not really.'

'Okay, fine.'

He breathed out through his nose. 'We were going to get married last year. It almost happened, too. But then, my life has a way of setting obstacles in my path.'

'Doesn't everyone's?' she said. 'It's like war. They say no strategic plan ever survives the first exchange of fire.'

'That's true enough,' he said. 'I should know.'

'I suppose you should,' she said. She paused, then asked, 'So, do you have any family?'

'My parents died a long time ago,' he replied. 'I have a younger sister, Ruth, and a son, Jude. He's nearly twenty-one.'

'Then you were married before?'

He shook his head. 'Long, long story.'

'What does he do, your son?'

'He's back in England. Sort of in between things at the moment.'

'You say that as if you're worried about him,' Silvie said.

'I do worry about him. I'm scared he might end up like me.'

'That doesn't sound so bad,' she said.

'You wouldn't say that if you knew me better. But thanks anyway.' Thinking about his troubles had made Ben's mouth go dry. He reached in his pocket. Took out the bottle that Père Antoine had given him. There was still a little of the tonic left. He uncapped it and sipped some. The taste took him straight back to his time at the monastery.

'What is that?' Silvie asked.

'Kind of an elixir that one of the monks gave me. It's supposed to keep you healthy.'

'Does it?'

'It didn't do him much good,' Ben said.

'May I?' She took the bottle from his hand and uncapped it, sniffed and sipped. 'Tastes metallic,' she said.

'I think it's herbal,' he said. 'Not really sure.'

'Whatever.' She handed it back to him.

They lapsed into silence. The train rattled onwards, fields and the occasional village flashing by. Ben's mind had drifted a long way by the time he left his seat half an hour later and made his way towards the buffet car, lusting after coffee. Getting as bad as Luc Simon, he thought absently as he headed towards the front of the train. They were speeding at full pelt through the French countryside, still forty-five minutes from the Swiss border. He swayed along the aisle, using the headrests of the seats on each side to steady himself.

The buffet car was three carriages to the front, a long metal counter running down the right side and a small kitchen behind, a couple of bar-style stools and a window looking out on the left side of the train. A whole different proposition from British railway catering, offering real food, coffee freshly made from actual coffee beans, and wine that wasn't better employed for stripping paint.

Ben ordered cheese and ham baguettes and a couple of tall cups of coffee. Black for him, cream and sugar for Silvie. As he was paying, he noticed the train slow down, suddenly and quite dramatically. The sharp deceleration made him lurch and forced him to reach out to steady himself against the counter. The buffet car attendant had to do the same and muttered, 'Whoa. Easy there, fellas,' as items swayed and clinked on his shelves.

'Are we coming to a station?' Ben asked him.

The attendant shook his head. 'No, must be something on the line. Some cows got loose on this stretch, couple of months ago. Or could be maintenance works, maybe.'

Ben got his change, picked up his tray. The coffee smelled good. The train slowed down even more, until it ground to a complete halt.

'Weird,' the attendant said. Ben turned and looked out of the window, craning his neck so that he could see the curvature of the train's left flank stretching in a long tail behind. There was no sign of a station, not even of a tiny rural stop. Beyond a few metres of gravelled run-off along the edge of the tracks was a low barrier, and the other side of it a minor road curving parallel with the railway line.

Ben's eyes narrowed and a small voice of alarm inside his head began to grow in volume as he saw the two cars.

Looked as if he wasn't going to get to drink that coffee, after all.

Chapter Thirty-Nine

The cars had pulled up at the edge of the road, one close behind the other, parked facing in the same direction as the stationary train. The car in front was a black Citroën C5 sedan, the one behind a blue Subaru Impreza WRX STI, the high-performance model with the wing on the back to aid rear-end downforce at speed. Both cars were filmed with road dirt. As Ben watched, the doors opened and three men got out of each vehicle. Six men who might as well have had the word COP branded in big letters on their foreheads. Plainclothes detectives, riding in unmarked cars. The Subaru was some kind of high-speed interceptor. The Citroën was probably souped up well above standard specs, too. The men were dressed casually, in jeans and light summer jackets that didn't quite do enough to hide the bulges of concealed weapons. They looked serious. They hadn't stopped for a chat or a cigarette or a quick roadside piss. They were walking straight towards the train, and the train manager had got out and walked down the length of the carriages to meet them. The cops flashed badges at him. There was a lot of talking and pointing. It was clear that the train had been officially ordered to a halt via radio, as a matter of urgency.

And Ben knew why.

The little voice was screaming inside his head now. He

abandoned the tray on the counter and hurried back the way he'd come. Through the next carriage and the next one after that, able to move faster now that the train was standing still. Passengers were looking around them, wondering what was happening. Through the windows Ben saw the six cops split up into three pairs. Two men headed for the centre of the train, two went running towards the back and the third pair ran towards the front. The doors opened, the whole length of the train. Ben was hustling quickly from the third carriage to the fourth as the two men at the front end of the train boarded the third carriage in his wake. He had a short head start on them but knew they'd immediately start sweeping back towards him, while four more of them were combing the carriages from the opposite direction. It was a pincer movement from which Ben and Silvie could escape only if they moved very fast.

'I think this is our stop,' he said as he reached their seats. Silvie was already on her feet, realising that something was wrong. He mouthed, 'We've got company.' Reached up above the seat and hauled down their bags.

'How did—?' she began.

'No time to worry about that now,' Ben said. What Silvie had said before about no battle plan ever surviving the first exchange of fire had been right on the money. But at this moment Ben hadn't even the most sketchy plan in mind, other than the pressing need to get off the train. Where to from there, he had no idea.

Two men in front of them, four behind. Best way to go was forward. He led the way, jostling down the aisle with the heavy bags. At the end of the fourth carriage the connecting door slid open with a hydraulic whoosh to let them through to the open outer door on the left side of the train. At the same moment, Ben saw the two detectives who'd boarded at the front. They were halfway down the third carriage, just metres away through the glass of the connecting door. Their eyes met. A grim look of recognition appeared on the cops' faces. The lead man whipped out a small radio handset. They moved faster. Heads turned. Cries of fear from some of the passengers as it became obvious that a serious situation was developing.

Ben pushed Silvie out through the open exit. It was further to the ground than when the train was pulled up at a platform. She jumped down with a grunt. Ben tossed the bags out after her, followed, hit the ground running and scooped the bags up again.

They ran, but there was nowhere to run to. They were out in the open, totally exposed and visible from the entire length of the train. The gravel run-off was rough and uneven underfoot. Beyond the siding barrier and the road parallel to it were nothing but a thousand metres of open pasture-land, stretching to an upward sweep of pine forest and then to the mountains standing tall in the far distance. There wasn't a building, hiding place or scrap of cover in sight.

Behind them, the two cops burst out of the train and started racing in their direction, the lead man talking urgently on his radio. Thirty metres further down the train's length appeared the second pair of cops, apparently responding to the radio call. Guns drawn, they jumped to the ground and dashed to the lead car, the black Citroën. They piled inside. The car roared into life and took off, speeding up the length of the train. At the same moment, the third pair of cops emerged from one of the rearward carriages and ran for the blue Subaru. It fired up with a throaty exhaust blast, wheels spinning as the driver punched the gas.

The black Citroën overtook the running detectives and

screeched to a halt diagonally in the road, just a few metres behind Ben and Silvie on the other side of the barrier.

Ben stopped running. Escape wasn't an option. Not on foot, heavily laden, with two fast cars in pursuit. He turned. Tore open the zipper on the holdall, pulled out the FAMAS rifle and let both bags fall to the ground. 'Get behind me,' he told Silvie. 'Try to look like a hostage.'

'Ben,' she said urgently. 'Don't hurt anyone. You're not a criminal.'

He flashed a glance at her. No time to reply. He flipped the weapon's fire selector switch to three-shot bursts. Front and right, the Citroën's doors flew open and its occupants piled out, guns drawn. Front and left, the two on foot halted fifteen metres away and raised their pistols in two-handed grips, legs braced, knees bent, the classic combat shooting stance they'd been taught in police academy and maybe had cause to use in real-life confrontations before. Or maybe not. Either way, they looked ready to deliver the goods. Fingers on triggers. Sights lined up squarely on Ben. Screaming at him to drop the weapon.

The blue Subaru squealed to a halt behind the Citroën. The fifth and sixth cops tumbled out and aimed their guns from behind their open doors.

Six against one on open ground with no available cover. Six automatic weapons pointing his way. Escape impossible, capture out of the question. And he wasn't allowed to hurt anyone.

Here we go, he thought.

Chapter Forty

Ben had a mixed attitude towards self-knowledge. In many ways he was a mystery to himself. He often had little clue why he acted the way he did in his everyday life. He'd spent more sleepless nights than he could begin to count, staring up at the dark ceiling and trying to analyse his own behaviour, wondering who he really was, what it was he really wanted from life, where he was going and where he'd end up.

In paradoxical stark contrast were those areas of absolute rock-solid certainty. Aspects of his personality and behaviour that presented no mystery whatsoever. Qualities in himself that he could trust and rely upon with utter confidence and unshakable self-belief. And one of those things was his ability to remain ice-cool and focused in moments of extreme danger that would reduce most men to a mewling sack of jelly. He'd simply been born that way, with a natural ability that his SAS instructors had recognised in their young recruit right from day one, and trained up to off-the-charts levels of perfection even before years of experience had honed and refined it still further. He'd confounded army doctors in medical tests by showing an actual decrease in heart rate and blood pressure during simulated combat situations. At times like these, his mind was able to compress seconds into milliseconds, so that what seemed to a normal person like a sensory overload of frantically speeded-up film, he experienced in frame-by-frame slow motion, allowing him all the time he needed to think and act. Calm and smooth and controlled. Evaluation. Observation. Analysis. Decision. Execution. No stress. No panic.

Not like the six men in whose field of fire he was standing at this moment. Facing an opponent like him had each of them exploding with supercharged nervous tension, a tidal wave of adrenalin threatening to drown them at any instant. He could see it in their bulging eyes and their terror-white faces. This was a first time for them.

He'd evaluated the situation. Now it was time to make his move. Which he did in a heartbeat. He swung the rifle muzzle a few degrees left, pulled the trigger and the FAMAS rattled off a three-shot fully automatic burst that stitched the ground at the feet of Cops One and Two and sent them flying backwards for cover. One of them fell to his knees and scrambled and rolled under the train. The other collapsed on his face as if he was trying to press himself into the gaps in the gravel.

By then the FAMAS muzzle was already swinging to the right and Ben's finger was squeezing another burst out of it. The windscreen of the Citroën crumpled, its side mirrors exploded into shards of plastic and glass. Cops Three and Four dived around the back of the car. Ben paused momentarily to flip the fire selector switch to full-auto, pulled the trigger again and held it. The FAMAS spewed a deafening stream of copper-jacketed lead into the Citroën that perforated and crumpled the bodywork like paper and blew out the rest of the windscreen, shredded the plastic radiator grille, blasted the headlights apart. The front left corner of the car sank down on a shredded tyre. Then the right.

Then his gun was empty, the bolt locked back, smoke trickling from the open breech. The cops were cringing behind their cars. Not a single shot fired. Ben stood his ground in the open. Calmly dropped the empty twenty-five-round magazine from his rifle and inserted another from the holdall. Released the bolt with a smack of his palm and fired another sustained burst that chewed up the Citroën's left flank and blew out the rear tyre, weaved a snaking line of bullet strikes up the road and drove Cops Five and Six in a jittery panic away from the cover of their Subaru.

'Weapons on the ground,' he said in a strong, clear voice. The cops barely hesitated. Six clattering sounds, muted in Ben's ears after the heavy gunfire, as their pistols hit the dirt. He swept the rifle muzzle in a ninety-degree arc, left to right, covering them all. 'Out where I can see you. Nice and easy.'

The cop hiding under the train crawled out. The one lying in the gravel pushed himself up on to his knees. The two cringing behind the shattered Citroën emerged tentatively, arms raised submissively, eyes cowed. The two who'd made a break from their Subaru put their hands on their heads and walked slowly back towards the road.

Silvie was staring at Ben as if she'd never seen him before. In the background he faintly registered noises of alarm and chaos from the train as the traumatised passengers witnessed the spectacle taking place.

Ben herded all six cops together into a ragged line next to the train. Keeping the rifle trained on them he collected their fallen weaponry. Five of the cops' pistols were the ubiquitous ugly but functional Glocks. The sixth was an old Browning Hi-Power. Ben's favourite personal defence weapon from years back. He dropped all six in the bag.

'Phones and radios on the ground in front of you,' he

told the cops. 'Drop your trousers. Then get down on your knees.'

Hostile, glowering looks, but no resistance as they obeyed. First the radios and phones. Then they started undoing their belts and unzipping themselves and revealing an array of briefs and boxer shorts. One by one they knelt down gingerly on the stony ground with their trousers around their ankles, furious and humiliated.

Ben jerked the rifle brusquely at Silvie, the way he'd have done with a real hostage. 'You, pick that lot up and put it in the bag,' he commanded, and she nodded and meekly hurried over to collect the mobiles and radio handsets from the ground in front of the line of kneeling officers. She dropped them in the green bag.

'Now get in the car,' Ben told her, motioning towards the blue Subaru. Silvie hurried across to it and got into the passenger seat. The rifle trained on the cops, Ben picked up the holdall and walked over to the Subaru and slung it on to the rear seats. He walked back and did the same with his green bag, then tossed the rifle in after it. Quickly pulled Eriq Sabatier's Beretta from his belt and pointed it at his angry prisoners, in case they got any clever ideas as he stepped around to the open driver's door. The Citroën looked like wreckage from a war zone, but the Subaru was untouched. Exactly as Ben had intended.

He slid in behind the wheel next to Silvie, slammed his door, waved bye-bye to the cops through the window, twisted the key, and the engine burbled into life with a note that promised all the performance he could have wished for. He steered around the remains of the Citroën, then stamped on the accelerator. The Subaru's tyres squealed and spun, then dug in ferociously and the car took off with a roar, pressing them hard into their seats.

'Maybe you'll listen to me next time,' he said to Silvie as they sped away. The immobile train shrank in the mirror, until the road peeled off its parallel course with the railway tracks and Ben threw the Subaru into a series of bends that cut the train from sight.

'Shit,' she said. 'Okay, so that might have been a slight tactical miscalculation on my part.'

Ben fell silent and concentrated on driving. The Subaru was some kind of souped-up police interceptor, all right. The suspension was stiff and responsive, the steering quick and agile. It surged forward aggressively at the slightest touch of the throttle and stayed glued to the road no matter how recklessly he hurled it into the twisty bends. Scenery people would pay to see flashed past the windows in an invisible blur. The throaty roar of the turbocharged engine filled the cockpit.

But not quite loudly enough to drown out the thump of rotor blades overhead. Ben glanced upwards and glimpsed the dark shape of the chopper swooping down on them out of a sky that had been empty moments earlier, GENDARMERIE painted in bold white letters on its fuselage.

'Shit,' Silvie said again.

Chapter Forty-One

Ben nudged the gas a little more forcefully and felt the car draw on its apparently limitless power reserves as the twisting road carried them steeply upwards into mountainous terrain. Using the width of both lanes, he took a racing line through a set of S-bends; then the way ahead opened up into a long straight, with a drop-away view to their right and an upward-sloping rock wall to their left. The road was similar to the one he'd negotiated in the old Belphégor, except now he was tackling it several times faster.

Still the dark shadow of the police helicopter stayed right overhead, pursuing them like a bird of prey descending on a running hare. Ben floored the throttle hard in fourth at over a hundred and seventy kilometres an hour and the Subaru howled and leaped forwards, reeling the horizon in, the road ahead a flickering ribbon disappearing rapidly under their wheels. The shadow of the chopper dropped back momentarily and then crept back up.

'Might be worth fastening your seatbelt,' Ben said to Silvie over the engine roar. She quickly clipped it into place. Unfazed by the wild speed they were doing, she reached behind her into Ben's bag for one of the stolen police radios and checked it, scanning through the channels in the hope of tuning into their communications. She shook her head. 'Radio silence. They know we're listening in.'

Ben said nothing. The speedometer climbed past one-ninety. Two hundred. Two-two-five. About as fast as he had ever driven before, but the chopper was faster. It effortlessly overtook them, just metres above the Subaru's roof, then dropped down to half the altitude so that its skids almost skimmed the road surface and its sleek fuselage blocked out Ben's view through the windscreen. It was a highly dangerous manoeuvre. The slightest touch of the skids on the rushing tarmac and the aircraft would go nose-down into a tumble that would destroy it and the Subaru in a split second. But Ben could see what the pilot's strategy was even before it began to happen. The pilot eased off the throttle and the chopper's swaying tail rotor seemed to come rushing back-wards towards them, forcing Ben to scrub off some of his own speed. Then the pilot would keep throttling off, a progressive stranglehold that wouldn't slacken until they were at a standstill. Whereupon, armed men would come leaping down from the aircraft to arrest them.

No dice.

Ben kept his foot relentlessly down and twisted the wheel hard to the right, throwing the Subaru into a howling swerve that narrowly missed spearing the windscreen on the back of the chopper's right skid. Silvie let out a gasp as they shot through the gap between the low-flying aircraft and the vertiginous drop to their right. One tiny mistake, one twitch, they'd veer straight off the edge taking the flimsy crash barrier with them, and go plunging hundreds of feet to their deaths. The vicious hurricane from the rotors buffeted them as they screamed past. The steering wheel vibrated violently in Ben's clenched fists. He tightened his jaw and kept his eyes front and sped onwards. Felt the car clear the downdraught.

Twisted the wheel to the left and the Subaru swerved away from the edge, straddling the middle of the road at blistering speed with its rear wing just two or three metres from the nose of the pursuing helicopter.

Silvie was clutching the sides of her seat now, eyes screwed shut. The deafening thud of the rotors filled their ears once more as the chopper pilot drew level with them, trying a new tactic: to force them into the rocky left side of the road. The left wing mirror tore away with a loud bang and Ben sawed the wheel to control a wobble. Then, as if sensing the risk, the chopper rose a few metres before swooping back in overhead and attempting to slow them down by blocking the way once more. Twisting left and right in his seat to see past the swaying aircraft, Ben saw a long left curve come flashing towards them. He refused to slow down. Kept the needle steady at one-ninety; then another straight opened up ahead and suddenly there was a high rocky bank hurtling directly towards them as the road disappeared into a tunnel through the mountainside. Ben had time to smile, imagining the look on the pilot's face.

The chopper pulled up into a steep emergency climb, disappearing from view as the car rocketed ahead and roared into the mouth of the tunnel. Ben glanced back and saw no fiery carnage and conflagration in the mirror – the pilot must have managed to clear the slope. The slap of rotors from the hovering aircraft was faintly audible as the car raced through the long, winding tunnel.

Ben knew it was only a temporary reprieve. The chopper could simply wait for them on the other side. If Ben had been running their show, he'd have had the pilot hovering just beyond the end of the tunnel, blocking the whole width of the road and cutting off all chance of escape. Plus, he'd have whatever armed agents were on board already on the ground, ready to intercept and arrest the fugitives at gunpoint. A fail-safe strategy. Not one that he wanted to deal with.

He braked, hard. The speedometer reading dropped like a stone and the car came to a slithering halt.

'What are we doing?' Silvie asked.

'Getting out,' Ben said. He shut off the Subaru's engine. Plucked the key from the ignition and threw open his door.

There was a vehicle coming in the opposite direction, headlights blinking in the tunnel. Moving fast. A low-slung little wedge of a sports car. Ben stepped out of the Subaru, wrenched open the back door and grabbed the FAMAS rifle. Planted himself in the middle of the road, aiming it at the oncoming car. The approaching headlights wobbled. The engine note dropped in pitch and was replaced by the shriek of brakes. The sports car halted a few metres away. A white Peugeot RCZ two-seater convertible with the top down, showroom-shiny. Probably being taken on its maiden voyage by its proud owner, a snappy-looking young guy in a golf cap and designer sunglasses, who was staring in shock at this unexpected turn of events.

'Out of the car,' Ben said, aiming at his chest.

'Wh-what do you mean, out of the car?' the young guy stammered.

'I'm commandeering it,' Ben said, moving around the side. Silvie was already lifting their things out of the Subaru.

'You can't have it,' the guy said.

Ben whipped the golf cap off his head and put it on.

'Hey!'

'On the double now, there's a good chap,' Ben said. He opened the sports car's door and grabbed the guy's arm, hauling him out.

'This is robbery!'

'Call it a swap,' Ben said, tossing him the Subaru keys.

'Now shut your mouth before you start annoying me. And I'll have those sunglasses, too.' He snatched them off the guy's face and put them on. Passed the FAMAS to Silvie, who brandished it menacingly as Ben tossed the bags into the narrow space behind the RCZ's seats. There was a jacket neatly folded on the passenger seat. Probably silk, most likely Italian, undoubtedly expensive. Ben could think of a use for that, too. He got behind the wheel and gunned the engine. Silvie hurried round to the passenger side, flung the rifle in with the bags and piled in next to him and they took off, leaving the guy standing there clutching the keys to the stolen police car.

'That was a little bit mean,' Silvie said as they streaked back in the direction they'd come, her hair streaming in the breeze blowing through the open cockpit.

'I'm a very mean kind of person,' Ben said.

She smiled. 'You don't fool me.'

Chapter Forty-Two

The Peugeot burst out of the tunnel, back into the sunlight. They'd won three minutes, maybe five. The moment the young guy emerged from the other side in the Subaru and was accosted, the cops would be right back on them and they'd know exactly what they were looking for. Ben spotted a minor junction on the left that they'd blazed past earlier without seeing. He threw the nimble little sports car into it; the narrow road snaked steeply downwards.

'Sorry if you got a scare back there,' he said.

'That was nothing,' said Silvie.

'You had your eyes shut.'

'I did not.'

Within less than two kilometres they were descending into thick pine forest. Ben looked up. The trees formed a canopy overhead that would shield them effectively from watchers in the air. Another two kilometres and he took another junction that led down a single-track country lane with passing places every few hundred metres, alternating right and left. No sign of anyone following them, either by road or by air. That was good news, and he intended to keep it that way. He pulled up in the next passing place and hauled his bulging green bag out from the space behind the seats. The little car's engine idled in a civilised purr. He dumped the heavy bag on his lap, leaned it against the steering wheel and opened it up.

'Now what?' she asked.

'Not much point in depriving the enemy of their communications if they can use them to track us,' he said, rooting around inside. With six more fully loaded handguns to add to their arsenal, plus the money and the gold bar acting as ballast in the bottom of the strained canvas, the bag was getting pretty full. His fingers felt a familiar shape and he took out the Browning Hi-Power that he'd removed from one of the cops. Ben was no gun worshipper, but the Browning was an old friend from days gone by. Its shape, weight and balance fitted his hand like an extension of his arm after the countless hours of training he and it had put in together. It was good to feel one again. He slipped it in his pocket.

Then he sifted out the small collection of phones and radio handsets they'd captured from the cops and laid them in a row on the dashboard. He checked the radios. Still no activity. He flung each in turn high over the windscreen of the open-top Peugeot, watched it arc down and hit the road and bounce and break apart into shattered fragments of brittle plastic and circuit board. That left the phones. He smashed one, two, three, four. The road ahead was littered with debris.

'I'm sure there's a more environmentally friendly way to dispose of those,' Silvie said.

Ben just grunted. He picked up the fifth phone and was about to send it hurtling along the same destructive parabola as the others, when it started to ring shrilly in his fist. He stared at it, wondering who the hell could be calling.

'Should we answer it?' Silvie said.

Ben hesitated. It was just some cop's phone. Could be

the guy's wife calling, to remind him to pick up groceries on the way home from work, or to tell him the washing machine had started leaking, or the cat was sick again. Then again, it could be someone who knew he had the phone now. Someone in the loop. With something specific and important to say.

Ben hit the reply button and pressed the phone to his ear, waited for the caller to speak. He wasn't too surprised when he heard who was at the other end.

'We can't go on like this,' Luc Simon's voice said in his ear. He sounded harried and demoralised, as if he'd just received news of what had happened back there at the railway line.

'I can,' Ben said. 'For as long as it takes. If a hundred more of your goons have to end up stripped to their undies for Joe Public's entertainment, then that's what'll happen.'

'You're a loose cannon, Ben. I have a serious job to do, and you're not making it any easier. It's distracting my people from the main issue at hand and diverting resources that could be far better used elsewhere.'

'I could say the same,' Ben said. 'Last thing I needed was your Keystone Cops getting under my feet.'

'Then we agree that it has to end, for everyone's sake. Before this gets ugly.'

'I didn't hurt anyone,' Ben said. 'I hope you appreciate that.'

'But someone will get hurt. It's only a question of time. Help me stop this thing now, while it's still possible.'

'Are we negotiating?' Ben asked.

'I'm open to reasonable suggestions.'

'Such as?'

'Well, for a start, such as you agreeing to abandon this reckless course and releasing Agent Valois into the hands of

270

the authorities. In return for which, I'll agree to hold the dogs off as long as I possibly can. Give you time to disappear.'

'Like a sporting chance? Close your eyes and count to ten to give me a head start?'

'A count of ten would be more than a man like you needs.'

'I thought I could run but I couldn't hide? I thought the long arm of the law would reach out and scoop me up, wherever I went?'

Luc Simon chuckled. 'Well, you know how it is. That kind of talk usually intimidates people into giving themselves up. You can't blame me for trying.'

'Problem is,' Ben said, 'running and hiding isn't my thing. And I have a job to take care of.'

'Then let's deal,' Simon replied. 'We have a common objective. We both want Streicher. I know we have different approaches to achieving that goal. I want to see him brought to justice through the official channels and locked away for a very, very long time. You have something . . . shall we say . . . more permanent in mind.'

'That's for sure,' Ben said.

'But maybe we can worry about the details later. Leave our differences aside for now. In the meantime, we can work together. Call a truce. Pool our resources and our skills, instead of pitting them against each other.'

'Which would naturally involve me giving myself up at the nearest police station and cooling my heels in a cell until the government boys come for me.'

'Inevitably, that would have to be the first step.'

'Doesn't sound like much of a deal so far,' Ben said. 'And then what?'

'Arrangements could be made. Unofficially speaking. Wouldn't you rather be an accredited law-enforcement official than a fugitive?'

Ben smiled and shook his head. 'What are you trying to say, Luc? You want to pin a tin star on me? Deputise me, like in the Wild West?'

'There are ways and means,' Simon said. 'I have more influence than you perhaps realise.'

'You still haven't even told me what Streicher means to you people. Must be something pretty big, to be kept from DGSI undercover agents. What did he do . . . snatch a compromising photo of the French President snorting lines of coke with a couple of prostitutes?'

'You'll be fully briefed once you're on board. We can come up with a suitably euphemistic title for you. Advisory Consultant, or something.'

'I don't do advisory.'

'All right, then we could work out a better compromise.'

'I don't do much of that either,' Ben said. 'And the fact of the matter is, Luc, I don't really give a damn what Streicher's done that's such a big deal to you people. I know what he's done to my friends, and that's enough for me.'

Simon sighed. 'Play the game, my friend. There are checks and balances. There are rules. Even you have to respect those.'

'I have my own rules,' Ben said. 'You want co-operation from me? Then call off the heat and leave me alone to get on with this, my way. Carte blanche. No comebacks.'

'So I just sit back and give you free rein to devastate half of Europe, is that the idea?'

'Who said anything about half?' Ben said. 'Maybe just a third.'

'You're crazy. No chance.'

'Then no deal,' Ben said, and threw the phone. It flew up high in an arc and dropped and hit the road and smashed apart.

'That's one way to end a conversation,' Silvie said.

'Let's go,' Ben said, and slammed the RCZ into gear.

The road kept winding ever downwards, until they reached a small village filled with the kind of Alpine chalets that appear on postcards. 'Next right,' Silvie said, pointing. 'There's a bus.'

The silver tour coach was pulled up at a stop, its big diesel idling, indicator flashing. The name of a Swiss travel company emblazoned on its side. Ben parked behind it, killed the engine, and they climbed out of the car.

'You think it might be travelling our way?' Silvie said.

'We don't have much choice in any case,' he replied. He took off his leather jacket, stuffed it in his bag and put on the Italian silk one in its place. It was tailored for a scrawnier frame and too tight around the shoulders, as well as a bad clash with the cap he was wearing. But he was more concerned about disguising himself than about scoring fashion points. He discreetly stuffed the FAMAS into the holdall, zipped it up, and the two of them made a run for the coach before it pulled away from the stop.

'Heading over the border?' Ben asked the driver.

'All the way up to Lausanne,' the driver replied with a beaming smile. 'Due in at eight o'clock this evening.'

'Got room for two more?'

'Plenty. Hop aboard.'

Chapter Forty-Three

The coach finally rumbled into the main bus station in Lausanne just after eight o'clock that evening. Ben and Silvie kept their heads down and waited for the rest of the passengers to disembark before grabbing their bags and following in their wake.

Lausanne looked like a hillier version of Paris, without the grime. 'First priority is some walking-around money,' Ben said as they stepped out into the neat, clean streets. Their stacks of euros were useless in Switzerland, but in the nation of banks it wasn't long before they found a Bureau de Change still open, where they exchanged a fat wad of Rollo's greasy, well-thumbed and disreputable-looking cash for a bundle of crisp Swiss francs that looked and smelled as if they'd been printed that morning. From the change office they walked to a nearby taxi stand and bundled their gear into the first one in the line, which was a green and black Mercedes estate. One day, Ben thought, he was going to get a ride in a taxi in Europe that wasn't a Mercedes Benz.

'Where to?' the driver asked, eyeing them in the mirror.

'I'm not sure,' Silvie said. Both Ben and the driver looked at her in surprise. 'It's not like I could just wander freely about,' she explained to Ben. 'I was the newbie. I was on a tight leash. I don't know the house number, not even the street name.'

'You drove from there.'

'Breslin drove. In the dark.' Turning to the driver, she said, 'Can you take us to the cathedral, please?'

'Why the cathedral?' Ben asked her as the car took off.

'I could see the tips of the spires from the window,' she said. 'The place is probably no more than a kilometre or so away from there, as the crow flies. I'll know it when I see it, trust me.'

A quick mental calculation told Ben that the house could be anywhere within a circle six kilometres around the cathedral. Given a rough population density of around three thousand people per square kilometre, the circle would encompass the homes of about nine thousand citizens. Say four thousand properties. He could only hope she'd pinpoint the safe house more precisely when they got there.

As twelfth-century Gothic cathedrals went, Ben thought that Lausanne's was a disappointment. Perched on a hillside overlooking part of the city, it was bland and half-draped in scaffolding and plastic and surrounded by anodyne, uninspiring buildings. A little too sterile for his taste. A little too Swiss. It was no Notre-Dame de Paris, that was certain. But if he was looking to be impressed, it was more by Silvie's orienteering skills. 'Well?' he asked as the taxi pulled up in the Place de la Cathédrale. The driver was watching expectantly in the mirror.

'Hold on,' she said, getting out of the car. She set off down the curving slope of the road, peering to left and right.

The driver was drumming his fingers impatiently on the wheel and looking as if he was about to start whining about being kept waiting. 'How much do you earn on a good day?' Ben asked him. The answer sounded like a lot of money.

The guy must either hustle hard for at least twelve straight hours or he was lying outright, but Ben didn't hesitate to reel the notes off his crisp wad of Swiss francs, wave them at the guy in the mirror and pass half of them over. 'The rest when we're done, okay? Now wait there.'

He climbed out and followed Silvie down the hill. A panoramic slice of the city of Lausanne, about seventy degrees wide, was visible from their high vantage point. Hundreds of rooftops crammed together, thousands of windows, a packed huddle of sloping angles and chimneys and towers and tall yellow cranes and little churches and tiny cobbled squares. A road bridge cut across the foreground, signposted Pont Bessières. Silvie waited for a gap in the traffic and ran across to the other side.

Ben followed. She'd reached the iron railing and was leaning against it, scanning slowly left to right, scrutinising the view through narrowed eyes, trying to get her bearings. The look of uncertainty on her face disappeared and she pressed her lips together, nodding. 'Down there,' she said, pointing. 'That's it.'

Ben wasn't sure which of a hundred clustered old houses she could be pointing at, but he had to trust her judgement. He looked back over his shoulder, measuring the line of sight and estimating that the tops of the white cathedral spires should just about be visible from the distant windows. 'Our guy will know the way,' he said.

Which their guy did, now entirely happier with the situation and looking forward to collecting the second half of his easy money. They drove over Pont Bessières, crossing the city in a sweeping clockwise quarter-circle that would eventually carry them round to the district Silvie had pointed out. The taxi sped down streets and boulevards, past upmarket cafés and restaurants and Persian rug merchants and jewellers and fashion boutiques. Big, ostentatious names like Yves St Laurent and Louis Vuitton and Chanel and Rolex flashed up all over the place, but most buildings they saw seemed to be banks. It appeared as if the city council had organised death squads to patrol the streets and shoot litter droppers and graffiti artists on sight. Too sanitised. Too damn Swiss. Now and then they caught glimpses of Lake Geneva through the gaps between buildings, as big as an ocean, glittering in the evening sunshine.

Away from the centre, the taxi took them deep into a web of narrower streets where tall old-fashioned shuttered buildings loomed close together on either side. Silvie perched in the middle of the rear seat, leaning forward through the gap between the front seats and directing the driver left, right, left again. Finally she said, 'Here it is. This is the street. The house is down there, just around the next bend.'

They got the driver to stop eighty yards short of the place. 'We might be a while here,' Ben told him. 'Maybe an hour, maybe more, maybe less. You sit tight.'

The driver had no problems with that. He had his radio, his cigarettes and a paper to read. Ben said nothing about the possibility of the quiet street erupting into a violent firefight sometime in the next few minutes. He could only hope the guy wouldn't just scram at the first sign of trouble.

Ben lifted the green bag out of the back of the Mercedes while Silvie handled the holdall. They exchanged nods and started walking down the street. He looked at her. He could see the edginess in her step and in her face and knew her heart was thumping fast, but she was doing a fine job of containing it.

'Thanks,' he said.

'For what?'

'For being on my side.'

She smiled. 'Just being a good little hostage.'

'Best I've ever had,' he said.

'Then you're still glad you didn't have to shoot me?'

'You don't have to come in,' he said. 'Things could get hairy in there.'

'That's the whole point of having someone on your side, isn't it?' she said.

Ben took out a Gauloise and his Zippo, and lit up. The evening gloom was slowly beginning to fall, lights coming on one by one in the windows of the neighbouring houses. The street was empty. No traffic. Streicher's safe house was sixty metres on, all in darkness. Which could have been as much of a strategic precaution as a sign that the place was empty. If they ventured much closer to the front entrance, they risked being easily spotted by anyone lurking behind those unlit windows.

'What are your thoughts on how we do this?' she asked.

'We get as close as we can without being seen,' Ben said. 'Then we find a way in and kill everyone who tries to stop us. With any luck, then we get to Streicher. Then we kill him too.'

'That simple,' she said.

'Probably not,' he replied. 'What are yours?'

'I don't know. Seems quiet,' she said. 'Aside from Breslin's Nissan there's usually at least one vehicle parked outside, more often two or three. One of the black Range Rovers we used to cross the border, or the white BMW with the dented right wing. That one's Torben Roth's. But I can't see anything. Maybe they're parked around the back.'

'You can get around the back?' Ben said.

She nodded, pointed to a gap between the buildings, forty yards down on the left. 'Through that alleyway.'

'That's our way in,' Ben said.

278

The bare-brick alley was one place the anti-graffiti death-squad patrols obviously hadn't inspected. It was just wide enough for a single car to squeeze down, until it opened up into a distinctly un-Swiss no-man's-land with tufted weeds, litter and building rubble and a row of big-wheeled garbage bins. A rickety fence ran along the back yards of the houses.

'No vehicles,' she observed.

'Doesn't make the place empty,' Ben said. 'Not with that many of them living there.' He motioned to Silvie to dump the holdall. He dropped the green bag to the ground next to it and crouched down. Unzipped the holdall and lifted out the FAMAS rifle and Omar's Kalashnikov AK-47. 'Can you handle one of these?' he asked her.

'Like a violin,' she said, taking the AK-47 from him. He watched her slim, small hands flit smoothly over the controls, extending the folding stock into place, dropping out the curved magazine to check it, snicking it cleanly back into the receiver, racking in a round, flicking on the safety.

'You know how to sweep a house out?'

'Please,' she said. 'Think I haven't been on raid duty before?' Her breathing was coming slightly faster as the pre-operational adrenalin kicked in. He tossed her one of the Glocks from the green bag, and she caught it and stuffed it into her jeans waistband, behind the right hip. Ben took one for himself, as a backup to supplement the Browning Hi-Power that was already nestling under his belt. Finally, he switched the part-used magazine of the FAMAS for a fully loaded one, clicked it firmly home with a slap of his palm and cocked the bolt. They were as tooled up as they could reasonably be. Four weapons, eighty-six rounds of ammunition between them.

He flicked away his cigarette stub. 'Last chance to change your mind.'

'Get fucked,' she said, and grinned at him.

Chapter Forty-Four

They broke in through the back door. Ben felt the flimsy
lock give under the pressure of his shoulder. He stood back
with the rifle shouldered, safety off, and counted *one – two
– three*. No alarm or sudden yelling voices from inside. No
twelve-gauge shotgun blast from the hallway. Nothing. He
kicked the door open wider and marched into the murky
hallway with Silvie one step behind.

It was one of those townhouses that are narrow from side
to side, but deceptively deep and tall, on three floors with
a converted attic at the top. They swept through the ground
floor first, turning on lights as they went, covering each
other at every entrance. Back hall, living room, dining room,
kitchen, utility room, front hall, a downstairs shower room
with cracked tiling and a dripping tap. The place felt cold
and empty. There was no smell of cooking in the kitchen,
no crockery or cutlery lying about, no lingering coffee aroma
in the air, none of the subtle effects of human presence that
Ben's sharp instincts had been trained to detect. But those
same instincts told him never to trust an empty house until
he'd covered every square inch.

He led the way up the stairs, rifle at his shoulder, finger
on the trigger, senses fully alert. There were no guns poking
into the stairwell. At the head of the stairs, he motioned to

Silvie to go left, while he went right. Doorway to doorway, moving silently, nudging open the door to one empty first-floor room after another. Nobody in any of them. Beds had been stripped. Wardrobes and shelves laid bare. The place was cheaply and minimally furnished, as if most of the stuff had been picked up in second-hand or junk shops. Streicher might be a wealthy man, but he obviously didn't believe in luxurious accommodation for his faithful cohorts.

The first floor was clear. Five minutes later, the second floor proved to be too. Three more bedrooms, spaced out around a galleried landing. Ben moved fast from one empty room to the next.

The second was a bedroom that had been adapted into a recreation room, furnished with two mismatched sofas and a pine table in one corner surrounded by plain wooden chairs. There was a well-thumbed back issue of *American Rifleman* lying on the table, next to the half-eaten remains of a takeaway meal for two that had been consumed straight out of its packaging.

Ben walked over to the table. Four silvery aluminium trays, two more or less scraped empty and two still three-quarters uneaten. In one of those, the leftover noodles were slowly drying and going hard and crusty. The other was full of some kind of dark, congealing sauce with bits of what was presumably meat inside. He picked up the foil container, lifted it to his nose and sniffed. Smelled like chicken in oyster sauce. Or maybe alley cat in macerated fish paste. He dipped a finger and dabbed it against his tongue. It was virtually uneatable, but not because it had been sitting there rotting for days. Ben's guess was that it had been pretty uneatable to start with, and only about twenty-four hours old. When you spent some time in the British Army, you got to be a decent judge of things like that.

The white paper bag the food had come in was lying rumpled on the table. Ben straightened it out and saw the name of the takeaway, with an address printed on one side.

The house sweep was almost done. Ben left Silvie to check the last bedroom while he trotted up the final staircase to the attic space at the top of the house. He knew it would be empty before he got there. Turned on the light and looked around him. It had been converted into its own self-contained flat, with a single bedroom and a kitchenette and living space combined. No sign of habitation, not within the last few days.

'They're gone,' Silvie said from the stairs. 'Shit.'

'They must have been alerted when you and Breslin never returned,' Ben said, walking down to join her. He let the rifle hang loosely in his hands, the safety back on now that the danger was past.

'Then that's it,' she said. 'We're nowhere again.'

'Which room was yours?' Ben asked.

'The small one on the second floor. Breslin was next door.'

'Who used the upstairs flat?'

'Streicher and his girlfriend, when they were around. Never longer than a single night at a time.'

'What about the rec room?'

'It was a spare they used as a spillover living room when we had a full house,' she said. 'Or when Streicher was using the lounge downstairs for one of his private conferences with the inner circle. Torben Roth, Holger Grubitz and some of the other guys tended to use it as a drinking and chow den.'

'Chinese?'

'Pizza,' she said. 'There's a takeaway joint just up the street where they'd go for a quick run out.'

'Is it an okay kind of place?' he asked.

'I've had worse. Don't tell me you're hungry again.'

'Not exactly. Let me show you something.' Ben led her back into the rec room.

'Yuck,' she said, pulling a face at the sight and smell of the half-finished food. 'You'd have to be desperate.'

'Super Delight,' Ben said, pointing at the paper bag.

'Who are they trying to kid, with a name like that?'

'It didn't come from this neighbourhood,' Ben said. 'The address is in Ouchy, wherever that is. The cab driver will know, if he hasn't buggered off already.'

'It's a district of the city,' she said. 'An old port, a few kilometres to the south of here.'

He looked at her. 'I thought you said you didn't know the area.'

'History nerd, remember? October, nineteen-twelve. Signing of the First Treaty of Lausanne in Ouchy, between Italy and the Ottoman Empire, spelling the end of the Italo-Turkish War.' She smiled sheepishly. 'What a team, huh?'

'Nobody drives several kilometres for slush like Super Delight dishes out,' he said. 'Not when they've got a reasonably decent pizza joint close by. Which makes me think I'm right.'

'Right about what?'

'Where did they all go in such a hurry?' he said. 'My guess is they used a couple of cars to ferry everyone out, plus all their stuff. Maybe took them two or three trips. Which would suggest they didn't drive that far. The two guys driving could have picked up the food locally on their way back, for a quick snack before heading off. Except one of them didn't appear too keen on it. Maybe a sign of good taste.'

'Another safe house?'

'You said yourself, Streicher's rich enough to have properties all over the place.'

'Ouchy,' she said. 'It's worth a try.'

'It's all we've got,' he said.

Chapter Forty-Five

The taxi driver turned out to be still there waiting for them, slouched in his seat and half asleep behind his paper. He jerked upright when he saw his fares walking back towards the car, cranked up the engine and turned on the lights. Ben put their gear in the boot, got in the back with Silvie and tossed the crumpled paper bag into the driver's lap.

'You want Chinese food?' the guy said. 'I know a better place than that.'

'It's Super Delight in Ouchy, or nothing,' Ben said. 'Let's go.' He leaned back and closed his eyes. Didn't open them again until twenty minutes later, when he felt the Mercedes slow and pull in at the kerb.

'Here it is,' the driver said. Super Delight was situated halfway down a residential street of terraced houses, all lit up and clearly doing a reasonable trade that evening. Ben shook his head and wondered what the world was coming to. 'Keep going to the end of the street,' he told the driver. 'Nice and easy.'

Ben looked out of the left-side window and Silvie out of the right as the Mercedes rolled slowly down the street. Both kerbs were lined with parked cars. Neither a white BMW with a dented wing nor a black Range Rover was among them. They reached the end of the street and came to a three-way junction. The driver said, 'Now what?'

If in doubt, bear dead ahead. 'Straight on,' Ben said.

The next street looked just the same as the last. The house they were looking for could have been any single one of them, left or right. No white BMW. No black Range Rover.

'Damn it,' Silvie muttered. 'This isn't going to work.'

'Now what?' the driver said impatiently as they reached another three-way junction. Left, right, or dead ahead.

'Left,' Ben said.

'You sure about that?'

Ben said nothing. He wasn't sure at all. He was getting that hollow feeling in the pit of his stomach and a bitterness in his mouth that wasn't just the aftertaste of stale alley cat in fish sauce. The taste of failure.

The taxi took a left at the junction. Its headlights gleamed in the windows of the terraced houses and shone back at them in the reflectors of the vehicles parked nose to tail on both sides of the narrow street. They rolled onwards at a steady speed, the clattering sound of the Mercedes' diesel engine reverberating back at them off the houses. Some of the windows had their curtains drawn, the glow of TV screens flickering through the gaps. Others didn't and Ben saw people moving about inside their homes or sitting in their living rooms, settling down for the evening. In one house a party was going on, music blaring out into the street.

No white BMW. No black Range Rover. No safe house.

This wasn't going to work.

Then Silvie spoke up urgently and pointed, her finger jabbing the inside of the taxi's rear window. 'There.'

Ben followed the line of her finger and saw what she'd seen. Parked in the tight line of vehicles on the right side of the street.

A white 3-series BMW with a dented wing.

The house it was parked in front of had lights in one curtained downstairs window and one first-floor window. Someone was at home.

'Pull in fifty metres ahead,' Ben told the driver.

'No spaces,' the guy protested.

'Then double-park, genius.'

The driver resentfully double-parked fifty metres ahead. Ben and Silvie exchanged nods. 'Ready?' he said.

'Take two,' she said. 'Let's do it.'

They got out. Ben opened the Mercedes' boot. 'Doesn't look like there's any back way in this time,' Silvie said.

'Then we'll just walk right in the front door,' he said. He pulled the rifles out of the holdall and passed her the AK-47.

She stared at it, then at him. 'Are you nuts? We can't go strolling down the street with assault rifles on open display.'

'This is Switzerland. Everybody has them here.' He left the bags in the boot of the car with the lid open, to shield what they were doing from the driver's rear-view mirror in case the guy panicked and took off. Checked his weapon. Same routine as before, a round in the chamber and the safety on. Browning and Glock in his belt, fully loaded and ready to go.

'Let's get to work,' he said.

It was only at the moment he was kicking in the front door that he was hit by a tiny doubt that they might have the wrong house. Parking spaces seemed to be at a premium. The BMW could have been parked three doors up, three doors down or on the opposite side of the street. But as the door frame gave way with a splintering crack, it was too late for second thoughts.

Ben and Silvie burst inside the hallway. A dingy carpeted stairway lay ahead. A doorway to the left. The ground-floor room with the light on. The hallway was narrow and in two strides he was at the door. The third stride landed midway up the panelled wood, level with the handle. The door smacked open. He shouldered through, gun first.

It was a living room, lit by the glow of a lopsided standard lamp in one corner. Cheaply and minimally furnished. A plain coffee table in the middle of the room. On it, an opened can of Stella Artois and a copy of *Guns and Ammo*, lying open to reveal glossy images of the latest offering in bolt-action tactical rifles. Next to the magazine and the beer can, a Smith & Wesson Military and Police Model automatic pistol lay on its side with its muzzle pointed towards the door.

That was when Ben knew for sure he was in the right house.

Three feet beyond the coffee table was a wing armchair upholstered in faded brown corduroy, and in it sat a man. He was perhaps thirty-eight or forty years old. Coppery hair cropped short, military-style. His shoulders were broad and the arms revealed by his sleeveless T-shirt were muscled and stringy. The right side of his face had been mutilated long ago. The scar was pink and white, like a spider's web of thickened, sclerotic flesh that stretched from the corner of his eye to the corner of his mouth and made him look as if he was scowling.

He's got the look of a killer. Doesn't say much. Face is messed up by a bullet.

Torben Roth. Streicher's man. The mercenary.

At first Ben thought he was asleep. But Roth was conscious, sitting upright in the chair with his eyes open. His gaze drifted up to meet Ben's, then drifted down to stare impassively at the loaded battle rifle that Ben had aimed at his centre of mass.

Through the open doorway behind him, Ben heard the light patter of Silvie's footsteps racing up the stairs.

'Don't even think about it,' he said to Roth, anticipating that the guy was about to lunge forward in his chair and make a grab for the pistol. He took a step forward, the rifle trained steady on the mercenary's chest. At this range it would blow the man's spine out through the back of the chair. Overkill, but Ben wasn't taking any chances faced with an experienced and dangerous opponent.

Roth didn't move. Didn't make any attempt to reach for the gun. Ben took another step closer, and now he could see how pallid and grey Roth's complexion was. A sheen of sweat filmed his brow. His eyes looked blank and expressionless. Maybe he was drunk. Ben kicked over the coffee table and sent the pistol tumbling away over the thin carpet. The Stella can hit the floor and rolled, beer sloshing out of its keyhole spout. If the guy was drunk, he must have got started earlier.

'On your knees,' Ben said. 'Hands behind your head.'

Roth still didn't move.

Ben took another step towards him and clubbed him across the left temple with the rifle barrel. Not hard enough to inflict damage, but enough to galvanise him a little.

'I said, on your—' Ben started to repeat.

But he didn't finish the sentence. Roth slumped out of the chair as limply as if someone had filleted every bone from his body. He collapsed to the floor. Landed on his face and lay absolutely still.

Ben could hear Silvie moving about from room to room upstairs, doors opening and closing.

He stared down at the man on the floor. Nudged him with his foot. No response. The blow hadn't been anywhere near enough to knock the guy unconscious. He could be feinting, waiting for Ben to drop his guard and come close, so he could rear up at him with a knife in his hand. Very carefully, keeping the gun pointed where it needed to be, Ben crouched down and checked his pulse. It was weak and faint and irregular, like a coma victim. Like someone just barely clinging to life.

Then the body started heaving and thrashing and jerking. Roth's spine arched and his arms went as taut as steel cables, every muscle standing out as if it was about to snap. The spasms went on for a few seconds and then the body went limp again.

He wasn't faking it. Something was wrong with the guy. Something was *very* wrong with him.

'Ben,' Silvie's voice called down from the top of the stairs. She sounded worried. 'You'd better get up here fast.'

Ben stepped away from Roth's comatose body. The man genuinely wasn't going anywhere. He ran out of the living room and up the stairs. Silvie was standing at the top, her rifle dangling loose from one hand. Which Ben assumed meant she'd found nobody upstairs.

'Just the one guy below,' he said. 'Roth. He's in no fit state to give us any trouble.'

She shook her head. 'Just two guys. Holger Grubitz is up here. And he's in pretty bad shape too.'

He reached the top of the stairs and she led him along a half-lit passageway with peeling floral wallpaper towards an open door. Nodded through it. Ben walked into the room. It was simply furnished like the ones in the first property. Like a student bedroom, except this was a bunkhouse for wanted mass murderers. Just a chair and a junk-shop plywood wardrobe and a narrow bed with a sagging mattress.

The bed had a dead man lying on it. Ben didn't have to get close to know that for certain. He didn't particularly want to. It wasn't the most serene-looking corpse he'd ever seen. The bed was rumpled and stained with sweat and urine. Grubitz's body was all twisted up and contorted, as if he'd died thrashing about in feverish agony. No blood. No visible injury. Something else had killed him.

'I don't think it was the Chinese food,' Ben said.

Silvie looked at him. She was pale. 'Roth?'

'Alive, but going the same way fast.'

'What do we do?'

Ben shrugged. 'Nothing. Let him suffer. He has it coming. Search the house for any clues as to where the others went. If there aren't, we sit tight and wait for them.'

He'd barely finished speaking before the scream of sirens drowned him out. He ran to the window and saw a whole fleet of police cars and two SWAT team vans flood the street below from both directions. The walls of the houses became a swirling kaleidoscope of blue light.

The vehicle doors swung open. Armed officers in uniform and black-clad tactical response cops with submachine guns were suddenly all over the place. They knew exactly where to go. Within seconds Ben could hear them swarming into the hallway below. Rushing footsteps on the stairs. Radios crackling and fizzing. Agitated shouts of, 'Police! Give yourselves up!'

'What do we do?' Silvie said, wide-eyed and even paler than before.

Ben turned away from the window. He let the FAMAS rifle drop from his hand and fall to the floor. Drew the Glock from his belt and tossed it away. Then did the same with the Browning Hi-Power.

'Only one thing we can do, Agent Valois,' he said. 'You've got to arrest me.'

Chapter Forty-Six

She stared at him. 'Do what?'

'Don't be stupid,' he told her. 'Point the damn rifle at me. Do it now. Quickly, and like you mean it.' He dropped to his knees in front of her and put his hands behind his bowed head with his fingers laced together.

Silvie hesitated, but there was no time and no choice. She pointed the AK-47 at Ben's head.

'How the hell did they find us?' she asked.

'Don't speak to me,' he said.

At that moment, SWAT officers came thundering down the passageway with their machine guns raised. They reached the open doorway and burst into the room. Suddenly it wasn't just one gun pointing at Ben, but ten or a dozen. He kept his head down and stared fixedly at the floor. Heard Silvie identify herself to them as a DGSI agent. Heard the SWAT team CO congratulate her on her good work and tell her they were taking over from here.

Then Ben was shoved down roughly to the floor and had his arms jerked behind his back. His wrists were bound with a plastic tie. He said nothing, and did nothing to resist them. They stripped out his pockets and even took Père Antoine's little tonic bottle, handling it as though it was liquid nitroglycerine. Next he was being marched back along the floral passageway and down the stairs to the hallway, and out into the swirling blue lights and the sea of police vehicles. He glanced up the street and saw the armed cops circling the taxi. They had the driver trussed up flat on his face in the road, squirming like a grounded turtle and surrounded by guns while the bags were being removed from the back of the car. It wouldn't be long before the cops let him go.

Ben wasn't betting on the same happening to him.

How the hell did they find us?

He had no idea. But he was pretty certain it wouldn't be long before he found out.

Six officers hustled him to a black police van. Its back doors were open. The rear compartment was a windowless steel cage. He was shoved and jostled towards it. Standard arrest procedure. But something wasn't right. Ben could see it in the faces of the cops emerging from the house. He could see it in the way they were barking into their radios. A tone of urgency that was incongruous with a normal crime scene. Something was happening.

He looked around for Silvie but couldn't see her. Where had they taken her?

In the final fleeting moment before they slammed him inside the cage, an unmarked panel van came speeding down the street with its headlights blazing and concealed blues flashing from behind its radiator grille and its siren shrieking. It was white, not black. Police vehicles moved smartly aside to let it through. It skidded to a halt outside the house. Its side door slid open and four men got out. They weren't armed and they weren't wearing police or SWAT uniform.

They looked like astronauts clambering out of a moon lander. Clad in shimmering silvery-white from head to toe, bulky full-body suits made of exotic space-age materials

293

capable of withstanding any kind of nuclear, chemical or bacteriological contamination. The swirling blue lights reflected on their protective clothing and the thick visors that covered their faces. They were clutching cases of equipment in their heavily gauntleted hands.

A hazmat team.

There was no way they'd had time to respond to a radio call. They'd either been on their way already, or standing by a street or two away waiting for the order to move in.

As if they knew something. Which was a damn sight more than Ben did, at that moment. Back in the day, he'd seen hazmat suits deployed in combat zones thousands of miles away across the globe, during actual or anticipated chemical warfare attacks. Here, in the middle of a quiet residential area in a peaceful lakeside Swiss town, they were a shockingly incongruous sight.

Three more identical white vans came roaring down the street and screeched to a halt, nose to tail. And as they moved in, the police and SWAT units were clearing out. Fast. The street was too narrow for them to U-turn out of there. Transmissions whined under hard reversing and tyres squealed as they reached the top of the street and wrestled their vehicles around and sped off as though a megaton bomb was about to explode. The taxi driver and his Mercedes had already been whisked away into the night. Eight more of the shimmering, visored figures piled out of the white vans. One of them was waving his bulky, padded arms at the remaining cops on the scene and mouthing something urgently behind his mask, as if to say, *Get the hell out of here NOW!*

Then Ben saw no more. The doors slammed and he was closed in darkness. He heard running steps and the sound of more doors, and then felt the floor under his feet lurch violently as the vehicle took off. He sat on the hard bench inside the cage, tried to get as comfortable as possible with his wrists tied behind his back, and waited for whatever was going to happen next.

It was a longer wait than he'd expected. The motion of the van told him they were driving through the city, constantly shifting speed, braking and accelerating, pausing at lights, turning one way and the other. Ben assumed their destination was the nearest *préfecture de police*. Which shouldn't be a long trip.

But instead, the van just kept going. The stop-start, left-right motion died away to a steady tempo, telling him they were heading out of the city on the open road. The unwavering engine note and the thrum of the tyres resonated through the bodyshell and the steel cage bars around him. Ben sat quietly in the darkness, rocking gently to the sway of the vehicle, feet braced against the opposite bench, wondering where he was being taken.

An hour passed by, time that Ben used to try and make sense of what he'd seen back there. It had looked as if the hazmat team were intent on shutting the whole street down. Unquestionably, it had to do with the two occupants of the safe house. One dead, the other dying. Whatever had made them sick, it was something serious and infectious enough to spark off a major emergency response.

Then he went on to think about Silvie and what the next stage would be for her. No doubt she was in for a long night with her DGSI superiors, going over every detail of her undercover mission leading up to the point when she'd been lured away and taken hostage, and everything that had happened since. Ben wasn't worried about her ability to handle herself through it all. He wasn't even all that worried about himself. There wasn't a lot he could do, so why waste energy on fretting about the situation?

Another hour went by. The plastic cuffs were tight and chafed his wrists. His shoulders were screaming from the lactic acid build-up in his muscles. He breathed steadily through his nose and centred himself and managed to shut out the pain, but he couldn't control the thoughts that kept flitting through his head. Memories of his time at the monastery. Playing chess with Père Antoine, feeding the animals with Roby. Something that Roby had said was nagging at him, but he couldn't remember what or why. The memory hung there in the back of his mind, like a shadow, taunting him until he gave up trying to recall it. The mental tension just brought back the pain in his muscles. He closed his eyes, focused on his breathing and willed himself into a state of relaxation. Like a Zen master.

Except that Ben was no Zen master. But in time he settled and his muscles eased, his heartbeat slowed and he stopped thinking at all.

He was close to being asleep when the van finally reached the end of its journey. The rear doors opened and strong light flooded in, dazzling him after the long spell of darkness. He blinked at the two silvery-white-clad, visored figures who unlocked the cage and pulled him out. Six more were standing around the van, holding automatic weapons. The van had been driven inside a large empty space. Concrete walls, concrete ceiling, concrete pillars. A heavy-duty steel shutter had rolled down. Halogen spotlamps blazed from all around.

One of the men in hazmat suits stepped close behind him with a pair of cutters and snipped the tie binding his wrists while gun muzzles covered him from different angles. Then they closed around him in escort formation and marched him to a doorway in the concrete wall. Eight on one. He should be flattered. He rubbed his wrists and rolled his shoulders, felt the circulation returning to his stiff muscles.

The door led to a lift. Ben and his captors were whooshed up two, three, four, five floors. The lift glided smoothly to a halt and its doors hissed open to reveal a long, broad, bright corridor that definitely didn't look like the inside of any police station Ben had seen, in any country. It looked more like a hospital, but one apparently with neither wards nor patients.

'Where are we?' he asked his escorts. No response.

He was pretty sure he knew the answer anyway. If it wasn't a military establishment it was at the very least a government one. The kind of secure facility that was kept nicely quiet from members of the public; that was, until such time as their rulers saw fit to whisk them off at gunpoint in the dead of night too.

His guards walked him along the corridor, where they were joined by more men in identical suits but not carrying guns. Medical personnel, Ben thought, rather than security. They steered him towards a door with a sign that read DECONTAMINATION. One of them tapped a key code into a wall panel and the door slid open with a swish of hydraulics. They pushed him inside, and the door swished shut behind him.

The room was a tiled white cube, about two metres square. The outline of the doorway he'd just walked through was barely visible, as was the shape of another doorway opposite. Recessed spotlamps burned hot. The floor sloped gently down to a centre drain. As Ben gazed around him, a harsh voice from a hidden speaker ordered him in English to remove his shoes, his watch and his clothes. If there was a hidden speaker there was probably a hidden camera too, but Ben wasn't bashful. His years of military service had removed those kinds of inhibitions. He kicked off his shoes, took off his jacket, then the shirt and jeans that Silvie had bought for him, then his socks, then his underwear. A sliding compartment opened in the tiled wall to his right. The same harsh voice ordered him to place the items inside. He did what he was told. There seemed little value in resisting. The compartment clicked shut.

A second later, a stunningly powerful spray of liquid showered down on him from a hundred concealed holes in the ceiling, making him gasp at its intensity and its coldness. It wasn't water, but some kind of chemical wash that stung and seared his skin like ice. After five seconds, the shower stopped as abruptly as it had begun. He stood dripping and shivering, clutching at his sides. Then a concentrated hurricane-force blast of air hit him from all sides and pummelled him for ten more seconds. To his amazement, when it stopped he was totally dry, even his hair. The clothing compartment clicked back open. His things were gone. In their place was a hospital robe. The hidden voice told him to put it on. He reached inside and lifted it out. Clean, crisp cotton, soft and warm. He shrugged it over his head and let it fall down loosely around his body.

Then the opposite doorway hissed open. Ben took that as an invitation, and was happy to leave the white cube before it sprang any more surprises on him. He stepped through the doorway and it instantly hissed shut behind him.

He found himself in a strange kind of hospital room. The lights were bright and the air smelled of antiseptic. The room had a metal-framed bed made up drum-tight, a stand with bottles of drinking water and plastic cups in sealed bags, a wash unit and, in a nod to personal privacy that struck him as pretty insincere under the circumstances, a toilet with a wrap-around nylon curtain draped from a ceiling rail. Everything looked spotless and sterilised. The same gleaming white tiles covered the floor, ceiling and three of the room's walls. The fourth consisted entirely of a panel of two-way mirror.

Ben immediately knew that every move he made was under constant surveillance.

He walked to the glass panel and rapped on it with his knuckles. It felt as thick and unyielding as armour plate. No point in trying to use the bed as a battering ram or ripping out the toilet bowl as a missile to smash his way out. 'Hey,' he said. 'Where the hell am I? What's going on here?'

No response.

Ben glared hard at the unseen faces he sensed were scrutinising him from the other side of the glass. Then he snorted in contempt and walked back to the bed and stretched out comfortably on it, figuring that he wasn't going to give these people the pleasure of seeing him lose his temper or pace anxiously about the room like a caged tiger. He breathed slowly and let his muscles relax against the firm mattress. Closed his eyes.

The watchers remained silent and hidden.

They remained silent and hidden for the next twenty-four hours.

Chapter Forty-Seven

He knew what was happening. He was in quarantine, being kept under observation to see if he collapsed dead of whatever had afflicted Torben Roth and the other guy at the safe house in Lausanne. He supposed the same was being done with Silvie. Maybe she was just next door, in an identical room the other side of the tiled wall.

But knowing what was happening didn't make it easier to bear. Hours dragged torturously by. The lights stayed on brightly the entire time, making it impossible to tell day from night, and before too long it became hard to preserve his outwardly cool attitude. Ben was no Zen master. And this place lacked the serenity of Chartreuse de la Sainte Vierge de Pelvoux that had taught him to quieten his thoughts. Frustration and anger began to gnaw increasingly at him. Anxiety about Silvie. Impatience at being cooped up helplessly in here while Streicher was still out there somewhere, getting harder to find by the minute and the hour.

He slept, tossing and turning a while, then sat a while, then paced and banged on the window and demanded a response, then got none and went back to pacing and doing press-ups and sit-ups, until he was tired out and sweaty and had a wash and went back to bed with his back defiantly turned to the two-way mirror.

He was sleeping when the doctors came into his room. He woke with a start to see three of them standing around the bed, accompanied by a nurse. They weren't wearing protective suits.

'Either you people are being really careless about exposure, or I'm in the clear,' he challenged them. 'Which is it?'

They said nothing. Just studied him curiously for a few moments, then nodded to one another and left the room. The nurse stayed behind, produced a syringe and drew blood from him.

'Can I smoke in here?' he asked her.

No response.

'How about something to eat?' he said.

Three hours later, the nurse returned with a tray. Coffee, fruit juice, a tasteless bit of brioche and a banana.

Three hours after that, Ben was given a fresh set of clothes and released from the observation room. He might be in the clear, but they still didn't trust him without an armed escort as he was taken down a series of corridors to a room. A guard knocked once on the door, then showed him in.

Two men were sitting at a circular office table inside the room.

'Hello, Ben,' said Luc Simon. He looked weary and drawn and his tie was loosened and crooked, which for Luc Simon was the equivalent of a ripped jacket sleeve or a sole flapping off his shoe. He was making inroads into the large pot of coffee that stood on a tray in the middle of the table. His companion hadn't touched any. He was an older man with thinning black hair, tall and gaunt in a dark suit. He was peering curiously at Ben.

For a moment or two, Ben considered kicking the table over. But he didn't want to spill the coffee. It smelled like the good stuff. He sat in one of the two empty chairs at the round table, grabbed one of the two spare cups from the tray and poured it full to the brim from the pot. Black, no sugar. It *was* the good stuff, strong and hot. He drank it greedily and felt better right away.

'I suppose you have a lot of questions, don't you?' Luc Simon said. 'That's understandable. For instance, I'm sure you'd like to know where you are and why you were subjected to all these medical indignities. All very necessary, I'm afraid. But before we start getting into it, I'd like to thank you for leading us to Streicher's safe house.' He smiled. 'You're the best unpaid agent I could have wished for,' he added, as if he couldn't resist saying it.

'Careful, you might upset me,' Ben said. 'I'm a loose cannon, remember.'

'I apologise,' Luc Simon said with a gracious nod.

'So how did you do it?'

'Trace your movements? By knowing how you think, Ben.'

'Am I that predictable?'

'No,' Luc Simon said. 'I'm just that good. Recalling your fondness for the prehistoric Grande Puissance 1935 Model Browning pistol – you once carjacked me with one – and knowing, naturally, that you'd easily get the better of them, I arranged for one of our agents who intercepted your train journey to be carrying one fitted with a miniature GPS tracking device. You'd have to take the grips off to find it.'

Crafty bastard, Ben thought. 'And the helicopter chase. That was just a decoy, wasn't it?'

'I couldn't let you think you'd got away *too* easily,' Luc Simon said. 'I wanted you to feel like you'd earned your freedom. The pilot was under orders to back off and make it appear as if you'd given him the slip. Meanwhile we were tracking you all the way to Lausanne, knowing you'd waste no time finding Streicher's people.'

'I only found two of them.'

'But you uncovered so much more. I'm relieved that Agent Valois didn't find an opportunity to arrest you sooner.'

Ben smiled inwardly at that, but showed nothing on his face. He finished his cup of coffee and refilled it from the pot without offering any to anybody else. The older man with the thinning dark hair still hadn't said a word, or been introduced. Ben didn't much care for the way the guy was sitting watching him. He had beady dark little eyes, like a crow.

'If you're wondering where she is, by the way,' Luc Simon said, 'like you she's come through the twenty-four-hour observation period with no problems and her blood tests negative. Although you were both exposed, you were lucky. Luckier still that we brought you here for assessment. It might have gone very differently.'

'You'll have to pardon me for not turning cartwheels of joy and gratitude,' Ben said. 'I don't know where I am. I don't know what any of this is about. I don't even know if it's day or night, because they junked my watch. I liked that watch. I had it a long time.'

'We'll get you a new one just like it,' Luc Simon reassured him. 'For the record, it's two-thirty-seven a.m. and our present location is a government science facility a few kilometres from our Interpol HQ in Lyon, one whose existence is not exactly secret but not exactly widely publicised either. As for the rest, I told you I'd fill you in when we were face to face. And I was being honest. I've been rethinking your offer. Whether we like it or not, right now you're possibly our best asset in this investigation. And my superiors now think likewise. Thanks to you, in the last twenty-four hours our worst fears about Streicher have been confirmed. I'm afraid the stakes are very high. It's time you knew a few things.'

'So fill me in,' Ben said.

'Better you hear it from my colleague here,' Simon said, motioning at the older man. 'Allow me to introduce Professor Jean-Pierre Oppenheim.'

'Professor of what?' Ben said, looking at him suspiciously.

Oppenheim made no reply and only gave a thin, frosty smile.

'Oh, of many things,' Luc Simon said. 'Take it from me, his experience and credentials are second to none. But the less you know about his exact professional role, the better. Let's just say he's our foremost authority on this matter.'

'Then let's hear it,' Ben said.

Oppenheim pursed his lips and shifted in his chair. He looked down at his long, bony hands and very carefully laced his fingers together over his knee. His dark crow's eyes regarded Ben for a moment and then he spoke for the first time. His voice was dry and crackling.

'The contingency we're dealing with here can easily be summed up in a single word,' he said. 'But first, I feel it necessary to provide you with the relevant background information.' Oppenheim paused for a few moments, as if weighing his words, chewing over what he was about to divulge. His eyes bored deep into Ben.

'How much do you know about bioterrorism?' he asked.

Chapter Forty-Eight

Ben was taken aback by this question so out of the blue. 'I know what my pay grade in the military allowed me to know,' he replied after a beat. 'That some people say it's a ticking time bomb waiting to explode. While others say that despite all the scaremongering, it's never resulted in a single successful attack or a single fatality anywhere in the world. A paper tiger.'

Oppenheim nodded gravely. 'Paradoxically, one might say that both of those statements are true,' he said. 'By a combination of vigilance and sheer good old-fashioned luck, we've so far managed to avoid disaster. But it's not been for lack of trying on the part of our enemies. And it would be a serious misjudgement to regard it as a paper tiger. In fact, there exists a long history of private individuals attempting to release biological attacks on the public at large, using agents that can be dispersed through the air, through water or by other means. The first significant attempt took place in Chicago in 1972, when a shoestring "terror" group calling themselves RISE tried to contaminate the city's drinking water with typhoid virus stolen from a hospital lab where one of them worked. The attack was thwarted before it ever happened. Then there was the 1984 incident in Oregon, an attempt to cause widespread food poisoning from salmonella, which resulted in several cases of illness.'

Oppenheim paused, then went on. 'Nine years later, in July 1993, a liquid suspension of *Bacillus anthracis* – that's anthrax – was aerosolised from the roof of a high building in Kameido, Tokyo, by a religious enclave called Aum Shinrikyo, a potentially devastating attack that only failed because they mistakenly used an attenuated and relatively harmless strain of the disease agent. Then in 2001, anonymous letters mailed to officials in Washington, DC and Santiago, Chile, were found to be contaminated with anthrax spores. Again, thankfully, nobody was hurt. But it gets more serious. The following year, US military and intelligence officials obtained a secret dossier from the Afghanistan home of a Pakistani nuclear physicist and then associate of Osama bin Laden, containing evidence that Al-Qaeda was targeting the Biohazard Level Four facility at Plum Island near New York as a potential source of bio-warfare materials. Then in 2008, the Pakistan-born and US-educated neuroscientist Aafia Siddiqui was sentenced to eighty-six years in prison for conspiracy to commit acts of bioterrorism.'

'The Grey Lady of Bagram,' Ben said. 'Otherwise known as Prisoner six-five-o. There are plenty of psychopathic mass murderers who've been put away for just a fraction of that time. Not what you might call entirely fair.'

Oppenheim shrugged his bony shoulders. 'You could say the Americans treated her a little harshly, overreacting in the wake of nine/eleven. Then again, you could say that a known associate of Al-Qaeda caught in possession of significant quantities of highly toxic substances and plotting mass-casualty attacks on US soil wasn't exactly a minor offender.'

'Did it ever occur to these scientists that they're asking for trouble, creating and stockpiling the damned things in the first place?' Ben said.

'It's certainly a point of view,' Oppenheim said with a dry smile. 'The potential threat of a serious bioterror attack is in direct proportion to the number of government laboratories worldwide handling, storing or manufacturing deadly disease-causing agents, which continues to increase year on year, along with the number of security lapses and un-answered calls for tighter regulation. That being said, as you rightly pointed out, to this day there still has never been a single attempted biological terror attack in Europe. Now . . .'

Oppenheim paused to lean his gaunt frame over the edge of his chair and reach down into an open briefcase at his feet. It was made of shiny black leather, like his shoes. His long fingers lifted out an A4-sized manila envelope, which he laid on the tabletop and skimmed over the polished surface towards Ben. 'Everything I've said thus far is just to set the scene. I want to focus now on this man.'

Ben picked up the envelope. It was unsealed and contained a single glossy photo print, which he slipped out. It was a grainy three-quarter shot of a tall, slim man in early middle age, taken from a distance with a long lens. He was standing by the door of a car, in conversation with another man whose back was turned to the camera. The photo had been taken during the cold months, judging from the way they were dressed. The man was wearing a long dark overcoat that looked expensive, maybe cashmere, and tan leather gloves. He was neat and clean-shaven with even features and a high forehead from which his hair was swept thickly back, a touch of grey around the temples. Half the car number plate was visible at the bottom of the photo. It was a Swiss registration.

'Is this who I think it is?' Ben said, laying the photo back on the table.

Luc Simon nodded.

'The last few decades have seen the rise of a strange and perplexing phenomenon,' Oppenheim said, leaning back in his chair and pressing his fingertips together, as if he were praying. 'A very particular neurosis of the human mind whose sufferers, overcome by their belief in a dark and uncertain future, are consumed by the need to do everything possible to *prepare* for it. Such forms of behaviour can assume a religious significance, marked by evangelical fervour, often with the desire to preach their apocalyptic convictions to all who'll listen. Such as the belief in floods and tidal waves of epic biblical proportions, set to sweep humanity away. Or the belief that God is imminently about to manifest his wrath against us, as in the Old Testament's destruction of Sodom and Gomorrah, to punish us for the sinful and debauched ways of modern society. Of a more secular nature are beliefs concerning the coming of natural disasters such as super storms, solar magnetic flares that will destroy the fabric of civilisation and plunge us back into the Dark Ages, and so on and so forth.'

Oppenheim paused, moistened his thin lips with the tip of his tongue in a way that made him look oddly reptilian, then continued. 'For many, these are genuinely terrifying prospects that they hope never to have to face in this lifetime. But there are some who secretly or perhaps even openly wish for the chance to witness these apocalyptic events first-hand. Perhaps simply to vindicate the personal convictions for which people have scorned and laughed at them all these years. Or perhaps just because they've been watching too many American TV shows about the dead rising to walk the earth, and think it would be a great game to go charging about blasting bullets everywhere with impunity.' Oppenheim smiled. 'We generally don't take that kind of person seriously. Their psychological profiles tend to indicate a cowardly streak that would have them running and hiding in terror at the first real sign of their fantasies coming true. But then,' he said, 'there are the serious ones. Those who would genuinely love nothing more than for the whole of human civilisation to be plunged into chaos and darkness. Who relish it so much, in fact, that they'd jump at the chance to be part of the process.'

'And Udo Streicher is one of those,' Ben said. 'That's what you're saying, correct?'

Luc Simon refilled his own coffee and Ben's, and savoured a long sip. 'Streicher's first appearance on our radar was eleven years ago, when Interpol operatives monitoring the Deep Web picked up talk of a new organisation calling itself Exercitus Paratorum. Roughly translated, "The Army of the Prepared". Now, as you might already know, our boy was born into wealth. Cosseted upbringing, the best private schooling Switzerland has to offer. As a teenager he received a top-notch classical education. Hence, presumably, the Latin name he later went on to choose for his group. But after a year he seemed to decide that Exercitus Paratorum was too much of a mouthful, or maybe sounded too elitist or intellectual, so he changed it simply to the Parati. The Ready or Prepared Ones.'

'Agent Valois told me,' Ben said. 'But ready for what? The end of the world? Armageddon? Is this a religious group, like Aum Shinrikyo?'

Luc Simon shook his head. 'From what we can gather, Streicher's a committed atheist. There's no apparent religious motivation behind his ideals.'

'This is an individual who fantasises day and night about

309

the coming of a new era for mankind, Mr Hope,' Oppenheim said. 'The Parati website, buried deep in the dark side of the internet and accessible only via specialised software, has described a future where the global population is reduced by seventy-five per cent. No more government, the monetary system gone, the rule of law no longer applicable. In his sick and very minutely detailed fantasy, the human race would be broken down to small, disparate, leaderless and helpless groups of people worldwide who had failed to prepare for the coming disaster, whatever form it might have taken. All except him and his followers, needless to say, who thanks to their strategic foresight and planning would now be in a position to unite them, and dominate them.'

'To dominate them?' Ben said.

'Streicher sees his future role as some kind of feudal overlord,' Luc Simon said. 'A king, you might say, with autocratic power over a huge army of followers in what he describes as the "afterworld". It's an all-consuming obsession. And the clock is ticking for him. Like all these Doomsday-preparation types, he's been waiting and hoping for years that some global crisis might bring him the opportunity he craves. At the age of forty-six, we can easily speculate that he's no longer content to wait passively. He wants it to happen while he's still young enough to enjoy and make the most of it. He desperately needs to control the situation. Hence, to find a way to actually *make it happen*, and soon. These factors are what make him such a prime concern to us.'

'Bullshit,' Ben said.

'You don't believe what we're telling you?'

'It's what you're not telling me,' he said. 'The part that would explain how some nutjob Doomsday fantasist managed to become Interpol's public enemy number one, justifying an operation on this kind of scale. It didn't make sense to me before, and it doesn't make sense to me now.'

Luc Simon and Oppenheim exchanged glances. Oppenheim's seemed to signify, *Are we okay divulging classified information to this man?* Luc Simon's quick affirmative nod said, *Go ahead, he needs to know.*

Chapter Forty-Nine

Oppenheim turned to Ben. 'In June 2011 an incident that was never released to the world media occurred in a classified location near a place called Kwanmo-Bong. You know where that is?'

'It's a mountain in North Korea,' Ben said.

'Surrounded by impenetrable forest, and believed to be the site of one of numerous military installations in that country devoted to the development of bioweapons. I'm sure you know that the so-called Democratic People's Republic of Korea is strongly suspected of flouting both the Geneva Protocol and the Biological Weapons Convention, in addition to the chemical weapons and nuclear arsenal they've already admitted to stockpiling. All part of their *Songun* or military-first policy to arm themselves to the teeth while their people are starving in the fields. Intelligence agencies believe that dozens of facilities scattered about the country posing as ordinary military bases may in fact be disguising hidden labs for the purpose of creating and storing biological threat agents of various kinds.

'According to intelligence reports, the June 2011 incident was an attempt by an outside group to break into one of those secret labs and obtain a quantity of such agents. Specifically what they were looking for, we don't know. We can only speculate that their target might have been a Level Three biohazard agent, classed as extremely serious but treatable, such as West Nile virus or anthrax. More disturbingly, it could equally have been a Level Four agent, for which no known treatment exists. Ebola virus, or Marburg virus, or Crimean-Congo haemorrhagic fever. Take your pick. All potentially devastating.' Oppenheim paused. 'As to who carried out the attack – there's very little uncertainty on that score.'

'Streicher,' Ben said.

Both men nodded. 'In a nutshell, you have one unhinged lunatic attempting to steal from a whole army of other unhinged lunatics,' Oppenheim said.

Ben saw the sneer on the guy's face, and felt a jolt of annoyance at the hypocrisy. 'Let's not get too smug,' he said. 'The North Koreans are what they are, but they're hardly the only ones with their finger in the pie. Don't tell me the Brits aren't doing exactly the same thing at Porton Down in Wiltshire. The USA and Russia are no different.'

'You're right about that,' Oppenheim admitted. 'The Russians were intensely hot on biowarfare research throughout the Soviet era. Western powers weren't slow to lure their scientists to defect over to us and then magic them away to work in rather secretive capacities behind closed doors, developing nobody quite knows what.' The way Oppenheim said it, it sounded to Ben as if he belonged to the ultra-exclusive club of people who knew *exactly* what. Maybe he really did, or maybe he just liked to give that impression. Either way, it made Ben wonder about the man's mysterious background that Luc Simon had avoided mentioning in any kind of detail.

'Like it or lament it,' Oppenheim said, 'that's the world we live in. The raiders must have thought that the Korean facility would be an easy target. In the event, they turned out to be very wrong. The attempt was not a success.'

'It was worse than unsuccessful,' Luc Simon put in. 'In fact, it was a perfect storm of failure. Streicher completely underestimated the strength of the military presence guarding the facility. Several of his people were killed and the rest only just managed to escape empty-handed by helicopter as far as the coast, from where it's believed they fled to Japan. When the first intelligence reports about the attack began filtering through, the line of thinking among Western agencies was that this could be Al-Qaeda, or perhaps some other jihadist splinter group, renewing its stated intention to unleash a whole new kind of WMD on the infidel West. Panic buttons were being hit all over the place. Then leaked information started coming through that the bodies of the raiders killed in the incident weren't your typical Muslim terrorists. They were white Europeans.'

'That led to some consternation in certain circles,' Oppenheim said, picking up the baton. 'Discounting the various factions within Northern Ireland, who all have their own localised agenda and their own habitual ways of operating, there hasn't been a significantly ambitious white European terror group since the days of Baader-Meinhof and the Red Army Faction, back in the seventies. With the current near-exclusive focus on Islamic jihadists, frankly, nobody knew where to look. Not until our sources in North Korea began releasing the identities of the dead. All of them, it turned out, connected to this little-known group called the Parati that European intelligence services had been keeping half an eye on for years. Until then, the Parati were only a theoretical, low-grade threat. They'd done nothing, at least nothing that we were aware of, that could justify any action being taken against them. Suddenly, it was confirmed beyond reasonable doubt that they were responsible for the North Korea raid. And there can be only one possible reason for such a raid. Streicher's intention was to deploy biological weapons in mainland Europe.'

Ben said nothing.

'So here's what we're looking at,' Luc Simon said. 'We know that Streicher failed in 2011 to obtain biological weapons that he intended to use to carry out his sick personal objectives. The failure cost him some of his best people, and an awful lot of money. He disappeared for a long time, and all efforts to locate him failed. It was as if he'd dropped off the face of the earth. Even his website disappeared, pulled down overnight from the Deep Web. Analysts came to the conclusion that the experience must have completely defeated him, perhaps driven him to drink or suicide. Or that someone within his organisation had killed him.

'It took many months of intensive police work to discover that he was still active. Whereupon, the joint operation was mounted between French, British and Swiss Intelligence services to plant undercover operatives into the organisation, with a twofold agenda. First, to discover where Streicher had been hiding, and second, to find out what he was up to. They failed on the first count. We still have no idea where he hides out. As for the second, Streicher answered it for us when he carried out the attack on the monastery. Now we know for a fact that he's by no means given up. All this time, he was simply lying low. Marshalling his forces, forming a new plan in the wake of the failed Korean attack. Looking for an alternative.'

'And now, it appears,' Oppenheim said, 'he's found it.'

Ben stared at the two of them. 'You said at the start that you could sum this up in just one word. So cut to the chase.'

Oppenheim glanced again at Luc Simon, as if looking for the green light. Luc Simon again quietly nodded his acquiescence.

Oppenheim turned to Ben and came out with the one word.

It was, 'Plague.'

Chapter Fifty

There was silence in the room. The two men were watching Ben closely for his reaction. He leaned back deeper in his chair and sipped his coffee. It was going cold and tasted suddenly bitter.

'Aren't you going to say anything?' Luc Simon asked him.

Ben waited another full minute before replying. He wanted to be sure he understood this right. 'The two of Streicher's men we found at the safe house, Roth and Grubitz. Were they infected with what you're talking about?'

'And now both dead,' Oppenheim said with a nod. 'The entire area has been evacuated and sealed off by specialist biohazard teams. It's a particularly virulent strain that attacks the system with extreme aggression.'

'And if you're not showing signs of infection within twenty-four hours, you never will,' Ben said. 'Hence the short quarantine period. Correct?'

'Correct.'

Ben was silent a while longer. Thinking hard. Whichever way he came at it, the conclusion seemed inescapable. He could only pray he was wrong. 'How long can something like this remain dormant and still survive?' he asked Oppenheim.

'Plague is a bacterial disease,' Oppenheim said. 'Its active agent is the bacterium *Yersinia pestis, Y pestis* for short. Unlike a virus, even without being kept sustained by a host, it can stay buried in the ground for centuries. Far from losing in virulence, it can actively evolve and mutate during that time, ready to spring back into action in strengthened form as and when the opportunity arises. Basically, it's a survivor.'

Ben sucked in a deep breath. He hadn't been wrong, and it wasn't a good feeling. 'The monastery,' he said. 'It was the source, wasn't it?'

Luc Simon nodded gravely. 'That's what we believe, too.'

'I lived there for seven months,' Ben said. 'There was nothing, no mention, no clue. Except for the walled-up crypt.' He spent the next few minutes explaining to them what he'd found down there. Père Antoine's reticence about discussing the monastery's past. The dark secrets on which he wouldn't be drawn. Then Ben told them about the errand that had taken him away from the monastery during the crucial hours of Streicher's attack. He described what he'd found on his return. The slaughtered monks, the skeletal remains of the plague dead. And the gold bars.

'We found one in your bag,' Luc Simon said.

'They were scattered about the place,' Ben said. 'The way they would be, if you were in a hurry to transfer a large haul of them from deep underground to a waiting truck, with the clock ticking. As if one accidentally dropped here or there didn't really matter because there were so many of them.' He shook his head. 'I was so sure. And I was so wrong.'

'Streicher is a man of many parts,' Oppenheim said. 'Not least of which are that he's extremely wealthy and extremely cunning. Red herrings don't come much more expensive than planting gold bars about your crime scene to create a false trail.'

'But it worked,' Ben said. 'It worked very bloody well indeed. It stopped me from thinking about the reason for the second explosive charge. The one that sealed up the hole and nearly buried me. He didn't want the cops to see what was down there. The bastard covered his tracks beautifully.'

And the cigarette too, Ben thought. The planted black Sobranie that had almost led him to declare war against every Russian mafioso from Nice to Marseille. Another piece of artful distraction dreamed up by a deviously calculating mind. Ben almost had to admire it.

'Let me reveal some further information I don't think you'll be aware of,' Oppenheim said. 'Very few people are. It concerns a discovery made in 2012 by an ecological survey team in the mountains surrounding Chartreuse de la Sainte Vierge de Pelvoux, who were there to assess the increasing wolf population in the Hautes-Alpes area. Since it became illegal to hunt the damn things, they've turned into more and more of a problem for livestock farmers. Anyway, during an expedition on foot, the survey team came across the body of a strange creature. A rat, physically very deformed and apparently eyeless.'

'I saw rats like that in the crypt before it blew up,' Ben said. 'They must have been breeding down there for a thousand generations.'

'When the rodent's body was taken for analysis, it was found to be harbouring a rare and aggressive strain of plague bacterium,' Oppenheim said, 'which in fact infected the survey team leader and two of his colleagues. None of them survived,' he added dryly. 'The incident was given only light coverage in a handful of scientific journals and wasn't allowed to reach the mainstream media, for fear that it could affect the Alpine tourism industry.'

'But the information is out there nonetheless,' Luc Simon said. 'And we think that it was while he was holed up in

319

hiding after the crushing defeat of his failed Korean mission that Streicher must have come across it, and it pricked his interest.'

If Streicher makes it his business to find out about something, believe me, he does. Silvie's words echoed in Ben's mind.

And: *Ancient secrets. Ones that had been almost completely forgotten over the course of centuries. Only he had been able to connect the facts. How he was going to make history. How he was going to be remembered.*

'Streicher's a researcher,' Ben said. 'He must have devoured everything he could find about the area, to figure out where that rat had come from. Starting with internet searches using obvious keywords like "rat" or "plague". That's how he eventually worked out that the source of the infection was right underneath the monastery, that the rat must have crawled through a crack in the mountain and died out there in the open. It was the connection with the old forgotten story of the martyr's curse.'

'The what?' Luc Simon said. Oppenheim was quiet, listening.

'The prophecy of a dying man as he burned at the stake,' Ben said. 'That a thousand years of pestilence would descend upon the land and bring his revenge on the descendants of the people who'd betrayed him. It was only six hundred odd years ago. Maybe Salvator's timing wasn't so wrong, after all.'

'What are you talking about, Ben?' Luc Simon said.

'The reason the contamination was down there in the first place,' Ben said, 'is that within just a few months, in 1348, the curse appeared to come true. It was a Plague year. The dead and the dying alike were walled up in the crypt underneath Sainte Vierge de Pelvoux. Sealed off from the outside world and left there for their bones to be gnawed by a thousand generations of rats. One of which happened to escape centuries later, giving Streicher the tip he'd been waiting for. It was an easy target. All he needed were the right people for the job, which he already had. Plus the right equipment.'

Now Ben realised what had been haunting him. Roby's last words as he'd lain bleeding to death from the gunshot wound in his belly. He'd said, *I saw ghosts. All white.*

Not strictly white. More silvery-white. Streicher's team members in hazmat suits, foraging deep under the monastery to gather all the toxic samples of dead and decomposed rat tissue they could pack into the white cases Silvie had later seen inside the assault vehicle. Containers for the transportation of biohazard materials. Meanwhile, the hazmat suits, masks, footwear and gauntlets had been in the bags that she had been tasked to burn after the raid.

'So now you understand what we're dealing with,' Luc Simon said. 'A lethal infectious pathogen in the hands of a maniac who wants to rule the world.'

'It was a devastatingly simple plan,' Oppenheim said. 'If you can't get hold of modern biological warfare agents, you source some ancient ones of your own. We can only assume that Streicher must have on his payroll at least one expert capable of processing the material. A chemist, or a biologist, or both. We can further speculate that he may have these people at work, even as we speak, on a vaccine or serum that he intends to use to protect himself and his fellow Parati members before unleashing this thing.'

'Which potentially buys us time,' Ben said.

'Potentially, yes. How much time is an open question. If our speculations are correct, Streicher must have access to some kind of private laboratory facilities. We don't know what, or where.'

'But you do know that what he's got is the same pathogen

as the medieval Black Death,' Ben said. 'Bubonic plague. Which is presumably a disease well known to medical science, and highly treatable.'

Luc Simon looked down at his feet.

Oppenheim pursed his lips.

'What?' Ben said.

'Mr Hope,' Oppenheim said. 'I wish it *were* bubonic plague.'

Chapter Fifty-One

'Then what the hell is it?' Ben asked, staring from Oppenheim to Luc Simon and back again.

'You need to understand that there are various forms of plague,' Oppenheim said. 'The so-called bubonic variety, named after the "buboes" or black lumpy spots that are a characteristic symptom of that particular strain of the disease, is spread by fleas infected with the *Y pestis* bacterium. It can't be contracted directly from a victim, which significantly reduces the rate and efficiency of the contamination. In effect, the disease is hamstrung by its own infection mechanism. It's just not enough of a killer to fully account for the appalling virulence of the medieval Black Death, which spread like a bush fire through Europe and beyond and claimed some two hundred million lives during its short but nefarious history. Many scientists now think that the Black Death is more likely to have been a form of *pneumonic* plague.'

'I'm not a doctor,' Ben said impatiently. 'These terms mean little to me.'

'The diseases have plenty in common,' Oppenheim explained. 'Both have been used in biological warfare. In the fourteenth century, the Tartars catapulted corpses of bubonic plague victims over the city walls during the Siege of Kaffa. In World War Two, the Japanese packed infected fleas into bombs with the aim of spreading the disease among allied troops. Suitably callous tactics, but crude and limited due to their reliance on parasitic organisms to carry the contagion. By contrast, when the Soviets experimented with aerosolised *Y pestis* during the Cold War, they discovered they'd created a weapon of a whole other magnitude of lethality.'

'Pneumonic plague?'

Oppenheim nodded. 'Same active bacterial agent, our old friend *Yersinia pestis*. But what makes all the difference is that in the pneumonic variety, it's airborne. You don't need to be bitten by an infected flea to contract it. This thing is directly communicable from one living being to another, humans and animals alike. Proximity is all it takes. It can spread with incredible speed over a large area, the rate of infection continually multiplying as it takes hold. In short, pneumonic plague is to its bubonic sibling what a nuclear missile is to a handgun.'

Ben stared at him. 'And this is what we're dealing with here?'

'Going by the pathology we've seen in both victims, Roth and Grubitz, then I'm very much afraid that that's *exactly* what we're dealing with,' Oppenheim said. 'It enters the lungs and swiftly takes over the entire system. Coughing and sneezing tend to be the first symptoms, quickly followed by violent fever and nausea, then uncontrollable bouts of seizures and bloody vomiting. Soon afterwards the system collapses into septic shock. Tissues break down and become necrotic and gangrenous. A horrible and agonising death ensues within hours.'

'If that's what happened to Roth and Grubitz, they had it coming,' Ben said.

'So does half of Europe, if we don't do something to stop it,' Oppenheim said. 'Consider the mortality rates. Bubonic plague kills between one to fifteen per cent of victims if treated, and between forty to sixty per cent in untreated cases. In other words, even without medical aid, your chances can be better than fifty-fifty. Contrast that to pneumonic plague, which has a one hundred per cent fatality rate if the patient isn't treated within the first twenty-four hours.'

'Maybe it's not as infectious as you think it is,' Ben said, shaking his head. 'I'm living proof of that. I wasn't just exposed for those few moments at the safe house. I was down there in that hole, knee-deep in infected rat shit and breathing in God knows what kind of dust and spores and bacteria. So why didn't I get it?'

Oppenheim spread his hands, as if to say *good question*. 'Studies have been done that suggest some Europeans have a genetic immunity to plague bacteria, going back to medieval times. That's one possible explanation. Another is the medication you were taking.'

Ben frowned. 'What medication?'

'Whatever the substance is inside the small brown glass dropper bottle that the arresting officers found on you at the safe house,' Luc Simon said.

'What, that? It's just some kind of traditional tonic that Père Antoine gave me,' Ben said. 'I never really thought of it as medication.'

'How much of it were you taking?'

'Just a few drops every day,' Ben said. 'I gave some to Silvie Valois, too.'

'Why?'

'I like to keep my hostages in tip-top condition.'

'What's in it?'

'I never asked.'

'We're having it analysed anyway,' Luc Simon said. 'I'm expecting a full chemical breakdown in the next few hours. It could be critical data for us.'

Ben was baffled by their interest in it. 'Wait a minute. Are you trying to say there's no modern drug treatment lined up to fight this disease?'

Oppenheim said nothing.

'It *is* treatable?' Ben repeated.

Oppenheim was quiet for a moment longer. 'We've got a long history of combating plague, sure enough,' he said. 'And in recent times we learned to become more relaxed about what had long been a dreaded disease. As long as it was caught early, it was readily treatable with antibiotics. You'll note my use of the past tense. *Was.* Because things are changing. In fact, they've already changed. We have a major problem. One that we were warned about, way back at the turn of the twentieth century, and happily ignored, when many doctors predicted that the antibiotic panacea wouldn't last. In fact they warned that these sensational new wonder drugs could even do harm in the long run. Firstly, by causing people to become dependent on them for even the most minor infection, potentially compromising their natural immunity. The natural law of use it or lose it. Secondly, even back then they knew how fast microbes could mutate, adapt and evolve. The fear was that they could develop ways of resisting the drugs. But they were laughed at, and we went on to spend the entire twentieth century and the first decade of this century abusing the drugs wholesale. Now we know the doomsayers were absolutely right.'

Ben said nothing.

'It's happening right before our eyes,' Oppenheim went on. 'In the last fifteen years, we've seen a seventy per cent increase in deaths from antibiotic-resistant infection, and that figure is set to get much worse. Hospitals will soon become no-go areas due to the hazard of MRSA and other powerfully evolved micro-organisms. It's a two-pronged problem. One, we've become weaker. Two, the enemy has become stronger. We underestimated the bugs, far more than we could have even imagined.'

'I'm afraid it's true,' Luc Simon said. 'I've read the reports myself.'

'Microbes are incredibly adaptable things,' Oppenheim said, almost glowing with admiration for the critters. 'They're smarter than us in a lot of ways. Some can even repair their own DNA, an incredible feat of bioengineering. Ultimately, they will be the downfall of humanity. In the short term, things aren't looking so great either. The medical profession doesn't want to admit it, but right now, we're like deer in the headlights. In fact, there's never been a worse time for a bacterial pandemic to happen. Our populations are at an all-time high, with unprecedented concentrations of people between whom disease can spread more efficiently than ever before. International travel makes our efforts to contain an outbreak practically impossible. Combine that with our lack of viable treatments and the majority of the population's lowered immunity to infection . . .' Oppenheim cracked a grim smile. 'In short, we're one small step away from being comprehensively screwed. My job is to stop us from taking that one small step.'

'You said Streicher could be preparing a vaccine or a serum to protect himself and his own people,' Ben said. 'Couldn't we do the same from this end?'

'It's a possibility,' Oppenheim said. 'But not a promising one. As unbelievable as it may sound, plague vaccines are still in their infancy. Drugs prepared from attenuated live *Y pestis* samples have only ever been tested on mice, and even then with limited efficacy. There are no guarantees of their success on humans, which goes for Streicher and his gang too. They could very well be dead already. Which would account for their disappearance, wouldn't it? As for us, even if we were able to develop a workable antiserum to protect the public, what are the chances we could produce enough, and fast enough, to control a major outbreak?'

'There has to be something that works,' Ben said. 'Did Torben Roth receive treatment before he died?'

Oppenheim nodded gravely. 'Every antibiotic drug that's ever been used to combat plague. Gentamicin, Streptomycin, Chloromycetin, Doxycycline, Ciprofloxacin, Tetracycline, you name it. Zero effect. The bacteria just marched on through. Like trying to hold off a tank division with a child's popgun.'

'It could be that he was too far gone already,' Luc Simon said. 'Perhaps if we'd been able to intervene sooner, he'd have survived.'

'Or perhaps not,' Oppenheim said. 'It could simply be that our last line of defence has failed before the war has even begun.' It was the first sign of friction Ben had seen between the two.

'We can contain it,' Luc Simon said firmly.

'I'd love to say I could believe that,' Oppenheim sighed, closing his eyes and pinching the bony bridge of his nose.

'Plus, there are all kinds of other possibilities,' Luc Simon said. 'Consider the fact that Roth and Grubitz managed to contract the infection in the first place. How did that happen? Was their protective clothing compromised in some way? Grubitz was the first to catch it, so maybe his hazmat suit was faulty or got damaged during the raid, exposing him, and then Roth caught it from him afterwards.'

'Anything's possible,' Oppenheim said.

'Alternatively, it could have been one of the others,' Luc Simon continued, leaning forward animatedly in his chair. 'Roth or Grubitz could have caught it from any of them. Which could mean they're all infected, one way or another. You said yourself, Streicher and his entire team could be dead already, precluding any attack from taking place.'

'But what if they're not?' Oppenheim countered. 'How much are we prepared to risk on wishful thinking? And then, what if they are dead? The bodies could be anywhere, leaking infection to any living thing that comes into contact with them.'

Luc Simon shrugged. 'We need to hope for the best, that's all.'

'And plan for the worst,' Ben said. He turned to Oppenheim. 'What's our darkest possible scenario here?'

Oppenheim shook his head. 'Don't even ask. You don't want to know.'

'I can take it,' Ben said.

'All right, then. Let's say this lunatic is indeed still alive out there somewhere, and that he goes ahead with his plans, by whatever means, such as poisoning the water supplies or exploding a dirty bomb or spraying the stuff out of a heli-copter. Let's say he successfully kicks off the beginnings of an epidemic, and that it takes a hold and spreads rapidly, displaying the same extremely aggressive traits we've already seen in the two confirmed victims to date. Moreover, let's say that our worst fears are confirmed, and the disease is resistant to even our most powerful antibiotics. And that we're unable to produce effective substitute treatments such as vaccinations in time . . .'

'Then?'

'Then Europe might be about to see something it hasn't seen for six centuries,' Oppenheim said. 'The outcome would be nightmarishly predictable. Widespread panic. Desperate crowds swarming the hospitals while others fled the cities altogether in the hope of avoiding the infection, jamming the roads and the transport systems solid. The emergency services strained far beyond capacity. The death toll rising faster than we can count it as the infection spreads exponentially. Thousands dead, virtually overnight. Then tens of thousands, then hundreds of thousands. People collapsing and dying even as they queue for useless treatments. Within months, or possibly just weeks, the number of dead rising into seven figures and still climbing. Meanwhile, a total breakdown of law and order. Riots and looting breaking out in every major city. Ultimately, police and medical services deserting their posts en masse to look out for themselves and their families. Or sick. Or dead already.'

Oppenheim paused and breathed out heavily. His face took on a pinched look that made it appear even more gaunt. 'Then, suddenly, silence. No more sirens, no more helicopters in the air. Airports and railway stations, cities and motorways, all deserted. The streets empty, apart from the bodies strewn in the road and the vermin and scavengers come to feast on their rotting flesh.

'Apocalypse.'

Chapter Fifty-Two

Oppenheim's words hung in the air like a knell of doom. Ben was the one who broke the silence. 'And then, out of the darkness come Streicher and his followers, ready to gather together the survivors and form a new world with him as its leader.'

'So his fantasy goes,' Oppenheim said. 'If he gets that far. Either way, the damage will have been done. He'll have won.'

The three men fell back into their separate reflections for a long minute. Finally Ben said, 'What do you want me to do?'

'To carry on as before,' Luc Simon said. 'To locate Udo Streicher's hideout and take him down before the worst happens. And this time, it'll be with our full co-operation. Your way. No interference, no comebacks.'

'Whatever it takes?' Ben said.

'Whatever it takes. Just one condition.'

Ben looked at him suspiciously. 'Which is what?'

'I'd like to assign you a partner. One of our top anti-terrorist agents, recently promoted in rank. Someone who already knows the score, who knows Streicher and can identify him on sight. Which is an essential advantage for the success of this mission, I hope you'll agree.'

'I need to move fast,' Ben said. 'I can't be lumbered with some by-the-book government type weighing me down every step of the way.'

Luc Simon smiled. 'I think you'll find this particular agent is anything but "by the book". They've shown ample evidence of that already. As well as the highest level of skill you could wish for in a partner. Expert in fieldcraft. Top of their class in armed and unarmed combat, if it comes to that. As well as being the only government agent who's personally known Udo Streicher and survived to tell the tale.' He turned towards the door and called out, 'You can come in, Special Agent Valois.'

The door opened.

Silvie looked as Ben had never seen her before. The battered biker jacket and faded jeans were gone, replaced by a smart dark grey trouser suit. Designer, for all Ben knew. It wasn't his particular area of knowledge, but whatever it was, she looked good in it. Capable, professional and more attractive than he'd realised when they'd been on the run together. Maybe he just hadn't had time to notice before. Her hair was loosely tied back and she was wearing just enough make-up to be discernible.

Neither of them quite managed to keep the smile off their face as she stepped into the room.

'Congratulations on your promotion, Special Agent,' Ben said. 'You must have hooked a pretty big fish.'

'Huge,' she said.

'It seems we'll be working together on an equal footing from now on.'

'As opposed to kidnapper and hostage?'

'My apologies for the harsh treatment.'

'No harm, no foul,' she said. 'I can take the knocks.'

If Luc Simon was wise to the play-acting between them,

nothing showed on his face. Nothing except the pallor and sunken eyes of a man under a great deal of stress. He yawned and said, 'It's nearly three a.m. Dr Oppenheim and I have to leave shortly. A car has been arranged to collect the two of you.'

'Where are we going?' Ben asked.

'To the Crowne Plaza hotel in Lyon. Your new temporary base. It's an Interpol perk. I trust you'll be comfortable there.'

'Very temporary,' Ben said.

'Whatever your requirements,' Luc Simon said, 'I can have everything ready by morning.'

'It won't be a long list,' Ben said. 'A new watch, to start with. Omega Seamaster automatic, steel, with the blue dial, like the one your medicos put in the trash.'

'Why not trade up to a Rolex Submariner?' Luc Simon said without skipping a beat. French tax euros at work.

'The Omega's always done a good job for me,' Ben said. 'And I'll need a car. Something rugged, up to a bit of punishment. Big enough to kip in, too, if it comes to it. That's if Special Agent Valois doesn't object to roughing it a little.'

Silvie said, 'I'm a big girl.'

'I was thinking,' Luc Simon said. 'There's a fellow in Briançon who seems to have mislaid a H1 Hummer, except he seems rather vague about the details. Name's Omar Adeyemi. A friend of yours, by any chance?'

Ben said nothing.

'The Hummer is in the police pound. I get the impression Monsieur Adeyemi isn't in a desperate hurry for it back. I can have it released to you with one call.'

'Then do it,' Ben said. 'And lastly, I wouldn't mind that FAMAS back. And the Browning, minus the GPS tracking gizmo inside.'

'Consider it done,' Luc Simon said. 'On the understanding that you won't go shooting the place up.'

Ben looked at him. 'I thought we agreed. My way.'

It took the Frenchman a moment to get the humour. He smiled. 'It's good to be working with you, Ben. We can stop this bastard.'

'Let's not get too excited about our chances,' Ben said. 'The trail's cold. We're out of leads. All we have left is an empty safe house that's now part of a biohazard evac zone, and a couple of dead men. I'm good at what I do, but I can't work miracles. We're going to have to do this the hard way. Go back to the drawing board and start again, looking for any little thread that can lead us to where Streicher's hiding out.'

'It's your call.'

'Has he got any surviving family?'

'None,' Luc Simon said. 'Parents died within eighteen months of one another. The father of leukaemia aged sixty-nine, the mother of acute heart failure at only sixty-two. No siblings, no children, no former spouses.'

'The footwear empire?'

'Sold off cheap for two hundred million to an Italian conglomerate in 2006,' Luc Simon said.

'What about Streicher's private dental practice in Geneva?' Ben asked. 'Strikes me as the kind of place you could set up a makeshift laboratory.'

'He quit that line of work years ago,' Luc Simon said. 'The building now operates as a cosmetic plastic surgery practice. Belonging to a Dr Emil Zucker, who was very startled to receive a visit from our agents. He thought they were tax auditors.'

'Then run up the list of names of Streicher's known followers,' Ben said. 'Starting with this Hannah Gissel.

Somewhere down the line there'll be a weak link, someone who knows something or who can at least lead us to someone else.'

'You think those avenues haven't already been thoroughly investigated?' Silvie said.

'Fine,' Ben said. 'Then the trail gets thinner still. All we have is two gangrenous corpses and a list of ghosts.'

'Not quite all,' Silvie said. She turned to Luc Simon. 'Have you told him about Donath?'

'I was about to get to that,' Luc Simon said.

'Who?' Ben asked.

'Miki Donath was one of Streicher's closest associates,' Luc Simon explained to Ben. 'Born in Dresden in 1976. Served in the German army for sixteen years, nine of them in the KSK, Kommando Spezialkräfte. Speaks fluent French and English. He seems to have been recruited to the Parati while still on active service. Left the military in 2010, and the following year is believed to have been part of the team put together for the abortive Korea mission. Returned to Europe as a diehard core member of the Parati, dealing in illegal weaponry on the side. We think he also supplied a large quantity of arms and ammunition to Streicher's people, hence the close rapport between the two men. In April 2013, Donath was suspected of the murders of two rival small-arms dealers in Berlin, but the charges didn't stick due to lack of evidence. Back in Switzerland, he was arrested five months later for his involvement in the brutal gang rape and mutilation of a thirteen-year-old girl in Lucerne.'

Ben felt his fists tighten. He clenched his jaw and let the Frenchman go on.

'On that occasion, the evidence against him was plentiful. He's currently serving a fifteen-year sentence at a low-security prison in Altdorf, though he may not be there much longer.

From what I gather, there have been some issues with his behaviour towards other inmates.'

'Has anybody been there to speak to him?' Ben asked.

Luc Simon nodded. 'Jürgen Ganz of the FIS, the Swiss Federal Intelligence Service, sent a pair of agents to interview him. That's the term they prefer, by the way. The concept of interrogation doesn't go down well with the liberal penal system there.'

'Result?' Ben asked, though he already knew the answer.

'Donath's a tough nut, pretty much as you'd expect from someone with his background. The agents came away with nothing. He wouldn't even speak to them.'

'I'd like to have a try,' Ben said.

'Your way?'

'Whatever works.'

Luc Simon shook his head. 'Sorry, Ben. Whatever exceptional leeway I'm authorised to grant you extends strictly within EU territory only. As far as Switzerland is concerned, being outside the Union, there are very specific limitations to be observed. If we're seen to overstep the mark even in the slightest degree, there'll be hell to pay. I can get you in to see him, no problem. But absolutely no forceful tactics will be permitted in the handling of the prisoner. I hope I'm being totally clear about this.'

'So you're saying we can't waterboard him,' Ben said.

'I hope you're kidding. He's not at Guantanamo Bay, Ben. And the Swiss penal system authorities pride themselves on their focus on progressive, humane social rehabilitation, as opposed to anything that carries even the faintest whiff of punishment. It's all about therapeutic communities and supervised holidays, windy walks and horse-riding in the countryside. What other approach could turn hardened criminals into responsible citizens?'

'They're way ahead over there,' Silvie said, with a blandly neutral expression.

'Fine,' Ben said. 'Let's go and ask him nicely, pretty please with icing on top, if he happens to know where his old pal Udo is hanging out these days.'

Chapter Fifty-Three

Luc Simon and the enigmatic Dr Jean-Pierre Oppenheim left, and a pair of large, taciturn twenty-something security goons in dark suits escorted Ben and Silvie outside to the waiting car, a long, low, black government Citroën DS5 with smoked windows, the same model that the President of France was chauffeured around in. The night was dark and damp. The first goon got in the front of the car alongside the driver while the second showed Ben and Silvie into the back. Ben could see the lump under his jacket where he was concealing a small submachine gun, maybe a Skorpion or a Micro Uzi, next to his ribs. The second goon stepped away from the car and muttered something into a radio. The driver took off and drove fast through the secret science facility's maze of buildings. They reached an armed checkpoint brightly illuminated by floodlights on tall masts. The security guy whirred down his window and flashed a pass at the guards, and they were waved briskly through two sets of tall steel-mesh gates. The night closed in around the speeding car.

'I'm glad you're okay,' Silvie said, too softly to be heard up front.

'I'm glad you are too,' Ben said. He could see her eyes shining in the darkness and the play of a smile on her lips.

Very tentatively, she reached out and her fingertips touched the back of his hand.

Nothing more was said until they reached the hotel. The Interpol ticket got them straight past the desk and into the lift to their rooms, which were part of a double suite that was spacious and comfortable and a far cry from the roadside motel room they'd shared two days earlier. More spacious and comfortable than were strictly necessary for the interests of national security, Ben thought, but at least he wasn't footing the bill. The two bedrooms were at opposite ends, separated by a lounge and open-plan adjoining dining area. There was a large fruit bowl on the dining table. Elegant lighting. Vases of flowers filled the room with sweet perfume. Ben walked over to the bedroom door at the lounge end and peered inside. There was a double bed and a small en suite bathroom, and a mock-Persian rug and French windows that looked as if they led out to a balcony.

A canvas and leather travel bag sat at the foot of the bed. He unzipped it and saw it was full of female clothing. Neatly folded blouses. Lacy underwear. A light, delicate and insubstantial pale silk nightdress that seemed to be more holes than material. He quickly shut the bag, feeling like he was intruding.

Silvie's room, evidently. The Interpol guys had thought of everything. He stepped back out of the room and closed the door. At the far side of the suite, Silvie was coming out of the other bedroom. 'This one's yours,' she said. 'That horrible musty old green sack is in there.'

They approached each other and stopped two steps apart in the middle of the suite. There was a strange awkwardness in the air. As if neither of them knew just what to say, like a couple of gauche teenagers hovering tentatively around one another, each terrified of making any kind of move.

'It's late,' Silvie said. 'I suppose we should get some rest. Nothing much we can do until morning, anyway.'

Ben wasn't remotely tired. He'd had enough enforced rest during his twenty-four-hour quarantine to last him a week. He'd be counting the night down, one minute at a time, until he could press on again with what he had to do.

'See you in the morning, then,' he said. Neither of them moved, as if neither wanted to be the first to turn away and head for their own bedroom. As if there was something stopping them.

'Well, goodnight,' Silvie said.

'Goodnight, Silvie.'

More awkward seconds passed as they stood there in the middle of the huge suite.

She raised an eyebrow and grinned. 'Why do you suppose they put us together, anyway?'

'Bureaucratic efficiency,' he said.

'Don't you just love it?'

'More tax euros at work.'

'Whatever. It's nice to be here with you.'

'Go and get some sleep,' he said. 'It's going to be a long day tomorrow.'

'I'm not really that sleepy,' she said.

He said nothing.

'There's bound to be some wine in the minibar. Maybe something a little stronger. Care for a midnight drink?'

'It's long past midnight,' he said. 'Besides, I more or less quit.'

She was just a couple of paces away, looking up at him with an expression he couldn't quite make out. Her hair was shining in the suite's soft lighting. There was a glow in her eyes, a half-smile on her lips.

He suddenly could imagine how easy it would be to step

forward those two paces and kiss her. The thought startled him. But it also appealed to him. Too much. Too damn much. He tried not to let her see him swallow.

'Goodnight, Silvie,' he said again, and this time he managed to turn and walk to his room. He opened the door and slipped inside without looking back. Clicked it shut behind him.

His room was just the same as hers, except for the baggage and fresh clothes that had been left there waiting for him. He'd miss the old leather jacket. In its place was a black synthetic military-style number, with a pair of jeans and a change of underwear. He turned off the main light and dimmed the bedside lamp to its lowest setting, just a halo of light, like a candle's. Sat on the bed and gave his bag a playful nudge with his foot. 'Horrible musty old green sack, indeed,' he murmured. Some people just didn't understand. He reached inside and found that they'd left him his cigarettes. Considerate, those Interpol guys. Aside from the fact that they'd quietly relieved him of the remainder of the stolen money. Maybe that was what was paying for the rooms.

He spent twenty minutes under the shower with the water turned up hot, blasting off the last of the chemical wash he could still smell on his skin. He used one of the tiny complimentary bottles of shampoo to wash his hair. Then he towelled himself off, rubbed a hole in the condensation on the mirror and rasped his hand over his jaw. He decided shaving could wait a couple more days and put on a hotel dressing gown.

Back in the bedroom, he turned off the light. Walked over to the French window via a detour over to his bag, stepped out on to the railed balcony and lit up a Gauloise. A cool breeze rustled the satin drapes and carried his wisps of smoke gently away, melting them into the night air. He savoured

341

the cigarette for as long as he could make it last, leaning on the railing and gazing out over the twinkling city lights. A siren was wailing in the distance. Somewhere out there, an unseen night train was rumbling out of the city. He thought about the passengers on board, and where their journey might be taking them. He thought about all the people asleep in their homes across Lyon, across France, across Europe. So many innocent lives out there. So fragile, so vulnerable, so ignorant of the lunatic destructiveness that threatened them and of the unravelling thread from which the stability and security of their world was hanging.

He smoked the cigarette down to a stub, until the heat of its glowing tip singed his fingers. Then he crushed it against the iron railing and the orange glow died away to nothing. He flicked the stub into the night and walked back into the darkened bedroom, leaving the French window open to allow the cool breeze inside.

He stopped.

Silvie was lying stretched out in his bed. The nightdress he'd found in her bag was a small pool of pale material on the rug nearby. Her hair was fanned out, dark against the pillow. He could see the curve of her bare shoulders above the sheet. She had one knee bent, the thin cotton draped over it like a tent. The light from the open window was reflected as bright little pinpoints in her eyes.

'I didn't hear you come in,' he said after a beat.

'I couldn't sleep,' she said.

'Me neither,' he said.

He took a step towards the bed. Then another. Lifted the edge of the sheet and peeled it back. Let the hotel gown slip off him and fall to the rug.

And it wasn't until a long time afterwards, lying there in the stillness of the night with Silvie's head nuzzled against his left shoulder and the warmth of her skin against his, listening to the soft, steady rhythm of her breathing as she slept, that he realised he couldn't remember the last time he'd thought about Brooke Marcel.

Chapter Fifty-Four

Altdorf, Switzerland

The place didn't even look like a prison until they were almost at the entrance. It was tucked away in what seemed like an ordinary street, among what seemed like ordinary buildings and offices and homes. Barely anything to differentiate it from its surroundings, apart from the heavy iron gate, and the bars on the upper windows, and the few token coils of razor wire that discreetly adorned the roof, gleaming dully in the morning sunshine.

As Ben and Silvie walked up to the gate, it clicked open by some remote mechanism and whirred aside on smooth tracks. It was 9.24 a.m., and they were expected. Silvie was wearing the same dark trouser suit as yesterday, somehow unrumpled despite that morning's helicopter ride from Lyon. Ben had nothing more formal to wear than his new jeans and black jacket. Not that it seemed to matter.

No passes or ID were needed. The magic ticket from Interpol was opening all the doors for them. Wherever the road might be heading, so far it was green lights all the way.

'I'm Special Agent Silvie Valois of DGSI and this is Major Hope, attached to Interpol,' Silvie said in French to the woman who met them inside the gate. 'We're here to see the prisoner Miki Donath.'

The woman shook their hands and introduced herself as Leila Amacker. She was tall and severe, threads of grey in the dark hair she wore tightly scraped back under a clasp. 'Please follow me,' she said. Ben wasn't sure if she was offended or not by the use of the term 'prisoner'. Inmate might have worked better. Or guest, maybe.

She led them through the main double doors of the unlikeliest prison Ben had ever seen. He'd beheld the inside of a few penal establishments in his time, more than once from the wrong side of the bars. He'd never been in one like this before, not least because it didn't appear to have any.

'Why is everything pink?' he asked Frau Amacker as she led them at a brisk walk through the corridors. Because everything was, the same way everything from the walls to the doors to the window frames of any military facility in the world was covered in gallons of generic drab olive green. Except this was fresh, bright pink, like the inside of a little girl's bedroom. All that was missing were the spangly pendants and fluffy toy horses.

'Colour psychology studies have shown that it reduces hostility levels in the inmates and promotes calmness,' Frau Amacker said, as if explaining the obvious to a rather dim-witted child.

'I see,' Ben said. 'And the pris— the inmates are free just to wander about the place?'

'Of course.' Frau Amacker cracked a frosty smile. 'Now, before we proceed, the governor wishes to have a word with you.'

She led them up another shining neon-lit pink corridor to a door, knocked softly and a man's voice answered from inside. Frau Amacker showed Ben and Silvie into the large, comfortable, plant-filled office. At least that wasn't pink, too.

'*Guete Morge*,' the governor said in Swiss-German, rising up from his desk, a small, wiry man with a worried look creasing his brow like rice paper. He sat them down, then mercifully switched to English and introduced himself as Mathias Heckethorn, governor of the Bezirksgefängnis Altdorf. After a few moments of pleasantries, he explained to them the reason for the worried look. A shocking, *shocking* incident had taken place just yesterday, during the inmate Miki Donath's weekly reintegration session with the young woman who was his regular visiting sociotherapist. The upshot of which was that the sociotherapist was now in hospital with a broken collarbone and half an ear missing from where Donath's teeth had severed it in a single bite.

'I'm afraid it's not the first time,' Governor Heckethorn said nervously. 'There have been five prior incidents, the last of which was when Donath almost blinded another inmate and destroyed all of his teeth. It's an intolerable situation; I have been compelled to arrange an immediate transfer to a more secure facility in Regensdorf.'

'Maybe the paint scheme isn't working too well, after all,' Ben said.

Silvie shot him a look. 'Does that mean we won't be able to see him?' she asked Heckethorn.

'No, but regrettably the interview will have to take place in a secure room, for your personal safety. You may also be pressed for time. Donath is scheduled to be out of here by midday.'

'We just have a few questions,' Ben said. 'It shouldn't take long.'

'Thank you so much for your co-operation,' Heckethorn simpered, virtually wringing his hands in relief. This guy

346

would have gone down a storm in charge of Alcatraz, Ben thought.

Ten minutes later, they were sitting in the interview room. Ben had studiously avoided using the word *interrogate*, on Luc Simon's advice. The room smelled of antiseptic and was bare apart from two plastic chairs and a plain table. Miki Donath was seated in an identical chair, separated from his interviewers by a thick Perspex security window drilled with sound holes. A pair of prison guards stood behind him, looking just a little wary of the prisoner and clearly ready to jump him in case he tried to headbutt his way through the glass.

Donath appeared perfectly calm. He looked older than his thirty-nine years, with a deeply lined face and hooded dark eyes that seemed as expressionless as a shark's. His hair was cut as short as an electric trimmer would go. He was wearing jeans and a T-shirt. Maybe the Swiss authorities believed that uniforms were disempowering, Ben thought.

Silvie began the dialogue, leaning close to the security screen and talking slowly and clearly. 'Herr Donath, as I'm aware that you speak English, I'm choosing to conduct this interview in that language. Is that acceptable to you?'

Donath made no reply. The shark eyes were staring at Silvie as if wondering which part of her to eat first. Ben stared back at him.

Silvie went on. 'Okay, Herr Donath, my name is Special Agent Silvie Valois, and I'm here on behalf of the French General Directorate of Homeland Security to speak with you regarding the whereabouts of your former associate, Udo Streicher.'

Donath smiled. Only his lips moved, curling in disdain. His eyes stayed blank. 'Who's the guy with you?'

'You don't want to know,' Ben said.

Silvie flashed Ben a furious sideways glare. Calmly resuming, she said to Donath, 'It's vitally important that we locate him. Your assistance in the matter would be greatly valued.'

No reply. Donath kept staring, completely still, like a lizard on a rock.

'I know what you're thinking, Miki,' she said, switching tack. 'I may call you Miki? Everybody hates a snitch, yes? But in fact you wouldn't be informing on him. You'd be helping him. You see, we have reason to believe that Udo is involved in activities that could get him into a lot of trouble. We only wish to speak to him about what would be in his best interests.'

Ben was deeply impressed with her professional aplomb in these surroundings. Warm and reassuring, the lies smoothly and believably delivered, her manner accommodating and reassuring, her body language relaxed. But Donath wasn't taking the bait. Ben watched those still, dead eyes. In the absence of a loaded and cocked pistol shoved under his chin, you could glean a great deal about a man's thoughts from his eyes. And Donath's revealed a lot. There was a knowing look at their inscrutable heart, a muted glow of satisfaction, almost of pride, as if he were thinking to himself, *Go get 'em, Udo!*

'I'm asking you to help us,' Silvie said in a softer tone. 'And your friend. Aren't you interested in helping him?'

Ben wanted to say something. Possibilities entered his mind, such as: *Listen, arsehole. Co-operate and we'll guarantee that your sentence is reduced to five years.* That might work, and who cared if it was true or not? *Tell us where Streicher is or I'll stamp your spine into little pieces* might work even better. Ben didn't foresee any theoretical difficulty in putting the two guards out of action, if it came to it. It was the impenetrable Perspex security window that might cause more problems.

But as the interview ticked by, it was Donath himself who proved the most impenetrable. Sylvie kept gamely trying. Ben admired her tenacity and inventiveness as she kept switching from one approach to another. In the end, nothing worked. After twenty-five minutes, the session was called to an end. Donath said nothing as the guards led him away. Ben and Silvie left the interview room empty-handed.

'That didn't go so well, did it?' she muttered as they walked back towards the official car that had brought them from the airport. She was agitated and flushed. 'You weren't much help in there,' she snapped at him.

Ben didn't speak. 'I didn't mean that,' she added a moment later, quickly regretting her words. She reached out her arm and let her fingers brush his, softly, lingering just a fraction longer than they needed to. She managed a brief, unhappy smile. 'It wasn't your fault. I shouldn't lash out at you to cover my own failure. I messed up. Damn it, our one chance and I totally dropped the ball.'

Ben paused in his stride and gently clasped her arm, easing her to a halt on the pavement and turning her round to face him. 'You did fine,' he said. 'Don't beat yourself up. It was an impossible job to start with. Suicide missions have had better odds than we had in there.'

She shook her head, staring down at her feet. 'You're just saying that.'

'No, I'd have been extremely surprised if it had gone any other way, under the circumstances. Because Donath knows perfectly well what this is really about. Whatever else he may be, he's not an idiot. He was there in Korea, risking getting shot to pieces by People's Army troopers for the sake of the Parati. He's probably every bit as committed to the whole

349

insane plan as Streicher is. And now, thanks to both FIS and us landing on him in quick succession, he knows that panic buttons have been pressed and that Streicher must somehow have succeeded in getting what he's been after all this time. We might as well have typed up the whole report for him. Which makes it even less likely that he'd spill the beans on his old pal. Our timing couldn't have been less subtle. So relax. This approach never stood a chance in hell.'

She looked at him with a frown of consternation. 'If you knew that all along, then why did you come here?'

'I felt I had to,' Ben replied simply. 'Because what the governor told us just now only confirmed what Luc Simon mentioned in Lyon, about the problems they've had keeping Donath in this place. He obviously needs something more calming than four pink walls to quell his less peaceable tendencies.'

'I know they're moving him,' she said. 'What difference does that make for us? We can't make him talk either way.'

They walked slowly on towards the waiting car. It was another black DS5. Rudy, their designated driver, had spotted them coming and fired up the motor.

'It's like Luc said,' Ben told her. 'This isn't Guantanamo Bay.'

'So?'

'So, the kind of penal system that allows dangerous and violent criminals to enjoy supervised holidays and horse-riding in the country isn't exactly going to transport this guy between prisons in an armoured truck with a full complement of gunned-up guards and a police motorcycle escort. It'll most likely be an ordinary prison service van with a driver and co-driver and nobody else. Which means a degree of vulnerability in transit. An easily exploited opportunity, for someone with the right motivation.'

Silvie paused with her hand on the car door handle. 'Shit. Do you think that's Streicher's next move? To try to get him out?'

Ben made a non-committal gesture. 'Hijacking a prison van wouldn't be a one-man job. Minimum of two, I'd say. It's been done plenty of times before. In the UK, springing fellow thugs out of the hands of private security firms is down to a fine art.'

Silvie reflected. 'Streicher and Hannah Gissel. I can see it. But Jesus, do you think they'd have the balls to pull it off? In broad daylight?'

'I think it's highly likely that somebody crazy enough would be seriously tempted to give it a bash,' Ben said.

'You could be right,' Silvie said. 'In which case, we haven't got a lot of time to prepare. Heckethorn said Donath would be out of there by midday.'

Ben glanced at his new watch. It was identical to the one he'd lost, minus a few scuffs and scratches that wouldn't take long to reappear. He said, 'We have a little under two hours. Call Luc Simon. Get him to lean on FIS and arrange for the Hummer to be flown right away to Emmen Air Base, which is the nearest military airfield from here. Tell him to load into it that equipment we talked about. He's got to move fast.'

Silvie whipped out her phone and started hitting keys. 'What about us?'

Ben opened the car door. 'We're going to go and grab some breakfast,' he said.

Chapter Fifty-Five

At precisely 11.58 that morning, Bezirksgefängnis Altdorf waved a relieved farewell to its former inmate Miki Donath. Guards stood by, trying not to smile with pleasure, and Governor Heckethorn watched from the safety of his window as the prison van drove out of the gates. Donath was finally off their hands. In two hours or less, he'd be arriving at his new home in Regensdorf, where the stricter regime might keep him in check as he served out the rest of his sentence.

The prison van was manned by a driver and co-driver. It was a simple short-distance transfer, meaning no stops were required, meaning no extra manpower. They cut through the quiet streets of Altdorf and headed out of town, south-eastwards on Seedorferstrasse towards Bahnhofstrasse and then through a series of roundabouts and junctions to catch the A4 motorway heading up towards Zurich and Regensdorf a little way further north.

It never made it as far as the motorway.

The incident would later be described in detail to the Swiss police by a number of badly shaken eye-witnesses, among them a travelling British wine buyer named Greg Turnbull who'd been taking an easy, meandering route through Switzerland with a couple of days in hand before meeting a client in Italy. Turnbull's police statement related how he'd been driving through the outskirts of Altdorf when his Jaguar had been overtaken by a speeding black Mercedes saloon that had cut him up badly and then swerved unexpectedly and violently across the road, forcing dozens of cars to slam on their brakes. Turnbull's Jaguar had been among the snarled-up mass of traffic that ended up strewn all over the road.

Forty yards ahead, the Mercedes had skidded to a halt at an angle, blocking the path of an unmarked white van. Turnbull said he'd been vaguely aware of the van's heavy-built, boxy shape and reinforced window frames with unusually small, thick panes of glass. Only when it had been forced to a standstill did it strike him that it was a prison vehicle. That was when his heart started thumping and he began to realise what he was witnessing. Some drivers had been honking their horns in anger, unaware of the dynamics of the unfolding situation. They quickly stopped after what happened next.

The doors of the black Mercedes opened and two people got out. Turnbull described them accurately as wearing black jackets and ski-masks. One was taller, perhaps six feet or a little under. The other was a few inches shorter and more slightly built. Turnbull wasn't the only witness who thought it could have been a woman. The two figures strode quickly up to the prison van. The taller one pulled out a handgun and stood in front of the van with the weapon pointed at the windscreen. The second figure produced a hammer, smashing the driver's window and then yanking open his door.

They bundled the terrified driver out and forced him down on his knees on the road, together with his co-driver. The masked man with the gun stood threateningly over them. Moments later, the second attacker disappeared inside the van, reappearing after a few seconds and then striding briskly to the back doors and hauling them open.

From that point, due to the relative angle of the vehicles, it was unclear exactly what had happened. All that the witness statements could verify was that the single prisoner the van had been transporting had been quickly, efficiently transferred into the black Mercedes. Turnbull only caught a glimpse of the man, late thirties, jeans, T-shirt, cropped hair, being manhandled towards the car. The Mercedes then took off at high speed, wheels spinning and leaving trails of rubber on the road. Within seconds it was gone, leaving behind it an empty prison van, two very stunned guards and a whole crowd of shocked onlookers.

None of the witnesses had ever seen a hijack before. And it was unlikely that any of them would do so again in their lifetimes. Especially one so brazenly, swiftly and professionally carried out in broad daylight. Long after Turnbull and the others had finished giving their statements and been released to go their separate ways, the police still had no clue as to who could have snatched the violent offender Miki Donath so soon after his departure from Bezirksgefängnis Altdorf.

The search for the missing prisoner was soon underway. It wouldn't take long to find him.

Chapter Fifty-Six

Silvie peeled off her mask and shook her hair free. 'I can't believe we did it.'

Ben had already removed his and tossed it into the back seat of the stolen Mercedes, where the claw hammer and the toy Airsoft Colt .45 replica lay. When all you had was a plastic gun, you needed to make a bit of a show by smashing things up with a good strong hammer. The intimidation factor was surprisingly effective. 'You don't spend years taking down kidnappers without learning a few tricks from them,' he said, driving fast.

'Now we're in deep shit,' she said.

Ben shook his head. 'No, Miki Donath's the one in deep shit. Besides, right now we could abduct the UN Secretary General and nobody would even slap our wrists.'

'I don't think the Swiss authorities will see it that way.'

'Not my business,' Ben said. A set of junctions flashed up. He piled through them, left, right, left again, tyres screeching. Horns wailed in protest. He didn't blink or glance back. 'My business is what we're carrying in the boot of this car.'

'What are we going to do with him?' she asked.

'Threaten him that he'll get nothing from Santa this year if he doesn't tell us where Streicher's hiding out.'

'You really think he knows?'

'He knows more about it than we do,' Ben said. 'I'm sure of it. I saw it in his eyes.'

'How could you see that in his eyes?'

'Mirrors of the soul,' Ben said. 'You should pay more attention to those things.'

'Donath's a psychotic child rapist and arms dealer. He doesn't have a soul.'

'Then they're the mirrors of whatever other evil shit he's got stashed away in there. I guarantee that whatever we get from him will advance our knowledge. And that's good enough for me.'

'Meanwhile, we're driving a stolen car.'

'A stolen car with plates borrowed from a T-boned wreck of a BMW in a scrapyard in Altdorf,' he reminded her. 'Not one that's going to come up on the radar any time soon.'

'These methods don't bother you?'

'You mean stealing cars? I don't generally make a habit of it.'

'I noticed.'

'Anyway, that's what insurance is for. And whoever owns this thing can afford taxis.'

'We should leave the owner a note,' she said.

'Saying "thank you for doing your part for national security"?' he said. 'We'll ditch it as soon as we get to Emmen Air Base and pick up the Hummer. After that, we need to keep our eyes peeled for lonely farm buildings, derelict factories or disused warehouses.'

'You have this all worked out,' she said. 'But have you given any serious thought to how you're going to extract information from a former KSK special forces hard case?'

'Don't need to,' Ben said. 'I'm a former special forces hard case myself. And my unit could have wiped the floor with those KSK boys, any day of the week, with our arms tied behind our backs and bags over our heads.'

Silvie looked doubtful.

'He'll talk,' Ben said.

Silvie said nothing.

Altdorf to Lucerne was a forty-kilometre drive, mostly by motorway. From Lucerne, the town of Emmen was only a short distance, and Militärflugplatz Emmen lay close by. They reached it just before two o'clock that afternoon. It was almost exclusively a military airbase, with limited commercial or civilian use, not the kind of place the public could just show up unannounced and expect to be let into. But Interpol's magic ticket worked once again, the gates buzzed open without questions being asked, and they found the H1 Hummer waiting for them inside a green prefab building, the key in the ignition, freshly rolled off a French military Airbus transport plane that had come in late that morning.

Luc Simon had come through for them, even better than his word. Two heavy-duty NATO-issue kitbags sitting side-by-side in the back contained more stuff than Ben had requested. Inside one was a Ziploc plastic pouch full of walking-around money, a thick bundle of mixed euros and Swiss francs. New phones and radios. An SOG tactical knife with a rubber handle and razor-sharp blackened blade, and a pair of strong aluminium police handcuffs, perhaps included just as a reminder to Ben to bring Streicher in alive. The second bag was heavier, containing a shiny, oiled pair of latest-generation FAMAS rifles and enough fresh ammunition to furnish a platoon, along with Ben's requested Browning pistol, minus GPS tracker. Five spare magazines, thirteen rounds apiece, all fully loaded with shiny new nine-millimetre full-metal jackets. Perhaps

Luc Simon didn't care about Streicher being brought in alive after all.

Ben cocked and locked the handgun and shoved it into its usual nestling place behind his right hip, where he was convinced he had a natural hollow from all the years of carrying one. Then all he had to do was sign a release form and Omar's gunmetal-grey monster and all its contents were his. He jumped up behind the controls and fired it up. The powerful engine burst into life with a roar at the first twist of the key. The fuel tank was full to the brim. Ben drove it out of the airbase with Silvie following in the Mercedes.

A kilometre up the road, by the side of the base's wire-mesh fence, they stopped again. Ben jumped down from the Hummer and they opened the boot of the stolen car. Any illusions Miki Donath might have been entertaining that the dramatic hijacking of his prison van was a rescue mission were, by now, completely dispelled. 'You're a dead man,' he growled as Ben cuffed his hands behind his back and then dragged him out of the Mercedes to frogmarch him to the Hummer. 'You should just blow your own brains out right now. You're fucked for this. You hear me?'

'And you're not in your little pink cell any more,' Ben said. Before Donath could reply, he whacked him sharply over the back of the head with the Browning. Donath went as limp as a wet towel and collapsed face down in the back of the Hummer. Ben used the same roll of duct tape left over from before to bind up his ankles and his torso, round and round until he looked like a giant cocooned insect. He slapped another four-inch length over his mouth. Then they emptied out the Mercedes, wiped down the interior surfaces, shut it up and abandoned it.

Silvie clambered into the passenger seat of the Hummer. 'Where it all began,' she said with a lopsided grin.

'I still have plenty of tape left,' he said. 'So don't you give me any trouble.'

'Careful. I might have to arrest you again.'

'Now for the hard part,' Ben said as they took off.

'He won't talk,' she said, shaking her head and looking serious.

'Hard for him,' Ben said. 'Not for us.'

'He won't talk,' Silvie said again.

Chapter Fifty-Seven

For anyone driving an enormous military-style four-wheel-drive laden with automatic weapons, a stack of ammunition and a hijacked prisoner, it made sense to steer largely clear of the prying eyes of civilisation and its polite citizens. Something that should have been easy in the central Swiss canton of Uri. It stretched for over a thousand mountainous square kilometres, of which almost a fifth was covered in thick pine forest and less than two per cent was inhabited. They passed through verdant valleys and skirted glittering blue lakes over which lazy paddle steamers scudded in the distance. The road rose and fell dramatically; now offering spectacular lofty views of the jagged mountain peaks, now dropping steeply to be swallowed by green tunnels of foliage. The sunny afternoon was wearing on. Three o'clock came and went and Ben was getting impatient. He considered stopping half a dozen times, but could see nowhere ideal. What he had in mind couldn't be done at the side of the road.

'Hell,' he muttered as they unexpectedly hit a town. It was a small, rural place comprised mostly of neat, decorative little gingerbread houses, with a church whose ornate spire poked up through the trees, and a flagpole in the square proudly flying the bull's head on a yellow background, the symbol of the canton. Next to the pole was a neat wooden sign with arrows pointing in three different directions towards narrow roads that led off the square. One said *Rathaus*, town hall; one said *Bahnhof*, railway station; another said *Ärztezentrum*, health centre. Ben pressed on.

It was Silvie who spotted the abandoned cottage in deep countryside a few kilometres further on, half hidden among the leafy undergrowth to their right, several hundred metres from the twisting road.

'Back up,' she said, pointing. Ben hit the brakes and reversed until he could see it, too. He nodded and twisted the wheel and bumped the Hummer off the road and on to the rutted earth track that led to the old house. As they approached they could see the decaying wooden shutters hanging off the windows, the sagging roofline and the weeds growing up around the front door. The corroded shell of a dead Simca was the only motor vehicle in sight. Nobody had lived here for a long time.

At the end of the track, Ben killed the engine and kicked open his door, walked round to the back of the Hummer and opened it up to reach inside and grab the prone Donath by the tape that bound him. The German was awake and struggling, muttering incomprehensibly behind the gag over his mouth. His eyes were bulging and his face was livid, a road map of veins swollen up all over his temples and forehead as he strained pointlessly to free himself. Ben used the SOG knife to slash through the tape binding his legs and dragged him out. Donath was unsteady on his feet as Ben steered him roughly in the direction of the derelict cottage.

'What are we going to do with him?' Silvie said again, biting her lip and looking at Ben with uncertain eyes.

'William Tell was supposed to have lived in these parts,' Ben said. 'If we had a crossbow, we could honour the legend by standing matey boy up against a tree and taking turns shooting apples off his head. That might loosen him up a bit.'

Silvie didn't look amused. 'We don't have a crossbow, Ben.'

'Shame.'

He kicked the cottage's front door. It burst in, flakes of old paint and slivers of rotting wood falling to the floor. The hallway smelled of damp and mice. Plaster was peeling off the walls and the bare wooden boards felt soft and loose underfoot. A doorway at the end of the hall, rodent-gnawed and ragged along its bottom edge, opened up into a gloomy room that had been stripped of its furniture, apart from a pair of ancient wooden chairs. Broken light peeped in through the cracks in the closed shutters.

Ben shoved Donath towards one of the chairs and pressed his shoulders down hard to force him to sit, with his cuffed hands looped behind the backrest. He tossed Silvie the tape, and held the Browning at Donath's head while she fastened the man's ankles to the chair legs and wrapped two lengths around his torso.

Ben pulled the other chair up and sat opposite Donath, two metres away with the gun in his right hand aimed squarely at the man's chest. He reached out with his left hand and ripped the four-inch length of tape from Donath's mouth. 'Now let's get started,' he said.

Donath gave him the shark eyes. 'You're a condemned man.'

'We've already covered that part,' Ben said. 'What comes next is, you tell us exactly where your friend Udo Streicher's gone to ground, and we don't leave you here for the maggots. How does that sound?'

'You want to find Streicher,' Donath said.

'You're a really fast learner,' Ben said. 'No wonder your pal thought you were good Parati material.'

Donath smiled. 'You've gone to all this trouble, it means you have no idea at all where he is, do you?'

'We'll find him, one way or another,' Silvie said.

Donath's gaze swivelled sideways to peer at her. He smiled more broadly, with the same smug expression he'd shown during the prison interview. *Go, Udo.* 'No chance. He's smarter than all of you fuckers put together.'

Ben raised the Browning a few degrees higher, so that it pointed at Donath's forehead. 'Talk,' he said. 'Now.'

The German appeared unmoved. The smile stayed on his lips, as if nothing could give him more pleasure than sitting here taunting these two idiots, knowing they were in a jam and that he held all the cards. 'Go ahead and shoot me, *Arschloch.* Not going to change a thing. Udo's got a little surprise for everyone.'

'We know about his plans,' Silvie said. 'I can assure you, they won't happen.'

'Is that a fact? How're you going to stop him? Or don't you think he means business? Then you don't know him.'

'I asked you to help us. You want millions of people to die, is that it?' Silvie said.

Donath just shrugged. 'What the fuck do I care what happens to them?'

Nobody spoke. Silence in the gloomy cottage. The overpowering stink of rot crowded in on them. Ben looked at the pistol in his hand, and gave it a waggle. 'This doesn't really scare you, does it, Miki?' he said.

'I've had guns pointed at me before,' Donath growled. 'Plenty of times. By men a lot harder than you, and I'm still here.'

'That's the problem with these things,' Ben said, lowering

the pistol. He rested it on his knee. Clicked on the safety. 'They're all or nothing. There's no middle ground with them. Even if I shoot you in the legs, you'll be in shock and bleed out too quickly to be of any use to me.'

'Bluffer,' Donath said. 'I knew it.'

'I don't need a gun to make you talk to me,' Ben said. 'And you will talk. Even if I have to hurt you. Do you understand that?'

Donath's satisfied little smile broadened out into a grin. 'You think you can hurt me, prick?'

'I get it,' Ben said. 'You're a proper tough guy. The real deal. You're not scared of a little roughing up, because you've been through all that and you were taught how to handle it, back in the day. RTI, we used to call it. Resistance to interrogation training.'

Donath's grin slackened off into a sour grimace. He spat. The shark eyes watched Ben.

'I've been through it myself,' Ben said. 'Not much fun, but you get over it. It teaches you a lot of useful lessons, too. About yourself. About human frailty. Because no matter how tough we are, we're all human and there's a limit to what each and every one of us can take. Even you, Miki. Don't kid yourself about that. Or about who I am. Not for one second. It would be a serious error of judgement.'

'Why, who the fuck are you?' Donath growled.

'I'm the guy who knows where the limits are,' Ben said. 'Trust me, I'll drive right through them and break you into a hundred pieces without thinking twice. I'll feel absolutely no remorse afterwards. Just like you, after what you and your friends did to the little girl.'

Donath said nothing.

Silvie stepped around the chair to face him. She rested a hand lightly on Ben's shoulder and bent down so that her face was at the same level as the German's. 'Miki, listen to us, please. You don't have to stand up for Streicher. He's not your friend. He could have used this opportunity to get you out of jail, but he didn't. If he releases this plague, you're just another victim as far as he's concerned.'

Donath's face worked for a few moments as he turned that thought over. He shook his head. 'Go play your mind games somewhere else, bitch. Think I'm a retard or something?'

'Last chance,' Ben said. 'Where is he?'

Donath shook his head again and clamped his mouth shut, turned his head away and stared resolutely into the murky corner of the room. Silvie stood up, biting her lip, and looked at Ben, as if to say, I can't talk to this guy.

The clock was ticking. Every moment that passed, Udo Streicher could be getting ready to drop his bomb on hundreds, thousands, millions of innocent people.

'Nobody just disappears,' Ben said. 'Not while they're still alive. But you will. Take it from me. So answer me. Where's Streicher hiding out?'

Donath turned his gaze back on Ben. The shark eyes seemed to twinkle for a moment. 'Somewhere you'll never get to him, that's for sure. He'll know you're coming. One whiff of your stink from a mile away and he'll lock down and stay buried for as long as it takes. He can stay down there a year if he has to.'

'I'm not going anywhere,' Ben said. 'I'll be there waiting for him when he sticks his head out of whatever foxhole he's cowering in. And you're going to tell me where to be standing.'

'You're so fucking stupid. Nobody's going to stop him. He's been waiting for this all his life.'

'I know what impatience feels like,' Ben said. 'I've been

waiting since this morning to start breaking bones, and now I don't think I can stand the suspense any longer. I won't ask you again. Where is he?'

Donath tossed his head and snapped out a defiant, '*Fuck* you.'

'I give up,' Ben said. 'This isn't working. I see I'm going to have to let you go.'

The prisoner's eyes gave another victorious little twinkle. Ben stood up. Slipped the Browning back into his belt and took the handcuff keys from his pocket. Silvie gave him an incredulous look as he walked around the back of Donath's chair and unlocked the cuffs. The linked aluminium bracelets hit the bare floorboards with a thump.

The German's arms fell loose down the sides of the chair. He sighed with relief and rolled his shoulders to loosen the stiff muscles.

Ben turned to Silvie. 'Maybe you'd like to get some air. It stinks in here.'

'I'm fine,' she said, catching his look and returning it with a questioning raised eyebrow.

'Up to you,' Ben said. And then he grabbed Donath's left hand and twisted it sideways and down, and felt the joint fail under the sudden violent pressure. There was a crackle of cartilage and a muted snap, like the crunch of a stick of celery breaking. Donath cried out sharply in pain.

Ben could feel Silvie's horrified look, but he didn't look back at her. 'There are three hundred and sixty joints in the human body, Miki. We don't have all day, so I'll just stick to the major ones to save time. Wrists, ankles, elbows and knees for starters. Then we're on to hips and shoulders. Then spinal vertebrae. I'll even let you choose. So, next wrong answer, what's it to be?'

Veins stood out like tug ropes on Donath's neck and

366

forehead. His eyes were bulging with agony as he nursed his broken wrist.

'You prefer surprises,' Ben said. 'That's fine by me.' Before Donath could twist away, he stepped around the right side of the chair and took hold of the man's right wrist. Cupped his other hand tightly around the bicep and pulled back, hard, and simultaneously drove forwards with his knee with a slamming impact that punched right through the joint and caved it in the wrong way.

Donath's piercing scream didn't quite drown out the sickening crack of bone. Ben felt the arm go floppy in his hands. There was nothing except a strand or two of muscle and some torn sinews connecting the humerus above the joint to the ulna and radius below it. Nothing except a lot of catastrophic damage that was going to require intricate surgery and months of healing to repair. Maybe an artificial elbow joint to replace the shattered original. Ben let go, and the useless arm flopped into Donath's lap. Donath was beating his head from side to side, snorting and groaning and gnashing his teeth. Mucus and drool were running down his chin.

'Ben—' Silvie started.

'You can make this stop whenever you want,' Ben said, ignoring her.

'Go – and – fuck – yourself,' Donath managed to say in between gasps.

It was hard not to admire his courage. Donath was tough, all right. Ben looked at him for a moment, then kicked over the chair and Donath went toppling sideways. Ben stepped over him. He took out the SOG tactical blade and slashed the tape binding Donath's right ankle to the chair leg. He flicked the knife down at the floor, where it stuck point-first in the boards, quivering. Caught the man's freed leg as it began to kick and thrash, and held the foot by the toe and ankle, ready to start twisting.

'Ben, please,' Silvie said. 'Not like this.'

'Do you hear that, Miki? Agent Valois would like me to treat you with more human empathy. Just like your friends treated mine.' Ben twisted the ankle, hard enough to threaten the joint and put serious secondary strain on the knee. Donath squirmed and tried to snatch his leg away, but Ben's grip on it was tight. He twisted a little harder, just to the point of breaking, but no more. 'But there's a difference between me and your friends,' he said. 'I don't enjoy this one bit. Them? Pain and suffering is what they're all about. They're even worse pieces of shit than a child rapist like you. They're not worth putting yourself through this. So I'm asking. I'm begging. Answer the question, while there's still a chance that a surgeon can put you back together again.'

Ben's heart thudded as he waited for Donath to defy them once more. If that happened, things were going to start getting properly ugly. Once you crossed the line, you couldn't go back. You just had to live with it for the rest of your life. Ben had enough to live with already.

Two long seconds passed. Then three more, then five more.

It didn't happen.

Every man has his limit.

And, to Ben's immense secret relief, Donath's had finally been reached. Sweat beading in huge droplets from every pore of his face and his chest heaving with tortured breath, the German told them everything.

Chapter Fifty-Eight

Silvie was very quiet as they drove away from the ruined cottage. 'That was awful,' she breathed at last, barely audible over the rumble of the Hummer's engine.

Ben nodded. 'Yes. It was.' He reached the bottom of the track and turned left, back towards the little town they'd passed through on their way here.

Silvie watched the road for a minute, deep in thought, then turned to look at him with questioning eyes. 'There was no other way, was there?'

'No,' he said. 'Not really.'

'Are we bad people?'

'Maybe,' he said.

Saving the lives of the innocent is not something of which you should be ashamed, Père Antoine had said to him that day. But Ben was. He felt tainted by what he'd had to do. He knew he'd always feel that way. Because things weren't about to get any better. The door was open now, and only darkness lay beyond it, waiting to swallow him up.

'No,' Silvie said resolutely, frowning and squeezing a fist, as if she was making a life-changing decision in which there was no room for self-doubt. 'It just fell on us. It was our moral duty. You did the right thing, no question.'

Ben said nothing more until they reached the outskirts

of the small town. They passed the pretty church and the first of the gingerbread houses, then came to the square where the flagpole stood, and next to it the three-pronged sign. Ben followed the direction for *Ärztezentrum* up a narrow, tree-lined street. The medical centre was a prim white cottage hospital, set off the road among neat lawns and trimmed hedges. Ben screeched the Hummer to a stop in the little car park outside and said, 'Be right back.' He jumped out, flung open the back and hefted Donath's limp, unconscious form over his shoulder, carried him a few paces and dumped him on the grass within sight of the entrance. He walked back to the Hummer and they U-turned out of the car park with a squeal and a roar as the cottage hospital door burst open and two medical staff rushed out to attend to the unconscious man. The word 'SCHWERVERBRECHER', scrawled in marker pen across his forehead from temple to temple, was there to warn them that their patient was a dangerous criminal. But not even a tough guy like Miki Donath was going anywhere with two broken arms.

Driving fast through the little town, Ben made a ten-second call to Luc Simon, to tell him where the Swiss cops could find their missing fugitive. He could have told Luc where he was going from here, but had already decided that could wait.

Reaching the square, Ben checked the wooden sign again. This time, he took the direction for *Bahnhof*.

'The railway station?' Silvie said, turning to stare at him. 'What do we need a train for?'

'We don't,' Ben told her. 'You do. This is where we part ways.'

She looked at him blankly. 'Where am I going?'

'Back to base. Home. Wherever you want, except where I'm going.'

'Are you kidding me?'

'I need to finish this by myself,' he said.

'You can't leave me hanging.'

'I can't be responsible for what happens to you.'

'Don't patronise me.' Her jaw clenched, making her face look tight and hard. 'This wasn't the deal, Ben.'

'There is no deal,' he said. 'There's just me and Streicher.'

'And upward of a dozen more Parati, tooled up and ready to die to defend him.'

'They'd better be ready to die,' he said. 'Because that's what's going to happen to them.'

'You go in there alone,' Silvie said, 'you'd better be ready to die too.'

Chapter Fifty-Nine

Many kilometres away, deep below the Swiss countryside, Udo Streicher walked down the white-tiled corridor and entered the laboratory. It consisted of an outer chamber, in which it was unnecessary to wear protective clothing, and a maximum-containment inner chamber from which it was securely sealed off by thick glass and an airlock chamber. The walls were bare except for a large clock. Down here where the generator-fed neon lights worked twenty-four-seven, you soon lost track of day and night.

On the other side of the glass, Anton Lindquist looked like a spaceman inside the same model of BSL-4 positive pressure protection suit he'd worn during his days as a lab technician at the European Centre for Disease Control in Stockholm, the job he'd been in when Streicher had first recruited him to the Parati. He was hooked up to his air supply via a curly plastic hose long enough to allow him to move freely about the room, and able to talk over the speaker system via the mic behind his PPPS suit visor. He had his back to the glass, intent on working at a massive stainless-steel bench that stretched from wall to wall and was covered in a range of equipment whose purpose Streicher could only guess at, even if he had paid for it all. There were incubators and vaccine baths, a huge vacuum pump, a centrifuge, a microscope wired up to a computer screen, racks of container jars and Petri dishes and all kinds of assorted tools and gadgets strewn everywhere. Streicher wasn't too interested in knowing what any of it did. The end result was his only real concern, and that end result was taking far longer to achieve than he'd initially been given to understand.

Streicher rapped on the glass. Lindquist didn't hear because the rush of his air supply tended to drown out most background sounds. Streicher rapped the glass harder, and the figure in the moon suit suddenly stiffened and spun around like a startled rabbit.

'You frightened me,' he said, his voice sounding scratchy and metallic through the speaker in the outer chamber. His glasses were steamed up behind the visor. He'd been expecting this visit from his boss, only not so soon.

'What progress are we making?' Streicher asked, laying emphasis on the *we*.

'Oh, er, some. I mean, we are. It's getting there.'

'It's been days,' Streicher said. 'You promised me this wouldn't take long.'

'I'm on my own here,' Lindquist replied, careful not to let the irritation show in his voice. The fear he could do nothing to hide. Back in his ECDC days in Stockholm, the most dangerous thing he'd ever had to work with was smallpox, which was technically classed Biosafety Level 3 because treatments existed for it. By contrast, this was like scaling the north face of the Eiger with no safety rope. If even a small needle punctured his suit, he might as well put a pistol in his mouth there and then, because at that point he was condemned to a horrible and irreversible death. He was sweating, hot and itchy inside the protective material. He couldn't scratch, couldn't go to the bathroom without getting fully decontaminated first; he was feeling dehydrated and hadn't eaten for many hours.

But when Udo Streicher was your boss, you didn't whinge and you didn't stop for tea. You just kept going, and prayed that he wouldn't be displeased with your efforts.

'How hard can it be?' Streicher demanded. 'The bulk of the work has already been done for you. Surely once you have the material—'

'This isn't exactly first-year science,' Lindquist explained, trying to remain calm. 'It's taken me long enough to process the raw samples to extract the pure bacteria and convert them into an aerosolised form. That part's finished.' He pointed at a row of unmarked aluminium canisters lined up inside a thick glass cabinet in the corner. Twelve of them, as Streicher had specified, to correspond with his much-revised world-wide list of cities that now comprised two targets in the United Kingdom as well as major centres all across mainland Europe.

All he needed was to confirm the dates, work out the travel itinerary and put the plan into action. It was just days away.

Streicher had to smile. Eight inches high, plain brushed metal, each no larger than a cocktail shaker, the canisters looked innocuous. Even he found it hard to imagine the lethal power of what was inside them.

'Easy to deploy,' Lindquist said with a nervous twitch. 'Just remove the retaining clip and depress the nozzle to release the contents under high pressure. Dropping the canister on its nose does the job just fine. It'll fill a large room in seconds. Or a concert hall, a cinema, a train, a dirty great ocean liner.'

'Does it work?'

'That would be an understatement,' Lindquist said. Before he'd started testing, the secondary lab next door had housed sixteen rhesus monkeys in cages and thirty white rats in glass tanks. Most were dead now, and the manner of their death hadn't been a pleasant thing to witness. 'The aerosolised strain seems to attack the monkeys' systems even faster than it does the rats'. Initial symptoms are coming on within the first hour after exposure to the gas.'

'Survival time?'

'Shortest recorded so far is five hours and forty-seven minutes. Of course, it could take a little longer for humans. Maybe an extra hour.'

Streicher had read every scrap of research ever published on weaponised plague. Such efficiency was rarely heard of in the scientific literature. 'It's aggressive.'

'Terrifyingly aggressive,' Lindquist said, with absolute sincerity. Even thinking about it made him sweat harder inside the suit. He was standing only a metre from the glass but he felt as if he were stranded all alone in the infinity of space, naked and vulnerable and very, very mortal.

'And the antitoxin? How soon will you have it?' Streicher's impatience was gnawing at him. To release the bacteria without self-protection would be worse than amateurish. It would be plain suicide.

Lindquist puffed out his cheeks behind the visor. His suit crinkled as he shrugged his shoulders. 'I'm going as fast as I can, but it's tough. The chromosome of *Yersinia pestis* carries about ten known toxin-antitoxin modules and two solitary antitoxins that belong to five different TA families, higBA, hicAB, RelEB, Phd/Doc and MqsRA—'

'Yes, yes, yes. Talk in plain language, can't you?'

'In plain language, it's a highly complex process. I've had to culture the organism in artificial media, inactivate it with formaldehyde and preserve it in nought point five per cent phenol. If I don't get each step of the sequence exactly right, it won't work. Or worse, we'll end up injecting ourselves with the live disease, and it's thank you and goodnight. The finished vaccine will also contain trace elements of beef-heart extract, yeast extract, agar, soya and casein.'

'Why those?'

'Do you really want to know?'

Streicher shrugged. 'No, I don't.'

'The bad news is that it's possible that not everyone will develop the passive haemagglutination antibody. Meaning I can't guarantee that it'll protect everyone who's exposed to the actual toxin. There could be a five to seven per cent failure rate.'

'It's an acceptable risk,' Streicher said with a dismissive gesture.

'And everyone who's injected with it will feel like shit afterwards,' Lindquist said. 'Headache, fever . . . nothing to worry about, but it won't be an easy ride for a few hours.'

'I think we can deal with that. When will it be ready?'

'I'm tired. I really should sleep. I could have an accident in here.'

'Sleep when you're done,' Streicher said.

'Twelve more hours,' Lindquist said wearily. 'Then we can start testing how well it works on what's left of the animals.'

Streicher shook his head, slowly. He had that burning light in his eye that Lindquist had seen before.

Lindquist swallowed. 'Okay, give me six more hours.'

'You have three,' Streicher told him. 'Get it done.' He smiled. Raised his right hand, extended his index finger and tapped his fingertip against the centre of his brow.

'Or I'll put a bullet in your brain,' he added casually, and left the outer chamber.

Chapter Sixty

'I'm the only one,' Silvie said as he drove. 'I'll bet I am.'

'The only what?'

'The only woman who ever drummed any sense into that thick skull of yours.'

Ben looked at her. She was giving him that knowing smile again, the one she'd been giving him ever since she'd won the argument back at the railway station. 'Don't get all smug on me, just because I let you tag along,' he said.

She cocked an eyebrow. 'Tag along?'

'I could have insisted,' he said. 'I didn't want you here. Now you are. So keep your eye on the map and don't distract me.'

'Yessir,' she grunted, smiling even more.

It had been a long, fast drive. Donath's directions had taken them west, back past Geneva and into picture-perfect rolling green hills to the north. The Hummer was a useful motorway tool and its intimidating size and looks were the best thing for bludgeoning through city traffic, but it was at the limits of its handling abilities as Ben gunned it mercilessly along the narrow country lanes.

It was after five by now. The late-afternoon sun glittered over the ever-present mountain backdrop and shone golden light across undulating pastureland that was broken here and there by patches of serrated dark green pine forest. Cattle grazed peacefully in fields bordered by neat white picket fences, cowbells dangling from their necks. Isolated farmhouses appeared in the distance. Nothing that looked remotely like the hideout of a terrorist group intent on destroying civilisation. Ben ground his teeth and kept driving, trying to block out the nagging thought that Donath could have tricked them.

'We're close,' Silvie said, bent over the map she had opened out over the centre console and tracing a route along it with her finger. 'Should be coming up on the place any moment now.'

Two kilometres on, the entrance to the organic dairy farm was pretty much as Donath had described it. The Hummer rattled over a cattle grid and bumped along a track that carried them perpendicular to the road until they glimpsed the farmhouse and the cluster of neat wooden outbuildings that circled the yard. Well-tended farmland stretched out beyond, overlooked by the sunlit mountains. A bright red tractor was ambling over the fields, tiny in the distance, like a ladybird crawling across a giant rippled sheet of green felt.

Silvie shook her head, bemused. 'Some terrorist stronghold. It's like a scene from a calendar.'

'Would you have preferred fortified defences, razor wire and men with machine guns?'

'At least we'd know for sure, then.'

'He's here,' Ben said.

'You don't sound convinced.'

'I have to believe it,' he said.

A little further up the track, they came to a side gate that opened on to a field of tall grass bordered along its western edge by a strip of woodland. Taking a chance that nobody was watching from the farmhouse, they passed through the gate and crossed the field, the Hummer bumping and lurching over the rough ground and leaving wide flattened tracks in its wake. They reached the trees, and Ben rolled it as deep under cover as he could and then shut off the engine. 'This is it.'

'If Donath was jerking our chain, I'm going back there to kill him,' Silvie said.

'One way or the other, we'll soon find out,' Ben replied. 'Grab your stuff. We walk from here.'

Neither of them spoke as they equipped themselves from the kitbags in the back of the Hummer. Ben slipped three of the fully loaded FAMAS magazines into his pockets and clicked a fourth into the rifle's receiver. Worked the bolt and felt the well-oiled action carry the top round snugly into the chamber. He set the three-way fire selector to single shots. Forget full-automatic. Even three-shot bursts would chew through ammo too quickly, and he worried about things like running out of bullets. Especially when he had no idea how many opponents he was going up against. If Streicher had called in extra muscle, it could be fifty. If Donath had played Ben and Silvie for fools, it could be none. Then they'd have all kinds of other problems, not least of which would be knowing where to pick up the thread again.

Ben checked his pistol and loaded a couple of spare mags into his pockets for that too, then fitted the SOG knife in its sheath to his belt. Took one of the radios and handed the other to Silvie. He gave the handcuffs a miss. Whatever might happen today, one thing was for certain: Streicher wouldn't be needing them.

'Ready?' he asked her.

'Ready.' Silvie slung her loaded rifle over her shoulder,

then quickly stepped close and put her hand against his cheek. She kissed him once, briefly but warmly, on the lips.

'For luck,' she said.

They slipped through the trees and emerged on the other side of the strip of woodland. The sun was still bright but a fresh breeze coming down from the mountains felt cool on their faces. Ahead of them was a wide expanse of fields dotted with grazing cattle. Beyond it, right off in the distance, due west across the gently waving grass, a larger, thicker section of forest stood fenced off from the pasture. It looked just the way Miki Donath had described it. If he'd told them everything he knew, then the ten-acre compound the other side of those pines was where Streicher had his hideout.

It was a quarter-hour hike across the fields. They walked in silence, single-file. A couple of big, placid-looking cows with swaying haunches and clunking bells around their necks wandered across to check them out, then quickly lost interest and moved off again.

Ben reached the wooded perimeter and turned round to scan the horizon. The farmhouse and buildings were well out of sight and a long way off. Silvie joined him. Up close, the forest looked like an enormous green fortress wall, curving round in a lazy circle to surround whatever lay behind the trees. 'This has got to be it,' Silvie said.

They padded single-file through the shadowy thicket, like a two-man jungle patrol. The ground was spongy with moss. The tall trunks creaked and swayed gently in the breeze.

They didn't have far to walk. After fifty metres, Ben held up a closed fist and whispered, 'Stop.' Up ahead, the dense screen of foliage ended abruptly at a high wire-mesh fence suspended from metal posts concreted into the ground. Ben moved cautiously to the fence and peered through the mesh. From where he stood, he could see the barrier stretched for about half a mile, with galvanised steel-framed mesh gates set into it at intervals of every four posts, padlocked shut. On the other side of the fence, the forest had been completely levelled and cleared in a circular plot about ten acres in size. But it wasn't the huge clearing that interested him. It was what stood at its centre.

He drew the SOG knife and, clutching it by its rubber handle, touched the blade against the wire. No flash, no spark. He brushed his fingers against it. It wasn't electrified. One less obstacle to worry about. He slipped the knife back in its sheath and whistled softly for Silvie to join him.

'Shit,' she breathed as she peered through the fence and saw what he'd seen. A straight concrete road marked the radius of the circle from a main gateway thirty degrees anticlockwise around the inside perimeter from where they stood. The road led to the single building inside the vast clearing. It was the size of a large square house, clad in dark wood, with white windows and a pitched roof and a huge steel shutter door, standing on a concrete apron roughly as large as a football field.

Streicher's hangar.

'Exactly as Donath described it,' Silvie whispered. She turned to Ben, her face full of expectation, as if to say, *Let's go for it.*

Ben gazed up at the fence, then around him at the trees, then back at the building. His instinct and training both told him to hang back and wait for nightfall before climbing the wire. If Streicher made a move before then, they'd be ready to make theirs.

'Not now,' he whispered. 'Better under cover of darkness.'

'How do we find a way in?' she breathed.

His smile was dry and without any trace of humour. 'There's always a way in.'

They backed away from the fence and settled in the shadows of the trees, and waited, and watched.

Without knowing that, from almost the moment they'd got here, they themselves were being observed.

Chapter Sixty-One

'Lindquist!' Streicher yelled as he flung open the laboratory door. In his hand was the nine-millimetre Beretta he'd personally used to execute the suspected spy in their midst, Dexter Nicholls. He fully intended to do the same to Anton Lindquist, if the man let him down. He could be replaced. Anyone could be, except Udo Streicher.

The inner containment chamber was empty. No sign of Lindquist. 'Fine,' Streicher said. He racked the slide on the Beretta, clicked off the safety and went looking for him.

Lindquist wasn't far away. Streicher found him next door, in the adjacent lab where the test animals were housed. Still wearing his PPPS suit, the Swede was standing watching a black-and-white monkey in a cage. The animal was resting on its haunches, munching on a slice of apple. At the sight of Streicher, it threw down the food and gripped the bars of its cage, screeching loudly. Lindquist turned in surprise. He was pale with exhaustion, both from lack of sleep and the prolonged terror of his ordeal, but he was suddenly very much awake and his eyes opened wide at the sight of the gun in Streicher's hand.

'A man's trust is a precious thing, Anton,' Streicher said. 'Especially mine, as your life happens to depend on it. You promised to deliver. Your time is up.'

'Jesus Christ, you can't come in here without protection,' Lindquist rasped behind the suit visor. 'The monkey – it's infected.'

Streicher took a step back, whipped a handkerchief from his pocket and pressed it over his nose and mouth. He gazed at the table near the cage, on which was a small amber-coloured bottle and a pack of disposable syringes. 'Is that what I think it is?'

'The antitoxin,' Lindquist said. 'I finished it sooner than expected. But the test isn't complete. I only administered the drug to the monkey ninety minutes ago, alongside the live bacteria.'

The monkey was still screeching wildly inside the cage. Streicher hated monkeys, mainly because they were too similar to humans. He pointed the gun at it. 'Make it shut the hell up.'

'I don't know how.'

'Is it sick?'

'It's just afraid of you,' Lindquist said. 'These aren't disease symptoms.'

A surge of elation stabbed through Streicher's heart. 'Then the antitoxin's working. It's been ninety minutes. You said the first symptoms appear within an hour.'

'Generally. But ninety minutes isn't long enough to be certain.'

Streicher considered, but only for a second. Triumph was blazing through him like a river of fire. He couldn't wait any longer. 'It's good enough,' he said, grabbing the bottle and syringes from the table. 'Will this provide doses for everyone?'

'Plenty,' Lindquist said. 'But—'

Streicher pointed the pistol at him. 'Take off your suit.'

'What?'

384

Streicher aimed the gun carefully at Lindquist's side, where the silvery material hung loose and baggy. He squeezed the trigger. The gunshot was deafening in the hard-surfaced lab. A nine-millimetre hole appeared in the loose folds of the PPPS suit. Passing straight through with no resistance, the bullet smashed a computer screen on a bench behind where Lindquist was standing. The monkey screamed even louder, and shook hysterically at its bars. Streicher swung the gun and fired again, and the monkey was blown against the back of the cage, crumpled and silenced, its fur bloody.

'Take off your suit,' Streicher repeated. 'It's useless to you now, anyway.'

Lindquist gaped at the hole in the material where the bullet had passed within two inches of his flesh, then turned and gaped again at the dead monkey. He clawed at the neck fastening of his headgear and removed it, pale and shaking. Then undid the fastenings of the rest of the suit and let it slip to the floor. He was mouthing the words he didn't dare speak out loud. 'You're fucking insane.'

Streicher tossed him the antitoxin bottle, then the syringes. 'Do you trust it?' he said.

'I-I did everything right. I know I did.'

'Then take a shot. The test is over. The operation starts here.'

Lindquist's hands were fluttering so badly that he could barely get the needle into his arm. He winced as he pressed the plunger.

'Good,' Streicher said. 'Now my turn.' Drawing a fresh needle from the pack, he administered his own dose without a flinch. Lindquist was staring at him, unable to speak. 'You did good work, Anton,' Streicher told him with a smile. He sounded like a benevolent schoolteacher after scoring a breakthrough with a recalcitrant pupil. 'Your contribution will go down in history. It won't be forgotten.'

Streicher left the lab and went striding rapidly down the corridor. Suddenly remembering what the Swede had said about the nausea and headaches that might come on as side effects of the antitoxin, he took a detour through the bunker and went to his personal office. He knew what would fix the side effects. Couldn't be seen throwing up and acting all weak and pathetic in front of the others. Not even in front of Hannah. It wouldn't become a man of his stature.

The office was a large room, with an oriental rug and leather chairs and a fine teak desk at which he often sat to gaze at the bank of security monitors mounted in a double row on the wall above a control panel, showing constantly switching high-definition images from inside the bunker and various points along the perimeter. He ignored them at this moment, because he had more pressing business on his mind.

Laying the antitoxin and needles on the desk, he opened a drawer and took out a plastic sachet of cocaine, a credit card and a short straw. Scattered fine white powder on the desktop, shaped it into three generous lines with the credit card, then bent over the desk and snorted them up in quick succession.

He straightened up, gasping at the sudden heady rush and dropping the straw. Coloured lights spangled in front of his eyes. His whole being tingled with a champagne fizz and a grin wider than a piano keyboard spread over his face. He breathed out with deep satisfaction and felt as if he was already king of the world. Which he already was, of course. His destiny was assured now. Nothing was going to—

That was when he happened to glance at the security monitors and something caught his eye that wiped the grin off his face.

The pair of intruders were standing at the fence and peering through the wire into the compound, filmed from above and to the side, clearly unaware of the miniature camera concealed overhead in the branches of a tree. Both carried automatic weapons. The man was blond and lean, about forty. Looked tough and able to handle himself. Streicher had never seen him before, but he knew the woman, all right. He'd have known her anywhere.

Michelle Faban.

Fury rose up inside Udo Streicher with volcanic intensity, fuelled by the cocaine rush.

The bitch.

The traitorous, treacherous, lying piece of shit bitch!

He stared enraged at the monitor for nearly two full minutes. The intruders were talking to one another, making him wish he'd installed microphones into his surveillance system. They seemed to be conferring. They seemed to be alone. As he watched, they drew back from the fence, but he could still see them lingering among the trees, on the edge of his screen. He reached to the control panel and nudged a stubby lever below the monitor that looked like a miniature joystick. The hidden camera panned a few degrees, bringing the concealed figures back to the centre of the screen. The bastards were obviously planning something.

Streicher tore at his pocket and snatched out the radio handset. He barked into it in a furious gabble.

'Wolf, we have a security breach in progress near Perimeter Gate Seventeen. The Faban woman is out there with some guy. I know why they're here, and they have to be stopped.

Do you hear me, Wolf? I want you to take a four-man team out there and deal with it, right this very minute. I'll be watching from the monitors. I want them *dead*. I want that bitch's head personally delivered to me on a *plate*, five minutes from now. Understand? Over and out.'

Chapter Sixty-Two

Wolf Schilling dropped his radio and ran along the corridor to the rec room where Dominik Baiza, Riccardo Cazzitti, Silvain Chavanne and Stefan Ringler were stretched out on sofas and armchairs watching a favourite post-apocalyptic thriller movie on the fifty-inch Panasonic.

'Where are the others?' Schilling said, standing in the doorway.

Baiza looked up from the sofa. 'Zwart's taking a shit. Lindquist's still in the lab. As for Wokalek, he was working out in the gym last time I saw him. Hannah's off somewhere, doing what Hannah does. What's up?'

'Situation. I'm picking a four-man team to join me out there. You guys are elected. C'mon, on your feet. Work to do.'

'Watching the movie, man,' Ringler groaned.

Wolf Schilling clapped his hands. 'Shift your arses, people. Go, go, go. Cazzitti, run to the armoury and break out the MP5s. You should be pleased, Ringler. Faban's back and you get to do what you want with her. Let's move it!'

Once they were fully tooled up, the hit squad raced through the tunnels in three electric buggies and came out through the hangar. The boss had reset the six-digit bunker entry/exit code again that morning. It was hard to keep up with all his frequent changes.

Inside the hangar, the five jumped out of the buggies. Wolf Schilling activated the control to lock down the bunker, then aimed the remote towards the steel shutters and stabbed the green button. With a jerk of steel cables followed by an electric whirr, the lower sill of the shutter rolled up just far enough for them to slide under, scraping their weapons as they went. The shutter whirred down behind them.

Keeping close to the building, they darted around to the far side to cut across the grass unseen from Perimeter Gate 17. They ran to the fence and Schilling undid the padlock on the nearest gate, allowing them access to the surrounding ring of woodland. The intruders were nearly a quarter of a mile away on the far side of the perimeter, so they had to move fast.

Wolf Schilling unslung his Heckler & Koch MP5SD submachine gun. It was the sound-suppressed version with the fat silencer that completely shrouded the barrel, one of the specialised military items provided for the Parati by their old pal Miki Donath. The four other men were carrying the same model, all fully bombed up with EOTech red dot optics and C-Mag hundred-round magazines, enough to start and finish a small war. They moved through the trees at a loping stride, their footsteps silent on the mossy ground, and covered the quarter mile in just under four minutes.

As they approached Perimeter Gate 17, they spread out. Riccardo Cazzitti had learned more than just chopper mechanic skills in the Italian Parachute Infantry Brigade. He prided himself on being able to sneak up on anything that lived and breathed. Taking the outside flank, his alert gaze darted to left and right, the fat muzzle of the H&K moving instinctively wherever he looked and his trigger finger optically connected to his brain, so that all he had to do was lock eyes on his target and it would go down in a silenced purr of machine-gun fire. Fifteen metres to his left crept Dominik Baiza, who was strictly more of a vehicles man and less comfortable on combat detail. Fanning out from Baiza's left, Schilling and Ringler and Chavanne spanned the remaining woodland. Nothing could escape them as they combed through the trees.

Chavanne reached the point of the fence where the intruders had been sighted. He gave a low whistle. *Nada.* Maybe the boss had been dreaming. Maybe this was just some drill he'd concocted to keep them from getting fat and dull watching movies all the time. He grinned at the thought.

Then something impacted the back of his neck very hard and his vision exploded white like a magnesium flare. He barely registered hitting the ground, and didn't register the cold steel blade slipping between his ribs as more than a momentary flash of agony.

Then he knew nothing at all.

Stefan Ringler caught the movement out of the corner of his eye and turned to his left, frowning hard and pointing his weapon in the direction of where Chavanne had been just a moment ago. He couldn't see him any more. He changed course, cutting ninety degrees towards the fence. The trigger pull on his MP5 weighed in at about six pounds, and he had about four pounds of pressure on it as he stalked through the trees.

Two metres closer. Still no sign of Chavanne.

Three metres closer. Where the hell was he? This was no time to nip behind a pine trunk for a slash. He opened his mouth, but knew he had to stay silent.

Stefan Ringler stayed silent for the rest of his life, which lasted less than four seconds. Technically, long enough to yell out and alert his teammates, but the black-clad forearm that whipped around his neck from behind and locked itself in a boa constrictor grip around his throat made any kind of sound impossible, apart from the thrashing of his legs as he was swiftly dragged to the mossy ground and the life choked out of him. Then, a terrible pain as his neck was twisted left and right and something snapped deep inside, and the lights went out.

Ben let the body fall limply away from him and got back on his feet. Silvie Valois was just a shadow among the trees, five metres away. He tossed Ringler's MP5 and the shadow reached nimbly out and caught it without a sound. He pointed at her, then motioned past her through the trees, then tapped his watch and held up five fingers, and the shadow nodded imperceptibly in reply. He crept along the line of the fence as Silvie moved silently at a perpendicular angle away from him and curved round to her left to come up behind the wing man on the far side.

Ben counted down the last of the five seconds, heard the sharp metallic purr of suppressed gunfire twenty metres away through the trees, and then opened up with the submachine gun he'd taken from the first dead guy. The Heckler & Koch *Maschinenpistole* was even more familiar to him than the Browning Hi-Power. He'd carried it in deserts and jungles and urban war zones, fired it in snow and underwater and in total darkness. He was as proficient with it as it was possible to be.

But even for a novice shooter, the enemy were too close and distinct to be missable. That was all they were in that moment: the enemy. Not men, not people. Three remaining, and none of them had the slightest inkling what was happening until the angled crossfire of two shooters mowed them down, left to right, right to left. The MP5SD silencer was highly effective. He felt the gun judder in his hands and the muzzle try to climb under the combined recoil of fifteen nine-millimetre Parabellum rounds a second. Five solid seconds of automatic fire. A combined total of one hundred and fifty copper-jacketed bullets zipping through the foliage and clipping leaves and punching through vital organs and bone and soft tissue as the men crumpled and fell amid almost eerie silence.

Ben would never know their names or care one way or the other, but Dominik Baiza, Wolf Schilling and Riccardo Cazzitti all died within five seconds of one another. Which was a far shorter and more merciful interval than Streicher's victims at Chartreuse de la Sainte Vierge de Pelvoux had had to endure.

It would have been more like two seconds, but Wolf Schilling didn't die right away. Ben walked over to the fallen man as he twitched and kicked face down on the mossy ground. He stepped on the submachine gun still clenched in the man's hand. Crouched down and drew the SOG once more. He slipped it up into the soft spot behind the man's ear and buried it deep inside the base of his brain. The blade found its mark with surgical precision and the kicking stopped.

Ben withdrew the knife, wiped the blade on the dead man's sleeve, then sheathed it and stood and stepped away, feeling nothing much except the quiet knowledge that every opponent no longer walking equalled one less obstacle between him and the end of this.

He looked over at Silvie as she stepped out from between the trees. She had her rifle slung over her back and the submachine gun cradled in front of her, a wisp of smoke still curling up from the muzzle of the hot silencer. All the ugly black hardware dangling from her body made her look smaller and slighter than she was.

Ben said, 'Okay?'

She nodded, pale but handling it. 'I'm fine.'

He studied her face for a moment and believed that she wasn't about to start shaking and collapse in shock.

'I guess they know we're coming now, don't they?' she said.

'I would imagine so,' he said.

She gazed down at the bodies. Liquid sadness in her eyes, the wistful expression of a young veterinarian who'd been compelled to euthanise a litter of kittens. 'You've done this before,' she said, turning the look on him.

He nodded. It would get worse from here on in, he thought. But he didn't say it.

'Not me,' she said. 'Not like that. It was self-defence, those other times.'

Welcome to my world, Ben thought, but didn't say that either. He switched his submachine gun for a fully loaded one from one of the dead men, then started frisking the bodies. Nothing on the first two, apart from a stick of gum and some cigarettes, loose change, a Bic lighter. He moved to the third and rolled him over. Like the others he was a white European, late thirties or so, short brown hair, ruddy features. Ben found a remote-control handset in his pocket. Some kind of custom-produced unit, with no maker's name anywhere on it. It had a keypad and two coloured buttons, one red, one green. Ben didn't know what to make of it.

The dead man's right arm was draped limply across his chest. Ben brushed it aside so he could check the rest of the pockets. The dead arm flopped to the ground, the fingers slightly clawed. Ben noticed a stain on the palm of his hand, like oil, or smeared ink. He picked up the limp hand and uncurled the fingers.

It wasn't a stain. It was the sweat-smudged remnants of a six-digit number hastily scribbled on the dead man's palm in biro.

Ben looked at it, then at the remote, and realised what he was seeing. The kind of raging paranoiac Streicher was would spare no effort in constantly changing passwords and numbers for everything he did, just like he kept issuing new phones to his people. Security numbers would be no different. Or the passcode to open an electronic lock. He'd reset them so often that even his closest aides couldn't keep track.

Unless they wrote them down. Human error. The fallibility principle. No matter how secure the system, there was always a weak link somewhere.

'I think we just found our way inside,' he said to Silvie.

Chapter Sixty-Three

The steel shutter was solid and immovable. It looked and felt as if it would take an armour-piercing rocket to get through it. Unless you happened to be holding the key.

'Here goes,' Ben said. He pointed the remote and pressed the red button.

Nothing happened. One down, one to go. He pressed the green button, and something went *click*, an electric motor whined and the shutter began to roll up. So far, so easy. But they still had no idea what to expect inside. As the shutter cranked upwards like the portcullis of a fortress, they jumped to the sides with their guns ready.

There was no violent response. No explosion of enemy gunfire spraying out of the entrance to repel the intruders. Nothing at all. There wasn't a living soul inside the hangar.

But it was far from empty.

'Jesus,' Silvie said as they stepped inside the cavernous space. 'It's like a damn auto museum.'

Ben looked across the gleaming red-painted concrete floor at Streicher's assembled fleet: the Bell 429 chopper resting on its wheeled undercarriage in one corner. The Volvo articulated lorry and trailer parked along the opposite wall. The collection of expensive motorcycles sparkling under the lights, all chrome and lustrous paintwork. The three identical black Range Rovers, and the exotic sports car that looked like something from a science-fiction movie. Finally, the menacing dark hulk of the Lenco BearCat assault truck.

Ben walked over to it, feeling a tightening in his muscles. He touched the massive battering ram welded to its front. There were splinters of the monastery gate still embedded in the rivet heads. He plucked one out and gazed at it for a moment.

'Just a big empty space,' Silvie said, gazing around them. 'Where's the rest of it? It's as if those guys came from nowhere.'

Ben pointed straight down at the floor between his feet. 'They came from underneath. Streicher's down there too.'

'Under the ground?'

'It's just like Donath said.'

'I know he did. It sounded weird to me at the time. Now we're here and it seems even weirder.'

'They're here,' Ben said. 'I know it.'

'Where? You see any kind of trapdoor or opening?'

Ben didn't reply. He tapped the six-digit code into the keypad. The green button had worked for the shutter, so he guessed that red was for something else. He pressed red.

Nothing happened.

Maybe the red button didn't do anything, he thought. A wire could be loose inside.

Silvie frowned at him and opened her mouth to speak. Probably to express more scepticism.

Then fifty tons of thick concrete slab seemed to lurch under their feet, to the sudden sucking *whoosh* of hydraulics and the rotation of unseen gears. A deep bass throb filled the air. The power of the mechanism made the walls tremble and their ribs vibrate. Invisible seams cracked wider and wider as a whole central section of the floor opened up in front of them, twenty metres long by five wide, hinging at one end to form an enormous ramp that sloped steadily downwards to connect flush with the hidden tunnel beneath. The operation took more than fifteen seconds, during which time all Ben and Silvie could do was stare. Finally, the mechanism came to rest with a soft thud that resonated all through the building.

'Is that what I think it is?' she breathed when there was silence again.

'One of the world's best-kept little secrets,' Ben said. 'How the other half live while the rest of us perish among the ruins of the post-nuclear wasteland.'

'Streicher built *this*?'

'Or bought it. I gather he's not short of a bob or two.'

'It's incredible.'

'I get the feeling there's a lot more to it,' Ben said. 'Only one way to find out.' He looked at the golf buggies that were parked by the mouth of the gaping hole, and saw that all three had the keys in them. Transportation for their welcoming committee, he guessed. Each had a soft double seat and a polished fibreglass bodyshell and shiny chrome wheels with chunky tyres. Stylish.

Ben unslung his rifle and submachine gun and stowed them in the carrying space behind the seat of the nearest buggy, then clambered aboard, put his foot on the pedal and the electric motor kicked silently in. He powered round in a tight U-turn and paused at the top of the ramp, waiting for Silvie to get on. She peered uncertainly into the tunnel. Light shone from the depths. Nothing but silence from down below.

'It looks like the entrance to hell,' she said.

'Then let's get down there and join the party,' Ben replied.

Udo Streicher had witnessed the whole thing unfold on the bank of monitors in his office. First the merciless slaughter of his men. Next, the Faban bitch and her unknown companion breaching hangar security as if it were nothing. Now he watched helplessly as the insolent bastards boarded one of his own golf buggies and disappeared down the mouth of the tunnel, heading straight into the heart of his hitherto undiscovered and totally inviolate sanctuary.

Now Streicher was gripped by terror at the question revolving in his mind: *who was Michelle Faban?* Clearly, that wasn't her real name, just as Streicher was certain that Dexter Nicholls had been a fake identity created to dupe him. Were they police? Government spies? Then more would come. A whole host of them could be set to descend on him at any moment. They could be on their way right now.

He snatched the bottle of antitoxin and the remaining syringes from the desk. They were too precious to let out of his sight. He burst out of the office at a run. 'Hannah!' he yelled, even though she couldn't possibly hear him in the vast network of tunnels. Where could she be? 'Hannah!'

He stopped, his brain speeding from the combined effects of panic and cocaine. Hannah didn't matter. Only one thing really mattered. He turned in the opposite direction and sprinted down a brightly lit corridor to the nearest buggy station. A whole fleet of them were stationed at various points around the nuclear bunker, plugged into the juice from the underground diesel generators to keep them topped up. He was breathless by the time he got to the charging bay. Unhooking the power cable of the first buggy in the line, he threw himself aboard and floored the pedal, urging the thing on as fast as it would go.

He rushed towards the laboratory.

Chapter Sixty-Four

Anton Lindquist felt exactly as predicted, like shit. He'd noticed the first hint of the antitoxin's side effects while he was still disposing of the dead monkey. By the time he'd finished up in the lab and was finally ready to head for his quarters to get some badly needed rest, his head had started pounding and the nausea was coming on strong.

Udo Streicher's sudden appearance was the very last thing Lindquist needed. The buggy tore up the corridor and screeched to a halt outside the lab window. Streicher leaped out. His hair was dishevelled, his eyes wild and his nostrils rimmed with white powder. 'The canisters!' he yelled. 'I need the canisters!'

Lindquist showed him where he'd put them in the outer chamber of the main lab room, carefully wrapped in packaging material and protected inside a plastic crate. Streicher ordered him to load it on the buggy. 'Hurry. Are you sick? Get a grip on yourself, man.'

'What's happening?' Lindquist asked in a faint voice, struggling to keep from vomiting. His face was a ghastly shade of white.

'We're under attack by government agents. Take this.' Streicher drew his pistol and held it out butt-first. 'You have to protect me. We're leaving. If we run into trouble along the way, you know what to do.'

'I'm a technician, not a fighter,' Lindquist protested, staring at the gun.

Streicher pressed his face so close to Lindquist's that their noses almost touched. 'I am your leader,' he hissed through bared teeth. 'You will do your duty by me, science boy, or I'll snap your scrawny neck.'

As the buggy sped through the tunnels with Lindquist riding shotgun, Streicher managed to raise another of his remaining men on the radio. 'Zwart? Is Wokalek with you? Now listen to me. The bunker has been breached by intruders. Arm yourselves and do whatever is required to repel this attack. That's an order.' Without waiting for Zwart's reply, he switched to the separate radio channel that he and Hannah used.

No response. Where the hell was she? He stuffed the handset in his pocket and yelled at the buggy to go faster.

'This place is unreal,' Sylvie said. 'No wonder we couldn't find the bastard. How long has he been living down here?'

They'd ditched their transport on penetrating the inner core of the nuclear bunker, and now they were moving on foot through an apparently endless web of rounded tunnels, sweeping from room to room. Ben had no idea exactly how deep they were underground, but an oppressive deadness about the atmosphere made him feel a long way from anywhere. They could have been orbiting Jupiter's moons, or encased inside a submarine combing the bottom of the world's deepest ocean trench. Silence, except for the background electrical hum from the generators and the whisper of the air conditioning.

The place seemed deserted. Ben's instincts told him otherwise.

He kicked open another door and pointed the MP5 into a room that looked like the dorms on board a naval battleship. Sleeping quarters for the men, and recently used by the look of the rumpled bedding and the smell of stale sweat. Next to it were five more identical rooms, then a canteen filled with tables and hard chairs, and next to that a mess lounge with a big-screen television.

They moved on. More tunnels, more doors. Comfortably appointed reception areas that could have been lifted straight from the corporate headquarters of a fancy legal firm in Zurich or New York. A dining room with a vast walnut table and Persian carpet, gleaming silverware, a marble fireplace, and what looked to Ben's unschooled eye like original Matisse and Cézanne works hanging on the walls. The post-nuclear holocaust, survived in style.

Further on, they discovered that the bunker wasn't all about comforts either. Ben had to whistle as they walked through a storage area that seemed to fill about a mile of corridor and contain a bewildering and highly organised inventory of edible and non-edible supplies. Even to begin to catalogue it all would have taken a month.

'He's been putting this together for years,' Silvie muttered, shaking her head.

The armoury section they came across further on beat it all. Ben had been in countless cathedral-sized military arms depots without ever batting an eyelid. He'd once seen inside a former Soviet atomic bunker that had been adapted by the Ukrainian military as a storehouse for more than ten thousand Kalashnikov rifles. That had been an impressive sight, but pound for pound, Udo Streicher's private small-arms arsenal was in another league just for the sheer dedication, persistence and financial commitment it must have taken to accumulate and gather together this much hardware, even in firearm-friendly Switzerland. Heavy machine guns. Shoulder-mounted rocket grenade launchers. Long-range sniper systems capable of taking out moderate-to-heavy armour from two miles away. Assault rifles from China, Russia and the USA. Submachine guns and combat shotguns and handguns of every make and calibre. Rack after rack after rack, standing both sides of the centre aisle and towering all the way to the curved ceiling.

Ben stopped. He bent down and picked up the small, hard object he'd just stepped on. It was a loose nine-millimetre round, shiny and new, recently unpacked from its crate. He turned it thoughtfully between finger and thumb.

Maybe it was because the moment took him straight back to when he'd stepped on the fired nine-mil casing on discovering the massacre at the monastery. Or maybe it was just some preternatural sixth sense developed over too many years of having to try hard to stay alive. But Ben felt the sudden frisson of tension in his back, in his neck and arms and guts, that alerted him.

He whirled round and found himself locking eyes with the two armed men who'd stepped out from behind storage units fifteen metres away.

It was difficult to tell who opened fire first. Ben squeezed the trigger of his MP5 and simultaneously grabbed Silvie's arm and propelled her hard behind a stack of ammo crates at pretty much the same instant as the incoming bullets ricocheted, sparking, off the gun racks where he'd been standing just milliseconds earlier. He hit the deck and rolled and kept firing, saw the men dive for cover. His weapon had a hundred-round magazine. But so did theirs.

Within seconds, the armoury was an unsafe place to be.

Chapter Sixty-Five

With the buggy speeding up the final stretch of tunnel before the exit ramp, Streicher was just minutes away from escape. He knew he would never return to the bunker, but it no longer bothered him. His work here was done. The plague canisters were nestled safely beside him in their crate, and the thrill of success was firing his blood.

Now the exit lay dead ahead. It only remained to open the hatch and get to the chopper, and he'd be gone before anyone could stop him. Streicher reached into his pocket for the remote and used his thumb to punch in the security code.

It was as he was about to key in the sixth and final number that he felt the hard steel press against his temple, and froze.

Anton Lindquist reached down with his other hand and plucked the key from the buggy's ignition. The power shut off, they coasted to a halt in the tunnel.

Lindquist was sweating from the nausea of the antitoxin, but also from fear. 'I'm sorry, boss,' he said in a hoarse, strained voice. 'But I can't allow you to go through with this. We're going back to the lab, and we're going to incinerate every last molecule of what's in those canisters.'

The gun muzzle felt cold against Streicher's skin. He gulped and tried to sound genial. 'Anton. What are you saying? It's almost as much your creation as it is mine.'

'Which gives me as much right to decide what happens to it,' Lindquist said, sounding more determined now. 'Every night I've lain awake thinking about the innocent lives we'd destroy if we went ahead and released those agents. It somehow never seemed quite real before. Now it is, I can no longer be a party to this insanity.'

'Anton—'

'Please throw down the remote, boss.'

Streicher hesitated and thought about trying to lash the gun out of Lindquist's hand. But that Beretta had a light trigger. Any sudden moves and the shot could go off, taking his head with it.

Streicher heaved a deep sigh and tossed the remote. Keeping the pistol pointed at him, Lindquist got out of the buggy and walked up to where the device lay on the floor. Then he aimed the gun downwards and fired, missed, fired again, three times, and his last two shots blew the remote control apart.

While the gun was pointed away from him, Streicher saw his chance. He leaped out of the buggy and hurled himself at the Swede. Lindquist was lightly built and went down hard with Streicher on top of him. Streicher knocked away the gun and punched him twice in the face. Lindquist's glasses broke. Blood specked his nose and lips. Streicher hit him again, then fastened both hands around his throat and strangled him to death.

Breathing hard, Streicher stood up and recovered his pistol. The remote was a hopeless mess of shattered plastic and circuit board. His only hope of leaving here was to get hold of the other remote, now in the hands of the enemy intruders.

This would not stop him. No setback, no obstacle, no man born of woman could deter him from the future that was written for him.

Streicher leaped back into the buggy, pulled a tight U-turn and raced back in the direction he'd come. As he made his way deeper into the bunker, his ears pricked at the sound of distant gunfire. He headed towards it.

A withering storm of machine-gun fire had Ben pinned behind the cover of the gun racks, sparks cracking off the steel framework and bullets pinging all around him. He'd survived numerous firefights by remaining calm, and he was calm now as he counted off the seconds before the two shooters would inevitably run their weapons dry. Because as exhilarating and empowering as it was to try to hose your opponent into submission by sheer mass of firepower, all good things came to an end sooner or later. Specifically, about 6.66 seconds when it came to emptying a hundred-round magazine through as hungry a weapon as an MP5.

Ben's count was off, but only by a second or two before he heard the pause, and rolled out of cover to let off a sustained return blast. A snaking line of bullet strikes chewed up the floor and the wall and sent the two shooters into a hasty retreat behind the storage units left and right of the centre aisle.

'You okay?' he called across to Silvie. She'd crawled in deeper behind the stack of ammo crates and he could no longer see her. Her hand appeared above the stack, giving him the thumbs-up and gesticulating towards the enemy position. He understood her signal. She was going to try and make her way through the narrow space between the gun racks and the curvature of the tunnel wall, and outflank them. Smart move.

In the meantime, things were set to get noisy. Ben ditched his near-empty submachine gun and unslung the FAMAS. High-velocity rifle bullets could punch their way into places where the nine-mil stuff just couldn't reach. He fired into the shelving units the two men had disappeared behind, right and left, a steady stream of single shots to keep them busy while Silvie worked on her surprise manoeuvre. Debris flew. Craters exploded out of the walls. The noise of an unsilenced battle rifle in such an enclosed space was punishing. His ears were ringing after five shots and hurting after ten. A splat of return fire told him the two men had reloaded and were back in the game. He saw movement as the shooter on the right ducked behind a row of boxes that covered a lower shelf. He fired straight into the boxes, figuring that whatever was inside them was unlikely to stop a 5.56 NATO round dead in its tracks.

The boxes erupted in a violent flash of blue flame and an explosion louder than the rifle, cardboard bursting apart and bits of twisted metal ricocheting everywhere. There was a scream, and the shooter who'd been hiding behind the boxes staggered out and fell into the centre aisle. His left arm and shoulder and one side of his head were on fire, and there was blood on his face. Ben swivelled the rifle, fixed the sights on him and without hesitation shot him twice through the chest. At the same instant, he heard the loud report of Silvie's FAMAS from the left side of the tunnel. Three rapid percussive blasts, BANGBANGBANG, and the second shooter came spinning out from cover, dropped his weapon and collapsed in a dead heap just a couple of metres from his companion.

The fire was spreading fast up the shelving unit. Ben spotted an extinguisher on a bracket, tore it down and sprayed foam over the flames. They died back almost instantly, leaving just guttering smoke. He looked at the tattered, singed remains of the box that had exploded and saw the legend CAMPING GAZ.

'That's what comes of hoarding hazardous materials,' Silvie said.

Ben looked down at the body of the man she'd shot. 'Self-defence that time?'

'He was aiming at you.'

'Thanks.'

'Tomasz Wokalek,' Silvie said, prodding the body with her gun barrel. He didn't move. 'The other one was Rutger Zwart.'

'I'm counting ten so far,' Ben said. 'Including Breslin and the two we didn't have to kill.'

Silvie nodded. 'Looks like Streicher didn't call up reserves, after all. The Army of the Prepared are getting a little thin on the ground.'

'It's not over until it's over,' said a voice behind them. 'To think otherwise would be a fatal mistake.'

Chapter Sixty-Six

Ben and Silvie turned. It was Streicher. Their guns were lowered, but his was raised and pointing right at them. In his other hand, he was clutching a plain metal canister that looked like a large stubby aerosol.

'I know you, bitch,' he said to Silvie.

'Not as well as you think, Udo,' she replied. 'Or you'd put that gun down and give this up, right now.'

Streicher sneered and ignored her. He turned the pistol a few degrees to point at Ben. 'And who the hell are you?'

'The guy you should have left alone,' Ben said. 'The guy whose friends you shouldn't have messed with. And the guy who's going to kill you. Apart from that, nobody much.'

'Think you can beat me?' Streicher said.

'It's a done deal,' Ben told him. 'Pull that trigger, you die. And I'll shoot you if you don't. You don't get a choice.'

'Maybe you think you can beat this, too.' Streicher held up the canister with a smile. It dangled lightly from his fingers, upside down with the high-pressure nozzle pointing at the floor. 'I only have to drop it, and this whole place will be contaminated instantly.'

'That'll make three of us dead,' Ben said. 'What about all the other millions of people you're planning on wiping out?'

Streicher shook his head and his smile broadened. 'No,

only two. That is to say, the two suckers who haven't had the antitoxin.'

'Then drop it,' Ben said. 'Go ahead, if you trust the anti-toxin so much. Let's see what happens.'

Streicher didn't move. His smile faltered, just a little.

'See, you don't look that confident to me,' Ben said. 'In fact, you look like you're about to crap your pants. You know you can't save yourself either way. Even if that was a grenade in your hand, you'd die with us. And if you drop it, we can still take our time shooting you to bits. Face it, there's just no way out for you.'

As Ben talked, his hand was inching towards the pistol grip of his rifle. He could see Streicher hesitating, baulking. Most of all, he could see that Streicher wasn't paying atten-tion to what Ben was about to do. The trick was going to be to shoot him before he could fire the pistol, and without letting him drop the canister.

Streicher's face twisted with sudden intent. Decision time. Ben went for his gun, jerking it into a centre-of-mass aim. His finger touched the trigger.

BOOM.

The heavy punch of the gunshot that filled the tunnel didn't come from Ben's rifle, or from Silvie's. Nor from Streicher's pistol. Ben was kicked forward by an impact that lifted him off his feet.

The rifle flew out of his hands and the ground rushed up to meet him. White light obliterated his vision for a moment and everything seemed far away and in slow motion. As if from the bottom of a murky pond, he heard Silvie scream out in fear and anger. Heard Streicher laugh, and another voice he didn't recognise.

Then the muffled clap of a pistol shot.

He felt no pain, but he was badly hurt and he knew it.

He rolled on his back, looked up and saw a woman in black standing over him with a combat shotgun in her hands.

Blond, spiky hair. Red lips. Pale grey eyes, narrowed and full of hatred.

Hannah Gissel.

Silvie was down and bleeding from Streicher's bullet. Ben tried to reach her, but he couldn't move. That was when he realised that his left arm and shoulder were broken. Warm blood was soaking his back and spreading in a pool under him.

Hannah Gissel stood over him and shouldered the shotgun for a second shot at close range that would take his head right off. Her cheek settled on the stock. Her knuckles whitened on the pistol grip and her finger began to curl around the trigger.

Then she keeled over sideways to the sharp crack of a rifle shot and a streak of blood flew from her mouth. Silvie struggled up on to one elbow and shot her again, one-handed. The bullet caught Hannah Gissel in the throat and blew it wide open in a bright red splash. Hannah crunched to the floor.

In the terrible moment before it happened, Ben saw Streicher's mouth open in a silent scream of fury and his gun come up as if in slow motion. He saw the jet of flame from the muzzle and the slide slam back and the fired case being ejected. Saw the recoil kick the muzzle in the air, and Silvie knocked back down as if she'd been punched, and the vertical splat of blood hit the wall behind her. Her rifle clattered out of her hands. Ben groaned and tried once more to reach out to her, but then the darkness came gushing in from everywhere and he was gone.

Udo Streicher could see that Hannah was finished. Blood was bubbling from her mouth and the mess of her throat.

Her eyes were rolling wildly in their sockets. Her lips moved, but all that came out of them was another gout of blood and a gurgling sound.

Streicher bent down over her. He put his pistol to her head and pulled the trigger. Goodbye, Hannah.

He stood. Looked down at the inert, bloody shapes of the Faban woman and her male friend. Streicher didn't know his name. What did it matter? Just another dead fool. There'd soon be plenty more.

He frisked the man's pockets and quickly found what he'd come looking for. The remote was slick with blood. He wiped it on his trousers, then turned and hurried back towards the buggy.

This was it. No more stop signs. If he was the last man standing, so be it. He'd release the plague on the world single-handed, one city at a time.

It wasn't over. It was just about to begin.

One eye fluttered open. Then the other. Light filtered through like a lantern in the mist, and slowly the darkness receded enough for him to understand where he was and what had happened. He moved, and the pain made him cry out.

He didn't care. He could worry about the pain later. He dragged himself up on his knees and elbows and managed to shuffle across the floor to where Silvie lay. So much blood. Hard to tell what was hers and what was his. They were mingling together with the spreading pool from the corpse of the woman with the spiky blond hair, now matted red around the massive gunshot wound to her skull.

Ben ran his hand over Silvie's pale, blood-spattered face, touched his dripping fingers to her neck and could feel the tiniest pulse. She was still holding on, but she might not for long.

Him too. He could feel strength ebbing out of him about as fast as his blood was leaking out. He was cold and his vision was blurring.

Streicher was gone.

He was escaping with the plague.

He was going to take off in the helicopter.

Ben blinked. He swayed to his feet and staggered a few steps, his feet slipping on the slick wet floor of the armoury. His left arm was dangling from what the shotgun blast had left of his shoulder. Fighting down the pain, he seized his useless hand and shoved it through his belt to stop it swinging about.

'This is nothing,' he said to himself, and smiled grimly.

It wasn't nothing. He knew the darkness would rise again soon, and that this time maybe it wouldn't give him up. He didn't give a damn, not about himself. Bring it on, he thought. But first, let's get this done.

The first thing he saw on the armoury rack was what he took down. It was heavy to carry in one hand. He gripped it tightly in his bloody fist and went after Streicher.

Chapter Sixty-Seven

No air had ever tasted sweeter than the gentle breeze that wafted into the hangar as the shutter door cranked open. Streicher filled his lungs and looked out at the evening light settling over the trees. The moon was out, the night's first stars appearing against the darkening blue. So beautiful. He laughed out loud and walked back to the chopper.

Within a couple of minutes, the turbine was powering up. He engaged the undercarriage gears and gently taxied out through the open shutter. The rotors began to turn, slowly at first but quickly gathering speed. He'd soon be out of here. The rest would be history.

Turning away from the controls, he made sure that his priceless payload was securely tied down and that none of the twelve canisters could roll or fall out of their crate. Everything was looking good. He turned back to the controls. *Here we go*, he thought. Freedom and victory. It was a wonderful feeling.

The rotor was almost at full speed now.

As an afterthought, Streicher reached into his pocket and took out the little cocaine bottle. Tapped some out on top of the dashboard, poked it into a crooked little line with his finger, then lowered his face to the dash and snorted the powder up. He gasped and threw his head back, closed his eyes and had never felt so elated and happy in his life.

He opened his eyes.

A figure was standing in front of the chopper. Ragged and bloody and unsteady on his feet.

'You,' Streicher breathed.

The weight of the ex-Soviet rocket-propelled grenade launcher over his good shoulder was almost more than Ben's weakening legs could bear. The wind from the chopper's rotors was like standing on a mountaintop in the middle of a storm. He swayed, then blinked and righted himself. The weapon was angled over his shoulder and pointing straight at the helicopter's cockpit. At this range, he wasn't going to need the flip-up sights, even if he'd been able to see them. His vision was badly blurred and darkening around the edges.

Streicher clambered out of the chopper and jumped down on the concrete apron, staring at Ben with an incredulous grin and crazy eyes. His nose and upper lip were dusted with something white.

'You're going nowhere, Streicher,' Ben shouted. The effort it cost him to speak was enormous.

'You fool!' Streicher yelled over the din of the rotors, his shirt crackling and hair whipping in the powerful draught. 'Fire that thing and you'll blow the canisters. You'll release the plague anyway.'

Ben was beginning to shake with the feverish cold that was spreading through him and the wind that was chilling his blood-soaked clothes against his flesh. He knew that Streicher was right. Not even an RPG blast at close range could be guaranteed to incinerate all the disease agent. He could visualise the unburned bacteria whipped up and carried high in the smoke from the explosion before slowly dissipating to drift gently on the evening breeze, with nothing but a prayer to stop them from carrying to nearby farms, villages, towns.

'You're right,' he said. 'I can't use this thing.'

He let go of the RPG and it slid off his shoulder and hit the ground with a dull metallic thud.

Streicher laughed again.

Ben felt himself losing balance. The darkness was encroaching further around the edges of his vision. He wobbled on his feet and managed to stay upright, the pain getting bad now. Getting worse than anything he'd ever felt before.

'I'll just have to use this,' he heard himself say.

He saw Streicher's expression change. The man took a step away. Then another, ducking back towards the helicopter.

As if in a dream, Ben felt his good arm reach back to that familiar place behind his right hip and his fingers close on the chunky grip of the Browning Hi-Power. Felt the steel clear the holster, registered the gun appearing in front of his blurring vision as he thrust it out one-handed, barely aware of it except as just an extension of his arm.

The sound of the report was half-drowned by the rotor blast, but Ben might not even have heard it otherwise. He was only dimly conscious of the snap of the recoil in the palm of his hand, and of Udo Streicher's brains blowing out against the fuselage of his own chopper, and of the man's knees folding and twisting under him as he went straight down like a sack of laundry, twitched once on the ground and then lay still with blood and pulped cerebral matter spilling over the concrete.

By then, Ben was already falling, falling, backwards off the edge of a cliff and tumbling for ever into nothingness.

Chapter Sixty-Eight

'Come,' Roby said, with a sunburst smile, beckoning enthusiastically. 'This way, Benoît.'

Ben followed the boy over the meadow, wading through verdant grass and sunflowers that grew knee-high and filled the air with their perfume. The mountains twinkled and the sky was an unbroken blue. 'This way,' Roby called, further away now, and Ben quickened his pace to catch up with him. 'Wait for me,' he called back.

Then he was surrounded by a circle of pearl-white archways that seemed to grow out of the waving flowers, looming tall and splendid all around him. Roby stood waiting for him at their centre, smiling and extending his hand. He took Ben's arm.

'See,' he said, and pointed.

Ben looked, and saw all his old friends stepping through the archways and gathering round to greet him. There was Père Antoine, his flowing robe and mane of white hair catching the sunlight, and his eyes glowing with that inner joy that Ben remembered from another life. Behind him came Père Jacques, and Frère Patrice, and the lay brothers Gilles and Marc and Olivier, the whole gang, all smiling and happy to meet him again. Jeff Dekker was there, too. And Ben's son Jude, his blond hair shining like gold.

'Welcome home, Ben,' Père Antoine said.

Ben asked, 'Am I in heaven?'

Père Antoine just smiled. He held Ben's hand and squeezed it tightly with such love in his kind old eyes that Ben could feel his own tearing up and felt like a little boy again.

'It's all right, Ben,' Père Antoine said. 'It's all right.'

Then the old man's voice grew distant and his smiling face seemed to fade into the brightness of the sunlight. The circle of arches melted away, and all his friends, gradually merging into the light until they were gone and all that remained was the brightness.

Ben squinted up at it, blinking. 'Where did you go?' he said, confused.

'I'm right here, Ben,' said the same voice, only it was different somehow, closer and more immediate. The same warm hand gripped his tightly, fingers meshed with his own.

Ben's eyes fluttered shut, then reopened. 'Silvie?'

'Welcome back,' she said again, and tears spilled out of her eyes and fell on his skin like the dew from the wildflowers in his dream.

Ben closed his eyes and slept.

He drifted, sometimes on the edge of consciousness, other times floating through more strange dreams, though Père Antoine and the others did not reappear. He slowly became more aware of time passing, days merging into nights and back into days. Through it all he could sense the presence of people around him, and one presence especially.

On the fifth day, he was able to keep his eyes open for longer and sit propped up on an extra pillow in the hospital bed. The private room was white and shiny and full of flowers. Silvie sat at his bedside, where he now realised she'd been sitting for days. Her right arm was in a sling, as his left arm would be when it was out of traction. She moved stiffly, but she seemed not to notice the pain of her injuries now that Ben was going to live. She couldn't stop crying and apologising for being silly.

'I thought you were gone,' he said when he found the strength to speak.

'Wasn't as bad as it looked,' she replied, smiling at him. 'Streicher was a terrible shot. Both bullets went straight through without touching anything.'

'Lucky,' he whispered.

'It was you I was worried about,' she said.

He rested again a while. Later, when he was a little stronger, she calmly explained to him how the surgeons had rebuilt his shoulder blade and reset the joint. Hannah Gissel's shotgun had been loaded with small birdshot. The wound had been spectacular, but the force of the blast had been largely absorbed by muscle and bone and none of the tiny pellets had penetrated with enough energy to find their way to his heart or lungs. It had been the loss of blood that would have killed most men, and things had been touch-and-go for a while. Silvie had been in the room next door until three days ago, since when she'd been at his bedside for as many hours of the day as the nurses would allow her. 'I'm your guard dog,' she said.

'More like guardian angel,' he replied.

'Glad I was there after all?'

'Glad you're here now,' he said, and she squeezed his hand.

'You're going to be fine, Ben. And so is everybody else.'

He asked, 'How did we get here?'

'You can thank Luc Simon for that,' she said. 'He was the one who insisted on being kept informed of our movements. Didn't think you'd take kindly to it. I secretly texted him the location we got from Donath. The police helicopters reached Streicher's bunker just a few minutes after it all went down.' She ran through how the cops had safely secured the plague canisters and sealed off the whole area.

'That Luc Simon is something, isn't he?' Ben said, and laughed, and the laugh became a painful cough.

'You can tell him so yourself. He's pretty anxious to speak to you. Wants to give you the whole spiel on behalf of the French nation, thanking you for averting such a major disaster, etc., etc.'

'And then throw me in jail,' Ben said.

'I somehow don't think that's going to happen,' Silvie said with a chuckle.

Ben slowly recovered his strength over the next week. Luc Simon did come and see him, and did give him the whole spiel, and made it clear that no charges would be brought for any of the little misdemeanours Ben had committed in the course of saving the world.

'Cheers for that one,' Ben said.

'Oh, I almost forgot to mention. We finally got back the lab results with the analysis of that liquid you were taking. Ever heard of colloidal silver?'

'No,' Ben said.

'Tiny particles separated from pure silver by a simple electrical process, suspended in water. Your friend Antoine used an apparatus he built himself, powered by a nine-volt battery. I'd never heard of the stuff either, but I've been reading up on it. There have been a lot of scientific studies that seem to show it's a pretty potent antibacterial.' Luc Simon shrugged. 'Maybe that explains how you were protected from infection down in the crypt. But I guess we'll never know for sure.'

'Not while the pharmaceutical industry is calling the shots,' Ben said.

'So damn cynical,' Luc Simon said.

Epilogue

Nineteen days after the operation to put his shoulder back together, Ben was ready to leave hospital. Dressing took a long time, with his arm in a sling and thirty-five stitches pulling whenever he moved. But it felt good to be getting out of here.

'I suppose you'll be going home now,' Silvie said on her final visit to his room.

He replied, 'I don't have a home.'

Silvie looked as if she'd been expecting him to say that. 'But I do,' she said. 'Nothing special, but I'd like you to come and live in it with me until you get your strength back. You need someone to look after you.' She smiled and added in another tone, 'Besides, I kind of like your company.'

'What about your job?' he asked.

'I quit. Decided to move out of my apartment, too. Fresh start, new job. Full-time in charge of getting you fully recovered.'

'With just one arm?' he said, eyeing her sling.

'Hey, I'm not Superwoman for nothing, you know.' She looked at him. 'What do you say, Ben?'

He said yes.

They spent the next six weeks together. Silvie had rented a small beachside place in the Bay of Biscay, near La Rochelle, where she'd spent part of her childhood. As Ben gradually regained his strength, they went walking on the beach, watching the boats and the sunsets over the bay, and joking about how they could still hold hands with their good arms. Her sling came off soon afterwards. Ben was healing well, and not long after that, the doctors said he could start doing without his. His shoulder was very stiff at first, but with time and exercises, full mobility would eventually return.

In the meantime, they had nothing but the warm days, the sea, and the tasty French dishes Silvie regaled him with, to build up his strength and put back on the weight he'd lost. And they had each other. Gentle days, tender nights. For a time, it seemed as if it could go on for ever.

But they both knew that wouldn't happen. It was too good a thing to spoil it.

One sunny August morning, Silvie woke to find him gone. His sudden departure came as no surprise to her, and she smiled when she read his note. All it said was:

Take care of yourself
Ben

Where he'd gone, she had no idea and didn't try to guess. She didn't know if she'd ever see or hear from him again, and tried not to think about it too much.

Read on for an exclusive extract
from the new Ben Hope adventure by

SCOTT MARIANI

The Cassandra Sanction

Prologue

Rügen Island,
Baltic coast, northern Germany
16th July

The woman sitting at the wheel of the stationary car was thirty-four years of age but looked at least five years younger. Her hair was long and black. Her face was one that was well known to millions of people. She was as popular for her looks as she was for her intellect, her sharp wit and her professional credentials, and often recognised wherever she ventured out in public.

But she was alone now. She'd driven many miles to be as far away from anybody as she could, on this particular day.

This day, which was to be the last day of her life.

She'd driven the Porsche Cayenne four-by-four off the coastal track and up a long incline of rough grass, patchy and flattened by the incessant sea wind, to rest stationary just metres from the edge of the chalk cliff. The Baltic Sea was hard and grey, unseasonably cold-looking for the time of year. With the engine shut off, she could hear the rumble and crash of the breakers against the rocks far below. Evening was drawing in, and the rising storm brought strong gusts of salt wind that buffeted the car every few seconds and rocked its body on its suspension. Rain slapped the windscreen and trickled down the glass, like the tears that were running freely down her face as she wept.

She had been sitting there a long time behind the wheel. Reflecting on her life. Picturing in turn the faces of those she was leaving behind, and thinking about how her loss would affect them. One, more than anybody.

She knew how badly she was going to hurt him by doing this. It would have been the same for her, if it had been the other way round.

Catalina Fuentes gazed out at the sea and whispered, 'Forgive me, Raul'.

Then she slowly reached for the ignition and restarted the engine. She put the car into drive and gripped the wheel tightly. She took several deep breaths to steady her pounding heart and deepen her resolve. This was it. The time had come. Now she was ready.

The engine picked up as she touched the gas. The car rolled over the rough grass towards the cliff edge. Past the apex of the incline, the ground sloped downwards before it dropped away sheer, nothing but empty air between it and the rocks a hundred metres below. The Porsche Cayenne bumped down the slope, stones and grit pinging and popping from under its wheels, flattening the coarse shrubs that clung to the weathered cliff top. Gathering speed, rolling faster and faster as the slope steepened; then its front wheels met with nothingness and the car's nose tipped downwards into space.

As the Porsche Cayenne vaulted off the edge of the chalk cliff and began its long, twisting, somersaulting fall, Catalina Fuentes closed her eyes and bid a last goodbye to the life she'd known and all the people in it.

Chapter One

Ben Hope had been in the bar less than six minutes when the violence kicked off.

His being there in first place had been purely a chance thing. For a man with nowhere in particular to be at any particular time, and under no sort of pressure except to find a cool drink on a warm early October afternoon, the little Andalucian town of Frigiliana offered more than enough choice of watering holes to pick out at random, and the whitewashed bar tucked away in corner of a square in the Moorish Quarter had seemed like the kind of quiet place that appealed.

Pretty soon, it was looking like he'd picked the wrong one, at the wrong time. Of all the joints in all the pueblos of the Sierra Almijara foothills, he'd had to wander into this one.

He'd been picking up the vibe and watching the signs from the moment he walked in. But the beer looked good, and it was too late to change his mind. He didn't have anything better to do anyway, so he hung around mainly to see whether his guess would turn out right. Which it soon did.

The bar wasn't exactly crowded, but it wasn't empty either. Without consciously counting, he registered the presence of a dozen people in the shady room, not including the owner, a wide little guy in a faded polo shirt, who was lazily tidying up behind the bar and didn't speak as he served Ben a bottle of the local cerveza. Ben carried his drink over to a shady corner table, dumped his bag and settled there with his back to the wall, facing the door, away from the other punters, where he could see the window and survey the rest of the room at the same time.

Old habits. Ben Hope was someone who preferred to observe than to be observed. He reclined in his chair and sipped his cool beer. The situation unfolding in front of him was a simple one, following a classic pattern he had witnessed more often and in more places in his life than he cared to count, like an old movie he'd seen so many times before. What was coming was as predictable and inevitable as the fact that he wasn't just going to sit there and let it happen.

On the left side of the room, midway between Ben's corner table and the bar, a guy was sitting alone nursing a half-empty tumbler and a half-empty bottle of Arehucas Carta Oro rum that he looked intent on finishing before he passed out. He was a man around his mid-thirties, obviously a Spaniard, lean-faced, with a thick head of glossy, tousled black hair and skin tanned to the colour of café con leche. His expression was grim, his eyes bloodshot. A four-day beard shaded his cheeks and his white shirt was crumpled and grubby, as if he'd been wearing it for a few days and sleeping in it too. But he didn't have the look of a down-and-out or a vagrant. Just of a man who was very obviously upset and working hard to find solace in drink.

Ben knew all about that.

The Spanish guy sitting alone trying to get wrecked wasn't the problem. Nor were the elderly couple at the table in the right corner at the back of the barroom, opposite Ben. The old man must have been about a thousand years old, and the way his withered neck stuck out of his shirt collar made Ben think of a Galápagos tortoise. His wife wasn't much younger, shrivelled to something under five feet with skin like rawhide. The Moorish Sultans had probably still ruled these parts back when they'd started dating. Still together, still in love. Ben thought they looked like a sweet couple, in a wrinkly kind of way.

Nor, again, was any of the potential trouble coming from the man seated at a table by the door. With straw-coloured hair, cropped short and receding, he looked too pale and Nordic to be a local. Maybe a Swedish tourist, Ben thought. Or a Dane. An abstemious one, drinking mineral water while apparently engrossed in a paperback.

No, the source of the problem was right in the middle of the barroom, where two tables had been dragged untidily together to accommodate the noisy crowd of foreigners. It didn't take much to tell they were Brits. Eight of them, all in their twenties, all red-faced from exuberance and the large quantity of local brew they were throwing down their throats. Their T-shirts were loud, their voices louder. Ben had heard their raucous laughter from outside. Their table was a mess of spilled beer and empty bottles, loose change and cigarette packs. To the delight of his mates, one of them clambered up on top of it and tried to do a little dance before he almost toppled the whole thing over and fell back in his chair, roaring like a musketeer. They weren't as rowdy as some gangs of beery squaddies Ben had seen, but they weren't far off it. The barman was casting a nervous eye at them as he weighed up the risks of asking them to leave against what they were spending in the place. Next, they broke into a chanting rendition of *Y Viva España* that was too much for the ancient couple in the right corner. The barman's frown deepened as they made their shuffling exit, but he still didn't say anything.

The Dane never looked up from his paperback, as if the noisy bunch didn't even exist. Maybe he was hard of hearing, Ben thought, or maybe it was just a hell of an interesting book. The yobs gave him a cursory once-over, seemed to decide he wasn't worth bothering with, and then turned their attention on the solitary Spaniard sitting drinking on the left side of the room. The response they'd manage to provoke out of the old folks had whetted their appetite for more. A chorus of faux-Spanish words and calls of 'Hey, Pedro. Cheer up, might never happen', quickly graduated into 'You speaka da English?'; and from there into 'Hey, I'm talking to you. You fucking deaf?'

They didn't seem to notice Ben sitting watching from the shadows. All the better for them.

The lone Spaniard poured more rum and quietly went on drinking as the loutish calls from across the barroom grew louder. He was doing almost as good a job as the Dane of acting as if the yobs were just a mirage that only Ben, the barman and the elderly couple had been able to see. Or maybe he was just too drunk to register that the taunting was directed at him. Either way, if he went on ignoring them, there was a chance that the situation might dissipate away to nothing. The eight lads would probably just down a few more beers and then go staggering off down the street in search of a more entertaining venue, or local girls to proposition, or town monuments to urinate on. Just boys enjoying themselves on holiday.

But it didn't happen that way, thanks to the big porker who'd been the first to call out to the Spaniard. He had gingery hair cropped in a bad buzzcut and a T-shirt a size too small for him with the legend EFF YOU SEE KAY

OWE EFF EFF in block letters across his flabby chest. He nudged the guy sitting next to him and muttered something Ben didn't catch, then turned his grin on the Spaniard and yelled out, 'The fucking bitch ain't worth it, mate.'

The atmosphere in the room seemed to change, like a sudden drop in pressure. Ben sensed it immediately. He wasn't sure if the English boys had. *Here it comes*, he thought. He watched as the fingers clutching the Spaniard's glass turned white. The Spaniard's lips pursed and his brow creased. One muscle at a time, his face crumpled into a deep frown.

Then the Spaniard stood up. The backs of his legs shoved his chair back with a scraping sound that was as laden with portent as the look on his face. Still clutching his drink, he walked around the edge of his table and crossed the barroom floor towards the English boys. There was a lurch to his step, but he was able to keep a fairly straight line. There was something more than just anger in his eyes. Ben wasn't sure if the English boys could see that, either.

The Dane was still sitting there glued to his book, apparently oblivious. Not like Ben.

They all stared at the Spaniard as he approached. One of them elbowed his friend and said, 'Oooo. Touch a nerve, did we?'

'I'm shitting my pants,' said the big porker in a tremulous voice.

The Spaniard stopped three feet away from their table. The Arehucas Carta Oro was making him sway on his feet, not dramatically, but noticeably. He eyed the eight of them as if they were fresh dogshit, and then his gaze rested on the big porker.

Quietly, and in perfect English, he said, 'My name isn't

Pedro. And you're going to apologise for what you just called her.'

An outraged silence fell over the group. Ben was watching the big porker, whose grin had dropped and whose cheeks turned mottled red. The pack leader; and if he wanted to remain so, peer pressure now demanded that he make a good show of responding to this upstart who'd had the monstrous balls to stand up to him in front of his friends.

'My mistake,' the big porker said, meeting the Spaniard's eye. 'I shouldn't have called her a bitch. I should've called her a cheap fucking dago whore slut cocksucker bitch. Because that's what she is. Isn't that right, Pedro?'

For a guy with the better part of a bottle of rum inside him, the Spaniard moved pretty fast. First, he dashed the contents of his tumbler at the big porker. Second, he hurled the empty tumbler against the table, where it burst like a grenade and showered the whole gang with glass. Third, he reached out and scooped up a cigarette lighter from the yobs' table. Without hesitation, he thumbed the flint and tossed it at the big porker, whose T-shirt instantly caught light.

The big porker screamed and started clawing at his burning shirt. The Spaniard snatched a beer from the table and doused him with it. The big porker staggered to his feet and threw a wild punch that came at the Spaniard's head in a wide arc. The Spaniard ducked out of the swing, then stepped back in with surprising speed and jabbed a straight right that caught the big porker full in the centre of his face and sent him crashing violently on his back against the table. Drinks and empty bottles capsized all over the floor.

The Dane still didn't move, react or look up. This kind of thing must happen all the time where he lived.

Then it was just seven against one. The rest of the gang

were out of their seats and converging on the Spaniard in a chorus of angry yelling. The barman was banging on the bar and yelling that he was going to call the police, but nobody was listening and the situation was already well out of control. The Spaniard ducked another punch and returned it with another neat jab to the ribs that doubled up his opponent. But the alcohol was telling on him, and he didn't see the next punch coming until it had caught him high on the left cheek and knocked him off his feet.

The five who could still fight closed in on him, kicking him in the stomach and legs as he fought back furiously and tried to get up. One of them grabbed a chair, to slam it down on the Spaniard's head. Raising the chair high in the air, he was about to deliver the blow when it was snatched out of his hands from behind.

He turned, just long enough to register the presence of the blond stranger who'd got up from the corner table. Then the chair splintered into pieces over the crown of his skull and he crumpled at the knees and hit the floor like a sandbag.

The English boys stopped kicking the Spaniard and stared at Ben as he tossed away the broken remnant of the chair and stepped over their fallen friend towards them.

'All of you against one guy,' Ben said. 'Doesn't seem fair to me.'

One of them pointed down at the Spaniard, who was struggling to his feet now that the kicking had stopped. 'What you taking his side for?'

Ben shrugged. 'Because I've got nothing better to do.'

'You saw what he did to Stu,' said another.

'Looked to me like Stu had it coming,' Ben said. 'So do the rest of you, unless you do the sensible thing and leave now, while you still have legs under you.'